Aunt Phil'

Proudly Presents

The Iron Trail

Written By
Rex Beach

Edited By
Laurel Downing Bill

Cordova To Kennecott Railway
Alaska's Irish Prince
The Man Behind The Words

By
Laurel Downing Bill

The Iron Trail originally published 1913
by Harper & Brothers, New York

Reprint from Public Domain 2022
by Aunt Phil's Trunk LLC
Anchorage, Alaska
www.AuntPhilsTrunk.com

ISBN: 978-1-940479-37-8

Rex Ellingwood Beach became one of the most famous novelists of his time. Along with Robert Service and Jack London, he helped form the general public's opinions about life in Alaska in the early 1900s.

TABLE OF CONTENTS

TABLE OF CONTENTS

MAP TO COPPER RICHES

EDITOR'S NOTES

The Iron Trail, published by Rex Beach in 1913, is based on the true story of the men who built the Copper River and Northwestern Railway between Cordova and the rich copper ore deposits at Kennecott between 1906 and 1911.

Beach's main fictional character, Murray O'Neil, was fashioned after railroad contractor Michael James "Big Mike" Heney (born October 24, 1864 and died October 11, 1910). Henry is best known for his work on the first two railroads built in Alaska – the White Pass and Yukon Route and the Copper River and Northwestern Railway.

The fictitious towns in this tale in reality are Valdez, Katalla and Cordova. Other actual people, places and events are listed on the next page. I share the real story of building the Copper River and Northwestern Railway in "Cordova To Kennecott Railway" beginning on page 307. Once you read the true account, I think you will agree that Beach captured the tenacity and dangers of the real story in *The Iron Trail*.

As with other writings of the early 1900s, many words now considered archaic were used throughout this book. I took the liberty of replacing them with more modern language in order to keep the story flowing. For instance, "sanguine affray" became "bloody battle."

I hope you enjoy this version of Rex Beach's *The Iron Trail!*

Laurel Downing Bill
Author, *Aunt Phil's Trunk*
Alaska history series

Real-Life Names	Names in *The Iron Trail*
Valdez	Cortez
Katalla	Kyak
Cordova	Omar
Eyak Lake	Omar Lake
Kennecott coalfield	Kyak coalfield
Prince William Sound	King Phillip Sound
Copper River	Salmon River
Miles and Childs glaciers	Jackson and Garfield
Copper River &	Salmon River &
Northwestern Railway	Northwestern Railway
Alaska Home Railway	Cortez Home Railway
Alaska Syndicate	Copper Trust
Guggenheims	Heidlemanns
Railroad builder Michael James Heney	Murray O'Neil
Dr. F.B. Whiting	Dr. Stanley Gray
Chief Engineer Erastus Hawkins	Mr. Parker

1

THE TIDE TAKES A HAND

The ship stole cautiously through the darkness, feeling her way past bay and promontory. Around her was no phosphorescent glow that lies above the open ocean, even on the darkest night, for the mountains ran down to the channel on either side. In places they overhung, and where they lay upturned against the dim sky, they were mantled with heavy timber. All day the *Nebraska* had made her way through an endless succession of straits and sounds, now squeezing through an inlet so narrow the somber spruce trees seemed to be within a short stone's throw, again plowing across some open reach where the pulse of the north Pacific could be felt. Out through the openings to seaward stretched the restless ocean, on across uncounted leagues, to Saghalien and the rim of Russia's prison yard.

Always near at hand was the deep green of the Canadian forests, denser, darker than a tropic jungle, for this was the land of "plenty waters" where hillsides were carpeted knee deep with moss, wet to saturation. Out of every gulch came a brawling stream whipped to milk-white frenzy; snow lay heavy upon the higher levels, while now and then from farther inland peered a glacier, like some dead monster crushed between the granite peaks. There were villages, too, and fishing stations, and mines and quarries. These burst suddenly upon the view, then slipped past with dreamlike swiftness. Other ships swung into sight, rushed by, and were swallowed up in the labyrinthine maze astern.

Passengers of the *Nebraska* who had never traversed the Inside Passage were loud in the praises of its picturesqueness, while those to whom the route was familiar seemed to find an ever-fresh fascination in its shifting scenes.

Among the latter was Murray O'Neil. The whole north coast from Flattery to St. Elias was as well mapped in his mind as the face of an old friend, yet he was forever discovering new vistas, surprising panoramas, amazing variations of color and topography. The mysterious rifts and passageways opened and closed as if to lure the ship astray, the trackless confusion of islets, the siren song of the waterfalls, the silent hills and glaciers and snow-soaked forests – all appealed to him, for he was at heart a dreamer.

Yet he did not forget that scenery such as this, lovely as it is by day, may be dangerous at night, for he knew the weakness of steel hulls.

On some sides his experience and business training had made him sternly practical and prosaic. Ships aroused no manner of enthusiasm

Courtesy University of Alaska Anchorage

Steamships, like the SS *Alaska* shown here on a voyage from Seattle to Cordova in the early 1900s, often plied the waters of Prince William Sound as they brought passengers to and from America's resource-rich northland.

in him except as a means to an end. Railroads had no glamour of romance in his eyes, for, having built several of them, he had outlived all poetic notions regarding the iron horse, and once the rails were laid, he was apt to lose interest in them. Nevertheless, he was almost poetic in his own quiet way, interweaving practical thoughts with fanciful visions, and he loved his dreams. He was dreaming now as he leaned upon the bridge rail of the *Nebraska*, peering into the gloom with watchful eyes. From somewhere to port came the occasional commands of the officer on watch, echoed instantly from the inky interior of the wheelhouse. Up overside rose the whisper of rushing waters; from underfoot came the rhythmic beat of the engines far below. O'Neil shook off his mood and began to wonder idly how long it would be before Captain Johnny would be ready for his nightcap.

He always traveled with Johnny Brennan when he could manage it, for the two men had become friends. O'Neil usually lived in Johnny's cabin, or on the bridge, and their nightly libation to friendship had come to be a matter of some ceremony.

The ship's master soon appeared from the shadows — a short, trim man with gray hair.

"Come, it's waiting for us," he told his frequent traveler.

O'Neil followed into Brennan's luxurious, well-lit quarters, where on a mahogany sideboard sat a tray holding decanter, siphon, and glasses, together with a bottle of ginger ale. The captain, after he had mixed a beverage for his passenger, opened the bottle for himself. They raised their glasses silently.

"Now that you're past the worst of it, I suppose you'll turn in," O'Neil said. "You're getting old for a hard run like this, Johnny."

Captain Brennan snorted. "Old? I'm a better man than you, yet. I'm a teetotaler, that's why. I discovered long ago that saltwater and whiskey don't mix."

O'Neil stretched himself out in one of Brennan's easy chairs. "Really." he said. "I don't understand why a ship carries a captain. Now of what earthly use to the line are you, for instance, except for your beauty, which, no doubt, has its value with the women? I'll admit you preside with some grace at the best table in the dining salon, but your officers know these channels as well as you do. They could make the run from Seattle to Juneau with their eyes shut."

"Indeed they could not; and neither could I."

"Oh, well, of course I have no respect for you as a man, having seen you without your uniform."

The captain grinned in thorough enjoyment of this teasing. "I'll say nothing at all of my seamanship," he said, relapsing into the faintest of brogues. "But there's no denying the master of a ship has many unpleasant and disgusting duties to perform. He must amuse the prominent passengers who can't amuse themselves, for one thing, and that takes tact and patience. Why, some people make themselves at home on the bridge, in the chartroom, and even in my living quarters, to say nothing of consuming my expensive wines, liquors, and cigars."

"Meaning me?"

"I'm a brutal seafaring man, and you'll have to make allowances for my well-known brusqueness. Maybe I did mean you. But I'll say, next to you, Curtis Gordon is the worst grafter I ever saw."

"You don't like Gordon, do you?" O'Neil said with a change of tone.

"I do not! He went up with me again this spring, and he had his widow with him, too."

"His widow?"

"You know who I mean—Mrs. Gerard. They say it's her money he's using in his schemes. Perhaps it's because of her that I don't like him."

"Ah-h! I see."

"You don't see, or you wouldn't grin like that. I'm a married man, I'll have you know, and I'm still on good terms with Mrs. Brennan, thank God. But I don't like men who use women's money, and that's just what our friend Gordon is doing. What money the widow didn't put up he's grabbed from the school ma'ams and servant girls and society matrons in the East. What has he got to show them for it?"

"A railroad project, a copper mine, some coal claims...."

"Bah! A menagerie of wildcats!"

"You can't prove that. What's your reason for distrusting him?"

"Well, for one thing, he knows too much. Why, he knows everything, he does. Art, literature, politics, law, finance, and draw poker have no secrets from him. He's been everywhere — and back — twice; he speaks a dozen different languages. He out argued me on poultry raising – and I know more about that than any man living. He can handle a drill or a coach and four horses; he can tell all about the art of ancient Babylon; and he beat me playing cribbage, which shows that he ain't on the level. He's the best-informed man outside of a university, and he drinks tea in the afternoon — with his legs crossed and the saucer balanced on his heel. Now, it takes years of hard work for an honest man to make a success at one thing, but Gordon never failed at anything. I ask you if a living authority on all the branches of human endeavor and a man who can beat me at 'crib' doesn't make you suspicious."

"Not at all. I've beaten you myself!"

"I was sick," Captain Brennan said.

"The man is brilliant, well educated, and wealthy. It's only natural that he should excite the jealousy of a weaker intellect."

Johnny opened his lips for an explosion, then changed his mind and agreed sourly.

"He's got money, all right, and he knows how to spend it. He and his valet occupied three cabins on this ship. They say his quarters at Hope are palatial."

"My dear grampus, the mere love of luxury doesn't argue that a person is dishonest."

"Would you let a hired man help you on with your underclothes?" demanded the mariner.

"There's nothing criminal about it."

"Humph! Mrs. Gerard is different. She's all class! You don't mind her having a maid and speaking French when she runs short of English. Her daughter is like her."

"I haven't seen Miss Gerard."

"If you'd stir about the ship instead of wearing out my Morris chair, you'd have that pleasure. She was on deck all morning." The captain fell silent and poked with a stubby forefinger at the ice in his glass.

"Well, out with it," O'Neil said after a moment.

"I'd like to know the inside story of Curtis Gordon and this girl's mother."

"Why bother your head about something that doesn't concern you?" The speaker rose and began to pace the cabin floor.

"Tell me, are you going to land me and my horses at Kyak Bay?" he asked as he changed the subject.

"That depends on the weather. It's a rotten harbor; you'll have to swim them ashore."

"Suppose it should be rough?"

"Then we'll go on and drop you there coming back. I don't want to be caught on that shore with a southerly wind, and that's the way it usually blows."

"I can't wait," O'Neil said. "A week's delay might ruin me. Rather than go on I'd swim ashore myself, without the horses."

"I don't make the weather at Kyak Bay. Satan himself does that. Twenty miles offshore it may be calm, and inside it may be blowing a gale. That's due to the glaciers. Those icefields inland and the warm air from the Japanese current offshore kick up some funny atmospheric pranks. It's the worst spot on the coast and we'll lose a ship there some day. Why, the place isn't properly charted, let alone buoyed."

"That's nothing unusual for this coast."

"True for you. This is all a graveyard of ships and there's been many a good master's license lost because of half-baked laws from Washington, D.C. Think of a coast like this with almost no lights, no beacons nor buoys; and yet we're supposed to make time. It's fine in clear weather, but in the dark, we go by guess and by God. I've stood the run longer than most of the skippers, but...."

Even as Brennan spoke the *Nebraska* seemed to halt, then jerk backward under his feet. O'Neil, who was standing, flung out an arm to steady himself; the empty ginger ale bottle fell from the sideboard. Loose articles hanging against the side walls swung to and fro; the heavy draperies over Captain Johnny's bed swayed.

Brennan leaped from his chair; his ruddy face mottled, his eyes wide and horror stricken.

"Damnation!" he gasped. The cabin door crashed open ahead of him and he was on the bridge, with O'Neil at his heels. They saw the first officer clinging to the rail; from the pilot house window came an excited burst of Norwegian, then out of the door rushed a quartermaster.

Brennan cursed and met the fellow with a blow that drove him sprawling back.

"Get in there, Swan," he bellowed. "Take your wheel."

"The tide swung her in!" the mate cried. "The tide—My God!"

"Sweet Queen Anne!" Brennan said quietly. "You've ripped her belly out."

"It—was the tide," the officer whispered.

The steady, muffled beating of machinery ceased, the ship seemed suddenly to lose her life, but it was plain she was not aground, for she kept moving through the gloom. From down forward came excited voices as the crew poured up out of the forecastle.

Brennan leaped to the telegraph and signaled the engine room. He was calm now. His voice sharp and steady.

"Go below, Mr. James, and find the extent of the damage."

A moment later the hull began to throb once more to the thrust of the propeller. Inside the wheelhouse Swan had recovered from his panic and mechanically repeated the master's orders.

The second and third officers arrived on the bridge, dressing as they came, and were followed by the chief engineer. Johnny spoke to them, his words crackling like sparks from a wireless. In an incredibly short time, he had the situation in hand and turned to O'Neil, who had been a silent witness of the scene.

"Glory be!" the captain said. "Most of our good passengers are asleep; the jar would scarcely wake them."

"Tell me where and how I can help," Murray said. His first thought had been of the possible effect of this catastrophe on his plans, for time was pressing. As for danger, he had looked upon it so often and in so many forms it had little power to stir him; but a

THE TIDE TAKES A HAND

shipwreck, which would halt his northward rush, was another matter. Whether the ship sank or floated could make little difference now the damage had been done. She was crippled and would need assistance. His fellow passengers, he knew, were safe enough. Fortunately there were not many of them — about 200 — and if worse came to worst there was room in the lifeboats for all. But the *Nebraska* had no watertight bulkheads and the plight of his 20 horses between decks filled him with alarm and pity. There were no lifeboats for those poor animals penned down in the rushing waters.

Brennan had stepped into the chartroom but returned in a moment.

"There's no place to beach her this side of Halibut Bay."

"How far is that?" O'Neil asked.

"Five or six miles."

"You'll—have to beach her?"

"I'm afraid so. She feels queer."

Up from the cabin deck came a handful of men passengers to inquire what had happened; behind them a woman began calling shrilly for her husband.

"We touched a rock," the skipper explained. "Kindly go below and stop squawking. There's no danger."

A few minutes later James, the first officer, came to report.

"She loosened three plates on her port quarter and she's filling fast."

"How long will she last?" Brennan asked.

"Not long, sir. Half an hour, perhaps."

The captain rang for full speed, and the decks began to strain as the engine increased its labor.

"Get your passengers out and stand by the boats," he ordered. "Take it easy and don't alarm the women. Have them dress warmly, and don't allow any crowding by the men. Mr. Tomlinson, you hold the steerage gang in check. Take your revolver with you." He turned to his silent friend, in whose presence he seemed to feel a cheering sympathy. "I knew it would come sooner or later, Murray," he said. "But—magnificent mummies! To touch on a clear night with the sea like glass!" He sighed. "It'll be tough on my missus."

O'Neil laid a hand on the captain's shoulder. "It wasn't your fault, and there will be room in the last boat for you. Understand?" Brennan hesitated, and O'Neil continued. "No nonsense, now! Don't make a darned fool of yourself by sticking to the bridge. Promise?"

"I promise."

"Now what do you want me to do?"

"Keep those dear passengers quiet. I'll run for Halibut Bay, where there's a sandy beach. If she won't make it, I'll turn her into the rocks. Tell 'em they won't wet a foot if they keep their heads."

"Good! I'll be back to see that you behave yourself," O'Neil said with a small chuckle. He then descended to the deck, where he found an incipient panic. Stewards were pounding on stateroom doors, half-clad men were rushing about aimlessly, pallid faces peered forth from windows, and there was the sound of running feet, slamming doors, and shrill, hysterical voices.

O'Neil saw a waiter thumping lustily on a door and heard him shout.

"Everybody out! The ship is sinking!"

As he turned away, Murray seized him roughly by the arm and thrust his face close.

"If you yell again like that, I'll toss you overboard," he warned.

"God help us, we're going...."

O'Neil shook the fellow until his teeth rattled; his own countenance, ordinarily so quiet, was blazing.

"There's no danger. Act like a man and don't start a stampede."

The steward pulled himself together and answered in a calmer tone.

"Very well, sir. I—I'm sorry, sir."

Murray O'Neil was known to most of the passengers, for his name had gone up and down the coast, and there were few places from San Francisco to Nome where his word did not carry weight. As he went among his fellow travelers now, smiling, self-contained, unruffled, his presence had its effect. Women ceased their shrilling, men stopped their senseless questions and listened to his directions with some comprehension. In a short time the passengers were marshaled to the upper deck where the lifeboats hung between their davits. Allotted crewmembers oversaw each little craft, electric lights continued to burn brightly, and panic gradually wore itself out.

Meanwhile the ship was running a desperate race with the sea, striving with every ounce of steam in her boilers to find a safe berth for her mutilated body before the inrush of water drowned her fires. The race was close, even the dullest understood, for the *Nebraska* was settling forward. The ship plowed into the night head down, like a thing maddened with pain. She was becoming unmanageable, too, and O'Neil thought with pity of that little iron-hearted skipper on the bridge who was fighting her so furiously.

There was little confusion, little talking upon the upper deck now; only a child whimpering or a woman sobbing hysterically. But down forward among the steerage passengers the case was different. These were mainly Montenegrins, Poles, or Slavs bound for the construction camps to the west, and they surged from side to side like cattle, requiring Tomlinson's best efforts to keep them from rushing aft.

O'Neil had employed thousands of such men; in fact, many of these very fellows had cashed his time checks and knew him by sight. He went forward among them, and his appearance proved instantly reassuring. He found his two hostlers, and with their aid he soon reduced the mob to comparative order.

But despite his confident bearing, he felt a great uneasiness. The *Nebraska* seemed close to the point of diving; he judged she must be settling fast and wondered that the forward tilt did not lift her propeller out of the water. Fortunately, however, the surface of the water was like a polished floor and there were no swells to submerge her.

Overside to starboard he could see the dim black outlines of mountains slipping past, but where lay Halibut Bay or what distance remained to be covered, he could but vaguely guess.

In these circumstances the wait became almost unbearable. The race seemed hours long, the miles stretched into leagues, and with every moment of suspense the ship sank lower. The end came unexpectedly. There was a sudden startled outcry as the *Nebraska* struck for a second time that night. She rose slightly, rolled, bumped, grated briefly, then came to rest.

Captain Brennan shouted from the bridge:

"Fill your lifeboats, Mr. James, and lower away carefully."

A cheer rose from the huddled passengers.

The boiler room was still dry, it seemed, for the incandescent lights burned without a flicker, even after the grimy oilers and stokers had come pouring up on deck.

O'Neil climbed to the bridge. "Is this Halibut Bay?" he asked Captain Johnny.

"It is. But we're piled up on the reef outside. She may hold fast—I hope so, for there's deep water astern, and if she slips off, she'll go down."

"I'd like to save my horses," the younger man said. Through all the strain of the past half hour or more his uppermost thought had been for them. But Brennan had no sympathy for such sentiments.

"Hell's bells!" he exclaimed. "Don't talk of horses while we've got women and children aboard." He hastened away to assist in transferring his passengers.

Instead of following, O'Neil turned and went below. He found the water was kneedeep on the port side of the deck where his animals were quartered, which showed the ship had listed heavily. He judged she must be deeper by the head than he had imagined, and her nose was crushed in among the rocks. Until she settled at the stern, therefore, the case was not totally hopeless.

His appearance, the sound of his voice, were the signals for a chorus of eager whinnies and a great stamping of hoofs. Heads were thrust toward him from the stalls, alert ears pricked forward, satin muzzles rubbed against him as he calmed their terror. This blind trust made the man's throat tighten. He loved animals as he loved children, and above all he cared for horses. He understood them, he spoke their language as nearly as any human can be said to do so. Quivering muscles relaxed beneath his soothing palm; he called them by name, and they answered with gentle twitching lips against his cheek. Some of them even began to eat and switch their tails.

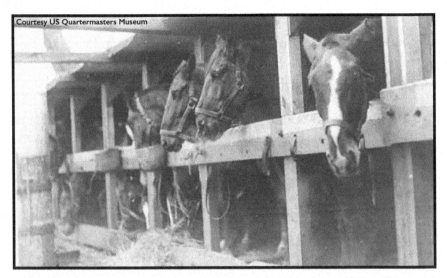

Thousands of horses were sent to Alaska via steamship after gold was discovered in the Klondike region in 1897. They were instrumental in helping to build transportation routes to resources.

He cursed aloud and made his way down the sloping deck to the square iron door, or port, through which he had loaded them. But he found it was jammed, or held fast by the pressure outside, and after a few moments' work in water above his knees he climbed to the starboard side. Here the entrance was obstructed by a huge pile of baled hay and grain in sacks. It would be no easy task to clear it away. He fell to work with desperate energy, for the ship was slowly changing her level. Her stern, which had been riding high, was filling; the sea stole in upon him silently. It crept up toward him until the horses, stabled on the lower side, were belly deep in it. Their distress communicated itself to the others.

O'Neil knew his position might prove perilous if the hulk should slip backward off the reef, yet he continued to toil, hurling heavy sacks behind him, bundling awkward bales out of the way, until his hands were bleeding, and muscles ached. He was perspiring furiously; the commotion around him was horrible. Then abruptly the lights went out, leaving him in utter blackness; the last fading yellow gleam was photographed briefly upon his retina.

Tears mingled with the sweat that drained down his cheeks as he felt his way slowly out of the place, splashing, stumbling, groping uncertainly. A horse screamed in a loud, horribly human note, and he shuddered. He was sobbing curses as he emerged into the cool open air on the forward deck.

His eyes were accustomed to the darkness now, and he could see something of his surroundings. He noted numerous lights out on the placid bosom of the bay, evidently lanterns on the lifeboats, and he heard distant voices.

He swept the moisture from his face; then with a start realized his situation. He listened intently. His eyes roved back along the boat deck. There was no doubt about it—the ship was deserted. Stepping to the rail, he observed how low the *Nebraska* lay and her bow was higher than her stern. From somewhere beneath his feet came a muffled grinding and a movement that told him the ship was seeking a more comfortable berth. He recalled stories of explosions and of the boiling eddies that sometimes accompany sinking hulls. Turning, he scrambled up to the cabin deck and ran swiftly toward his stateroom.

2

A GIRL APPEARS

O'Neil felt for the little bracket lamp on the wall of his stateroom and lit it. By its light he dragged a life preserver from the rack overhead and slipped the tapes about his shoulders, reflecting Alaska waters are disagreeably cold. Then he opened his traveling bags, dumped their contents on the white bedspread, and selected certain documents and trinkets. The latter he thrust into his pockets as he found them, the former he wrapped in handkerchiefs before stowing them away. The ship had listed now so it was difficult to maintain footing; the lamp hung at a grotesque angle and certain articles had become dislodged from their resting places. From outside came the gentle lapping of water, a gurgling and hissing as of air escaping through the decks. He could feel the ship strain. He acknowledged it was not pleasant to be left alone on a sinking hulk, particularly on an ink-black night.

All at once he whirled and faced the door with an exclamation of astonishment, for a voice had addressed him.

There, clinging to the casing, stood a woman—a girl—evidently drawn out of the darkness by the light that streamed down across the sloping deck from his stateroom. Plainly she just had awakened, for she was clothed in a silken nightrobe that failed to conceal the outlines of her body, the swelling contour of her bosom, the ripened fullness of her limbs. She had flung a quilted dressing gown of some sort over her shoulders and with one bare arm and hand strove to hold it in place. He saw her pink feet were thrust into soft, heelless slippers and her hair, black in this light, cascaded down to her waist. Her wide, dark eyes fixed on him with a stare like that of a sleepwalker.

"It is so dark—so strange—so still," she murmured. "What has happened?"

"God! Didn't they waken you?" he asked.

"Is the ship sinking?" Her odd bewilderment of voice and gaze puzzled him.

"We struck a rock," he said as he nodded. "The passengers have been taken off. We're the only ones left. In Heaven's name where have you been?"

"I was asleep."

He shook his head in astonishment. "How you failed to hear that hubbub...."

"I heard something, but I was ill. My head—I took something to ease the pain."

"Ah – medicine. It hasn't worn off yet, I see. You shouldn't have taken it. Drugs are nothing but poison to young people. Now at my age there might be some excuse for resorting to them, but you ...." He was talking to cover the panic of his thoughts, for his own predicament had been serious enough, and her presence rendered it doubly embarrassing. What in the world to do with her? His lips were smiling, but his eyes were grave as they roved over the cabin and out into the blackness of the night.

"Are we going to drown?" she asked, dully.

"Nonsense!" He said and laughed in apparent amusement, showing his large, strong teeth.

She came closer, glancing behind her and shrinking from the oily waters that could be seen over the rail and had crept up nearly to the sill of the door. She steadied herself by grabbing him uncertainly. Involuntarily he turned his eyes away, for he felt shame at profaning her with his gaze. She was soft and white, a fragile thing utterly unfit to cope with the night air and the freezing waters of Halibut Bay.

"I'm wretchedly afraid...," she whispered through white lips.

"None of that!" he said. "I'll see that nothing happens to you." He slipped out of his life preserver and adjusted it over her shoulders, first drawing her arms through the sleeves of her dressing gown and knotting the cord snugly around her waist. "Just as a matter of precaution," he assured her. "We may get wet. Can you swim?"

She shook her head.

"Never mind; I can." He found another lifebelt, fitted it to his own form, and led her out on the deck. The scuppers were awash now, and she gasped as the sea licked her bare feet. "Cold, isn't it?" he said. "But there's no time to dress, and it's just as well, perhaps, for heavy clothes would only hamper you."

She strove to avoid the icy waters and finally paused.

"I can't! I can't go on!"

Slipping his arm about her, he bore her to the door of the main cabin and entered. He could feel her warm, soft body quivering against his own. She had clasped his neck so tightly that he could scarcely breathe, but, lowering her until her feet were on the dry carpet, he gently loosed her arms.

"Now, my dear child," he told her. "You must do exactly as I tell you. Come! Calm yourself or I won't take you any farther." He held her off by her shoulders. "I may have to swim with you; you mustn't cling to me so!"

He heard her gasp and felt her draw away abruptly. Then he led her by the hand onto the starboard deck, and together they made their way forward toward the bridge.

The lights he had seen coming from the forward hold were still in view and he hailed them at the top of his voice. But other voices were calling through the night, some of them comparatively close at hand, others answering faintly from far inshore. The boats first launched were evidently landing, and those in charge of them were shouting directions to the ones behind. Some women had started singing and the chorus floated out to the man and the girl.

"Pull for the shore, sailor, pull for the shore."

It helped to drown their cries for assistance.

Women and children historically have been the first to be saved from sinking ships, as seen in this photo of passengers escaping the *Titanic* in April 1912.

O'Neil judged the ship was at least a quarter of a mile from the beach, and his heart sank, for he doubted that either he or his companion could last long in these waters. It occurred to him Brennan might be close by, waiting for the *Nebraska* to sink — it would be unlike the little captain to forsake his trust until the last possible moment — but he reasoned the cargo of lives in the skipper's boat would induce him to stand well off to avoid accident. He called lustily time after time, but no answer came.

Meanwhile the girl stood quietly beside him.

"Can't we make a raft?" she suggested, timidly, when he ceased to shout. "I've read of such things."

"There's no time," he told her. "Are you very cold?"

She nodded. "Please forgive me for acting so badly just now. It was all so sudden and — so awful! I think I can behave better. Oh! What was that?" She clutched him nervously, for from the forward end of the ship had come a muffled scream, like that of a woman.

"It's my poor horses," said the man. She looked at him curiously, prompted by the catch in his throat.

There followed a wait that seemed long, but was only a few minutes, for the ship was sliding backward and the sea was creeping upward faster and faster. At last they heard a shuddering sigh as she parted from the rocks and air rushed up through the deck openings with greater force. The *Nebraska* swung sluggishly with the tide; then, when her upper structure had settled flush with the sea, Murray O'Neil took the woman in his arms and leaped clear of the rail.

The first gasping moment of immersion was paralyzing; after that the reaction came, and the two began to struggle away from the sinking ship. The water was cruelly cold, and their bodies ached in every nerve and fiber. O'Neil did his best to encourage his companion. He talked to her through his chattering teeth, and once she had recovered from the mental shock of the first fearful plunge, she responded pluckily. He knew his own heart was normal and strong, but he feared the girl's might not be equal to the strain. Had he been alone, he felt sure he could have made it to shore, but with her upon his hands he only made a little headway.

The expanse of water seemed immense; it fairly crushed hope out of him. The lights on the shore were as distant as fixed stars. This was a country of heavy tides, he reflected, and he began to fear the current was sweeping them out. He turned to look for the ship, but could see no traces of her, and since it was inconceivable the *Nebraska* could have sunk so quietly, her disappearance confirmed his fears. More than once he thought he heard an answer to his cries for help — the rattle of rowlocks or the splash of oars — but his ears proved unreliable.

After a time the girl began to moan with pain and terror, but as numbness gradually robbed her of sensation, she became quiet. A little later her grip on his clothing relaxed and he saw she was collapsing. He drew her to him, held her so her face lay upturned, and her hair floated about his shoulders. In this position she could not drown, at least while his strength lasted. But he was rapidly losing control of himself. His teeth clicked loosely, his muscles shook and twitched. It required a great effort to shout, and he thought his voice did not carry as far as at first. Therefore he fell silent, paddling with his free arm and kicking to keep his blood stirring.

Several times he gave up and floated quietly, but courage was ingrained in him. Deep within his consciousness was a vitality, an inherited stubborn resistance to death, of which he knew nothing. It was that unidentified quality of mind that supports one man through a great sickness or a long period of privation, while another of more robust physique succumbs. That same quality brings one man out from desert wastes, or the white silence of the polar ice, while the bodies of his fellows remain to mark the trail. This innate power of supreme resistance is found in chosen individuals throughout the animal kingdom, and it was due to it alone that Murray O'Neil continued to fight the tide long after he had ceased to exert conscious control.

At length there came through the man's dazed sensibilities a different sort of sound – a human voice, mingled with the measured thud of oars in their sockets. It roused him like an electric current and gave him strength to hoarsely cry out. Someone answered him. Then out of the darkness to seaward emerged a deeper blot. It loomed large and proved to be a lifeboat full of people. It came to a stop within an oar's length of him. From the babble of voices he distinguished one that was familiar and cried the name of Johnny Brennan. His brain cleared. A great dreamlike sense of thanksgiving warmed him, and he felt equal to any effort. He was vaguely amazed to find his limbs refused to obey him, however.

His own name was being pronounced in shocked tones. The splash from an oar filled his face and strangled him, but he managed to grab onto the blade and was drawn in until outstretched hands seized him.

"Be careful, there!" an oarsman said. "We can't take him in without swamping."

"Make room or I'll bash in your bloody skull," Brennan demanded.

Another protest arose, and O'Neil saw the craft was indeed loaded to the gunwales.

"Take the girl," he implored. "I'll hang on. You can tow me."

The limp form was removed from his side and dragged over the wooden rower's bench while a murmur of excited voices went up.

"Can you hold out for a minute, Murray?" Brennan asked.

"Yes — I think so."

"I'd give you my place, but you're too big to be taken in without danger."

"Go ahead," chattered the man in the water. "Look after the girl before it's too late."

The captain's stout hand was in his collar now and he heard him crying.

"Pull, you muscle-bound heathens! Everybody sit still! Now away with her, men. Keep up your heart, Murray, my boy. Remember it takes more than water to kill a good Irishman. It's only a foot or two farther, and they've started a fire. Serves you right, you big idiot, for going overboard with all those boats. Man, you're pulling the arm out of me; it's stretched out like a garden hose! Hey! Cover up that girl, and you, lady, rub her feet and hands. Good! Move over, please, so the men can bail."

The next O'Neil knew he was feeling miserable and cold, notwithstanding the fact he was wrapped in dry clothing and laying so close to a roaring spruce fire its heat blistered him.

Brennan was bending over him with eyes wet. He was swearing, too, in a weak, faltering way, calling upon all the saints to witness the prostrate man was the embodiment of every virtue, and his death would be a national calamity. Others were gathered about, men and women, and among them O'Neil saw the doctor from Sitka whom he had met on board the *Nebraska*.

As soon as he was able to speak, he asked about the girl he had helped rescue. Johnny promptly reassured him.

"Man, she's doing fine. A jigger of brandy brought her to, gasping like a blessed mermaid."

"Was anybody lost?"

"Praise God, not a soul! But it's lucky I stood by to watch the old tub go down, or we'd be mourning two. You'll be well by morning. There's a cannery in the next inlet and I've sent a boat's crew for help. And now, my boy, lay yourself down again and take a sleep, won't you? It'll do you a lot of good."

But O'Neil shook his head and struggled to a sitting position.

"Thanks, Johnny," he said. "But I couldn't. I can hear those horses screaming, and besides — I must make new plans."

3

THE IRISH PRINCE

As dawn broke, the cannery tender from the station nearby nosed her way up to the gravelly shore where the castaways were gathered and blew a cheering toot-toot on her whistle. She was a flat-bottomed, wet-sterned craft, and the passengers of the *Nebraska* trooped onto her deck over a gangplank. As Captain Brennan had predicted, not one of them had wet a foot, except for the two who had been left aboard through their own carelessness.

By daylight, Halibut Bay appeared an idyllic spot, quite innocent of the terrors with which the night had endowed it. A pebbled half-moon of beach set in among rugged bluffs; the verdant forest crowded down to it from behind. Tiny crystal wavelets lapped along the shingle, swaying the brilliant sea mosses that clung to the larger rocks. Altogether the scene gave a strong impression of peace and security, yet just in the offing was one jarring contrast — the masts and funnel of the *Nebraska* slanting up out of the blue serenity, where she lay upon the sloping bottom in the edge of deep water.

The reaction following a sleepless night of anxiety had replaced the first feeling of thankfulness at deliverance, and it was not a happy cargo of humanity the rescuing boat bore with her as the sun peeped over the hills. Many of the passengers were only half dressed, all were exhausted and hungry, each one had lost something in the catastrophe. The men were silent, the women hysterical, the children fretful.

Murray O'Neil had recovered sufficiently to go among them with the same warm smile that had made him friends from the first. In the depths of his cool gray eyes was a sparkle that showed his unquenchable Celtic spirit, and before long smiles answered his smiles, jokes rose to meet his pleasantries.

It now was his turn to comfort Captain Johnny Brennan, who had yielded to the blackest despair once his responsibility was over.

"She was a fine ship, Murray," the master lamented, staring with tragic eyes at the *Nebraska's* spars.

"She was a tin washtub, and rusted like a sieve," O'Neil teased.

"But think of me losing her on a still night!"

"I'm not sure yet that it wasn't a jellyfish that swam through her."

"Humph! I suppose her cargo will be a total loss. Around $200,000...."

"Insured for $300,000 no doubt. I'll warrant the company will thank you."

"It's kind of you to cheer me up," said Brennan, a little less gloomily. "Especially after the way I abandoned you to drown, but the missus won't allow me in the house at all when she hears I left you in pickle. Thank God the girl didn't die, anyway! I've got that to be thankful for. Curtis Gordon would have broken me."

"Gordon?"

"Sure! Man, don't you know who you went bathing with? She's the daughter of that widow Gerard, and the most prominent passenger aboard, outside of your blessed self. Ain't that luck! If I was Japanese samurai, I'd split myself open with a breadknife."

"But, fortunately, you're a sensible 'harp' of old Ireland. I'll see the papers get the right story. So buck up."

"Do you think for a minute that Mrs. Brennan will understand why I didn't hop out of the lifeboat and give you my place? Not at all. I'm ruined nautically and domestically. I may live it down during the next 10 years, but meanwhile I'll sleep in the woodshed and speak when I'm spoken to."

Murray knew that Miss Gerard had been badly shaken by her ordeal, hence he made no attempt to see her even after the steamer had reached the fishing village and the rescued passengers had been taken in by the residents. Instead, he went directly to the one store in the place and bought its entire stock, which he turned over to the sufferers. It was well he did so, for the village was small and, although the townspeople were hospitable, both food and clothing were scarce.

A southbound steamer was due the next afternoon, it was learned, and plans were made for her to pick up the castaways and return them to Seattle. At the same time, O'Neil discovered a freighter heading west was expected some time that night. And since she did not call at this port, he arranged for a launch to take him out to the channel where he could intercept her. The loss of his horses had been a serious blow. It was now more imperative he should go on, since he would have to hire men to do horses' work.

During the afternoon, Miss Gerard sent for him. He went to the house of the cannery superintendent, where she had been staying. The superintendent's wife had clothed her, and she seemed to have recovered her poise of body and mind. O'Neil was surprised to find her quite a different person from the frightened and disheveled girl he had seen in the yellow lamplight of his stateroom the night before. She was as pale now as then, but her expression of terror and bewilderment had turned into one of reposeful confidence. Her lips were red and ripe and of a somewhat haughty turn. She was attractive, certainly, despite the disadvantage of the borrowed garments, and though she struck him as being possibly a little proud and cold, there was no lack of warmth in her greeting.

For her part, she beheld a man of perhaps 40, of commanding height and heavy build. He was gray about the temples; his eyes were gray, too, and rather small, but animated and kindly, with many little lines penciled about their corners. These were evidently marks of expression, not of age, and although the rugged face itself was not handsome, it had a degree of character that compelled her interest. His clothes were good, and despite their recent hard usage, lent him the appearance of a man habitually well dressed.

She was vaguely disappointed, having pictured him as being in the first flush of vigorous youth, but the feeling soon disappeared under the charm of his manner. The ideal figure she had imagined began to seem silly and school-girlish, unworthy of the man himself. She was pleased, too, by his faint though manifest embarrassment at her thanks, for she had feared a lack of tact.

Above all things she abhorred obligation of any sort, and she was inclined to resent masculine protection. This man's service filled her with real gratitude, yet she rebelled at the position in which it placed her. She preferred granting favors to receiving them.

But he dismissed the whole subject so brusquely he almost offended her, and when she realized how incomplete had been her acknowledgment, she said, with an air of pique:

"You might have given me a chance to thank you without dragging you here against your will."

"I'm sorry if I seemed neglectful."

She fell silent for a moment.

"Do you detest me for my cowardice?" she asked. "I couldn't blame you for never wanting to see me again."

"You were very brave. You were splendid," he said. "I simply didn't wish to intrude."

"I was terribly frightened," she confided. "But I felt I could rely on you. That's what everyone does, isn't it? You see, you have a reputation. They told me how you refused to be taken into the boat for fear of capsizing it. That was fine."

"Oh, there was nothing brave about that. I wanted to get in badly enough, but there wasn't, room. Jove! It was cold, wasn't it?" His ready smile played whimsically about his lips, and the girl felt herself curiously drawn to him. Since he chose to make light of himself, she determined to allow nothing of the sort.

"They have told me how you bought out this whole funny little place and turned it over to us," she said. "Is it because you have such a royal way of dispensing favors that they call you 'The Irish Prince'?"

"That's only a silly nickname."

"I don't think so. You give people food and clothes with a careless wave of the hand; you give me my life with a shrug and a smile; you offer to give up your own to a boatful of strangers without a moment's hesitation. I—I think you are a remarkable person."

"You'll turn my head with such flattery if you aren't careful," he said with a slight flush. "Please talk of something sensible now, for an antidote—your plans, for instance."

"My plans are never sensible, and what few I have are as empty as my pockets. To tell the truth, I have neither plans nor pockets since this is a borrowed gown," she said with a laugh.

"Pockets in gowns are entirely matters of hearsay, anyhow; I doubt if they exist. You are going back to Seattle?"

"Oh, I suppose so. It seems to be my fate, but I'm not a bit resigned. I'm one of those unfortunate people who can't bear to be disappointed."

"You can return on the next ship at the company's expense."

"No. Mother would never allow it. In fact, when she learns I'm out here she'll probably send me back to New York as fast as I can go."

"Doesn't she know where you are?"

"Indeed no! She thinks I'm safely and tamely at home. Uncle Curtis wouldn't object to my visit, I fancy; at any rate, I've been counting on his good offices with mother, but it's too late now."

"I'm like you," he said. "I can't brook disappointment. I'm going on."

In answer to her questioning look he explained his plan of intercepting the freight-steamer that night, whereupon her face brightened with sudden hope.

"Can I go, too?" she implored, eagerly. She was no longer the haughty young lady he had met upon entering the room, but a wistful child.

"I'm afraid that's hardly...."

"Oh! If only you knew how much it means! If only you knew how badly I want to! I'm not afraid of discomforts."

"It's not that...."

"Please! Please! Be a real prince and grant me this favor. Won't you? My heart is set upon it."

It was hard to resist her imploring eyes—eyes that showed they had never been denied. It was hard for O'Neil to refuse anything to a woman.

"If your uncle is willing...." he began.

"He isn't my real uncle—I just call him that."

"Well, if Mr. Gordon wouldn't object, perhaps I can manage it, provided, of course, you promise to explain to your mother."

Miss Gerard's frank delight showed she was indeed no more than a child. Her changed demeanor awakened a doubt in the man's mind.

"It will mean that you'll have to sit up all night in an open launch," he cautioned her.

"I'll sit up for a week."

"With the creepy water all about, and big black mountains frowning at you."

"Oh, fiddle!" she exclaimed. "You'll be there if I get frightened." Rising, she laid her hand on his arm and thanked him with an odd mingling of frankness and shyness, as if there could be no further doubt of his acquiescence. He saw her eyes were the color of shaded woodland springs and her hair was not black, but of a deep, rich brown where the sun played upon it, the hue of old mahogany, with the same blood-red flame running through it. He allowed himself to admire her in silence, until suddenly she drew back with a startled exclamation.

"What is it?"

"I forgot—I have no clothes." Her words came with a doleful cadence.

"The universal complaint of your sex," he said as a smile spread across his face. "Allow me to talk with your hostess. I'm sure she will let you walk out with your borrowed finery, just like Cinderella. You'll need a nice thick coat, too."

"But this is her very, very best dress."

"She shall receive, on the next ship, a big box all lined with tissue paper, with the imprint of the most fashionable dressmaker in Seattle. I'll arrange all that by cable."

"You don't know how she loves it," the girl said.

"Come! Call her in. If I'm to be a prince, you mustn't doubt my power."

Nor did the event prove him overconfident. Before he had barely made known his request, the good lady of the house was ready to surrender not only her best Sunday gown, but her fluttering heart as well. Murray O'Neil had a way of making people do what he wanted, and women invariably yielded to him.

4

A JOURNEY ENDS AT HOPE

To Natalie Gerard, the trip down the bay and into the Sound that night was a wonderful adventure. She remembered it afterward far more vividly than the shipwreck, which became blurred in retrospect. She soon began to think of it as of some half-forgotten nightmare. To begin with, the personality of Murray O'Neil intrigued her more and more. The man was so strong, so sympathetic, and he had such a resistless way of doing things. The stories she had heard of him were romantic, and the superintendent's wife had not allowed them to suffer in the telling. Natalie felt elated that such a remarkable person should exert himself on her behalf. And the journey itself impressed her imagination deeply.

Although it was nine o'clock when they boarded the launch, it was still light. The evening was yellow with the peculiar, diffused radiance of high latitudes, lending a certain someberness to their surroundings.

The rushing tide, the ragged rock teeth that showed through it, the trackless, unending forests that clothed the hills in every direction, awed her a little, yet gave her an unaccustomed feeling of freedom and contentment. The long wait out between the lonely islands, where the tiny cockleshell rolled strangely, although the sea seemed as level as a floor, held a subtle excitement. Darkness crept down out of the unpeopled gorges and swallowed them up, thrilling her with a sense of mystery.

When midnight came, she found she was ravenously hungry, and she was agreeably surprised when O'Neil produced an elaborate lunch. There were even thermos bottles filled with steaming hot coffee, more delicious, she thought, than anything she had ever before tasted. He called the meal their after-theater party, pretending they had just come from a Broadway melodrama of shipwreck and peril. The subject led them naturally to talk of New York, and she found he was more familiar with the city than she.

"I usually spend my winters there," he explained.

"Then you have an office in the city?"

"Oh yes. I've maintained a place of business there for years."

"Where is it? On Wall Street?"

"No." he said and smiled. "On upper Fifth Avenue. It's situated in the extreme southwest corner of the men's cafe at the Holland House. It consists of a round mahogany table and a leather settee."

"Really!"

"That's where I'm to be found at least four months out of every twelve."

"They told me you build railroads."

"I do—when I'm lucky enough to underbid my competitors. But that isn't always, and railroads aren't built every day."

"Mr. Gordon is building one."

"So I'm told." O'Neil marveled at the trick of fortune that had entangled this girl and her mother in the web of that brilliant and unscrupulous adventurer.

"Perhaps it will be a great success like your famous North Pass & Yukon Railway."

"Let's hope so." He was tempted to inquire what use Gordon had made of that widely advertised enterprise in floating his own undertaking, but instead he asked another question.

"Your mother has invested heavily, has she not?"

"Not in the railroad. Her fortune, and mine too, is all in the coal mines."

O'Neil smothered an exclamation.

"What is it?" she asked.

"Nothing, only — are you sure?"

"Oh, quite sure! The mines are rich, aren't they?"

"There are no mines, thanks to our misguided lawmakers at Washington," he told her. "There are vast deposits of fine coal that would make mines if we were allowed to work them, but we are not allowed."

"We? Are you a — a coal person, like us?"

"Yes. I was one of the first men in the Kyak fields, and I invested heavily. I know Mr. Gordon's group of claims well. I have spent more than $100,000 trying to perfect my titles and I'm no nearer patent now than I was to begin with — not so near, in fact. I fancy Gordon has spent as much and is in the same fix. It is a coal matter that brings me to Alaska now."

"I hardly understand."

"Of course not, and you probably won't after I explain. You see the government gave us — gave everybody who owns coal locations in Alaska — three years in which to do certain things; then it extended that time another three years. But recently, a new Secretary of the Interior has come into office. He has just rescinded that later ruling, without warning, which gives us barely time to comply with the law as it first stood. For my part, I'll have to hustle or lose everything I have put in. You see? That's why I hated to see those horses drown, for I intended to use them in reaching the coalfields. Now I'll have to hire men to carry their loads. No doubt Mr. Gordon has arranged to protect your holdings, but there are hundreds of claimants who will be ruined."

"I supposed the government protected its subjects," the girl said.

"One of the illusions taught in the elementary schools," O'Neil said with a laugh. "We Alaskans have found it does exactly the opposite! We have found it a harsh and unreasonable landlord. But I'm afraid I'm boring you."

He wrapped her more snugly in her coverings, for a chill had descended with the darkness, then strove to enliven her with stories garnered from his rich experience — stories that gave her fascinating glimpses of great undertakings and made her feel personally acquainted with people of unfamiliar type, whose words and deeds, mirthful or pathetic, were always refreshingly original. Of certain individuals he spoke repeatedly until their names became familiar to his hearer. He called them his "boys" and his voice tender as he told of their doings.

"These men are your staff?" she ventured.

"Yes. Everyone who succeeds in his work must have loyal hands to help him."

"Where are they now?"

"Oh, scattered from Canada to Mexico, each one doing his own work. There's Mellen, for instance; he's in Chihuahua building a cantilever bridge. He's the best steel man in the country. McKay, my superintendent, is running a railroad job in California. 'Happy Tom' Slater...."

"The funny man with the blues?"

"Exactly! He was at work on a hydraulic project near Dawson the last I heard of him. Dr. Gray is practicing in Seattle, and Parker, the chief engineer, has a position of great responsibility in Boston. He is the brains of our outfit, you understand; it was really he who made the North Pass & Yukon possible. The others are scattered out in the same way, but they'd all come if I called them." The first note of pride she had detected crept into his voice when he said: "My boys are never idle. They don't have to be, after working with me."

"And what is your part of the work?" the girl asked.

"Me? Oh, I'm like Marcelline, the clown at the Hippodrome — always pretending to help, but forever keeping underfoot. When it becomes necessary, I raise the money to keep the performance going."

"Do you really mean that all those men would give up their positions and come to you if you sent for them?"

"By the first train, or afoot, if there were no other way. They'd follow me to the Philippines or Timbuctoo, regardless of their homes and their families."

"That is splendid! You must feel very proud of inspiring such loyalty," Natalie said. "But why are you idle now? Surely there are railroads to be built somewhere."

"Yes, I was asked to figure on a contract in Manchuria the other day. I could have had it easily, and it would have meant my everlasting fortune, but...."

"But what?"

"The country is sickly and unsafe. Some of my boys would die before we finished it, and the game isn't worth that price. No, I'll wait. Something better will turn up. It always does."

As Natalie looked upon that kindly, square-hewn face with its tracery of lines about the eyes, its fine, strong jaw, and its indefinable expression of power, she began to understand more fully why those with whom she had talked had spoken of Murray O'Neil with an almost worshipful respect. She felt insignificant and purposeless as she huddled there beside him, and her complacence at his attentions deepened into a vivid sense of satisfaction. Thus far he had spoken entirely of men; she wondered if he ever thought of women and thrilled a bit at the intimacy that had sprung up between them so quickly and naturally.

It confirmed her feeling of prideful confidence in the man that the northbound freighter should punctually show her lights around the islands, and she should pause in her majestic sweep at the signal of this pigmy craft. The ship loomed huge and black and terrifying as the launch at length drew in beneath it; its sides towered like massive, unscalable ramparts. There was a delay; there seemed to be some querulousness on the part of the officer in command at being thus halted, some doubt about allowing strangers to come aboard. But the girl smiled to herself as the voices flung themselves back and forth through the night.

Once they learned who it was that called from the sea, their attitude would quickly change. Sure enough, in a little while orders were shouted from the bridge; she heard men running from somewhere, and a rope ladder came swinging down. O'Neil was lifting her from her warm nest of rugs and telling her to fear nothing. The launch crept closer, coughing and shuddering as if in terror at this close contact.

There was a brief instant of breathlessness as the girl found herself swung out over the waters; then a short climb with O'Neil's protecting hand at her waist and she stood panting, radiant, upon steel decks that began to throb and tremble to the churning engines.

One further task remained for her protector's magic powers. It appeared there were no quarters on the ship for women, but after a subdued discussion between Murray and the captain, she was led to the cleanest and coziest of staterooms high up near the bridge. Over the door she glimpsed a metal plate with the words "First Officer" lettered upon it. O'Neil was bidding her good night and wishing her untroubled rest, then almost before she had accustomed herself to her new surroundings an immaculate, though sleepy Japanese steward stood before her with a tray. He was extremely cheerful for one so lately awakened, being still aglow with pleased surprise over the banknote that lay neatly folded in his waistcoat pocket.

Natalie sat cross-legged on her berth and munched with the appetite of a healthy young animal at the fruit, biscuits, and lovely heavy cake the steward had brought. She was glad now she had disobeyed her mother. It was high time, indeed, to assert herself, for she was old enough to know something of the world, and her judgment of men was mature enough to ensure perfect safety—that much had been proved. She felt her adventure had been a great success practically and romantically. She wanted to lie awake and think it over in detail, but she soon grew sleepy. Just before she dozed off, she wondered drowsily if "The Irish Prince" had found quarters for himself, then reflected that undoubtedly the captain had been happy to tumble out of bed for him. Or perhaps he felt no fatigue and would watch the night through. Even now he might be pacing the deck outside her door. At any rate, he was not far off. She closed her eyes, feeling deliciously secure and comfortable.

In one way, the southern coast of Alaska may be said to be perhaps a million years younger than any land on this continent, for it is still in the glacial period. The vast alluvial plains and valleys of the interior are rimmed in to the southward and shut off from the Pacific by a well-nigh impassable mountain barrier, the top of which is capped with perpetual snow. Its gorges, for the most part, run rivers of ice instead of water. Europe has nothing like these glaciers that overflow the Alaska valleys and submerge the hills, for many of them contain more ice than the whole of Switzerland. This range is the Andes of the north, and it curves westward in a magnificent sweep, hugging the shore for a thousand leagues. Against it the sea beats, its frozen crest played upon by constant rains, fogs, and blizzards. But over beyond lies a land of sunshine, of long, dry, golden summer days.

Into this chaos of cliff and peak and slanting canyon, midway to the westward, is King Phillip Sound, a sheet of water dotted with islands and framed by forests. It reaches inland with long, crooked tentacles that end like talons, in living ice. Hidden some 40 miles up one of these, upon the moraine of a receding glacier, sits Cortez, a thriving village and long the point of entry to the interior, the commencement of the overland trail to the golden valleys of the Yukon and the Tanana. The government wagon trail winds in from here, tracing its sinuous course over one pass after another until it emerges into the undulating prairies of the "inside country."

Looking at the map, one would imagine an easier gateway to the heart of Alaska would be afforded by the valley of the Salmon River, which enters the ocean some few miles to the eastward of King Phillip Sound, but there are formidable difficulties. The stream bursts the last rampart of the Coast Range asunder by means of a canyon down which it rages in majestic fury and up which no craft can navigate. Then it spreads itself out through a dozen shallow mouths across a 40-mile delta of silt, sand, and glacial wash. As if Nature feared her arctic strongbox still might be invaded by this route, she has placed additional safeguards to the approach in the form of giant glaciers, through the bowels of which the Salmon River is forced to burrow.

Men had attempted to ascend the valley in the early days of the Klondike gold rush, but they had succeeded only at the cost of such peril and disaster that others were warned away. The region became the source of many weird stories, and while the icefields could be seen from the Kyak coalfields, and on still days their cannonading could be heard far out at sea, there were few who had ventured to cross the

40-mile morass that lay below them and thus attempt to verify or to disprove the rumors.

It was owing to these topographical conditions that Cortez had been established as the point of entry to the interior; it was because of them she had grown and flourished, with her sawmills and her ginmills, her docks, and her dives. But at the time when this story opens Alaska had developed to a point where an overland outlet by winter and a circuitous inlet, by way of Bering Sea and the crooked Yukon, in summer were no longer sufficient. There was need of a permanent route for men and freight to come and go throughout the year. The famous North Pass & Yukon Railway, far to the east, afforded transportation to Dawson City and the Canadian territory. It had proven itself such a financial success that builders began to look for a harbor more to the west from which they could tap the great heart of Alaska. Thus it was that Cortez awoke one morning to find herself selected as the terminus of a new line. Other railway propositions followed, flimsy promotion schemes for the most part, but among them two that had more than paper and hot air behind them. One of these was backed by the Copper Trust, which had made heavy mining investments 200 miles inland, the other by Curtis Gordon, a promoter, who claimed New York as his birthplace and the world as his residence.

Gordon had been one of the first locaters in the Kyak coalfields, and he also had purchased a copper prospect a few miles down the bay from Cortez, where he had started a town called Hope. There were some who shook their heads and smiled knowingly when they spoke of that prospect, but no one denied it was fast assuming the outward semblance of a mine under Gordon's direction. He had erected a fine substantial wharf, together with buildings, bunkhouses, cottages, and a spacious residence for himself; and daily the piles of debris beneath the tunnel entries to his workings grew. He paid high wages, he spent money lavishly, and he had a magnificent and compelling way with him that dazzled and delighted the good people of Cortez. When he began work on a railroad, designed to reach far into the interior, his action was taken as proof positive of his financial standing, and his critics were put down as pessimists who had some personal grudge against him.

It was up to the raw, new village of Hope, with its odor of fresh cut fir and undried paint, the freight-steamer with Natalie Gerard and The Irish Prince aboard came gingerly one evening.

O'Neil surveyed the town with some curiosity as he approached, for Gordon's sensational doings had interested him greatly. He was accustomed to the rapid metamorphoses of a growing land. It was his business, in fact, to win the wilderness over to order, and therefore he was not astonished at the changes wrought here during his absence. But he was agreeably surprised at the businesslike arrangement of the place, and the evidence a strong and practiced hand had guided its development.

Even before the ship tied up, he had identified the tall, impressive man on the dock as the genius and founder of Hope, and the dark-haired, well-formed woman beside him as Natalie's mother. It was not until they were close at hand that the daughter made her presence known; then, unable to restrain herself longer, she shrieked her greeting down over the rail.

Mrs. Gerard started, then stared upward as if at an apparition; she stretched out a groping hand to Gordon, who stood as if frozen in his tracks. They seemed to be exchanging hurried words, and the man appeared to be reassuring his companion. It looked odd to O'Neil; but any suspicion Natalie was unwelcome disappeared when she reached the dock. Her mother's dark eyes were bright with unshed tears of gladness, her face was transfigured, she showed the strong, repressed emotion of an undemonstrative nature as they embraced. Natalie clung to her, laughing, crying, bombarding her with questions, begging forgiveness, and babbling of her adventures. Their resemblance was striking, and in point of beauty there seemed little to choose between them. They might have been nearly of an age, except the mother lacked the girl's restless vivacity.

O'Neil remained in the background, like an uncomfortable bridegroom, conscious meanwhile of the searching and hostile regard of Curtis Gordon. But at last his protegee managed to gasp out the main facts of the shipwreck and her rescue, whereupon Gordon's attitude abruptly altered.

"My God!" he said. "You were not on the *Nebraska*?"

"Yes, yes, yes!" Natalie cried. "The lifeboats went off and left me all alone — in the dark — with the ship sinking! Mr. O'Neil saved me. He took me up and jumped just as the ship sank, and we were all night in the freezing water. We nearly died, didn't we? He fainted, and so did I, mummie dear — it was so cold. He held me up until we were rescued, though, and then there wasn't room in the lifeboat for both of us. But he made them take me in, just the same, while he stayed in the water. He was unconscious when he reached the shore. Oh, it was splendid!"

O'Neil's identity being established, and the nature of his service becoming apparent, Curtis Gordon took his hand in a crushing grip and thanked him in a way that might have warmed the heart of a stone gargoyle. The man was transformed, now that he understood; he became a geyser of eloquence. He poured forth his appreciation in rounded sentences; his splendid musical voice softened and swelled and broke with a magnificent and touching emotion. Through it all the Irish contractor remained uncomfortably silent, for he could not help thinking this fulsome outburst was aroused rather by the man who had built the North Pass.

A crowd was collecting round them, but Gordon cleared it away with an imperious gesture.

"Come!" he said. "This is no place to talk. Mr. O'Neil's splendid gallantry renders our mere thanks inane. He must allow us to express our gratitude in a more fitting manner."

"Please don't," O'Neil begged.

"You are our guest; the hospitality of our house is yours. Hope would be honored to welcome you, sir, at any time, but under these circumstances...."

"I'm going right on to Cortez."

"The ship will remain here for several hours, discharging freight, and we insist you allow us this pleasure meanwhile. You shall spend the night here, then perhaps you will feel inclined to prolong your stay. All that Cortez has we have in double proportion — I say it with pride. Cortez is no longer the metropolis of the region. Hope — well, I may say that Cortez is, of all Alaska cities, the most fortunate, since it has realized its Hope." He laughed musically. "This town has come to stay; we intend to annex Cortez eventually. If you feel you must go on, I shall deem it a pleasure to send you later in my motorboat. She makes the run in 15 minutes. But you must first honor our house and our board; you must permit us to pledge your health in a glass. We insist!"

"Please!" Mrs. Gerard insisted.

"Do come, your Highness," Natalie urged from the shelter of the elder woman's arms.

"You're more than kind," O'Neil said, and together the four turned their faces to the shore.

5

CURTIS GORDAN MAKES PLANS

C urtis Gordon's respect for his guest increased as they walked up the dock, for, before they had taken many steps, out from the crowd that had gathered to watch the ship's arrival stepped one of his foremen. This fellow shook hands warmly with O'Neil, whereupon others followed, one by one — miners, day laborers, and roughnecks of many nationalities. They doffed their hats – something they never did for Gordon — and stretched out grimy hands, their faces lighting up with smiles. O'Neil accepted their greetings with genuine pleasure and called them by name.

"We just heard you was shipwrecked," said Gordon's foreman. "You wasn't hurt, was you?"

"Not in the least."

"God be praised! There's a lot of the old gang at work here."

"So I see."

"Here's Shorty, you may remember him from the North Pass." The speaker dragged from the crowd a red-faced, perspiring ruffian who had hung back with the bashfulness of a small boy. "He's the fellow you dug out of the slide at twenty-eight."

"Connors!" O'Neil cried. "I'm glad to see you. And how are the two arms of you?"

"Better 'n ever they was, the both av them!" Connors blushed, doubled his fists, and flexed his bulging muscles. "An' why shouldn't they be, when you set 'em both with your own hands, Misther O'Neil? 'Twas as good a job as Doc Gray ever done in the hospittle. I hope you're doin' well, sir." He pulled his forelock, placed one foot behind the other, and tapped it on the planking, grinning expansively.

"Very well indeed, thank you."

O'Neil's progress was slow, for half the crowd insisted upon shaking his hand and exchanging a few words with him. Clumsy Swedes bobbed their heads, dark-browed foreign laborers, whose nationality it was hard to distinguish, showed their teeth and chattered words of greeting.

"Bless my soul!" Gordon finally exclaimed. "You know more of them than I do."

"Yes – I seldom have to fire a man."

"Then you are favored of the gods. Labor is my great problem. It is the supreme drawback of this country. These people drift and blow on every breeze, like the sands of the Sahara. With more and better help I could work wonders here."

Unexpected as these salutations had been, O'Neil's greatest surprise came a moment later as he passed the first of the company buildings. There he heard his name pronounced in a voice that stopped him, and in an open doorway he saw a huge, loose-hung man of tremendous girth, with a warbag in his hand and a wide black hat thrust back from a shiny forehead.

"Why, Tom!" he exclaimed. "Tom Slater!"

Gordon groaned and went on with the women. "Come up to the house when you escape, Mr. O'Neil," he said. "I shall have dinner served."

Mr. Slater came forward slowly, dragging his clothes bag with him. The two shook hands.

"What in the world are you doing here, Tom?"

"Nothing!" Slater said. He had a melancholy cast of features, utterly out of keeping with his rotund form. In his eye was the somber glow of a soul at war with the flesh.

"Nothing?"

"I had a good job, putting in a power plant for his nibs," he said, indicating the retreating Gordon with a disrespectful jerk of the thumb. "But I quit."

"Not enough pay?"

"Best wages I ever got. He pays well."

"Poor grub?"

"Grub's fine."

"What made you quit?"

"I haven't exactly quit, but I'm going to. When I saw you coming up the dock I said: 'There's the chief! Now he'll want me.' So I began to pack." The speaker dangled his partly filled warbag as evidence.

"Ain't that just me?" he continued in a sour murmur. "I ain't had a day's luck since Lincoln was shot. The minute I get a good job, along you come and spoil it."

"I don't want you," O'Neil said with a laugh.

But Slater was not convinced. He shook his head.

"Oh yes, you do. You've got something on, or you wouldn't be here. I've been drawing pay from you now for over five minutes."

O'Neil made a gesture of impatience.

"No! No! In the first place, I have nothing for you to do; in the second, I probably couldn't afford the wages Gordon is paying you."

"That's the hell of it," gloomily agreed the man many called Happy Tom. "Where are your grips? I'll begin by carrying them."

"I haven't any. I've been shipwrecked. Seriously, Tom, I have no place for you."

The repetition of this statement made not the smallest impression upon the hearer.

"You'll have one soon enough," he replied. Then with a touch of spirit, added "Do you think I'd work for this four-flusher if you were in the country?"

"Hush!" O'Neil cast a glance over his shoulder. "By the way, how do you happen to be here? I thought you were in Dawson."

"I finished that job. I was working back toward ma and the children. I haven't seen them for two years."

"You think Gordon is a false alarm?"

Happy Tom spat with unerring accuracy at a crack.

"He's talking railroads. Railroads!" Slater said. "Why, I've got a boy back in the state of Maine, 14 years old...."

"Willie?"

"Yes. My son, Willie, could skin Curtis Gordon at railroad building—and Willie is the sickly one of the outfit. But I'll hand it to Gordon for one thing. He's a money getter and a money spender. He knows where the loose stone in the hearth is laid, and he knows just which lilac bush the family savings are buried under. Those poverty-stricken Pilgrim Fathers in my part of the country come up and drop their bankbooks through the slot in his door every morning. He's the first easy money I ever had; I'd get rich off him, but...." Slater sighed. "Of course you had to come along and wrench me away from the till."

"Don't quit on my account," urged his former chief. "I'm up here on coal matters. I can't take time to explain now, but I'll see you later."

"Suit yourself, only don't keep me loafing on full time. I'm an expensive man. I'll be packed and waiting for you."

O'Neil went on his way, somewhat amused, yet undeniably pleased at finding his boss packer here instead of far inland, for Slater's presence might, after all, fit well enough into his plans.

The Irish Prince had gained something of a reputation for extravagance, but he acknowledged himself completely outshone by the luxury with which Curtis Gordon had surrounded himself at Hope. The promoter had spoken of his modest living quarters—they actually consisted of a handsome 20 room house, furnished with the elegance of a Newport cottage. The rugs were thick and richly colored; the furniture was of cathedral oak and mahogany. In the library were deep leather chairs and bookcases, filled mainly with the works of French and German authors of decadent type. The man's taste in art was revealed by certain pictures, undeniably clever, but a little too daring. He was undoubtedly a sybarite, yet he evidently possessed rare energy and executive force. It was an unusual combination.

The dinner was notable mainly for its lavish disregard of expense. There were strawberries from Seattle, fresh cream and butter from

Gordon's imported cows, cheese prepared expressly for him in France, and a champagne the date of which he took pains to make known.

Overall, he played host agreeably enough and his constant flow of talk was entertaining. His anecdotes embraced three continents; his wit, though Teutonic, was genial and mirth provoking. When Mrs. Gerard took time from her worshipful regard of her daughter to enter the conversation, she spoke with easy charm and spontaneity. As for Natalie, she was intoxicated with delight; she chattered, she laughed, she interrupted with the joyful exuberance of youth.

Under such circumstances the meal should have proved enjoyable, yet the guest of honor had never been more ill at ease. Precisely what accounted for the feeling he could not quite determine. Somewhere back in his mind was a suspicion that things were not as they should be, here in this house of books and pictures and incongruities. He told himself he should not be so narrow minded as to resent Gloria Gerard's presence here, particularly since she had told him her friendship for Gordon dated back many years. Nevertheless, the impression remained to disturb him.

"You wonder, perhaps, why I have been so extravagant with my living quarters," Gordon said, as they walked into the library. "But it is not alone for me. You see I have people associated with me who are accustomed to every comfort and luxury, and I built this house for them. Mrs. Gerard has been kind enough to grace the establishment with her presence, and I expect others of my stockholders to do likewise. You see, I work in the light, Mr. O'Neil; I insist upon the broadest publicity in all my operations, and to that end I strive to bring my clients into contact with the undertaking itself. For instance, I am bringing a party of my stockholders all the way from New York, at my own expense, just to show them how their interests are being administered. I have chartered a special train and a ship for them, and of course, they must be properly entertained while here."

"Quite a scheme," O'Neil said.

"I wanted to show them this marvelous country, God's wonderland of opportunity. They will return impressed by the solidity and permanence of their investment."

CURTIS GORDON MAKES PLANS

Certainly the man knew how to play his game. No more effective means of advertising, no more profitable stock-jobbing scheme could be devised than a free trip of that sort and a tour of Alaska under the watchful guidance of Curtis Gordon. If any member of the party returned unimpressed, it would not be the fault of the promoter; if any one of them did not voluntarily go out among his personal friends as a missionary, it would be because Gordon's magnetism had lost its power. O'Neil felt a touch of unwilling admiration.

"I judge, from what you say, the mine gives encouragement," he ventured, eying his host curiously through a cloud of tobacco smoke.

"'Encouragement' is not the word. Before many years, Hope Consolidated will be listed on the exchanges of the world along with Amalgamated and the other great producers. We have here, Mr. O'Neil, a tremendous mountain of ore, located at tidewater, on one of the world's finest harbors. The climate is superb. We have coal near at hand for our own smelter. The mine only requires systematic development under competent hands."

"I was in Cortez when Lars Anderson made his first discovery here, and I had an option on all this property," O'Neil told his host. "I believe the price was $1,200; at any rate, it was I who drove those tunnels you found when you bought him out."

Gordon's eyes wavered briefly, then he laughed.

"My dear sir, you have my sincere sympathy. Your poison, my meat as it were, eh? You became discouraged too soon. Another 100 feet of work and you would have been justified in paying $12,000. This 'Eldorado' the Copper Trust has bought has a greater surface showing than Hope, I grant; but it lies 200 miles inland, and there is the all-important question of transportation to be solved. The ore will have to be hauled, or smelted on the ground, while we have the Kyak coalfields at our door. The Heidlemanns are building a railroad to it that will parallel mine in places, but the very nature of their enterprise foredooms it to failure."

"Indeed? How so?"

"My route is the better. By a rigid economy of expenditure, by a careful supervision of detail, I can affect a tremendous saving over their initial cost. I hope to convince them of the fact, and thus induce them to withdraw from the field or take over my road at a reasonable figure. Negotiations are underway."

O'Neil refrained from smiling, with difficulty, at this talk of economy from Curtis Gordon. He felt certain the man's entire operations were as unsound as his statement he could bring the Trust to terms. Yet Gordon seemed thoroughly in earnest. Either he expected to fool his present hearer, or else he had become hypnotized by the spell of his own magnificent twaddle. O'Neil could not tell which.

"Who laid out your right-of-way?" he asked.

"A very able young engineer, Dan Appleton. An excellent man, but unreliable in certain things. I had to let him go this very afternoon, in fact, for insubordination. But I discharged him more for the sake of discipline than anything else. He'll be anxious to return in a few days. Now tell me...." Gordon paused and fixed his visitor with a bland stare that failed to mask his gnawing curiosity. "What brings you to King Phillip Sound? Are we to be rivals in the railroad field?"

"No. There are enough projects of that sort in the neighborhood for the present."

"Five, all told, but only one destined to succeed."

"I'm bound for the Kyak coalfields to perfect and amend my surveys under the new ruling."

"Ah! I've heard about that ruling."

"Heard about it?" O'Neil said. "Good Lord! Haven't you complied with it?"

"Not yet."

"You surely intend to do so?"

"Oh yes—I suppose so."

"If you don't, you'll lose...."

"I'm not sure we can ever win."

"Nonsense!"

"I'm not sure it's wise to put more good money into those coal claims," Gordon said. "This ruling will doubtless be reversed as the others have been. One never knows what the Land Office policy will be two days at a time."

"You know your own business," O'Neil said. "But unless you have inside information, or a bigger pull in Washington than the rest of us, I'd advise you to get busy. I'll be on my way to Kyak in the morning with a gang of men." Gordon's attitude puzzled him, for he could not bring himself to believe such indifference was genuine.

"We have been treated unfairly by the government."

"Granted!"

"We have been fooled, cheated, hounded as if we were a crowd of undesirable aliens, and I'm heartily sick of the injustice. I prefer to work along lines of least resistance. I feel tempted to let Uncle Sam have my coal claims, since he has lied to me and gone back on his promise. I'd rather devote myself to other enterprises that offer a certainty of greater profits."

Then Gordon smiled deprecatingly. "I dare say, I shall hold on, as you are doing, until that fossilized bureau at Washington imposes some new condition that will ruin us all."

Remembering Natalie's statement her own and her mother's fortunes were tied up in the mines, O'Neil felt inclined to go over Gordon's head and tell the older woman plainly the danger of delay in complying with the law, but he thought better of the impulse. Her confidence in this man was supreme and it seemed incredible that Gordon should jeopardize her holdings and his own. More likely his attitude was just a part of his pose, designed to show the bigness of his views and to shed a greater luster upon his railroad project.

It was difficult to escape from the hospitality of Hope, and O'Neil succeeded in doing so only after an argument with Natalie and her mother. They let him go at last only upon his promise to return on his way back from the coalfields. Then they insisted on accompanying him down to the dock, whither Gordon had preceded them to have his motorboat ready.

As they neared the landing, they overheard the latter in spirited debate with Happy Tom Slater.

"But my dear fellow," he was saying, "I can't lose you and Appleton on the same day."

"You can't? Why, you've done it!" the fat man retorted.

"I refuse to be left in the lurch this way. You must give more notice."

Slater shrugged, and without a word tossed his bulging warbag into the motorboat moored beneath him. His employer's face was purple with rage as he turned to Murray and the ladies, but he calmed himself sufficiently to say:

"This man is in charge of important work for me, yet he tells me you have hired him away."

"Tom!" O'Neil exclaimed.

"I never said that," Slater protested. "I only told you I was working for Murray."

"Well?"

"I hired myself. He didn't have anything to say about it. I do all the hiring, firing, and boosting in my department."

"I appeal to you, O'Neil. I'm shorthanded," Gordon cried.

"I tell you he don't have a word to say about it," Slater said.

Natalie gave a little tinkling laugh. She recognized in this man the melancholy hero of more than one tale The Irish Prince had told her. Murray did his best, but knowing Happy Tom's calm obstinacy of old, he had no real hope of persuading him.

"You see how it is," he said, finally. "He's been with me for years and he refuses to work for anyone else while I'm around. If I don't take him with me, he'll follow."

Mr. Slater nodded vigorously, then imparted these tidings:

"It's getting late, and my feet hurt." He bowed to the women, then lowered himself ponderously yet carefully over the edge of the dock and into the leather cushions of the launch. Once safely aboard, he took a package of wintergreen chewing gum from his pocket and began to chew, staring out across the Sound with that placid, speculative enjoyment that reposes in the eyes of a cow at sunset.

Curtis Gordon's face was red and angry as he shook hands stiffly with his guest and voiced the formal hope they would meet again.

"I'm glad to be gone," Slater said as the speedboat rushed across the bay. "I'm a family man, and I've got principles. Gordon's got neither."

"It was outrageous for you to walk out so suddenly. It embarrassed me."

"Oh, he'd let me go without notice if he felt like it. He fired Dan Appleton this afternoon just for telling the truth about the mine. That's what I'd have got if I'd stayed on much longer. I was filling up with words and my skin was getting tight. I'd have busted, sure, inside of a week."

"Isn't the mine any good?"

"It ain't a mine at all. It's nothing but an excavation filled with darn fools and owned by idiots; still, I s'pose it serves Gordon's purpose." After a pause he continued. "They tell me snakes eat their own young – Gordon ought to call that mine the Anaconda, for it'll swallow its own dividends and all the money those Eastern people can raise."

"I'm sorry for Mrs. Gerard."

Slater emitted a sound like the moist exhalation of a porpoise as it rises to the surface.

"What do you mean by that snort?" Murray asked.

"It's funny how much some people are like animals. Now the ostrich thinks when his head is hid, his whole running gear is out of sight. Gordon's an ostrich. As for you — you remind me of a mud turtle. A turtle don't show nothing but his head, and when it's necessary he can yank that under cover. Gordon don't seem to realize he sticks up above the underbrush — either that or else he don't care who sees him. He and that woman...."

"Never mind her," O'Neil said. "I'm sure you're mistaken."

Mr. Slater grunted once more, then chewed his gum silently, staring mournfully into the twilight.

"Why don't you show these people how to build a railroad, Murray?" he asked after a moment.

"No, thank you! I know the country back of here. It's not feasible."

"The Copper Trust is doing it."

"All the more reason why I shouldn't. There are five projects underway now, and there won't be more than enough traffic for one."

Slater nodded. "Every man who has $2, a clean shirt, and a friend at Washington has got a railroad scheme up his sleeve."

"It will cost $30 million to build across those three divides and into the copper country. When the road is done it will be one of heavy grades, and...."

"No wonder you didn't get the contract from the Heidlemanns – if your estimate was $30 million."

"I didn't put in a figure."

Tom looked surprised. "Why didn't you? You know them."

"I was like the little boy who didn't go to the party – I wasn't asked." The speaker's expression showed his pride had been hurt and discouraged further questioning. "We'll hire our men and our boats tonight," he said. "I've arranged for that freighter to drop us off at Omar on her way out. We'll have to row from there to Kyak. I expected to land my horses at the coast and pack in from Kyak Bay, but that shipwreck changed my plans. Poor brutes! After my experience, I'll never swim horses in this water again."

An eleven-o'clock twilight enveloped Cortez when the two men landed, but the town was awake. The recent railway and mining activity in the neighborhood had brought a considerable influx of people to King Phillip Sound, and the strains of music from dancehall

Courtesy University of Alaska Fairbanks

Around the time Murray O'Neil arrived in Cortez (Valdez), the town was buzzing with railroad building.

The Valdez-Yukon Railroad Company, organized in 1905 to build a railroad from Valdez to Dawson, wanted to benefit from the rich copper and gold districts of the Copper, Chitina, and Tanana rivers.

doors, the click of checks and roulette balls from the saloons, gave evidence of an unusual prosperity.

O'Neil had no difficulty in securing men. Once he was recognized, the scenes at Hope were re-enacted, and there was a general scramble to enlist on his payroll. Within an hour, therefore, his arrangements were made, and he and Tom retired to Callahan's Hotel for a few hours' sleep.

A stud game was going on in the barroom when they entered. O'Neil paused to watch it while Slater spoke to one of the players, a clean-cut, blond youth of whimsical countenance. When the two friends finally faced the bar for their nightcap, Tom explained.

"That's Appleton, the fellow Gordon fired today. I told him I'd left the old man flat."

"Is he a friend of yours?"

"Sure. Nice boy — good engineer, too."

"Umph! That game is crooked."

"No?" Happy Tom displayed a flash of interest.

"Yes, Cortez is fast becoming a metropolis, I see. The man in the derby hat is performing a little feat that once cost me $4,000 to learn."

"I'd better split Dan away," Tom said.

"Wait! Education is a good thing, even if it is expensive at times. I fancy your friend is bright enough to take care of himself. Let's wait a bit."

"Ain't that just my blamed luck?" Slater said. "Now if they were playing faro, I could make a killing. I'd copper Appleton's bets and open the ones he coppered!"

O'Neil smiled, for Happy Tom's caution in money matters was notorious. "You know you don't believe in gambling," he said.

"It's not a belief, it's a disease," the fat man said. "I was born to be a gambler, but the business is too uncertain. Now that I'm getting so old and feeble that I can't work anymore, I'd take it up, only I broke three fingers, and when I try to deal, I drop the cards. What are we going to do?"

"Just wait," O'Neil said.

6

MURRAY O'NEIL DREAMS

Unobserved, the two friends watched the poker game that for a time proceeded quietly. But suddenly they saw Appleton lean over the table and address the man wearing the derby hat; then, thrusting back his chair, he rose and yelled.

"I tell you I saw it. I thought I was mistaken at first." His face was white, and he disregarded the efforts of his righthand neighbor to quiet him.

"Don't squeal," the dealer said with a smile. "I'll leave it to the boys if I did anything wrong."

"You pulled that king from the bottom. It may not be wrong, but it's darned peculiar."

"Forget it!" one of the others exclaimed. "Denny wouldn't double cross you."

"Hardly!" Mr. Denny agreed. "You're 'in' a $180, but if you're sore you can have it back."

Appleton flung his cards into the middle of the table and turned away. "It's a hard thing to prove, and I'm not absolutely sure I saw straight, or I'd take it back fast enough."

Denny shrugged and gathered in the discarded hand. "You've been drinking too much, that's all. Your eyesight is scattered."

Appleton's face flushed as he beheld the gaze of the company upon him and heard the laughter that greeted this remark. He turned to leave when O'Neil, who had continued to watch the proceedings with interest, crossed to the group and touched Denny on the shoulder.

"Give him his money," he quietly told the dealer.

"Eh?" The smile faded from the fellow's face. He looked up startled. "What?"

"Give him his money."

In the momentary hush that followed, Happy Tom Slater, who had frequently seen his employer in action and understood storm signals, sighed deeply, and then reached for the nearest chair. With a wrench of his powerful hands he loosened a leg. Although Mr. Slater abhorred trouble, he was accustomed to meet it philosophically. A lifetime spent in construction camps had taught him, of all weapons, the one best suited to his use was a pick handle; second to that he had come to value the hardwood leg of a chair. But his precaution proved needless, for the dispute was over before he had prepared himself.

Without waiting for O'Neil to put his accusation into words Denny had risen swiftly, and in doing so he had either purposely or by accident made a movement that produced a prompt and instinctive reaction. Murray's fist met him as he rose, met him so squarely and with such force that he lost all interest in what followed. The other cardplayers silently gathered Mr. Denny in their arms and stretched him on a disused roulette table. The bartender appeared with a wet towel and began to bathe his temples.

Appleton, dazed by the suddenness of it all, found a stack of gold pieces in his hand and heard O'Neil speaking to him in an everyday tone.

"Come to my room, please. I'd like to talk to you."

Something commanding in the speaker's face made the engineer follow against his will. He longed to loiter here until Denny had regained his senses, but O'Neil had him by the arm. A moment later he was being led down the hall away from the lobby and the barroom. As Slater, who had followed, closed the door behind them, Dan burst forth.

"By Jove! Why didn't you tell me? I knew he was crooked ... but I couldn't believe...."

"Sit down!" O'Neil said. "He won't pull himself together for a while, and I want to get to bed. Are you looking for a job?"

The engineer's eyes opened wide.

"Yes."

"Do you know the Kyak country?"

"Pretty well."

"I need a surveyor. Your wages will be the same Gordon paid, and they begin now – if it's agreeable."

"It certainly is!"

"Good! We'll leave at six o'clock, sharp. Bring your bedding and instruments."

"Thanks! I – this is a bit of a surprise. Who are you?"

"I'm O'Neil."

"Oh!" Mr. Appleton's expression changed quickly. "You're Murray...." He stammered an instant. "It was very good of you to take my part, after I'd been fool enough to...."

"Well, I didn't want to see you make a total idiot of yourself."

The young man flushed slightly then continued in a quieter voice.

"How did you know I was out of work?"

"Mr. Gordon told me. He recommended you highly."

"He did?"

"He said you were unreliable, disloyal, and dishonest. Coming from him I took that as high praise."

There was a moment's pause, then Appleton laughed boyishly.

"That's funny! I'm very glad to know you, Mr. O'Neil."

"You don't, and you won't for a long time. Tom tells me you didn't think well of Gordon's enterprise and so he fired you."

"That's right. I suppose I ought to have kept my mouth shut, but it has a way of flying open when it shouldn't. He is either a fool or a crook, and his mine is nothing but a prospect. I couldn't resist telling him so."

"And his railroad?"

Appleton hesitated. "Oh, it's as good a route as the Trust's. I

MURRAY O'NEIL DREAMS

worked on the two surveys. Personally I think both outfits are crazy to try to build in from here. I had to tell Gordon that, too. You see I'm a volunteer talker. I should have been born with a stutter — it would have saved me a lot of trouble."

O'Neil smiled. "You may talk all you please in my employ, so long as you do your work. Now get some sleep, for we have a hard trip. And by the way...."

The youth paused with a hand on the doorknob.

"Don't go looking for Denny."

Appleton's face hardened stubbornly.

"I can't promise that sir."

"Oh, yes you can. You must. Remember, you're working for me, and you're under orders. I can't have the expedition held up on your account."

The engineer's voice was heavy with disappointment, but a vague admiration was growing in his eyes as he agreed.

"Very well, sir. I suppose my time is yours. Goodnight."

When he had gone, Happy Tom turned to his boss.

"Now, why in blazes did you hire him? We don't need a high-priced surveyor on this job."

"Of course not, but don't you see? He'd have been arrested, sure. Besides, he's Irish, and I like him."

"Humph! Then I s'pose he's got a job for life," Tom said. "You make friends and enemies quicker than anybody I ever saw. You've got Curtis Gordon on your neck now."

"On account of this boy? Nonsense."

"Not altogether. Denny is Gordon's right bower. I think he calls him his secretary. Anyhow, he does Gordon's dirty work and they're thicker than fleas. First you come along and steal me, underhanded, then you grab his pet engineer before he has a chance to hire him back again. Just to top off the evening you publicly brand his confidential understrapper as a card cheat and thump him on the medulla oblongata."

"Are you sure it wasn't the duodenum?"

"Well, you hit him in a vital spot, and Gordon won't forget it."

Late the following morning, O'Neil's expedition landed at the deserted fishing station of Omar, 30 miles down the sound from Cortez. From this point, its route lay down the bay to open water and thence eastward along the coast in front of the Salmon River delta some 40 miles to Kyak. This latter stretch would have been almost impossible for open boats, but the numerous mud bars and islands thrown out by the river afforded a sheltered course. These inside channels, though shallow, were of sufficient depth to allow small craft to navigate and had long been used as a route to the coalfields.

Appleton, smiling and cheerful, was the first member of the party to appear at the dock that morning, and after landing at Omar, he showed his knowledge of the country by suggesting a short cut that would save the long row down to the mouth of the sound and around into the delta. Immediately back of the old cannery, which occupied a gap in the mountain rim, lay a narrow lake, and this, he declared, held an outlet that led into the Salmon River flats. By hauling the boats over to this body of water—a task made easy by the presence of a tiny tramway with one dilapidated push car that had been a part of the cannery equipment—it would be possible to save time and labor.

"I've heard there was a way through," O'Neil confessed. "But nobody seemed to know just where it was."

"I know," the young man assured him. "We can gain a day at least, and I judge every day is valuable."

"So valuable we can't afford to lose one by making a mistake," his employer said.

"Leave it to me. I never forget a country once I've been through it."

Accordingly, the boats were loaded on the handcar and transferred one at a time. In the interval, O'Neil examined his surroundings. He was surprised to find the dock and buildings in excellent condition, notwithstanding the station had lain idle for several years. A solitary Norwegian was watching the premises and managed to make known his impression that poor fishing had led the owners to abandon operations at this point. He, too, had heard that Omar Lake had an outlet into the delta, but he was not sure of its existence; he was sure of nothing, in fact, except it was lonesome here, and he had run out of tobacco five days before.

But Dan Appleton was not mistaken. A two-hour row across the mirrorlike surface of Omar Lake brought the party out through a hidden gap in the mountains and afforded them a view across the level delta. To their left the range they had just penetrated retreated toward the canyon where the Salmon River burst its way out from the interior. Beyond that point it continued in a coastward swing to Kyak, their destination. Between lay a flat, trackless tundra, cut by sloughs and glacial streams, with long tongues of timber reaching down here and there from the high ground and dwindling away toward the seaward marshes. It was a desolate region, the breeding place of sea fowl, the hunting ground for the great brown bear.

O'Neil had never been so near the canyon as this, although he'd heard wild stories. He surveyed the place curiously as the boats glided along, but he could see nothing more than a jumble of small hills and buttes. Beyond them he saw the dead, gray backs of the twin glaciers coming down from the slopes to east and west. Beyond the foothills and the glaciers themselves the main range was gashed by a deep valley, through which he judged the river must come, and beyond that he knew was a country of agricultural promise, extending clear to the fabulous copper belt where the railroads from Cortez were headed. Still farther inland lay the Tanana, and then the Yukon, with their riches untouched.

What a pity, what a mockery, that this obvious entrance to the country has been blocked by nature, O'Neil thought.

Just at his back was Omar, with its deep and sheltered harbor. The lake he had crossed gave passage through the guardian range, and this tundra — which O'Neil estimated he could lay a mile of track a day over — led up to the glaciers. Once through the Coast Range, building would be easy, for the upper Salmon was navigable, and its banks presented no difficulties to track laying.

He turned abruptly to Appleton, who was pulling an oar.

"What do you know about that canyon?" he asked.

"Not much. Nobody knows much, for those fellows who went

through in the gold rush have all left the country. Gordon's right-of-way comes in above, and so does the Trust's. From there on I know every foot of the ground."

"I suppose if either of them gets through to the Salmon the rest will be easy."

"Dead easy!"

"It would be shorter and much cheaper to build from Omar, through this way."

"Of course, but neither outfit knew anything about the outlet to Omar Lake until I told them—and they knew there was the canyon to be reckoned with."

"Well?"

Appleton shook his head. "Look at it! Does it look like a place to build a railroad?"

"I can't tell anything about it from here."

"I suppose a road could be built if the glaciers were on the same side of the river, but they're not. They face each other, and they're alive, too. Listen." The oarsmen ceased rowing at Dan's signal, and out of the northward silence came a low rumble like the sound of distant cannonading. "We must be at least 20 miles away, in an airline. The ice stands up alongside the river, hundreds of feet high, and it breaks off in chunks as big as a New York office building."

"You've been up there?"

"No. But everybody says so, and I've seen glacier ice clear out here in the delta. They're always moving, too—the glaciers themselves—and they're filled with crevasses, so that it's dangerous to cross them on foot even if one keeps back from the river."

"How did those men get their outfits through in '98?" O'Neil asked.

"I'm blessed if I know—maybe they flew." After a moment Dan added, "Perhaps they dodged the pieces as they fell."

O'Neil smiled. He opened his lips to speak, then closed them, and for a long time kept his eyes fixed speculatively in the direction of the canyon. When he had first spoken of a route from Omar, he had thrown out the suggestion with only a casual interest. Now, suddenly, the idea took strong possession of his mind. It fascinated him with its daring, its bigness. He began to dream.

The world owes all great achievements to dreamers, for men who lack vivid imaginations are incapable of conceiving big enterprises. No matter how practical the thing accomplished, it requires this faculty, no less than a poem or a picture. Every bridge, every skyscraper, every mechanical invention, every great work man has wrought in steel and stone and concrete, was once a dream.

O'Neil had no small measure of the imaginative power that makes great leaders, great inventors, great builders. He was capable of tremendous enthusiasm; his temperament forever led him to dare what others feared to undertake. And here he glimpsed a tremendous opportunity. The traffic of a budding nation was waiting to be seized. To him who gained control of Alaska transportation would come the domination of her resources.

Many were striving for the prize, but if there should prove to be a means of threading that Salmon River canyon with steel rails, the man who first found it would have those other railroad enterprises at his mercy. The Trust would have to sue for terms or abandon further effort. This route was shorter, it was level, it was infinitely cheaper to improve. The stakes in the game were staggering. The mere thought of them made his heart leap. The only obstacle, of course, lay in those glaciers, and he began to wonder if they could not be made to open. Why not? No one knew positively they were impregnable, for no one knew anything certainly about them. Until the contrary had been proven there was at least a possibility they were less formidable than rumor had painted them.

Camp was pitched late that night far out on the flats. During the preparation of supper Murray sat staring fixedly before him, deaf to all sounds and insensible to the activities of his companions. He had lost his customary breeziness and his good nature. He was curt, sullen, unsmiling. Appleton tried to arouse him from this abstraction, but Slater quickly drew the young man aside with a warning.

"Don't do that, son, or you'll wear splints for the rest of the trip."

"What's the matter with him, anyhow?" Dan asked. "He was

boiling over with enthusiasm all day, but now — why, he's asleep sitting up! He hasn't moved for 20 minutes."

Tom shook his head, dislodging a swarm of mosquitoes.

"Walk on your toes, my boy. Walk on your toes. I smell something cooking — and it ain't supper."

When food was served O'Neil made a pretense of eating, but then suddenly rose.

"I'll stretch my legs a bit." His voice was strangely listless; in his eyes was the same abstraction that had troubled Appleton during the afternoon. He left camp and disappeared up the bank of the stream.

"Nice place to take a walk," the engineer said. "He'll bog down in half a mile or get lost among the sloughs."

"Not him." Slater said. Nevertheless, his worried eyes followed the figure of his chief until he disappeared. "Something is coming, but what it is or where it's going to hit us I don't know," he added a little while later.

Their meal over, the boatmen laid down their beds, rolled up in their blankets, and soon were asleep. Appleton and Tom sat in the smoke of a smudge, gossiping idly as twilight approached. From the south came the distant voice of the sea, out of the north rolled the intermittent thunder of those falling bergs, and from every side sounded a harsh chorus of waterfowl. Ducks whirred past in bullet-like flight, honkers flapped heavily overhead, a pair of magnificent snow-white swans soared within easy gunshot of the camp. An hour passed, then another, and another; the arctic night descended. And through it all the mosquitoes sang their blood song and stabbed the watchers with tongues of flame.

Happy Tom sang his song, too, for it was not often he had a listener. It was a song of infinite hard luck. Mr. Slater, it seemed, was a creature of many ills - the wretched abiding place of aches and pains, colic, cramps, and rheumatism. He was the target of misfortune and the sport of fate. His body was the galloping ground of strange disorders that baffled diagnosis, and his financial affairs were dominated by an evil genius that betrayed him at every turn. To top it all, at that moment he suffered a violent attack of indigestion.

"Ain't that just my luck?" he lamented. "Old 'Indy's got me good, and there ain't a bit of soda in the outfit."

"Instead of dramatizing your own discomforts, you'd better be thinking of the boss. I'm going out to look for him," said Appleton, who'd been growing quite uneasy with O'Neil's absence.

"Now don't be a dam' fool," Slater advised. "It would be worth a broken leg to annoy him when he's in one of these fits. You'd make yourself as popular as a smallpox patient at a picnic. When he's dreamed his dream, he'll be back."

"When will that be?"

"No telling — maybe tonight, maybe tomorrow night."

"And what are we going to do in the meantime?"

"Sit tight." Mr. Slater chewed steadily and sighed. "No soda in camp, and this gum don't seem to lay hold of me. That's luck!"

Darkness had settled when O'Neil reappeared. He came plunging out of the brush, drenched, muddy, stained by contact with the thickets. But his former mood had disappeared and in its place was a harsh, explosive energy.

"Tom!" he cried. "You, Appleton, and I will leave at daylight. The men will wait here until we get back." His voice was incisive, its tone forbade question.

The youthful engineer stared at him in dismay, for only his anxiety had triumphed over his fatigue, and daylight was but four hours away. O'Neil noted the expression.

"You're tired, Appleton, I know, but in working for me you'll be called upon for extraordinary effort now and then. I may not demand more than an extra hour from you; then again, I may demand a week straight without sleep. I'll never ask it unless it's necessary and unless I'm ready to do my share."

"Yes, sir."

"The sacrifice is big, but the pay is bigger. Loyalty is all I require."

"I'm ready now, sir."

"We can't see to travel before dawn. Help Tom load the lightest boat with rations for five days. If we run short, we'll forage." He kicked off his rubber boots, upended them to drain out the water, then flung himself on his bed of boughs and was asleep almost before the two had recovered from their surprise.

"Five days — or longer," Slater said, gloomily, as he and Dan began their preparations. "And me with indigestion!"

"What does it mean?" Appleton asked.

"It means I'll probably succumb."

"No, no. What's the meaning of this change of plan? I can't understand it."

"You don't need to," Happy Tom said. There was a look of solicitude in his face as he added, "I wish I'd made him take off his wet clothes before he went to sleep."

"Let's wake him up."

But Slater shook his head. "I'd sooner wake a rattlesnake."

O'Neil roused the members of his expedition while the sky was reddening faintly, for he had a mind that worked like an alarm clock. All except Appleton had worked for him before, and the men accepted his orders to await his return with no appearance of surprise.

With the first clear light he and his two companions set out, rowing up the estuary of the Salmon until the current became too swift. Then landing, they rigged a "bridle" for the skiff, fitted their shoulders to loops in a 90-foot tow rope, and began to track their craft up against the stream. It was hard work. Frequently they were waist deep in the cold water. Long sweepers with tips awash in the flood interfered with their efforts. The many branches of the stream forced them to make repeated crossings, for the delta was no more than an endless series of islands through which the current swirled. When dusk overtook them, the men were wet, weary, and weak from hunger.

Then when dawn came, they were up and at it again, but their task became constantly more difficult because of the floating glacier ice, which increased with every mile. They were obliged to exercise the most extreme caution. Hour after hour they strained against the current until the ropes bit into their aching flesh, bringing raw places out on necks and palms. Hour after hour the ice went churning past, and through it all came the intermittent echo of the caving glaciers ahead of them.

Dan Appleton soon realized where the journey was leading, and at the thought of facing the terrors that loomed so large, his pulse began to leap. He had a suspicion of O'Neil's intent but dared not voice it. Though the scheme seemed mad enough, its audacity fascinated him. It would be worthwhile to take part in such an undertaking, even if it ended in failure. And somehow, against his judgment, he felt his leader would find a way.

For the most part, O'Neil was as silent as a man of stone, and only on those rare occasions when he craved relief from his thoughts would he encourage Dan to talk. Then he sometimes listened, but more frequently he did not. Slater had long since become a dumb draught animal, senseless to discomfort except in the hour of relaxation when he monotonously catalogued his ills.

"Are you a married man?" O'Neil once asked Dan.

"Not yet, sir."

"Family?"

"Sure! A great big, fine one, consisting of a sister. But she's more than a family — she's a religion." Receiving encouragement from his employer's look of interest, he continued. "We were wiped out by the San Francisco earthquake and stood in the bread line for a while. We managed to save $4,000 from the wreck, which we divided equally. Then we started out to make our fortunes. It was her idea."

"You came to Cortez?"

"Yes. Money was so easy for me that I lost all respect for it. The town rang with my mirth for a while. I was an awful fool."

"Education!"

"Now it's my ambition to get settled and have her with me. I haven't had a good laugh, a hearty meal, or a Christian impulse since I left her."

"What did she do with her half of the fortune?"

"Invested it wisely and went to work. I bought little round celluloid disks with mine, she bought land of some sort with hers. She's a newspaper woman, and the best in the world — or at least the best in Seattle. She wrote that big snowslide story for *The Review* last fall. She tells 'em how to raise eight babies on $7 a week, or how to make a full set of library furniture out of three beer kegs, a packing case, and an epileptic icebox. She runs the 'Domestic Economy' column; and she's the sweetest, the cleverest, the most stunning...."

Appleton's enthusiastic tribute ceased suddenly, for he saw O'Neil again was deaf and his eyes fixed dreamily upon the canyon far ahead.

As the current quickened, the progress of the little party became slower and more exhausting. Their destination seemed to retreat before them; the river wound back and forth in a maddening series of detours. Some of the float ice was large now, and these pieces rushed down upon them like charging horses, keeping them constantly on the alert to prevent disaster. It seemed impossible that such a flat country could afford so much fall. Happy Tom constantly suggested they tie up and pack the remaining miles overland, but O'Neil would not hear of it.

They had slept so little, their labors had been so heavy, they were dumb and dull with fatigue when they finally reached the first bluffs and worked their boat through a low gorge where all the waters of the Salmon thrashed, and icebergs galloped past like a pallid host in flight. Here they paused and stared with wondering eyes at what lay before them. A chill, damp breath swept over them, and a mighty awe laid hold of their hearts.

"Come on," O'Neil said. "Other men have gone through – we'll do the same."

On the evening of the sixth day a splintered, battered poling boat with its seams open swung into the bank where O'Neil's men were encamped, and its three occupants staggered out. They were gaunt, stiff, and heavy eyed. Even Tom Slater's full cheeks hung loose and flabby. But the leader was alert and buoyant; his face calm, his eyes smiling humorously.

"You'll take the men on to the coalfields and finish the work," he told his boss packer later that night. "Appleton and I will start back to Cortez in the morning. When you have finished, go to Juneau, and see to the recording."

"Ain't that my luck?" murmured the dyspeptic. "Me for Kyak where there ain't a store, and my gum all wet."

"Chew it, paper and all," Appleton cheerfully advised.

"Oh, the good has all gone out of it now," Slater said.

"Meet me in Seattle on the 15th of next month," his employer directed.

"I'll be there if old 'Indy' spares me. But dyspepsia, with nothing to eat except beans and pork bosom, will probably lay me in my grave long before the 15th. However, I'll do my best. Now, do you want to know what I think of this proposition of yours?" He eyed his superior somberly.

"Sure. I want all the encouragement I can get, and your views are always inspiriting."

"Well, I think it's nothing more nor less than hydrophobia. These mosquitoes have given you the rabies and you need medical attention. You need it bad."

"Still, you'll help me, won't you?"

"Oh yes," Tom said. "I'll help you. But it's a pity to see a man go mad."

7

A Dream Develops

The clerk of the leading hotel in Seattle whirled his register about as a man deposited a weather-beaten warbag on the marble floor and leaned over the counter.

"Is Murray O'Neil here?"

This question had been asked repeatedly within the last two hours, but heretofore by people totally different in appearance from the one who now spoke. The man behind the desk measured the stranger with a suspicious eye before answering. He saw a ragged, loose-hung, fat person of melancholy countenance, who was booted to the knee and chewing gum.

"Mr. O'Neil keeps a room here by the year," he said, guardedly.

"Show me up!" said the newcomer as if advancing a challenge.

A smart reply was on the lips of the clerk, but something in the other's manner discouraged flippancy.

"You are a friend of Mr. O'Neil's?" he asked.

"Friend? Um-m, no. I'm just him when he ain't around." Then he turned to the girl at the newsstand." "Have you got any wintergreen gum?"

"Mr. O'Neil is not here."

The fat man stared at his informant.

"Ain't this the 15th?" he asked.

"It is."

"Then he's here, all right!"

"Mr. O'Neil is not in," the clerk repeated, as he gazed over Mr. Slater's left shoulder.

"Well, I guess his room will do for me. I ain't particular."

"His room is occupied at present. If you care to wait, you will find...."

Tom never learned precisely what it was that he was to find, for at that moment the breath was driven out of his lungs by a tremendous whack, and he turned to behold Dr. Stanley Gray towering over him, an expansive smile upon his face.

"Look out!" Slater cried as he coughed and seized his Adam's apple. "You made me swallow my cud." The two shook hands warmly.

"We've been expecting you, Tom," the doctor said. "We're all here except Parker, and he wired he'd arrive tomorrow."

"Where's Murray?"

"He's around somewhere."

Slater turned a resentful, smoldering gaze upon the hotel clerk, and looked around for a chair with a detachable leg, but the object of his regard disappeared abruptly behind the key rack.

"This rat-brained party said he hadn't come."

"He arrived this morning, but we've barely seen him."

"I left Appleton in Juneau. He'll be down on the next boat."

"Appleton? Who's he?" Gray asked.

"Oh, he's a new member of the order — initiated last month. He's learning to be a sleep hater like the rest of us. He's recording the right-of-way."

"What's in the air? None of us know. We didn't even know Murray's whereabouts — thought he was in Kyak until he sounded the alarm from New York. The other boys have quit their jobs and I've sold my practice."

"It's a railroad!"

Dr. Gray grinned. "Well! That's the tone I use when I break the news that it's a girl instead of a boy."

"It's a railroad," Slater repeated. "Up the Salmon River."

"Good Lord! What about those glaciers?"

"Oh, it ain't so much the glaciers and the floating icebergs and the raging chasms and the quaking tundra — Murray thinks he can overcome them. It's the mosquitoes and the Copper Trust that are going to figure in this enterprise. One of 'em will be the death of me, and the other will bust Murray if he don't look out. Say, my neck is covered with bumps till it feels like a dog collar of seed pearls."

"Do you think we'll have a fight?" the doctor asked.

"A fight? It'll be the worst massacre since the Little Big Horn. We're surrounded already, and no help in sight."

O'Neil found his "boys" waiting for him when he returned to his room: Mellen, lean, gaunt, and serious-minded with the dust of Chihuahua still on his shoes; McKay, the superintendent, who had arrived from California that morning; Sheldon, the commissary man; Elkins; Doc Gray; and Happy Tom Slater. Only Parker, the chief engineer, was absent.

"I sent Appleton in from Cortez to come down the river and make the preliminary survey into Omar," O'Neil told them. "He cables me he has filed his locations, and everything is okay. On my way East, I stopped here long enough to buy the Omar cannery, docks, buildings, and town site. It's all mine, and it will save us 90 days' work in getting started."

"What do you make of that tundra between Omar and the canyon?" asked McKay, who had crossed the Salmon River delta and knew its character. "It's like calf's foot jelly — a man bogs down to his waist in it."

"We'll fill and trestle," O'Neil said.

"We couldn't move a piledriver 20 feet."

"It's frozen solid in winter."

McKay nodded. "We'll have to drive steam points ahead of every pile, I suppose, and we'll need Alaska Natives to work in that cold, but I guess we can manage somehow."

"That country is like an apple pie," Slater said. "It's better cold than hot. There's a hundred inches of rainfall at Omar in summer. We'll all have web feet when we get out."

Sheldon, the light-hearted commissary man, spoke up. "If it's as wet as all that, we'll need Finns instead of Natives." He was promptly hooted into silence.

"I understand those glaciers come down to the edge of the river," the superintendent said.

"They do," O'Neil acknowledged. "And they're the liveliest ones I ever saw. Tom can answer for that. One of them is fully 400 feet high at the face and four miles across. They're constantly breaking, too."

"Lumps bigger than this hotel," Slater added. "It's quite a sight — equal to anything in the state of Maine."

O'Neil laughed with the others at this display of sectional pride, and then explained his idea.

"The problem of passing them sounds difficult, but it isn't. If those other engineers had looked over the ground as I did, instead of relying entirely upon hearsay, we wouldn't be meeting here today. Of course, I realized we couldn't build a road over a moving river of ice, nor in front of one, for that matter. But I discovered that Nature had made us one concession. She placed her glaciers on opposite sides of the valley, to be sure, but she placed the one that comes in from the east bank slightly higher upstream than the one that comes in from the west. They don't really face each other, although from the sea they appear to do so. You see the answer?"

His hearers nodded vigorously.

"If we cross the river, low down, by a trestle, and run up the east bank past Jackson glacier until we are stopped by Garfield — the upper one — then throw a bridge directly across, and back to the side we started from, we miss them both and have the river always between them and us. Above the upper crossing there will be a lot of heavy rock work to do, but nothing unusual, and, once through the gorge, we come out into the valley, where the other roads run in from Cortez. They cross three divides, while we run through on a one percent grade. That will give us a downhill pull on all heavy freight."

"Sounds as simple as a pair of suspenders, doesn't it?" Slater said. "But wait till you see it. The gorge below Niagara is stagnant water compared with the cataract above those glaciers. It takes two looks to see the top of the mountains. And those glaciers themselves — well! Language just gums up and sticks when it comes to describing them."

Mellen, the bridge builder, spoke for the first time.

"As I understand it, we will cross the river between the glaciers and immediately below the upper one."

"Exactly!"

He shook his head. "We can't build piers to withstand those heavy bergs you tell me are always breaking off."

"I'll explain how we can," O'Neil said. "You've hit the bullseye — the tender spot in the whole enterprise. While the river is narrow and rapid in front of Jackson, the lower glacier — opposite Garfield - there is a kind of lake, formed, I suppose, when the glacier receded from its original position. Now then, here lies the joker, the secret of the whole proposition. This lake is deep, but there is a shallow bar across its outlet that serves to hold back all but the small bergs. This gives us a chance to cross in safety. At first, I was puzzled to discover why only the ice from the lower glacier came downriver; then, when I realized the truth, I knew I had the key to Alaska in my hands. We'll cross just below this bar. Understand? Of course it all depends upon Parker's verdict, but I'm so sure his will agree with mine that I've made my preparations, bought Omar, and gathered you fellows together. We're going to spring the biggest coup in railroad history."

"Where's the money coming from?" Slater asked.

"I'm putting in my own fortune."

"How much is that? I'm dead to all sense of modesty, you see."

"About a million dollars," O'Neil said.

"Humph! That won't get us started."

"I've raised another million in New York." The chief was smiling and did not seem to resent this inquisitiveness in the least.

"Nothing but a shoestring!"

"My dear Happy," the builder said. "I don't intend to complete the road."

"Then — why in blazes are you starting it?" demanded Slater in bewilderment that the others evidently shared. "It's one thing to build a railroad on a contractor's commission, but it's another thing to build it and pay your own way as you go along. Half a railroad ain't any good."

"Once my right-of-way is filed it will put those projects from Cortez out of business. Only an imbecile would think of building in from there with the Omar route made possible. Before we come to that Salmon River bridge the Copper Trust will have to buy us out!"

"Those are words I understand," Happy Tom said with admiration. "I withdraw my objections and give my consent to the deal."

"You are staking your whole fortune on your judgment, as I understand it," McKay ventured.

"Every dollar of it," Murray answered.

"Say, chief, that's gambling some!" young Sheldon said with a wondering look.

They were deep in their discussion when the telephone rang. Sheldon, being nearest to it, answered. "There's a newspaper reporter downstairs to interview you," he said.

"I don't grant interviews," O'Neil said. He could not guess by what evil chance the news of his plans had leaked out.

"Nothing doing!" Sheldon spoke into the transmitter. He turned again to his employer. "Operator says the party doesn't mind waiting."

O'Neil frowned.

"Throw him out!" Sheldon shouted, then suddenly dropped the receiver as if it had burnt his fingers. "Hell! It's a woman, Murray – she's on the wire. She thanks you sweetly and says she'll wait."

"A woman? A newspaper woman?" O'Neil rose and seized the instrument.

"Hello?" he said coldly. "I refuse to be interviewed. There's no use...." His tone suddenly altered. "Miss Appleton? I beg your pardon. I'll be right down." He then turned to his subordinates. "This seems to terminate our interview," he said with a wry smile. "She's Dan Appleton's sister, and therefore...." He shrugged in resignation. "Now run along. I'll see you in the morning."

The men made their way down to the street, talking guardedly as they went. All were optimistic except Slater, whose face remained shrouded in its customary gloom.

"Cheer up, Happy!" Dr. Gray said. "It's the biggest thing we ever tackled."

"Wait. Just wait till you've seen the place," Tom said.

"Don't you think it can be done?"

"Nope!"

"Come, come."

"It's impossible – of course we'll do it, but it's impossible, just the same. It will mean a scrap, too, like none of us ever saw, and I was raised in a logging camp where fighting is the general recreation. If I was young, like the rest of you, I wouldn't mind; but I'm old – and my digestion's gone. I can't hardly take care of myself anymore, Doc. I'm too feeble to fight or…." He signaled a passing car. It failed to stop, and he rushed after it, dodging vehicles with the agility of a rabbit and swinging his heavy warbag as if it weighed no more than a good resolution.

O'Neil entered the ladies' parlor with a feeling of annoyance, expecting to meet an inquisitive, bold young woman bent on exploiting his plans and his personality in the usual inane journalistic fashion. He was surprised and offended that Dan Appleton, in whom he had the utmost faith, should have betrayed his secret. Publicity was a thing he detested, and at present he particularly dreaded its effect. But he was agreeably surprised in the girl who came toward him briskly with hand outstretched.

Miss Appleton was her brother's double. She had his frank blue eyes, his straw-gold colored hair, his humorous smile and wide-awake look. She was not beautiful, as her features were too irregular, her nose too tip-tilted, her mouth too generous. She was crisp, clean cut, and wholesome.

What first struck O'Neil was her air of boyishness. From the crown of her plain straw sailor hat to the soles of her sensible walking boots, there was no suggestion of feminine frippery. She wore a plain shirtwaist and a tailored skirt, and her hair was arranged simply. The wave in its pale gold was the only concession to mere prettiness.

Yet she gave no impression of deliberate masculinity. She struck one as merely not interested in clothes, instinctively expressing in her dress her own boyish directness and her businesslike absorption in her work.

"You're furious, of course – anybody would be," she began, then laughed so frankly his eyes softened and the wrinkles at their corners deepened.

"I fear I was rude before I learned you were Dan's sister," he apologized. "But you see I'm a bit afraid of newspaper people."

"I knew you'd struggle—although Dan described you as a perfectly angelic person."

"Indeed!"

"But I'm a real reporter, so I won't detain you long. I don't care where you were born or where you went to school, or what patent breakfast food you eat. Tell me, are you going to build another railroad?"

"I hope so. I'm always building roads when my bids are low enough to secure the contracts. That's my business."

"Are you going to build one in Alaska?"

"Possibly. There seems to be an opportunity there—but Dan has probably told you as much about that as I am at liberty to tell. He's been over the ground."

She pursed her lips. "You know very well, or you ought to know, Dan wouldn't tell me a thing while he's working for you. He hasn't said a word, but...is that why you came in frowning like a thunder cloud? Did you think he set me on your trail?"

"I think I do know he wouldn't do anything really indiscreet," he said.

Murray regarded her with growing favor. There was something about this boyish girl that awakened the same spontaneous liking he had felt during his first meeting with her brother. He surprised her by confessing his plan.

"I am building a railroad—to the interior of Alaska. I've been east and raised the money, my men are here, and we'll begin operations at once."

"That's what Mr. Gordon told me about his scheme, but he hasn't done much, so far."

"My line will put his out of business, also that of the Trust, and the various wildcat promoters."

"Where does your road start from?"

"The town of Omar, on King Phillip Sound, near Hope and Cortez. It will run up the Salmon River and past the glaciers those other men refused to tackle."

"If I weep, it is for joy," the girl said. "I don't like Curtis Gordon. I call him Simon Legree."

"Why?"

"Well, he impresses me as a real old-time villain — with the riding boots and the whip and all that. *Uncle Tom's Cabin* is my favorite play, it's so funny. This is a big story you've given me, Mr. O'Neil."

"I realize that."

"It has the biggest news value of anything Alaskan that's broken for some time. I think you are a very nice person to interview, after all."

"Wait! I don't want you to use a word of what I've told you."

Miss Appleton's clearly penciled brows rose. "Then why didn't you keep still?"

"You asked me. I told you because you are Dan Appleton's sister. Nevertheless, I don't want it made public."

"Let's sit down," the girl said with a laugh. "To tell you the truth, I didn't come here to interview you for my paper. I'm afraid I've tried your patience awfully." A faint flush tinged her clear complexion. "I just came, really, to get some news of Dan."

"He's perfectly well and happy, and you'll see him in a few days."

Miss Appleton nodded. "So he wrote, but I couldn't wait. Now won't you tell me all about him — not anything about his looks and his health, but little unimportant things that will mean something. You see, I'm his mother and his sister."

O'Neil did as he was directed, and before long, found himself reciting the details of that trying trip up the Salmon River. He told her how he had sent the young engineer out to run the preliminary survey for the new railroad.

"He is in a fair way to realize his ambition of having you with him all the time," he added. "I'm sure that will please you."

"And it is my ambition to make enough money to have him with me," she said. With an air of some importance she continued. "I'll tell you a secret: I'm writing for the magazines—stories!" She sat back awaiting his enthusiasm. "My, how you do rave over the idea," she said when she saw no excitement on O'Neil's face.

"I congratulate you, of course, but...."

"Now don't tell me you tried it once. Of course you did. I know it's a harmless disease, like the measles, and everybody has it when they're young. Above all, don't volunteer the information that your own life is full of romance and would make a splendid novel. They all say that."

Murray O'Neil felt the glow of personal interest that results from the discovery in another of a congenial sense of humor.

"I didn't suppose you had to write," he said. "Dan told me you had invested your fortune and were on Easy Street."

"That was poetic license. I fictionized slightly in my report to him because I knew he was doing so well."

"Then your investment didn't turn out fortunately?"

Miss Appleton hesitated. "You seem to be a kindly, trusting person. I'm tempted to destroy your faith in human nature."

"Please don't."

"Yes, I shall. My experience may help you avoid the pitfalls of high finance. Well, then, it was a sad little fortune to begin with, like a boy in grammar school—just big enough to be of no assistance. But even a boy-size fortune looked big to me. I wanted to invest it in something sure—no national bank stock, subject to the danger of an absconding cashier, mind you. And no government bonds with the possibility of war to depreciate them, but something stable and agricultural, with the inexhaustible resources of nature back of it. This isn't my own language. I cribbed it from the apple man."

"Apple man?"

"Yes. He had brown eyes, and a silky mustache, and a big irrigation plan over east of the mountains. You gave him your money and he gave you a perfectly good receipt. Then he planted little apple trees. He nursed them tenderly for five years, after which he turned them over to you with his blessing, and you lived happily ever after. At least that was the idea. You couldn't fail to grow rich, for the water always bubbled through his little ditch and it never froze nor rained to spoil things. I used to love apples. And then there was my name, which seemed a good omen. But lately I've considered changing Appleton to Berry or Plummer or some other kind of fruit."

"I infer the scheme failed?" O'Neil's eyes were half closed with amusement.

"Yes. It was a good scheme, too – except the irrigation ditch ran uphill, there wasn't any water where it started from, apples never had been made to grow in that locality because of something in the soil, and Brown-eyed Betty's title to the land wouldn't hold water any more than the ditch. Otherwise I'm sure he'd have made a success and I'd have spent my declining years in a rocking chair under the falling apple blossoms, eating Pippins and Jonathan's and Northern Spies. I can't bear to touch them now. Life at my boarding house is one long battle against apple pies, apple puddings, apple tapioca. Ugh! I hate the word now."

"I can understand your aversion," O'Neil said with a chuckle. "I wonder if you would let me order dinner for both of us, provided I taboo fruit. Perhaps I'll think of something more to tell you about Dan. I'm sure he wouldn't object ...."

"Oh, my card is all the chaperon I need. It takes me everywhere and renders me superior to the smaller conventionalities." She handed him one.

Eliza V. Appleton
The Review

"May I ask what the V stands for?" He held up the card between his thumb and finger.

Miss Appleton blushed then answered.

"It stands for Violet. But that isn't my fault, and I'm doing my best to live it down."

A DREAM DEVELOPS

8

OMAR BECOMES HUB OF ACTIVITY

The editor of *The Review* asked his girl reporter a very important question. "Miss Appleton, would you like to take a vacation?"

"Is that your delicate way of telling me I'm discharged?" Eliza said.

"You know very well we wouldn't fire you. But you haven't had a vacation for three years, and you need a rest."

"I thought I was looking extremely well, for me."

"We're going to send you on an assignment—to Alaska—if you'll go."

"I'm thinking of quitting newspaper work for good. The magazines pay better, and I'm writing a book."

"I know. Perhaps this will fit in with your plans, for it has to do with your pet topic of conservation. Those forestry stories of yours and the article on the waterpower combination made a hit, didn't they?"

"I judge so. Anyhow the magazine people want more."

"Good! Here's your chance to do something big for yourself and for us. Those Alaska coal claimants have been making a great effort in Washington, D.C. to rush their patents through, and there seems to be some possibility of their succeeding unless the public wakes up. We want to show up the whole fraudulent affair, show how the entries were illegal, and how the agents of the Trust are trying to put over the greatest steal of the century. It's the Heidlemanns that are back of it—and a few fellows like Murray O'Neil."

"O'Neil?"

"You know him, don't you?"

"Yes. I interviewed him a year ago last spring when he started his railroad."

"He's fighting for one of the biggest and richest groups of claims. He's backed by some Eastern people. It's the psychological moment to expose both the railroad and the coal situation, for the thieves are fighting among themselves—Gordon, O'Neil, and the Heidlemanns."

"Mr. O'Neil is no thief," the girl said.

"Of course not. He's merely trying to snatch control of an empire, and to grab $10 million worth of coal for nothing. That's not theft, it's financial genius! Fortunately, however, the public is rousing itself— coming to regard its natural resources as its own and not the property of the first financier who lays hold of them. Call it what you will but give us the true story of the Kyak coal and, above all, the story of the railroad battle. Things are growing bitter up there already, and they're bound to get worse. Give us the news and we'll play it up big through our Eastern syndicate. You can handle the magazine articles in a more dignified way if you choose. A few good vigorous, fearless, newspaper stories, written by someone on the ground, will give Congress such a jolt no coal patents will be issued this season and no government aid will be given to the railroads. You get the idea?"

"Certainly! But it will take time to do all that."

"Spend a year at it if necessary. *The Review* is fighting for a principle. It will back you to any extent. Isn't it worth a year – two years – of hard labor to awaken the American people to the knowledge they are being robbed of their birthright? I have several men whom I could send, but I chose you because your work along this line has given you a standing. This is your chance, Eliza, to make a big reputation and to perform a real service to the country. It's a chance that may never come your way again. Will you go?"

"Of course I'll go."

"I knew you would. You're all business, and that's what makes a hit in this office. You're up against a tough proposition, but I can trust you to make good on it. You can't fail if you play one interest against the other, for they're all fighting like Kilkenny cats. The Heidlemanns are a bunch of bandits; Gordon is a brilliant, unscrupulous promoter; and O'Neil is a cold, shrewd schemer with more brains and daring than any of the others. He showed that when he walked in there and seized the Salmon River canyon. He broke up all their plans and set the Copper Trust by the ears, but I understand they've got him bottled up at last. Here's your ticket for transportation on Saturday's steamer."

The editor shook Miss Appleton's hand warmly as she rose.

"Good luck, Eliza. Remember, we won't balk, no matter how lively your stuff is. The hotter the better — and that's what the magazines want, too. If I were you, I'd gum-shoe it. They're a rotten crowd and they might send you back if they get wise."

"I think not," Eliza whispered.

The town of Omar lay drenched in mist as the steamer bearing the representative of *The Review* drew in at the dock. The whole region was rain-soaked, verdant with a lush growth. No summer sun shone here to bake sprouting leaves or sear tender grasses. Beneath the sheltering firs a blanket of moss extended over hill and vale, knee-deep and treacherous for walking. The mountain crests were white, and down every gully streamed water from the melting snows. The country itself lay on end, as if crumpled by some giant hand, and presented a tropical blend of colors. There was the gray of fog and low-swept clouds, the dense, dark green of the spruce trees, underlaid with the richer, lighter shades where summer vegetation rioted. And running through it all were the shimmering, silent reaches of the Sound.

Omar itself was a mushroom city, sprung up by magic, as if the dampness at its roots had caused it to rise overnight. A sawmill shrieked complainingly; a noisy switch-engine shunted rows of flat cars back and forth and tooted lustily; the rattle of steam-winches and the cries of stevedores from a discharging freighter echoed against the hillsides. Closely huddled at the waterfront lay the old cannery buildings, greatly expanded, multiplied, and glistening with fresh paint. Back of them lay the town, its stumpy, half-graded streets terminating in the forest like the warty feelers of a stranded octopus. Everywhere was hurry and confusion, and overall was the ever-present shroud of mist that thickened into showers or parted reluctantly to let the sun peep through.

Dan Appleton, his clothing dewy from the fog, his cheeks bronzed by exposure, was over the rail before the ship had made fast. Soon he had Eliza in his arms, crushing her with the hug of a bear.

"Come up to the house, Sis, quick!" he cried, when the first frenzy of greeting was over. "Your house and mine!" His eyes were dancing, his face alight with eagerness.

"But, Danny," she laughed, squeezing his arm tenderly. "You live with Mr. O'Neil and all those other men in a horrible, crawling bunkhouse."

"Oh, do I? I'll have you know our bunkhouses don't crawl. And besides ... but wait ... it's a surprise."

"A surprise?" she queried, eagerly. "For me?"

He nodded.

"Tell me what it is, quick. You know I never could wait for surprises."

"Well, it's a brand-new ultra-stylish residence for just you and me. When the chief heard you were coming, he had a cottage built."

"Danny, it was only five days ago that I cabled you!"

"That's really 10 days for us, for you see we never sleep. It is finished and waiting, and your room is in white, and the paint will be dry tomorrow. He's a wonder!"

Remembering the nature of her mission, Eliza demurred. "I'm afraid I can't live there, Dan. You know...," she hesitated. "I may have to write some rather dreadful things about him."

"What?" Dan's face fell. "You are going to attack the chief? I had no idea of that!" He looked genuinely distressed and a little stern.

She laid a pleading hand on his arm. "Forgive me, Dan," she said. "I knew how you would feel, and, to tell the truth, I don't like that part of it one bit. But it was my big chance—the sort of thing I have been waiting years for. I couldn't bear to miss it." There was a suspicion of tears in her eyes. "I didn't think it all out. I just came. Things get awfully mixed, don't they? Of course I wouldn't attack him unfairly, but I do believe in conservation — and what could I do but come here to you?"

Dan smiled to reassure her. "Perhaps you won't feel like excoriating him when you learn more about things. I know you wouldn't be unfair. You'd flunk the job first. Wait till you talk to him. But you can't refuse his kindness, for a time at least. There's nowhere else for you to stay, and Murray would pick you up and put you into the cottage, muckrake and all, if I didn't. He had to go out on the work this morning or he'd have been here to welcome you. He sent apologies and said a lot of nice things, which I've forgotten."

"Well...." Eliza still looked troubled. "All right. But wait," she cried, with a swift change of mood. "I've made a little friend, the dearest, the most useless creature. We shared the same stateroom and we're sisters. She says I'm pretty, so of course I'm her slave for life." She hurried away during Dan's loyal protestations that she was pretty — more beautiful than the stars, more pleasing to the eye than the orchids of Brazil. A moment later she reappeared to present Natalie Gerard.

Dan greeted the new arrival with a cordiality that had a trace of shyness — unusual with him. "We've made quite a change since you were up here, Miss Gerard," he said. "The ships stop first at Omar now, you see. I trust it won't inconvenience you."

"Not in the least," Natalie said. "I shall arrive at Hope quite soon enough."

"Omar Khayyam is out in the wilderness somewhere with his book of verses and his jug of wine, I suppose," Eliza told her girlfriend.

"Mr. O'Neil?"

"Yes. But he'll be back soon, and meanwhile you are to come up and see our paradise."

"It looks terribly wet," Natalie said. "Perhaps we'd better wait until the rain stops."

"Please don't," Dan said with a laugh. "It won't stop until autumn, and then it will only change to snow. We don't have much sunshine."

"You must — you're so suntanned," his sister said.

"That's rust! O'Neil wanted to get a record of the bright weather in Omar, so he put a man on the job to time it, but the experiment failed."

"How so?"

"We didn't have a stopwatch in town. Now come! Nobody ever catches cold here — there isn't time."

He led the two girls ashore and up through the town to a moss-green bungalow, its newness attested by the yellow sawdust and fresh shavings that lay about. Amid their exclamations of delight he showed them the neatly furnished interior, and among other wonders a bedroom daintily done in white, with white curtains at the mullioned windows and a suite of wicker furniture.

"Where he dug all that up, I don't know," Dan said, pointing to the bed and dresser and chairs. "He must have had it hidden out somewhere."

Eliza surveyed this chamber with wondering eyes. "It makes me feel quite ashamed," she said. "Though, of course, he did it for Dan. When he discovers my abominable mission, he'll probably set me out in the rain and break all my lead pencils. But — isn't he magnificent?"

"He quite overwhelms one," Natalie agreed. "Back in New York, he's been sending me American Beauties every week for more than a year. It's his princely way." She colored slightly, despite the easy frankness of her manner.

"Oh, he's always doing something like that," Dan told them.

"You see, Natalie? The man is a viper," Eliza said. "If he let his beard grow, I'm sure we'd see it was blue."

"You shall have an opportunity of judging," came O'Neil's voice from behind them, and he entered with hands outstretched, smiling at their surprise. When he had expressed his pleasure at Natalie's presence and had bidden both her and Eliza welcome to Omar, he explained.

"I've just covered 18 miles on a railroad tricycle and my back is broken. The engines were busy, but I came, anyhow, hoping to arrive before the steamer. Now what is this I hear about my beard?"

It was Eliza's turn to blush, and she outdid Natalie.

"They were raving about your gallantry," said Dan, with all a brother's ruthlessness. "Until I told them it was merely a habit of mind with you; then Sis called you a Bluebeard."

O'Neil smiled, stroking his stubbly chin. "You see it's only gray."

"I don't see," said Eliza, still flushing furiously.

"You would if I continued to let it grow."

"Hm-m! I think, myself, it's a sort of bluish gray," Dan said.

"You are still working miracles," Natalie told O'Neil an hour later while he was showing his visitors the few sights of Omar. "Miracles of kindness, as usual."

Dan and his sister were following at a distance, arm in arm and chattering like magpies.

"No, no! That cottage is nothing. Miss Appleton had to have some place to stop."

"This all seems like magic." Natalie paused and looked over the busy little town. "And to think you have done it in a year."

"It was not I who did it; the credit belongs to those boys of whom I told you. They are all here, by the way — Parker, McKay, Mellen, Sheldon, Doc Gray — he has the hospital, you know."

"And Mr. Slater?"

"Oh, we couldn't exist without Happy Tom! No, the only miracle about all this is the loyalty that has made it possible. It is that which has broken all records in railroad building and pushed our tracks forward until we're nearly up to one of Nature's real miracles. You shall see those glaciers one of these days. Sometimes I wonder if even the devotion of those men will carry us through the final test. But you shall meet them all tonight — my whole family."

"I can't. The ship leaves this afternoon."

"I've arranged to send you to Hope in my motorboat, just as Mr. Gordon sent me on my way a year ago. You will stay with the Appletons tonight and help at the housewarming, then Dan will take you on in the morning. Women are such rare guests at Omar that we refuse to part with them. You agree?"

"How can I refuse? Your word seems to be law here. I'll send word to mother by the ship that I am detained by royal decree."

She spoke with a gaiety that seemed a little forced, and at mention of her departure a subtle change had come over her face. O'Neil realized she had matured markedly since his last meeting with her; there was no longer quite the same effect of naive girlishness.

"This was a very unhappy year for your loyal subject, Mr. O'Neil."

"I'm sorry," he said with such genuine kindliness she was moved to confide in him.

"Mother and I are ruined."

"Will you tell me about it?"

"It's those wretched coal claims. I have a friend in the Land Office at Washington, and, remembering what you said, I asked him to look them up. I knew no other way to go about it. He tells me something was done, or was not done, by us, and we have lost all we put in."

"I urged Gordon to obey that ruling last spring."

Natalie saw his face become dark with indignation, and the knowledge that he cared set her heart pounding gratefully. She was half tempted to talk about that other, greater trouble that had stolen in on her peace of mind and robbed her of her girlhood, but she shrank from baring her wounds. Above all, a wound so vital and so personal as this.

"Does your mother know?" he asked.

"No, I preferred to tell her in Mr. Gordon's presence." Murray noticed she no longer called the man uncle. "But now the time has come, I'm frightened."

"Never allow yourself to be afraid. Fear is something false; it doesn't exist."

"It seems to me he was — unfaithful to his trust. Am I right?"

"That is something you must judge for yourself," he told her. "You see, I don't know anything about the reasons that prompted him to sacrifice your rights. He may have had good reasons. I dare say he had. In building this railroad I have felt but one regret — the indirect effect it may have upon you and your mother. Your affairs are linked closely with Gordon's and the success of my enterprise will mean the failure of his."

"You mustn't feel that way. I'm sure it won't affect us at all, for we have nothing more to lose. Sometimes I think his judgment is faulty,

OMAR BECOMES HUB OF ACTIVITY

erratic, wonderful man though he is. Mother trusts him blindly, of course, and so do I, yet I hardly know what to do. It is impossible that he did worse than make a mistake."

Her dark eyes were bent upon Murray, and they were eloquent with the question she could not bring herself to ask. He longed to tell her frankly that Curtis Gordon was a charlatan, or even worse, and his fairest schemes were doomed to failure by the very nature of his methods.

"I'm deeply distressed," he said instead. "I hope things are not as bad as you think, and Mr. Gordon will be able to straighten them out for you. If ever I can be of service, you must be sure to call upon me."

Her thanks were conventional, but in her heart was a deep, warm gratitude, for she knew he meant what he said and would not fail her.

Dan Appleton, eying Natalie and his chief from a distance, turned toward his sister.

"She's a perfect peach, Sis. She registered a homerun with me the first time at bat."

"She is nice," Eliza said.

"You know a fellow gets mighty lonely in a place like this. She'd make a dandy sister-in-law for you, wouldn't she?"

"Forget it!" Eliza said. "That's rank insubordination. Omar Khayyam snatched her from the briny and tried to die for her. He has bought her two acres of the most expensive roses and he remembers the date of her birthday. Just you keep your hands off."

"How does she feel about him?"

"Oh, she heroizes him, of course. I don't know just how deep the feeling goes, but I got the impression that it was serious. Two women can't borrow hairpins and mix powder puffs for a week and remain strangers."

"Then, as for Daniel Appleton, C.E., goodnight!" exclaimed her brother, ruefully. "If I were a woman, I'd marry him myself, provided I could get ahead of the rush. But, being a male of the species, I suppose I shall creep out into the jungle and sulk."

"Right-o! Don't enter this race, for I'm afraid you'd be a bad loser. Personally I can't see anything in him to rave about. What scares me pink is the knowledge I must tell him the wretched business that brings me here. If he strikes me, Danny, remember I'm still your sister."

When the big gong gave the signal for luncheon, Appleton escorted Natalie and Eliza to the company messroom, where the field and office force dined together, and presented them to his fellow lieutenants. At suppertime those who had been out on the line during the day were likewise introduced, and after a merry meal the whole party took the two girls back to the green bungalow.

"Why, here's a piano!" Eliza exclaimed when entering the parlor.

"I borrowed it for the evening from the Elite Saloon," O'Neil said. "It's a dissipated old instrument, and some of its teeth have been knocked out — in drunken brawls, I'm afraid — but the owner vouched for its behavior on this occasion."

"It knows only one tune — 'I Won't Go Home until Morning,'" Dan said.

McKay, however, promptly disproved this assertion by seating himself at the keyboard and rattling off some popular melodies. With music and laughter, the long twilight fled while O'Neil's boys flung themselves into the task of entertaining his guests with whole-souled enthusiasm.

So successful were their efforts even Happy Tom appeared to derive a mild enjoyment from them, which was a testimonial indeed. His pleasure was made evident by no word of praise, nor faintest smile, but rather by the lightened gloom in which he chewed his gum and he complained of nothing. In truth, he was not only entertained by the general gaiety, but he was supremely interested in Miss Appleton, who resembled no creature he had ever seen. He had met many girls like Natalie, and feared them, but Eliza, with her straightforward airs and her masculine mannerisms, was different.

She affected him in a way at once pleasant and disagreeable. He felt no diffidence in speaking to her, for instance — a phenomenon that was ground for suspicion. Then, too, her clothes — he could not take his eyes off her clothes — were almost like Dan's. That seemed to show common sense but was probably only the sign of an eccentric, domineering nature. On the other hand, the few words she addressed to him were gracious, and her eyes had a merry twinkle that warmed his heart. She must be all right, he reluctantly concluded, being Dan's sister and O'Neil's friend. But deep down in his mind he had doubts.

At her first opportunity, Eliza decided to confess what had troubled her all afternoon. Drawing O'Neil aside, she began with some trepidation.

"Have you any idea why I'm here?" she asked.

"I supposed either you or Dan had achieved your pet ambition."

"Far from it. I have a fell purpose, and when you learn what it is I expect you to move the piano out—that's what always happens in the play when the heroine is dispossessed. Well, then, I've been sent by *The Review* to bare all the disgraceful secrets of your life!"

"I'm delighted to learn you'll be here so long. You can't possibly finish that task before next spring." His manner, though quizzical, was genuinely hearty.

"Don't laugh!" the girl said. "There's nothing funny about it. I came north as a spy."

"Then you're a Northern Spy?"

"Apples!" she cried. "You remembered, didn't you? I never supposed men like you could be flippant. Well, here goes for the worst." She outlined her conversation with the editor of her paper.

"So you think I'm trying to steal Alaska," he finally said.

"That seems to be the general idea."

"It's a pretty big job."

"Whoever controls transportation will have the country by the throat."

"Yet somebody must build railroads, since the government won't. Did it ever occur to you there is a great risk involved in a thing of this sort, and capital must see a profit before it enters a new field? I wonder if you know how badly this country needs an outlet and how much greater the benefit in dollars and cents will be to the men in the interior than to those who finance the road. But I perceive you are a conservationist."

"Rabid!" Eliza bridled a little at the hint of amused superiority in his voice. "I'm a suffragist, too! I dare say that adds to your disgust."

"Nonsense," he protested. "I have no quarrel with conservation nor with votes for women. Neither have I anything to conceal. I'm only afraid that, like most writers, you will be content with half information. Incomplete facts are responsible for most misunderstandings. If you are in earnest and promise to take the time necessary to get at all the facts, I'll make an agreement with you."

"I promise. Time and a typewriter are my only assets. I don't intend to be hurried."

Dan approached, drawn by the uncomfortable knowledge of his sister's predicament, and broke in.

"Oh, Sis has time to burn. She's going to write a book on the salmon canneries. It's bound to be one of the six best smellers!"

O'Neil waved him away with the threat of sending him out among the mosquitoes.

"I'll agree to show you everything we're doing."

"Even to the coalfields?"

"Even to them. You shall know everything, then you can write what you please."

"And when I've exposed you to the world as a commercial pickpocket, as a looter of the public domain—after Congress has appropriated your fabulous coal claims—will you nail up the door of this little cottage and fire Dan?"

"No."

"Will you still be nice to me?"

"My dear child, you are my guest. Come and go when and where you will. Omar is yours so long as you stay, and when you depart in triumph, leaving me a broken, discredited wretch, I shall stand on the dock and wave you a bon voyage. Now it's bedtime for my boys, since we rise at five o'clock."

"Heavens – five! Why the sun isn't up at that time."

"The sun shines very little here; that's why we want you to stay at Omar. I wish we might also keep Miss Natalie."

When the callers had gone, Eliza confided in Natalie and Dan.

"He took it so nicely that I feel more ashamed than ever. One would think he didn't care at all. Do you suppose he does?"

"There's no denying you appeared at an unfortunate time," her brother said.

"Why?"

"Well—I'm not sure we'll ever succeed with this project. Parker says the glacier bridge can be built, but the longer he studies it the graver he gets. It's making an old man of him."

"What does Mr. O'Neil say?"

"Oh, he's optimistic, as usual. He never gives up. But he has other things to worry him—money! It's money, money, all the time. He wasn't terribly rich to begin with, and he has used up all his own fortune, besides what other people put in. You see, he never expected to carry the project so far. He believed the Trust would buy him out."

"Well?"

"It hasn't and it evidently doesn't intend to. When it learned of his plan, its engineers beat it out to the glaciers and looked them over. Then they gave up their idea of building in from Cortez, but instead of making terms with us, they moved their whole outfit down to Kyak Bay, right alongside the coalfields, and now it has become a race to the glaciers, with Gordon fighting us on the side just to make matters lively. The Trust has the shorter route, but we have the start."

"Why didn't Mr. O'Neil take Kyak as a terminus instead of Omar?"

"He says it's not feasible. Kyak is an open harbor, and he says no breakwater can be built there to withstand the storms. He still clings to that belief, although the Trust is building one. If they succeed, we're cooked. Meanwhile he's rushing work and straining every nerve to raise more money. Now you come along with a proposal to advertise the whole affair to the public as a gigantic graft and set Congress against him. I think he treated you mighty well under the circumstances."

"I won't act against my convictions," Eliza declared, firmly. "Even if it means calamity to everybody."

Natalie spoke for the first time, her voice tuned to a pitch of feeling that contrasted oddly with their conversational tones.

"If you hurt my Irish Prince, I shall hate you as long as I live."

9

GORDON SHOWS HIS TEETH

Affairs at Hope were nearly, if not quite, as prosperous as those at Omar, for Curtis Gordon's advertising had yielded large and quick returns. His experiment during the previous summer of bringing his richest stockholders north had been a great success. They had come, ostensibly at his expense, and once on the ground had allowed themselves to be hypnotized. They had gone where he led, had seen what he pointed out, had believed what he told them. Their imaginations were fired with the grandeur of an undertaking that would develop the vast resources of the north country for the benefit of the struggling pioneers of the interior and humanity in general. Incidentally they were assured over and over again in a great variety of ways the profits would be tremendous.

Gordon showed them Hope and its half-completed mine buildings, and he showed them the huge mountain behind. They noticed there were trees on the sides of it and snow on its top. They marveled. Gordon told them its heart was solid copper ore, and they gasped. Had he revealed in the same impressive manner the hill contained a vein three inches thick, they would have exhibited the same astonishment. They entered the dripping tunnels and peered with grave approval at the drills, the rock cars, and the Montenegrin miners. They rambled over the dumps, to the detriment of shoe leather and shins, filling their suitcases with samples of perfectly good country rock. They confessed to each other, with admirable conservatism, the proposition looked promising, very promising indeed, and they listened with appreciation to Gordon's glowing accounts of his railroad enterprise, the physical evidence of which consisted of a mile or two of track that shrank along the steep shorefront and disappeared into a gulch as if ashamed of itself. He had a wonderful plan to consolidate the mining and railroad companies and talked of a giant holding corporation that would share in the profits of each. The details were intricate, but he seemed to see them all with perfect clearness, and his victims agreed.

He entertained them on a scale that was almost embarrassing, and when they returned to their homes, they outdid one another in their praise of the financial genius who was leading them to the promised land of profits and preferred stock. As a matter of course, they one and all advised their friends to buy, vouching for the fabulous richness of Hope Consolidated, and since their statements were backed by a personal examination of the property, subscriptions came pouring in.

All in all, the excursion had proven so profitable that Gordon had arranged for another, designed to accommodate new investors and promising "prospects." Preparations for their welcome were underway when Natalie arrived.

The girl and her mother talked late that evening, and Gordon saw on the following morning that Gloria, at least, had passed a trying night; but he gave himself no uneasiness. Emotional storms were not unusual; he always disregarded them as far as possible, and usually they passed off quietly.

"I received a letter from Miss Golden in yesterday's mail," he told them at breakfast the next morning. "She is to be one of the new party."

"Did you invite her to return this summer?" Mrs. Gerard asked.

"Yes."

"I remember her well," Natalie said. "Too well, in fact. I thought her very bold."

"She is one of our largest investors, and she writes she would enjoy spending a fortnight here after the others go back."

"Will you allow it?"

"Allow it? My dear Gloria, I can't possibly refuse. In fact, it would be the height of inhospitality not to urge her to do so. She is welcome to stay as long as she chooses, for these quarters are as much hers as ours. I hope you will be nice to her."

Mrs. Gerard made no answer, but later in the morning sought Gordon in his private office.

"I preferred not to discuss the Golden woman before Natalie," she coldly told him. "But—you don't really intend to have her here, do you?"

"Most assuredly!"

"Then I shall have to tell her she is not welcome."

"You will do nothing of the sort, my dear. You will assume the duties of hostess, for which no one is more charmingly qualified."

Mrs. Gerard's lips became white with anger.

"I shall not allow that woman under the same roof with Natalie."

"As usual, you choose the most inconvenient occasion for insisting upon your personal dislikes."

"My dislike has nothing to do with the matter. I overlooked her behavior with you last year—as I have overlooked many things in the past—but this is asking too much."

Gordon's coldness matched her own.

"I repeat, this is no time for jealousy...."

"Jealousy! It's an insult to Natalie."

"Miss Golden is one of our largest stockholders."

"That's not true! I had Denny look up the matter."

"So!" Gordon flared up angrily. "Denny has been showing you the books, eh? He had no more right to do that than you had to pry into my affairs. While Miss Golden's investment may not be so large as some others', she has influential friends. She did yeoman service in the cause, and I can't allow your foolish fancies to interfere with my plans."

"Fancies!" cried the woman, furiously. "You behaved like a schoolboy with her. It was disgraceful. I refuse to let her associate with my daughter."

"Aren't we drawing rather fine distinctions?" Gordon's lip curled.

"In the first place, Natalie has no business here. Since she came, uninvited, for the second time, she must put up with what she finds. I warned you last summer that she might suspect...."

"She did. She does. She discovered the truth a year ago." Mrs. Gerard's usually impassive face became distorted, and she voiced her confession with difficulty.

"The devil!" Gordon yelled.

The woman nodded. "She accused me last night. I tried to lie, but—God! How I have lived through these hours I'll never know."

"Hm-m...," Gordon reflected, briefly. "Perhaps, after all, it's just as well that she knows; she would have found it out sooner or later, and there's some satisfaction in knowing the worst is over."

Never had his callous cynicism been so frankly displayed. It chilled her and made the plea she was about to voice seem doubly difficult.

"I wish I looked upon the matter as you do," she said, slowly. "But other people haven't the same social ideas as we. I'm crushed, and she ... poor child! I don't know how she had the courage to face it. Now that she has heard the truth from my own lips, I'm afraid it will kill her."

Gordon laughed. "Nonsense! Natalie is a sensible girl. Disillusionment is always painful, but never fatal. Sooner or later the young must confront the bald facts of life, and I venture to say she will soon forget her schoolgirl morality. Let me explain my views of...."

"Never!" cried the woman, aghast. "If you do, I shall...." She checked herself and buried her face in her hands. "I feel no regrets for myself, for I drifted with my eyes open. But this—this is different. Don't you understand? I am a mother. Or are you dead to all decent feeling?"

"My dear, I'm the most tender-hearted of men. Of course I shall say nothing, if you prefer, for I am subservient to your commands in all things. But calm yourself. What is done cannot be undone."

"You seem to think the matter is ended, but it isn't," Mrs. Gerard said in more even tones. "Natalie will never allow us to continue this way, and it isn't just to her that we should. We can't go on, Curtis."

"You mean I must marry you?"

She nodded.

He rose and paced the room before answering.

"I always supposed you understood my views on that subject. Believe me, they are unalterable, and in no way the result of a pose."

"Nevertheless, for my sake and Natalie's, you will do it. I can't lose the one thing I love best in the world."

"It would seem that Natalie has filled your head with silly notions," he exclaimed.

"She has awakened me. I have her life to consider, as well as my own."

"We are all individuals, supreme in ourselves, responsible only to ourselves. We must all live our own lives; she cannot live yours, nor you hers."

"I am familiar with your arguments," Mrs. Gerard said, wearily. "But I have thought this all out and there is no other way."

He frowned in his most impressive manner and his chest swelled ominously.

"I will not be coerced. You know I can't be bullied into a thing. I deny that you have any right to demand...."

"I'm not demanding anything. I merely ask this—this favor, the first one I have ever asked. You see, my pride is crumbling. Don't answer now; let's wait until we are both calmer. The subject came up, at least she approached it, by asking about the coal claims. She is worried about them."

"Indeed?"

"She was told by a friend in the Land Office that our rights had been forfeited. I assured her...."

"I refused to heed the absurd rulings of the department, if that is what she refers to."

"Then we have lost?" Mrs. Gerard's pallor increased.

"Technically, yes. In reality, I shall show that our titles were good, and our patents should issue."

"But...." The woman's bloodless fingers were tightly interlaced. "All I have, all Natalie has, is in those claims."

"Yes—and it would require another fortune the size of both to comply with the senseless vagaries of the U.S. Interior Department and to protect your interests. I grew weary of forever sending good hard-earned dollars after bad ones, merely because of the shifting whim of some theorist 5,000 miles away."

"Then I am afraid…." Mrs. Gerard's voice trailed off miserably. "It is all we have, and you told me…."

Gordon broke in irritably: "My dear Gloria, spare me this painful faultfinding. If I can win for you, I shall do so, and then you will agree that I acted wisely. If I lose, it will merely be the luck of the average investor. We played for big returns, and of course the risks were great."

"But Mr. O'Neil told her his claims…."

Gordon's blazing eyes warned her. "O'Neil, eh? So, he is the 'friend in the Land Office'? No doubt he also gave Natalie the suggestion that led to her scene with you. Tell her to occupy herself less with affairs that do not concern her and more with her own conduct. Her actions with that upstart have been outrageous."

"What about your own actions with the Golden woman?" cried Mrs. Gerard, reverting with feminine insistence to the subject of their first difference. "What are you going to do about her?"

"Nothing."

"Remember, I refuse to share the same roof with her. You wouldn't ask it of your wife."

This second reference to a disagreeable subject was unfortunate. Gordon was given to the widest vagaries of temper, and this interview had exasperated him beyond measure. He exploded.

"Please remember you are not my wife! My ideas on matrimony will never change. You ought to know by this time I am granite."

"I can't give up Natalie. I would give up much, for we women don't change, but…."

"A fallacy!" He laughed disagreeably. "Pardon me, Gloria, if I tell you that you do change; that you have changed; that time has left its imprint upon even you. A cruel fact, but true." He took savage pleasure in her trembling, for she had roused all the devils in him, and they were many.

"You are growing tired!"

"Not at all. But you have just voiced the strongest possible argument against marriage. We grow old! Age brings its alterations! I have ever been a slave to youth and beauty and the years bring to me only an increasing appreciation, a more critical judgment, of the beautiful. If I chose to marry … well, frankly, the mature charms of a woman of my own age would have slight attraction for me."

"Then, I will go," Mrs. Gerard whispered.

"Not by any wish of mine," he assured her. "You are quite welcome to stay. Things will run along in the usual way—more smoothly, perhaps, now we have attained a complete understanding. You have no place to go, nor means with which to insure a living for yourself and Natalie. I would hate to see you sacrifice yourself and her to a Puritanical whim, for I owe you much happiness and I'm sure I should miss you greatly. Someone must rule, and since nature has given me the right, I shall exercise it. We will have no more rebellion."

Mrs. Gerard left the room dazed and sick with despair.

"We must go! We must go!" she kept repeating, but her tragic look alarmed Natalie far more than her words.

"Yes, yes!" The girl took her in her arms and tried to still the ceaseless trembling that shook the mother's frame, while her own tears fell, unheeded.

"We must go! Now!"

"Yes, dearest. But where?"

"You love me still?" Gloria asked. "I suppose you need me, too, don't you? I hadn't thought of that."

"Every hour!" The round young arms pressed her closer. "You won't think of … of leaving me?"

Mrs. Gerard shook her head slowly. "No. I suppose that must be part of the price. But penniless? Friendless? Where can we go?"

"Mr. O'Neil, my Irish Prince," faltered the daughter through her tears. "Perhaps he would take us in."

"Omar Khayyam," said Eliza Appleton, entering O'Neil's office briskly. "You are the general trouble man, so prepare to listen to mine."

"Won't the kitchen flue draw or has a hinge come off the bungalow door?" Murray smiled. He was harassed by endless worries, a dozen pressing matters called for his instant attention; yet he showed no trace of annoyance. "If so, I'll be right up and fix it."

"The kitchen chimney has a draught that threatens to draw Dan's salary out with the smoke every time I cook a meal, and the house is dandy. This is a real man-size tribulation, so of course, I run to you. Simon Legree is at his tricks again."

"Legree!"

The girl nodded her blond head vigorously.

"Yes! He's stolen Mrs. St. Claire's slaves, and she and Little Eva are out in the cold."

"What the deuce are you talking about?"

"Gordon, of course, and the two Gerards, Natalie and Gloria— 'Town Hall, Tonight. Come one, Come all!'"

"Oh!" O'Neil's eyes brightened.

"There have been terrible goings-on over at Hope. I went up yesterday, in my official capacity, to reconnoiter the enemy's position and to give him a preliminary skirmish, but the great man was sulking in his tent and sent word by a menial for me to begone or look out for the bloodhounds. Isn't he the haughty thing? I don't like to 'begone'—I refuse to git when I'm told, so, of course, I paid my respects to Natalie and her mother. But what do you think I found? Mrs. St. Claire desolated, Eva dissolved in tears and her hair down."

"Will you talk sense?"

"Just try a little nonsense and see. Well, the great eruption has taken place and the loss of life was terrible. Among those buried in the cinders are the dusky-eyed heroine and her friend mother. It seems Eva had a hand in the overseer's exposure...."

"Yes, yes! It's about those coal claims. I knew it was coming."

"She told her mother of the horrid treachery, and mother lugged the complaint to Gordon and placed it in his lap. Result—confession and defiance from him. Even the family jewels are gone."

"Is Gordon broke?"

"He's weltering in money, but the coal claims are lost, and he wants to know what they're going to do about it. The women are ruined. He magnanimously offers them his bounty, but of course they refuse to accept it."

"Hasn't he made any provision for them?"

"Coffee and cakes, three times a day. That's all! He won't even provide transportation, and the troupe can't walk home. They refuse to stay there, but they can't get away. I've cabled *The Review*, overdrawing my salary scandalously, and Dan is eager to help, but the worst of it is neither of those women knows how to make a living. Natalie wants to work, but the extent of her knowledge is the knack of frosting a layer cake, and her mother never even sewed on a button in all her life. It would make a lovely Sunday story, and it wouldn't help Curtis Gordon with his stockholders."

"You won't write it, of course."

"Oh, I suppose not, but it's maddening not to be able to do something. Since there's a law against manslaughter, the pencil is my only weapon. I'd like to jab it clear through that ruffian." Eliza's animated face was stern, her generous mouth set firmly.

"You can leave out the personal element," he told her. "There's still a big story there, if you realize it runs back to Washington and involves your favorite policy of conservation. Those claims belonged to Natalie and her mother. I happen to know their locations were legal and there was never any question of fraud in the titles, hence they were entitled to patents years ago. Gordon did wrong, of course, in refusing to obey the orders of the Secretary of the Interior even though he knew those orders to be senseless and contradictory, but the women are the ones to suffer. The government froze them out. This is only one instance of what delay and indecision at headquarters has done. I'll show you others before we are through. As for those two—you say they want to do something?"

"It's not a question of wanting; they've *got* to do something—or starve. They would scrub kitchens if they knew how."

"Why didn't they come to me?"

"Do you need a cook and a dishwasher?"

Murray frowned. "Our new hotel is nearly finished; perhaps Mrs. Gerard would accept a position as—as hostess."

Courtesy University Alaska Anchorage

This photo taken in Porcupine shows what a typical interiorof an early Alaska hotel looked like in the early 1900s.

"*Hostess*! In a railroad camp hotel? Who ever heard of such a thing?" Eliza eyed him incredulously.

O'Neil's flush did not go unnoticed.

"It *is* unusual, but we'll try it," he said quietly. "She might learn to manage the business, with a competent assistant. The salary will be ample for her and Natalie to live on."

Eliza laid a hand timidly on his arm.

"Omar Khayyam, you're a fine old Persian gentleman!" she said. "I know what it will mean to those two poor women, and I know what it will mean to you, for of course the salary will come out of your pocket."

He smiled. "It's the best I can offer, and I'm sure you won't tell them."

"Of course not. I know how it feels to lose a fortune, too, for I've been through the mill. Don't laugh! You have a load on your shoulders heavier than Mr. Sinbad's, and it's mighty nice of you to let me add to the burden. I—I hope it won't break your poor back. Now I'm going up to your bungalow and lock myself into your white bedroom, and...."

"Have a good cry?" he said, noting the suspicious moisture in her eyes.

"Certainly not!" Eliza exclaimed, indignantly. "I'm not the least bit sentimental."

10

Doc Grey Shows His Wit

The talk between O'Neil and Mrs. Gerard upon her arrival from Hope was short and businesslike. Neither by word nor look did he show he knew or suspected anything of the real reason of her break with Gordon. Toward both her and Natalie he preserved his customary heartiness, and their first constraint soon disappeared. Mrs. Gerard had been plunged in one of those black moods where it seems no possible event can bring even a semblance of happiness. But it was remarkable how soon this state of mind began to give way before O'Neil's matter-of-fact cheerfulness.

He refused to listen to their thanks and made them believe they were doing him a favor by accepting the responsibility of the new hotel. Pending completion of that structure, he was hard pressed to find a lodging place for them until Eliza and her brother insisted they share the bungalow with them—a thing O'Neil had not felt at liberty to ask under the circumstances. Nor was the tact of the brother and sister less than his; they received the two unfortunates as honored guests.

Gradually the visitors began to feel they were welcome, needed, and had an important task to fulfill. Soon the sense they were really of service drove away depression. Night after night they lay awake, discussing the wonderful change in their fortunes and planning their future. Natalie at least had not the slightest doubt all their troubles were at an end.

One morning they awoke to learn O'Neil had gone to the States, leaving Dr. Gray in charge of affairs at Omar during his absence. The physician, who was fully in his chief's confidence, gravely discussed their duties with them. He was so discreet they had no suspicion he knew their secret. It was typical of O'Neil and his boys that they should show this chivalry toward two friendless outcasts; it was typical of them, also, that they all considered themselves protectors of Natalie and her mother, letting it be known through the town that the slightest rudeness toward the women would be promptly punished.

While O'Neil's unexpected departure caused some comment, no one except his trusted lieutenants dreamed of the grave importance of his mission. They knew the necessities that hounded him and were aware of the trembling insecurity in which affairs now stood. But they maintained their cheerful industry, worked with unabated energy, and the road crept forward foot by foot, as steadily and as smoothly as if he himself were on the ground to direct it.

Many disappointments had arisen since the birth of the Salmon River & Northwestern; many misfortunes had united to slow the development of its builder's plans. Climate was the first obstacle O'Neil encountered. Unceasing rains, mists, and fogs dispirited his workmen during summer and cut their efficiency in half. He had made certain allowances for this, of course, but no one could have foreseen so great a percentage of inefficiency as later developed.

The cold was intense during winter, and the snows were of remarkable depth, while outside the shelter of the Omar hills the winds howled and rioted over the frozen delta, chilling men and animals and paralyzing human effort. Under these conditions it was hard to get workmen, and harder to keep them. Progress was slower than had been anticipated.

Then, too, the physical difficulties of the country were almost insurmountable. The morass that comprised the Salmon River plain was a bottomless ooze in summer, over which nothing could be transported, yet in winter it became sheathed with a steel-hard armor against which piling splintered. It could be penetrated at that season only by the assistance of steam thawers, which involved delay and heavy expense. These were but samples of the obstacles that had to be met, and everyone realized the work thus far had been merely preparatory. The great obstruction, of which the success of the whole undertaking hinged, still lay before them.

But the most serious by far of all handicaps was the lack of capital. Murray had foreseen as inevitable the abandonment by the Trust of its Cortez route, but its change of base to Kyak had come as a startling surprise and as an almost crushing blow. Personally, he believed its present plan to be even more impracticable than its former one, but its refusal to buy him out had disheartened his financial associates and tightened their purse strings into a knot no argument of his could loosen. He had long since exhausted his own liquid capital, utilized all his available assets, and his personal credit was tottering.

He was obliged to finance his operations with new money — a task that became ever more difficult as the months passed and the Trust continued its work at Kyak. Yet he knew the briefest flagging, even a temporary abandonment of work, meant swift and utter ruin. His track must go forward, his labor must be paid, his supplies must not be interrupted. He set his jaw and fought on stubbornly, certain of his ultimate triumph if only he could hold out.

A hundred miles to the west was a melancholy example of failure in railroad building, in the form of two rows of rust upon a weed-grown embankment. It was all that remained of another enterprise that had succumbed to financial starvation, and the wasted millions it represented was depressing to consider.

Thus far O'Neil's rivalry with the Trust had been friendly, if spirited, but his action in coming to the assistance of Mrs. Gerard and her daughter raised up a new and vigorous enemy whose methods were not as scrupulous as those of the Heidlemanns.

Gordon was a strangely unbalanced man. He was magnetic, his geniality was heartwarming, yet he was perfectly coldblooded in his selfishness. He was cool and calculating, but interference roused him to an almost insane pitch of passion. Fickle in most things, he

DOC GREY SHOWS HIS WIT

was uncompromising in his hatreds. O'Neil's generosity in affording sanctuary to his defiant mistress struck him as a personal affront, it fanned his dislike of his rival into a consuming rage. It was with no thought of profit he cast about for a means of crippling O'Neil. He was quite capable of ruining himself, not to speak of incidental harm to others, if only he could gratify his spleen.

Denny, his trusted jackal, resisted stoutly any move against the Irish Prince, but his employer would not listen to him or consent to delay. Therefore, a certain plausible, shifty-eyed individual by the name of Linn was dispatched to Omar on the first steamer. Landing at his destination, Mr. Linn quietly effaced himself, disappearing out the right-of-way, where he began moving from camp to camp, ostensibly in search of employment.

It was a few days later, perhaps a week after O'Neil's departure, that Eliza Appleton entered the hospital to talk to Dr. Gray.

"I've finished my first story for *The Review*."

The big physician had a rapid, forceful habit of speech. "Well, I suppose you uncorked the vitriol bottle," he said.

"No. Since you are now the fount of authority here, I thought I'd tell you that I have reserved my treachery for another time. I haven't learned enough yet to warrant real fireworks. As a matter of fact, I've been very kind to Mr. O'Neil in my story."

"Let me thank you for him."

"Now don't be sarcastic! I could have said a lot of nasty things, if he hadn't been so nice to me. I suppose it is the corrupting influence of his kindness."

"He really will be grateful," the doctor assured her, seriously. "Newspaper publicity of the wrong sort might hurt him a great deal just now. In every big enterprise there comes a critical time when everything depends upon one man; strong as the structure seems, he's really supporting it. You see, the whole thing rests ultimately on credit and confidence. An ill-considered word, a little unfriendly shove, and down comes the whole works. Then some financial power steps in, reorganizes the wreckage, and gets the result of all the other fellow's efforts, for nothing."

"Dan tells me the affairs of the railroad are in just such a tottering condition."

"Yes. We're up against it, for the time being. Our cards are on the table, and you have it in your power to do us a lot of harm."

"Don't put it that way!" Eliza said. "You and Mr. O'Neil, and even Dan, make it hard for me to do my duty. I won't let you rob me of my liberty. I'll get out and camp in a tent first."

The physician laughed. "Don't mistake leaf mold for muck, that's all we ask. O'Neil is perfectly willing to let you investigate him."

"Exactly! And I could bite off his head for being so nice about it. Not that I've discovered anything against him, for I haven't— I think he's fine—but I object to the principle of the thing."

"He'll never peep, no matter what you do or say."

"It makes me furious to know how superior he is. I never detested a man's virtues as I do his. Gordon is the sort I like, for he needs exposing, and expects it. Wait until I get at him and the Trust."

"The Trust, too, eh?"

"Of course."

"Now what have the Heidlemanns done?"

"It's not what they have done; it's what they're going to do. They're trying to grab Alaska."

Dr. Gray shook his head impatiently, but before he could make answer Tom Slater entered and broke into the conversation.

"I've spotted him, Doc. His name is Linn, and he's Gordon's hand. He's at mile 24 and 50 men are quitting from that camp."

"That makes 200, so far," the doctor said.

"He's offering a raise of 50 cents a day and transportation to Hope."

Gray scowled and Eliza turned to Tom.

"What's wrong, Uncle Tom?"

"Don't call me 'Uncle Tom,'" Slater said. "I ain't related to you."

Miss Appleton smiled at him sweetly. "I had a dear friend once— you remind me of him, he was such a splendid big man."

Tom eyed her suspiciously.

"He chewed gum incessantly, too, and declared it never hurt anybody."

"It never did," Slater agreed.

"We pleaded, we argued, we did our best to save him, but...." She shook her blond head sadly.

"What happened to him?"

"What always happens. He lingered along for a time, stubborn to the last, then...." She then turned her attention to Dr. Gray. "Who is this man Linn, and what is he doing?"

"He's an emissary of Curtis Gordon and he's hiring our men away from us," snapped the physician.

"Why, Dan tells me Mr. O'Neil pays higher wages than anybody!"

"So he does, but Linn offers a raise. We didn't know what the trouble was till over 100 men had quit. The town is full of them, now, and it's becoming a stampede."

"Can't you meet the raise?"

"That wouldn't do any good."

Tom agreed. "Gordon don't want these fellows. He's doing it to get even with Murray for those wo...." He bit his words in two after a glance from Gray. "What happened to the man that chewed gum?" he asked.

"Oh yes! Poor fellow. We warned him time and again, but he was a sullen brute, he wouldn't heed advice. Why don't you bounce this man Linn? Why don't you run him out of camp?"

"Fine counsel from a champion of equal rights." Gray said with a smile. "You forget we have laws and Gordon has a press bureau. It would antagonize the men and cause a lot of trouble in the end. What O'Neil could do personally, he can't do as the president of the S. R. & N. It would give us a black eye."

"We've got to do something dam' quick," Slater said, "or else the work will be tied up. That would crab Murray's deal. I've got a pick handle that's itching for Linn's head." The speaker coughed hollowly. "I've got a bad cold on my chest—feels like pneumonia, to me. Wouldn't that just be my luck?"

"Do you have pains in your chest?" the girl asked.

"Terrible! But I'm so full of pains that I get used to 'em."

"It isn't pneumonia."

Slater flared up at this, for he was jealous of his sufferings.

"It's gumbago!" Eliza declared.

Dr. Gray's troubled countenance relaxed into a grin.

"I'll give you something to rub on those leather lungs," the doctor said. "Harness oil, perhaps."

"Is this labor trouble really serious?" Eliza asked.

"Serious? It may knock us out completely. Go away now and let me think. Pardon my rudeness, Miss Appleton, but...."

Slater paused at the door.

"Don't think too long, Doc," he said. "There's a ship due in three days, and by that time there won't be a roughneck left on the job. It'll take a month to get a new crew from the States, and then it wouldn't be any good till it was broke in."

The doctor sat down to weigh the news Happy Tom had brought, but the more squarely he considered the matter the more alarming it appeared. Thus far the railroad project had been remarkably free from labor troubles. To permit them to creep in at this stage would be extremely perilous. The briefest cessation of work might, and probably would, have a serious bearing on O'Neil's efforts to raise money. Gray felt the responsibility of his position with extraordinary force, for his chief's fortunes had never suffered in his hands and he could not permit them to do so now.

But how to meet this move of Gordon's he did not know; he could think of no means of keeping these men at Omar. As he had told Eliza, to meet the raise would be useless, and a new scale of wages once adopted would be hard to reduce. Successful or unsuccessful in its effect, it would run into many thousands of dollars. The physician acknowledged himself dreadfully perplexed. He racked his brain uselessly, yearning meanwhile for the autocratic power to compel obedience among his men. He would have forced them back to their jobs had there been a way, and the fact they were duped only added to his anger.

It occurred to him to quarantine the town, a thing he could easily do as port physician in case of an epidemic, but Omar was unusually healthy, and beyond a few surgical cases his hospital was empty.

His meditations were interrupted when Tom Slater returned.

"Give me that dope, Doc; I'm coughing like a switch engine."

Gray rose and went to the shelves upon which his drugs were arranged, while the fat man continued.

"That Appleton girl has got me worried with her foolishness. Maybe I *am* sick; anyhow, I feel rotten. What I need is a good rest and a nurse to wait on me."

The physician's eyes in running along the rows of bottles encountered one labeled "Oleum Tiglii," and paused there. "You need a rest, eh?" he asked.

"If I don't get one, I'll wing my way to realms eternal. I ain't been dried off for three months." Gray turned to regard his caller with a speculative stare, his fingers toyed with the bottle. "If it wasn't for this man Linn I'd lay off—I'd go to jail for him. But I can't do anything, with one foot always in the grave."

The doctor's face lightened with determination.

"Tom, you've been sent from heaven!"

"D'you mean I've been sent for, from heaven?" The invalid's red cheeks blanched, into his mournful eyes leaped a look of quick concern. "Say! Am I as sick as all that?"

"This will make you feel better," Gray said as he uncorked the bottle. "Take off your shirt."

"What for?"

"I'm going to rub your chest and arms."

Slater obeyed, with some reluctance.

"You ain't stripping me down so you can operate?"

"Nonsense!"

"I'm feeling pretty good again."

"It's well to take these things early. They all look alike at the beginning."

"What things?"

"Grippe, gumbago, smallpox...."

"God'lmighty!" exclaimed Slater with a start. "I haven't got anything but a light cold."

"Then this liniment ought to be just the thing."

"Humph! It don't smell like liniment," Tom said after a moment, but the doctor had fallen to work on him and he submitted with resignation.

Perhaps an hour later Dr. Gray appeared at the Appleton bungalow and surprised Eliza.

"I've come to you for some help. You're the only soul in Omar I can trust."

"Have you gone raving mad?" she asked.

"No. I must put an end to Linn's activity, or we'll be ruined. These workmen must be held in Omar, and you must help me do it."

"They have the right to go where they please."

"Of course, but Gordon will let them out as soon as he has crippled us. Tell me, would you like to be a trained nurse?"

"No, I would not," Eliza said.

"Nevertheless, you're going to be one — Tom needs you."

"Tom? What ails him?"

"Nothing at this moment, but wait until tomorrow." The physician's eyes were twinkling, and when he explained the cause of his amusement, Eliza laughed.

"Of course I'll help," she said. "But it won't hurt the poor fellow, will it?"

"Not in the least – unless it frightens him to death. Tom's an awful coward about sickness. That's why I need someone like you to take care of him. He'll be at the hospital tomorrow at three. If you'll arrange to be there, we'll break the news to him gently. I dare not tackle it alone."

Tom was a trifle embarrassed at finding Eliza in Dr. Gray's office when he entered the next afternoon. The boss packer seemed different than usual; he was much subdued. His cough had disappeared, but in its place, he suffered a nervous apprehension. His cheeks were pale, the gloom in his eyes had changed to a lurking uneasiness.

"Just dropped in to say I'm all right again," he said in an offhand tone.

"That's good!" Gray said. "But you don't look well."

"I'm feeling fine!" Mr. Slater hunched his shoulders as if the contact of his shirt hurt his flesh.

"You'd better let me rub you. Why are you scratching yourself?"

"I ain't scratching."

"You were!" The doctor was sternly curious. He had assumed his coldest and most professional air.

"Well, if I scratched, I probably itched. That's why people scratch, ain't it?"

"Let me look you over."

"I can't spare the time, Doc."

"Wait!" Gray's tone halted the speaker as he turned to leave. "I'm not going to let you out in this weather until I rub you."

This time there was no mistaking Happy Tom's pallor. "I tell you I feel great," he said with shaking voice. "I—haven't felt so good for years."

"Come, come! Step into the other room and take off your shirt."

"Not on your life."

"What do you mean?"

"I don't want no more of your dam' liniment."

"Why?"

"Because I'm—because I don't."

"Then I suppose I'll have to throw and hogtie you." The physician rose and laid a heavy hand on his patient's arm, at which Tom flinched.

"Ouch! Leggo! Gimme the stuff and I'll rub myself."

"Tom!" The gravity of the speaker's voice was grim, alarming. Mr. Slater hesitated, his gaze wavered, he scratched his chest unconsciously.

Eliza shook her head in pity and uttered an inarticulate murmur of concern.

"You couldn't get my shirt off with a steam winch. I tell you I'm feeling grand."

"Why *will* you chew the horrid stuff?" Miss Appleton asked.

"I'm just a little broke out, that's all."

"Ah ... you're broken out. I feared so," the doctor said.

The grave concern in those two faces was too much for Slater's sensitive nature. His stubbornness gave way, his self-control vanished.

"I spent an awful night, Doc," he confessed. "I'll burst into flame if this keeps up. What is it, anyhow?"

"Is there an eruption of the arms and chest?"

"They're all erupted to hell."

Dr. Gray silently parted the shirt over Slater's bosom. "Hm-m!" he said.

"Tell him what it is," urged Eliza, in whom mirth and pity were struggling for mastery.

"It has every appearance of smallpox."

The victim uttered a choking cry and sat down limply. Sweat leaped out all over his face, beads appeared on his round bald head.

"I knew I was a sick man. I've felt it coming on for three months, but I fought it off for Murray's sake. Say it's chickenpox," he pleaded.

"Never mind; it's seldom serious," Eliza endeavored to comfort the stricken man. "You wanted a good rest."

"I don't. I want to work."

"I'll have to quarantine you, Tom."

Slater was in no condition for further resistance; a complete collapse of body and mind followed the diagnosis of his illness. He began to complain of many symptoms, none of which were in any way connected with his fancied disease. He was racked with pains, he suffered a terrible nausea, his head swam. He spoke bravely of his destitute family and prepared to make his will. When he left the hospital an hour later, it was on a stretcher between four straining bearers.

That evening a disturbing rumor crept through the town of Omar. It penetrated the crowded saloons where the laborers who had quit work were squandering their pay, and it caused a brief lull in the ribaldry. But the mere fact that Tom Slater had come down with smallpox and had been isolated on a fishing boat anchored in the creek seemed, after all, of little consequence. Some of the idlers strolled down the street to stare at the boat, and upon their return verified the report. They also announced they had seen the yellow-haired newspaper woman aboard, all dressed in white. It was considered high time by the majority to leave Omar, for an epidemic was a thing to be avoided, and a wager was made that the whole force would quit in a body as soon as the truth became known.

On the second day, Dr. Gray undertook to allay the general uneasiness, but upon being pressed, reluctantly acknowledged his patient showed all the signs of the dread disease. This hastened the general preparations for departure, and when the incoming steamer hove in sight, every laborer was at the dock with his kitbag. It excited some idle comment among them to note Dr. Gray had gone down the bay a short distance to meet the ship, and his efforts to speak to its occupants were watched with interest and amusement. Obviously, it would have been much easier for him to wait until she landed, for she came right on and drew in toward the wharf. It was not until her bow line was made fast that the physician succeeded in hailing the captain. Then the deserters were amazed to hear the conversation that ensued.

"I can't let you land, Captain Johnny" came a voice from Dr. Gray's launch.

"And why can't you?" demanded Brennan from the bridge of his new ship. "Have you some prejudice against the Irish?" The stern hawser was already being run out, and the crowd was edging closer, waiting for the gangplank.

"There is smallpox here, and as health officer I've quarantined the port."

There came a burst of Elizabethan profanity from the little skipper, but it was drowned by the shout from shore as the full meaning of the situation finally came home. Then the waiting men made a rush for the ship. She had not yet touched, however, and the distance between her and the pier was too great to leap.

Above the confusion came Brennan's voice, through a megaphone, commanding them to stand back. Someone traitorously cast off the loop of the bow line, the ship's propellers began to thrash, and the big steel hull backed away inch by inch, foot by foot, until, amid curses and cries of rage, she made a majestic circle and plowed off up the Sound toward Hope.

By a narrow margin the physician reached his hospital ahead of the infuriated mob, and it was well he did so, for they were in a lynching mood. But, once within his own premises, he made a show of determined resistance that daunted them, and they sullenly retired.

That night Omar rang with threats and deep-breathed curses, and Eliza Appleton, in the garb of a nurse, tended her patient cheerfully.

To the delegation that waited for him the next morning, Dr. Gray explained the nature of his duties as health officer, informing them coolly that no living soul could leave Omar without incurring legal penalties. Since he could prevent any ships from landing, and as the U.S. marshal was present to enforce the quarantine, he seemed to be master of the situation.

"How long will we be tied up?" demanded the spokesman of the party.

"That is hard to say."

"Well, we're going to leave this camp!" the man announced.

"Indeed? Where are you going?"

"We're going to Hope. You might as well let us go. We won't stand for this."

The physician eyed him coldly. "You won't? May I ask how you are going to help yourselves?"

"We're going to leave on the next steamer."

"Oh, no you're not!" the marshal spoke up.

"See here, Doc! There's over 200 of us and we can't stay here; we'll go broke."

Gray shrugged his broad shoulders. "Sorry," he said, "but you see I've no choice in the matter. I never saw a case of smallpox that looked worse."

"It's a frameup," growled the spokesman. "Tom hasn't got smallpox any more than I have. You cooked it to keep us here." There was an angry second to this.

"You think so, eh?" the doctor said. "Then just come with me."

"Where?"

"Out to the boat where he is. I'll show you."

"You won't show me no smallpox," asserted one of the committee members.

"Then *you* come with me," the physician urged the leader.

"So you can bottle me up, too? No, thank you!"

"Get the town photographer with his flashlight. We'll help him take a picture. Then you can show it to the others. I promise not to quarantine you."

After some hesitation the men agreed to this. The photographer was summoned and joined the party on its way to the floating pest house.

It was not a pleasant place in which they found Tom Slater, for the cabin of the fishing boat was neither light nor airy, but Eliza had done much to make it agreeable. The sick man was propped up in his bunk and playing solitaire, but he left off his occupation to groan as the newcomers came alongside.

When the cause of the visit had been made known, however, he rebelled.

"I won't pose for no camera fiend," he shouted. "It ain't decent and I'm too sick. D'you take me for a bearded lady or a living skeleton?"

"These men think you're stalling," Dr. Gray told him.

"Who? Me?" Slater rolled an angry eye upon the delegation. "I ain't sick, eh? I s'pose I'm doing this for fun? I wish you had it, that's all."

The three members of the committee of investigation wisely halted at the foot of the companionway stairs where the fresh air fanned them. They were nervous and ill at ease.

Drawing his covers closer, Slater yelled to the men.

"Close that hatch, you boneheads! I'm blowing away!"

The photographer ventured to protest.

"It's mighty close in here, Doc. Is it safe to breathe the bugs?"

"Perfectly safe," Gray assured him. "At least Miss Appleton hasn't suffered yet."

As a matter of fact, the patient betrayed no symptoms of a wasting illness, for his cheeks were ruddy, he had eaten three hearty meals each day, and the enforced rest had done him good, so the committee saw nothing about him to satisfy their suspicions. But when Tom weakly called upon them for assistance in raising, they shrank back.

"I wouldn't touch you with a fishpole," one of them said.

Eliza came forward, however. She permitted her charge to lean on her while she adjusted the pillows at his back. But when Dr. Gray ordered him to bare his breast and arms Slater refused. He blushed, he stammered, he clutched his nightrobe with a hand that would have required a cold chisel to loosen, and not until Eliza had gone on deck would he consent to expose his bulging chest.

But Miss Appleton had barely left the cabin when she was followed by the most timid member of the delegation. He raced up the stairs.

"I've saw enough! He's got it and got it bad."

A moment later came the dull sound of the exploding flashlight, then a yell, and out of the smoke stumbled his two companions. The spokesman, it appeared, also had seen enough—too much—for with another yell he leaped the rail and made for shore. Fortunately the tide was out and the water low. He left a trail across the mud flat like that of a frightened hippopotamus.

When the two conspirators were finally alone on the deck they rocked in each other's arms, striving to stifle their laughter. Meanwhile from the interior of the cabin came the feeble moans of the invalid.

By evening, hastily made photographs of the sick man were shown on the streets. Nor could the most skeptical deny he presented a revolting sight and one warranting Dr. Gray's precautions. Despite this evidence, however, threats against the physician continued to be made freely. But when Eliza expressed fears for his safety he only smiled grimly, and he stalked through the streets with such defiance written on his heavy features that no man dared raise a hand against him.

Day after day the quarantine continued, and at length some of the men went back to work. As others exhausted their wages they followed. In a fortnight Omar was once more free of its floating population and work at the front was going forward as usual. Meanwhile the patient recovered in marvelous fashion and was loud in his thanks to the physician who had brought him through so speedily. Yet Gray stubbornly refused to raise the embargo.

Finally the cause of the whole trouble appeared at the hospital and begged to be released.

"You put it over me," Mr. Linn said. "I've had enough, and I want to get out."

"I don't know what you're talking about," the doctor said. "No one can leave here now."

"I know it wasn't smallpox at all, but it worked just the same, I'll leave your men alone if you'll let me go out on the next Seattle steamer."

"But—I thought you came from Hope?" Gray said.

Mr. Linn shifted his eyes and laughed uneasily. "I did, and I'm going to keep coming from Hope. You don't think I'd dare to go back after this, do you?"

"Why not?"

"Gordon would kill me."

"So! Mr. Gordon sent you?"

"You know he did. But—I've got to get out now. I'm broke."

"I didn't think it of Gordon...." The doctor shook his head sadly. "How underhanded of him!"

"Don't let's four-flush," Linn sid. "You were too slick for him, and you sewed me up. I've spent the money he gave me and now I'm flat."

"You look strong. We need men."

Gordon's emissary turned pale. "Say! You wouldn't set me to work? Why, those men would string me up."

"I think not. I've spoken to the shift boss at mile 30, and he'll take care you're not hurt so long as you work hard and keep your mouth shut."

An hour later Mr. Linn, cursing deeply, shouldered his pack and tramped out the grade, nor could he obtain food or shelter until he had covered those 30 weary miles. Once at his destination, he was only too glad to draw a numbered tag and fall to work with pick and shovel. But he estimated it would take him until late the following month to earn his fare to the States.

11

TWO SIDES OF ELIZA VIOLET APPLETON

Dan Appleton entered the bungalow one evening, wet and tired from his work, to find Eliza pacing the floor in agitation.

"What's the matter, Sis?" he asked.

"His sister pointed to a copy of *The Review* that day's mail had brought.

"Look at that!" she cried. "Read it!"

"Oh! Your story, eh?"

"Read it!"

He read a column, and then glanced up to find her watching him with angry eyes.

"Gee - that's pretty rough on the chief, Kid. I thought you liked him," he said.

"I do! I do! Don't you understand, dummy? I didn't write that! They've changed my story — distorted it. I'm — *furious!*"

Dan whistled softly. "I didn't suppose they'd try anything like that, but — they did a good job while they were at it. Why, you'd think O'Neil was a grafter and the S. R. & N. nothing but a land-grabbing deal."

"How dare they?" the girl cried. "The actual changes aren't so many — just enough to alter the effect of the story — but that's what makes it so devilish. For instance, I described the obstacles and handicaps Mr. O'Neil has had to overcome in order to show the magnitude of his enterprise. But Drake has altered it, so the physical conditions here seem to be insurmountable, and he makes me say the road is doomed to failure. That's the way he changed it all through."

"It may topple the chief's plans over; they're very insecure. It plays right into the hands of his enemies, too, and of course Gordon's press bureau will make the most of it."

"Heavens! I want sympathy, not abuse!" wailed his sister. "It's all due to the policy of *The Review*. Drake thinks everybody up here is a thief. I dare say they are, but ... how can I face Mr. O'Neil?"

Dan shook the paper in his fist. "Are you going to stand for this?"

"Hardly! I cabled the office this morning, and here's Drake's answer."

Dan read the telegram.

> Stuff colorless. Don't allow admiration warp judgment.
>
> – Drake, The Review

"Can you beat that?" Eliza asked him.

"He thinks you've surrendered to Murray, like all the others."

"I hate him! I detest him!"

"Who? O'Neil or Drake?"

"Both. Mr. O'Neil for putting me in the position of a traitor, and Drake for presuming to rewrite my stuff. I'm going to resign, and I'm going to leave Omar before Murray O'Neil comes back."

"Don't be a quitter, Sis. If you throw up the job the paper will send somebody who will lie about us to suit the policy of the office. Show 'em where they're wrong; show 'em what this country needs. You have your magazine stories to write."

Eliza shook her head. "Bother the magazines and the whole business! I'm thinking about Mr. O'Neil. I—I could cry. I suppose I'll have to stay and explain to him, but—then I'll go home."

"No! You'll stay right here and go through with this thing. I need you."

"You? What for?"

"You can perform a great and significant service for your loving brother. He's in terrible trouble!"

"What's wrong, Danny?" Eliza's anger gave instant place to solicitude. "You — you haven't *stolen* anything?"

"Lord, no! What put that into your head?"

"I don't know — except that's the worst thing that could happen to us. I like to start with the worst."

"I can't sulk in the jungle anymore. I'm a rotten loser, Sis."

"Oh! You mean — Natalie? You — like her?"

"For a writer you select the most foolish words! Like, love, adore, worship — words are no good, anyway. I'm dippy. I'm out of my head. I've lost my reason. I'm deliriously happy and miserably unhappy – I...."

"That's enough," the girl said. "I can imagine the rest."

"It was a fatal mistake for her to come to Omar, and to this very house, of all places, where I could see her every day. I might have recovered from the first jolt if I'd never seen her again, but...." He waved his hands hopelessly. "I'm beginning to hate O'Neil."

"You miserable traitor!" Eliza gasped.

"Yep. That's me. I'm dead to loyalty, lost to the claims of friendship. I've fought myself until I'm black in the face, but — it's no use. I must have Natalie!"

"She's crazy about O'Neil."

"Seems to be, for a fact, but that doesn't alter my fix. I can't live this way. You must help me, or I'll lose my reason."

"Nonsense! You haven't any or you wouldn't talk like this. What can I do?"

"It's simple. Be nice to Murray and — and win him away from her."

Eliza stared at him as though she really believed him daft.

"Is that all?" she asked in mockery. "Just make him love me?"

Dan nodded. "That would be fine, if you could manage it."

"Why — you — you — I —" She gasped uncertainly for terms in

which to voice her indignant surprise. "Idiot!" she finally exclaimed.

"Thanks for such glowing praise," Dan said. "I feel a lot worse than an idiot. An idiot is not necessarily evil. At heart he may be likable, and pathetic, and merely unfortunate...."

"You simply can't be in earnest!"

"I am, though!" He turned upon her eyes that had grown suddenly old and weary with longing.

"You poor, foolish boy. In the first place, Mr. O'Neil will hate me for this story. In the second place, no man would look at me. I'm ugly...."

"I think you're beautiful."

"With my snub nose, and big mouth, and...."

"You can make him laugh, and when a woman can make a fellow laugh the rest is easy."

"In the third place, I'm mannish and—vulgar, and besides—I don't care for him."

"Of course you don't, or I wouldn't ask it. You see, we're taking no risks! You can at least take up his attention and—and when you see him making for Natalie you can put out your foot and trip him up."

"It wouldn't be honorable, Danny."

"Possibly. But that doesn't make any difference with me. You may as well realize I've got beyond the point where nice considerations weigh with me. If you'd ever been in love, you'd understand such things don't count at all. It's your chance to save the reason and happiness of an otherwise perfectly good brother."

"There is nothing I wouldn't do for your happiness—nothing. But—oh, it's preposterous!"

Dan relapsed into gloomy silence, and they shared an uncomfortable meal. Unable to bear his continued lack of spirits, Eliza again referred to the subject, and tried until late in the evening to argue him out of his mood. But the longer they talked, the more plainly she saw his feeling for Natalie was not fanciful, but sincere and deep. She continued to discount his suggestion she could help him by captivating O'Neil, and stoutly maintained she had no attraction for men. Nevertheless, when she went to her room, she critically examined herself in her mirror. This done, she gave herself over to her favorite relaxation.

First, she exchanged her walking skirt, prim shirtwaist, and jacket for a rose-pink wrapper she furtively brought out of a closet. It was an elaborate wrapper, all fluffy lace and ruffles and bows, and it had cost Eliza a sum she strove desperately to forget. She donned silk stockings and a pair of tiny bedroom slippers. Then seating herself once more at her dresser, she let down her hair. She invariably wore it tightly drawn back—so tightly, in fact, that Dan had more than once complained that it pulled her eyebrows out of place. On this occasion, however, she crimped it, she curled it, she brought it forward about her face in soft riotous puffs and strands, patting it into shape with dexterous fingers until it formed a golden frame for her piquant features.

Now this was no unusual performance for her. In the midnight solitude of her chamber she regularly gave rein to the feminine side of her nature. By day she was the severe, matter of fact, businesslike Eliza Appleton, deaf to romance, lost to illusion, and unresponsive to masculine attention. But deep in her heart were all the instincts and longings of femininity, and at such times as this they came uppermost. Her bedroom had none of the Puritanical primness that marked her habit of dress. It was in no way suggestive of the masculine character she so proudly paraded on the street. On the contrary, it was a bower of daintiness, crowded with all the senseless fripperies of a schoolgirl. Carefully hidden away beneath her starched shirtwaists was much lingerie—bewildering creations to match the pink wrapper—and this she petted and talked to adoringly when no one could hear.

Eliza read romances and improbable tales of fine ladies and gallant squires when she was unobserved. There were times, too, when she wrote, chewing her pencil in the perplexities of vividly colored love scenes; but she always destroyed these manuscripts before the curious sun could spy upon her labors. In such ecstatic flights of fancy the beautiful heroine was a languorous brunette with hair of raven hue and soulful eyes in which slumbered the mystery of a tropic night. She had a Grecian nose, moreover, and her name was Violet.

From all this it may be gathered that Eliza Appleton was by no means the extraordinary person she seemed. Beneath her false exterior she was shamelessly normal.

In the days before O'Neil's return, she suffered constant misgivings and qualms of conscience, but the sight of her brother reveling, expanding, fairly bursting into bloom beneath the influence of Natalie Gerard led her to think perhaps she did have a duty to perform. Dan's cause was hers, and while she had only the faintest hope of aiding it, she was ready to battle for his happiness with every weapon at her command. The part she would have to play was not exactly nice, she reflected, but — the ties of sisterhood were strong, and she would have made any sacrifice for Dan. She knew Natalie was fond of him in a casual, friendly way, and although it was evident the girl accorded him none of that hero-worship with which she favored his chief, Eliza began to think there still might be some hope for him. Since we are all prone to argue our consciences into agreement with our desires, she finally brought herself to the belief that O'Neil was not the man for Natalie. He was too old, too confirmed in his ways, and too self-centered to make a good husband for a girl of her age and disposition. Once her illusions had been rubbed away through daily contact with him, she would undoubtedly awaken to his human faults, and unhappiness would result for both. What Natalie needed for her lasting contentment was a boy her own age whose life would color to match hers. So argued Eliza with that supreme satisfaction we feel in arranging the affairs of others to suit ourselves.

She was greatly embarrassed, nevertheless, when she next met O'Neil and tried to explain that story in *The Review*. He listened courteously and smiled his gentle smile.

"My dear," he said. "I knew there had been some mistake, so let's forget it ever happened. Now tell me about the smallpox epidemic. When I heard what Linn was doing with our men, I was badly worried, for I couldn't see how to checkmate him. But it seems you and Doc were equal to the occasion. He cabled me a perfectly proper announcement of Tom's quarantine, and I believed we had been favored by a miracle."

"It wasn't a miracle at all," Eliza said in a matter-of-fact tone. "It was croton oil. Nobody has dared tell him the truth. He still believes he could smell the tuberoses."

O'Neil seemed to derive great amusement from her account of what followed. He had already heard Dr. Gray's version of the affair, but Eliza had a refreshing way of saying things.

"I brought you a little present," he said when she had finished.

She took the package he handed her.

"A surprise! Nobody but Dan ever gave me a present," she said as she blushed. Then her eyes darkened with suspicion. "Did you bring me this because of what I did?"

"Now don't be silly. I knew nothing about your part in the comedy until Doc told me. You are a most difficult person."

Slowly she unwrapped the parcel, and then with a gasp lifted a splendidly embroidered kimono from its box.

"Oh-h!" Her eyes were round and astonished. "Oh-h! It's for *me*?"

It was a regal garment of heavy silk, superbly ornamented with golden dragons, each so cunningly worked it seemed upon the point of taking wing. "Why, their eyes glitter! And — they'd breathe fire if I jabbed them. Oh-h!" She stared at the gift in helpless amazement. "Is it mine, *honestly*?"

He nodded. "Won't you put it on?"

"Over these things? Never!" Again Miss Appleton blushed, for she recalled she had prepared for his coming with extraordinary care. Her boots were even stouter than usual, her skirt plainer, her waist more stiff, and her hair more tightly smoothed back. "It would take a fluffy person to wear this. I'll always keep it, of course, and — I'll worship it, but I'm not designed for pretty clothes. I'll let Natalie wear...."

"Natalie has one of her own, done in butterflies, and I brought one to her mother, also."

"And you bought this for me after you had seen that fiendish story over my signature?"

"Certainly!" He quickly forestalled her attempted thanks by changing the subject. "Now then, Dan tells me you are anxious to begin your magazine work, so I'm going to arrange for you to see the glaciers and the coalfields. It will be a hard trip, for the track isn't through yet, but...."

"Oh, I'll take care of myself; I won't get in anybody's way," she said.

"I intend to see you don't by going with you; so make your preparations and we'll leave as soon as I can get away."

After O'Neil departed, Eliza gave herself a pep talk for the job that lay ahead.

Eliza Violet, this is your chance. It's underhanded and mean, but—you're a mean person, and the finger of Providence is directing you.

She snatched up the silken kimono and ran into her room, locking the door behind her. Hurriedly she put it on, then posed before the mirror. Next down came her hair amid a shower of pins. She arranged it loosely about her face, and, ripping an artificial flower from her party hat, placed it over her ear, then swayed grandly to and fro while the golden dragons writhed and curved as if in joyous admiration. A dozen times she slipped out of the garment, and gathering it to her face, kissed it. A dozen times she donned it, strutting about her little room like a peacock. Her tip-tilted nose was red, and her eyes were wet when at last she laid it out upon her bed and knelt with her cheek against it.

"Gee...if only I were pretty," she said with a sigh. "I almost believe he—likes me."

Tom Slater laboriously propelled himself up the hill to the bungalow that evening and seated himself on the topmost step near where Eliza was rocking. She had come to occupy a considerable place in his thoughts of late, for she was quite beyond his understanding. She affected him as a mental gadfly, stinging his mind into an activity quite unusual. At times he considered her a nice girl, though undoubtedly insane; then there were other moments when she excited his deepest animosity. Again, on rare occasions she completely upset all his preconceived notions by being so friendly and so sympathetic she made him homesick for his own daughter. In his idle hours, therefore, he spent much time at the Appleton cottage.

"Where have you been lately, Uncle Tom?" she began.

Slater winced at the appellation but ignored it.

"I've been out on the delta hustling supplies ahead. Heard the news?"

"No."

"Curtis Gordon has bought the McDermott outfit in Kyak."

"That tells me nothing. Who is McDermott?"

"He's a shoe-stringer. He had a wildcat plan to build a railroad from Kyak to the coalfields, but he never got farther than a row of alder stakes and a book of press clippings."

"Does that mean Gordon abandons his Hope route?"

"Yep! He's swung in behind us and the Heidlemanns. Now it's a three-sided race, with us in the lead. Mellen just brought in the news half an hour ago; he was on his way down from the glaciers when he ran into a field party of Gordon's surveyors. Looks like trouble ahead if they try to crowd through the canyon alongside of us."

"He must believe Kyak Bay will make a safe harbor."

"Don't say it! If he's right, we're fried to a nice brown finish on both sides and it's time to take us off the stove. I'm praying for a storm."

"'The prayers of the wicked are an abomination unto the Lord,'" Eliza quoted.

"Sure! But I keep right on praying just the same. It's a habit now. The news has set the chief to jumping sideways."

"Which, translated, I suppose means he is disturbed."

"Or words to that effect. Too bad they changed that newspaper story of yours."

"Yes."

"It put a crimp in him."

"How — do you mean?"

"He had some California capitalists tuned up to put in $3 million, but when they read our plan was impracticable their fountain pens refused to work."

"Oh!" Eliza gasped.

Slater regarded her curiously, then shook his head. "Funny how a kid like you can scare a bunch of hard-headed bankers, ain't it?" he said. "Doc Gray explained it wasn't your fault, but — it doesn't take much racket to frighten the big fish."

"What will Mr. O'Neil do?"

"Oh, he'll fight it out, I s'pose. The first thing is to block Gordon. Say, I brought you a present."

"This is my lucky day," Eliza said with a smile as Tom fumbled in his pocket. "I'm sure I shall love it."

"It ain't much, but it was the best in the crate, and I shined it up on my towel." Mr. Slater handed Eliza a fine red apple of prodigious size, at sight of which the girl turned pale.

"I — don't like apples," she cried, faintly.

"Never mind – they're good for your complexion."

"I'd die before I'd eat one."

"Then I'll eat it for you. My complexion ain't what it was before I had the smallpox." When he had carried out this intention and subjected his teeth to a process of vacuum cleaning, he asked her a question: "Say, what happened to your friend who chewed gum?"

"Well, he was hardly a friend," Miss Appleton said. "If he had been a real friend he would have listened to my warning."

"Gum never hurt anybody," Slater argued.

"Not ordinary gum. But you see, he chewed nothing except wintergreen...."

"That's what I chew."

Eliza's tone was one of shocked amazement. "Not *really*? Oh, well, some people would thrive on it, I dare say, but he had indigestion."

"Me too! That's why I chew it."

The girl eyed him during an uncomfortable pause.

"Do you ever feel a queer, gnawing feeling, like hunger, if you go without your breakfast?"

"Uh-huh! Don't you?"

"I wouldn't alarm you for the world, Uncle Tom...."

"I ain't your uncle!"

"You might chew the stuff for years and not feel any bad effects, but if you wake up some morning feeling tired and listless...."

"I've done that, too." Slater's gloomy eyes were fixed upon her with a look of vague apprehension. "Is it a symptom?"

"Certainly! Pepsin poisoning, it's called. This fellow I told you about was a charming man, and since we had all tried so hard to save him, we felt terribly at the end."

"Then he died?"

"Um-m! Yes and no. Remind me to tell you the story sometime... here comes Dan, in a great hurry."

Young Appleton came panting up the hill.

"Goodbye, Sis," he said. "I'm off for the front in 10 minutes."

"Anybody hurt?" Slater asked quickly.

"Not yet, but somebody's liable to be. Gordon is trying to steal the canyon, and Murray has ordered me out with a car of dynamite to hold it."

"Dynamite! Why, Dan!" his sister exclaimed.

"We have poling boats at the lower crossing, and we'll be at the canyon in two days. I'm going to load the hillside with shots, and if they try to come through, I'll set 'em off. They'll never dare tackle it." Dan's eyes were dancing; his face was alive with excitement.

"But suppose they should?" Eliza asked.

"Then send Doc Gray with some stretchers. I owe one to Gordon, and this is my chance." Drawing her aside, he said in an undertone. "You've got to hold my ground with Natalie while I'm gone. Don't let her see too much of Murray."

"I'll do the best I can," she said. "But if he seems to be in earnest, I'll stop, no matter what happens to you, Danny."

He kissed her affectionately and fled.

12

CURTIS GORDON FAILS

The so-called canyon of the Salmon River lies just above the twin glaciers. Scenically, these are by far the more impressive, and they present a more complex engineering problem. Yet the canyon itself was the real strategic point in the struggle between the railroad builders. The floor of the valley immediately above Garfield glacier, though several miles wide, was partly filled with debris that had been carried down from the mother range on the east, and this mass had forced the stream far over against the westward rim, where it came roaring past the foot wall in a splendid cataract some three miles long. To the left of the river, looking upstream at this point, the mountains slanted skyward like a roof, until lost in the hurrying scud 4,000 feet above. To the right, however, was the old moraine, just mentioned, consisting of a desolate jumble of rock and gravel and silt overlaying the ice foot. Because of its broken character and the unstable nature of its foundation, this bank was practically useless for road building, and the only feasible route for steel rails was along the steep west wall.

On his first reconnaissance O'Neil had perceived that while there was room for more than one bridge across the Salmon between the upper and the lower ice masses, there was no room for more than one track alongside the rapids, some miles above that point. He knew, moreover, once he had established his title to a right-of-way along the west rim of the cataract, it would be difficult for a rival to oust him, or to parallel his line without first crossing back to the east bank—an undertaking at once hazardous and costly. For this reason, he had given Dan Appleton explicit instructions to be careful in filing his survey so no opportunity might be left open for a later arrival. The engineer had done his work well, and O'Neil rested secure in the belief he held possession of the best and least expensive route through to the open valleys above.

He had had no cause to fear a clash with the Heidlemann forces, for they had shown a strict regard for his rights and seemed content to devote themselves to developing their terminus before trying to negotiate the canyon. They were wise in taking this course, for their success would mean O'Neil's project would fall of its own weight. Kyak was nearer Seattle, by many miles, than Omar; it was closer to the coal and copper fields, and the proven permanence of their breakwater would render useless further attempts to finance the Salmon River & Northwestern.

But the entrance of Curtis Gordon into the field changed matters. O'Neil recognized danger. Gordon was swayed by no such business scruples as the Heidlemanns; he was evidently making a desperate effort to secure a footing at any cost. In purchasing the McDermott holdings, he had executed a coup of considerable importance, for he had placed himself on equal footing with the Trust and in position to profit by its efforts at harbor building without expense to himself. If, therefore, he succeeded in wresting from O'Neil the key to that upper passageway, he would be able to block his personal enemy and to command the consideration of his more powerful rival. No one, not even the Trust, had taken the McDermott enterprise seriously, but with Curtis Gordon in control, the wildcat suddenly became a tiger.

In view of all this, it was with no easy mind O'Neil dispatched Appleton to the front, and it was with no small responsibility upon his shoulders the young engineer set out in charge of those wooden boxes of dynamite. Murray had told him frankly what hung upon his success, and Dan had vowed to hold the survey at any cost.

Steam was up and the locomotive was puffing restlessly when he returned from his farewell to Eliza. A moment later the single flat car carrying his party and its dangerous freight, was being whirled along the shores of Omar Lake. On it rushed, shrieking through the night, out from the gloomy hills and upon the tangent that led across the delta. Ten minutes after it had rolled forth upon the trestle at the lower crossing, the giant powder had been transferred to poling boats and the long pull against the current had begun.

O'Neil had picked a crew for Dan, men upon whom he could depend. They were on double pay, and as they had worked on the North Pass & Yukon Railway, Appleton had no doubt of their loyalty.

The events of that trip were etched upon the engineer's mind with extraordinary vividness, for they surpassed in peril and excitement all his previous experiences. The journey resembled nothing but the mad scramble of a gold stampede. The stubborn boats with their cargoes had to be so gently handled, the ever-increasing fury of the river, the growing menace of those ghastly, racing icebergs, the taut-hauled towing lines, and the straining, sweating men in the loops, all made a picture hard to forget. Then, too, the uncertainty of the enterprise, the crying need of haste, the knowledge of those other men converging upon the same goal, lent a gnawing suspense to every hour. It was infinitely more terrible than that first expedition when he and Tom Slater and O'Neil had braved the unknown. It was vastly more trying than any of the trips that had followed, even with the winter hurricane-force winds streaming out of the north as from the mouth of a giant funnel.

Dan had faced death in various forms on this delta during the past year and a half. He had seen his flesh harden to marble whiteness under the raging north wind; his eyes and lungs had been drifted full of sand in summer storms that rivaled those of the Sahara. With transit on his back he had come face to face with the huge brown grizzly. He had slept in mud, had made his bed on moss that ran water like a sponge; he had taken danger and hardship as they came—yet never had he punished himself as on this dash.

Through his confusion of impressions, his intense preoccupation with present dangers and future contingencies, the thought of Natalie floated now and then vaguely but comfortingly. He had seen her for a moment, before leaving—barely long enough to explain the nature of his mission—but her quick concern, her unvoiced anxiety, had been pleasant, and he could not believe it was altogether due to her interest in the fortunes of O'Neil.

Dan knew Mellen's crew was camped at the upper crossing, busied in drilling for the abutments and foundations of the bridge. But he reasoned they would scarcely suspect the object of Gordon's party and, in any case, they were not organized or equipped to resist it. Moreover, the strategic point was four miles above the bridge site, and the surveying corps would hardly precipitate a clash, particularly since there was ample room for them to select a crossing place alongside.

It was after midnight of the second day when he and his weary boatmen stumbled into sight of the camp. Appleton halted his command and stole forward, approaching the place through the tangled alders that flanked it. He had anticipated the rival party would be up to this point by now, if not even farther advanced, and he was both angered and relieved to sight the tops of other tents pitched a few hundred yards beyond Mellen's outfit. So they were here – he had arrived in time! A feeling of exultation conquered the deathly fatigue that slowed his limbs. Although he still had to pass the invader's camp and establish himself at the canyon, the certainty he had made good thus far was ample reward for his effort.

A dog broke into furious barking as he emerged from cover, and he had a moment's anxiety lest it serve as warning to the enemy; but a few quick strides brought him to the tent of Mellen's foreman. Going in, he roused the man, who was sleeping soundly.

"Hello!" cried the foreman, jumping up and rubbing his eyes, "I thought Curtis Gordon had taken possession."

"Hush! Don't wake them up," Dan cautioned.

"Oh, there's no danger of disturbing them with this infernal cannonading going on all the time." The night resounded to a rumbling crash as some huge mass of ice split off, perhaps two miles away.

Courtesy Alaska State Library

Railroad workers spanned the canyon with bridges like the one seen in this photograph.

"When did they arrive?"

"Night before last. They've located right alongside of us. We were surprised when they showed up. They expect to break camp in the morning." He yawned widely.

"Hm-m! They're making tracks, aren't they? Were they friendly?"

"Oh, sure – so were we. There was nothing else to do, was there? We had no orders."

"I have two dozen men and four boatloads of dynamite with me. I'm going to hold that mountainside."

"Then you're going to fight!" All vestige of drowsiness had fled from the man's face.

"Not if we can help it. Who's in charge of this crew?"

"Gordon himself."

"Gordon!"

"Yes. And he's got a tough gang with him."

"Armed?"

"Sure. This is a bear country, you know."

"Listen – I want you to tell him, as innocently as you can, that we're on the job ahead of him. Tell him we've been there for a week and have loaded that first rock shoulder and expect to shoot it off as soon as possible. You can tell him, too, that I'm up there and he'd better see me before trying to pass through."

"I've got you – but that won't stop him."

"Perhaps. Now have you any grub in camp?"

"No."

"We threw ours overboard, to make time. Send up anything you can spare; we're played out."

"It'll be nothing but beans, and they're moldy."

"We can fight on beans – we'll eat the paper off those giant cartridges if we must. Don't fail to warn Gordon the hillside is mined and warn him loud enough for his swampers to hear."

Appleton hastened back to his boats, where he found his men sprawled among the boulders sleeping the sleep of complete exhaustion. They were drenched, half numbed by the chill air of the glacier, and it was well that he roused them.

"Gordon's men are camped just above," he told them. "But we must get through without waking them. No talking, now, until we're safe."

Silently the crew resumed their towlines, fitting them to their aching shoulders; gingerly the boats were edged out into the current.

It was fortunate the place was noisy, and the voice of the river and the periodic bombardment from the glaciers drowned the rattle of loose stones dislodged by their footsteps. But it was a trying half hour that followed. Dan did not breathe easily until his party had crossed the bar and were safely out on the placid waters of the lake, with the last stage of the journey ahead of them.

About mid-forenoon of the following day Curtis Gordon halted his party at the lower end of the rapids and went on alone. To his right lay the cataract and along the steep slope against which it chafed wound a faint footpath scarcely wide enough in places for a man open to pass.

This trail dipped in and out, wound back and forth around frowning promontories. It dodged through alder thickets or spanned slides of loose rock until, three miles above, it emerged into more country back of the parent range. It had been worn by the feet of wild animals and it followed closely the right-of-way of the S. R. & N. To the left the hills rose swiftly in great leaps to the sky; to the right, so close that a false step meant disaster, roared the cataract, muddy and foam flecked.

As Gordon neared the first bluff he heard, above the clamor of the flood, a faint metallic "tap-tap-tap" as of hammer and drill, and, drawing closer, he saw Dan Appleton perched on a rock that commanded a view in both directions. Just around the shoulder, in a tiny gulch, or gutter from the slopes above, were pitched several tents, from one of which curled the smoke of a cookstove. Close at hand were moored four battered poling boats.

"Look out!" Appleton shouted from on high.

Gordon flushed angrily and kept on, scanning the surroundings with practiced eye.

"Hey, you!" Dan called, for a second time. "Keep back! We're going to shoot."

Still heedless of the warning, Gordon held stubbornly to his stride. He noted the heads of several men projecting from behind boulders, and his anger rose. How dared this whipper-snapper shout at him! He felt inclined to toss the insolent young scoundrel into the rapids. Then suddenly his resentment gave place to a totally different emotion.

The slanting bank midway between him and Appleton lifted itself bodily in a chocolate-colored upheaval, and the roar of a dynamite blast rolled out across the river. It was but a feeble echo of the majestic reverberations from the glacier across the lake, but it was impressive enough to send Curtis Gordon scurrying to a place of safety. He wheeled in his tracks, doubling himself over, and his long legs began to thresh wildly. Reaching the shelter of a rock crevice, he hurled himself into it, while over his place of refuge descended a shower of dirt and rocks and debris. When the rain of missiles had subsided, he stepped forth, his face white with fury, his big hands twitching. His voice was hoarse as he shouted his protest.

Appleton scrambled carefully down from his perch in the warm sunshine and approached with insolent leisure.

"Say – do you want to get your fool self killed?" he cried. "Oh … is it you, Gordon?" he then said in an altered tone.

"You knew very well it was I." Gordon swallowed hard and partially controlled his wrath. "What do you mean by such carelessness?" he demanded. "You ought to be hung for a thing like that." He brushed the dirt from his expensive hunting suit.

"I yelled my head off," Dan said. "You must be deaf."

"You saw me coming! Don't say you didn't. Fortunately I wasn't hurt." In a tone of command he added, "You'll have to stop blasting until I go through with my party."

"Sorry. Every day counts with us," Appleton said with a grin. "You know how it is—short season, and all that."

"Come, come! Don't be an idiot. I have no time to waste,"

"Then you'll have to go around," Dan said. "This isn't a public road, you know."

Gordon had come to argue, to pacify, to gain his ends by lying, if necessary, but this impudent jackanapes infuriated him. His plans had gone smoothly so far, and the unexpected threat of resistance momentarily provoked him beyond restraint.

"You scoundrel," he cried. "You'd have blown me into the river if you could. But I'll go through this canyon…."

"Go as far and as fast as you like," Dan interrupted with equal heat. "Only take your own chances and have a net spread at the lower end of the rapids to catch the remains."

They eyed each other angrily.

"This is ridiculous," Gordon said, more quietly. "You can't stop me."

"Maybe I can't and maybe I can. I'm under orders to rush this work and I don't intend to knock off to please you. I've planted shots at various places along our right-of-way and I'll set 'em off when it suits me. If you're so anxious to go upriver, why don't you cross over to the moraine? There's a much better trail on that side. You'll find better walking a few miles farther up, and you'll run no danger of being hurt."

"I intend to run a survey along this hillside."

"There isn't room; we beat you to it."

"The law provides...."

"Law? Jove! I'd forgotten there is such a thing. Why don't you go to law and settle the question that way? We'll have our track laid by the time you get action, and I'm sure Mr. O'Neil wouldn't place any obstacles in the way of your free passage back and forth. He's awfully obliging about such things."

Gordon ground his fine, white, even teeth. "Don't you understand that I'm entitled to a right-of-way through here under the law of common user?" he asked, with what patience he could muster.

"If you're trying to get a legal opinion on the matter, why don't you see a lawyer? I'm not a lawyer, neither am I a public speaker nor a piano tuner, nor anything like that—I'm an engineer."

"Don't get funny. I can't send my men in here if you continue blasting."

"So it seems to me, but you appear to be hell bent on trying it."

Dan was enjoying himself and he deliberately added to the other's anger by inquiring, as if in the blinding light of a new idea, another option.

"Why don't you bridge over and go up the other side?" He pointed to the forbidding, broken country that faced them across the rapids.

Gordon snorted. "How long do you intend to maintain this preposterous attitude?" he asked.

"As long as the powder lasts—and there's a good deal of it."

The promoter chewed his lip for a moment in perplexity.

"Appleton, you're all right!" he said with a geniality he was far from feeling. "I admire your loyalty, even though it happens to be for a mistaken cause. I always liked you. I admire loyalty—it's something I need in my business. What I need I pay for, and I pay well."

"So your man Linn told us."

"I never really discharged you. In fact, I intended to re-employ you, for I need you badly. You can name your own salary and go to work any time."

"In other words, you mean you'll pay me well to let you through."

"Fix your own price and I'll double it."

"Will you come with me up this trail a little way?" Dan inquired."

"Certainly."

"There's a spot where I'd like to have you stand. I'll save you the trouble of walking back to your men—you'll beat the echo."

There was a pause while Gordon digested this.

"Better think it over," he said at length. "I'll never let O'Neil build his road, not if it breaks me, and you're merely laying yourself open to arrest by threatening me."

"Please come with me!" urged Appleton. "You'll never know what hit you."

With a curse the promoter wheeled and walked swiftly down the trail by which he had come.

"Get ready to shoot," Dan ordered when he had returned to his vantage point. A few moments later, he saw the invading party approach, but he withheld his warning shout until it was close at hand. Evidently Gordon did not believe he would have the reckless courage to carry out his threat and had determined to put him to the test.

The engineer gauged his distance nicely, and when the newcomers had fairly passed within the danger zone, he gave the signal to fire.

A blast heavier than the one that had discouraged Gordon's advance followed his command, and down upon the newcomers rained a deluge that sent them scurrying to cover. Fortunately no one was injured.

An hour later the invaders had pitched camp a mile below, and after placing a trusted man on guard, Appleton sent his weary men to bed.

It was Curtis Gordon himself who brought O'Neil the first tidings of this encounter, for, seeing the uselessness of an immediate attempt to overcome Dan's party by force, he determined to make formal protest. He secured a boat, and a few hours later the swift current swept him down to the lower crossing, where McKay put a locomotive at his disposal for the trip to Omar. By the time he arrived there he was quite himself again, suave, self-possessed, and magnificently outraged at the treatment he had received. O'Neil met him with courtesy.

"Your man Appleton has lost his head," Gordon began. "I've come to ask you to call him off."

"He is following instructions to the letter."

"Do you mean that you refuse to allow me to run my right-of-way along that hillside? Impossible!" His voice betokened shocked surprise.

"I am merely holding my own survey. I can't quit work to accommodate you."

"But, my dear sir, I must insist that you do."

O'Neil shrugged.

"Then there is but one way to construe your refusal—it means that you declare war."

"You saved me that necessity when you sent Linn to hire my men away."

Gordon ignored this reference. "You must realize, O'Neil, that I am merely asking what is mine. I have the right to use that canyon—the right to use your track at that point, in fact, if it proves impracticable to parallel it—under the law of common user. You are an experienced contractor; you must be familiar with that law."

"Yes. I looked it up before beginning operations, and I found it has never been applied to Alaska."

Gordon started. "That's a ridiculous statement."

"Perhaps, but it's true. Alaska is not a territory, it's a district, and it has its own code. Until the law of common user has been applied here, you'll have to use the other side of the river."

"That would force me to bridge twice in passing the upper glacier. We shall see what the courts have to say."

"Thanks! I shall be grateful for the delay."

Gordon rose with a bow. The interview had been short and to the point. O'Neil put an engine at his service for the return trip, and after a stiff adieu the visitor departed, inwardly raging.

It was his first visit to Omar, and now that he was here, he determined to see it all. But first another matter demanded his attention—a matter much in his mind of late, concerning that he had reached a somewhat satisfactory decision during his journey.

He went directly to the new hotel and inquired for Gloria Gerard.

Beneath the widow's coldness when she came to meet him, he detected an uncertainty, a frightened indecision that assured him of success, and he set himself to his task with the zest he always felt in bending another to his will.

"It has been the greatest regret of my life we quarreled," he told her when their strained greeting was over. "I felt I had to come and see with my own eyes you are well."

"I am quite well."

"Two people who have been to each other as much as we have been cannot lightly separate; their lives cannot be divided without a painful readjustment." He paused, then reflecting he could afford a little sentimental extravagance, added, "Flowers cannot easily be transplanted, and love, after all, is the frailest of blooms."

"I—think it is perennial. Have you—missed me?" Her dark eyes were strained and curious.

"My dear, you can never know how much, nor how deeply distressing this whole affair has been to me." He managed to put an affecting pathos into words sufficiently banal, for he was an excellent actor. "I find I am all sentiment. Under the shell of the hard-headed businessman beats the heart of a schoolboy. The memory of the hours we have spent together, the places we have seen, the joys and discouragements we have shared, haunts me constantly. Memory can glean but never renew: 'joy's recollection is no longer joy while sorrow's memory is sorrow still.'"

The spell of his personality worked strongly upon her. "Recollection is the only paradise from which we cannot be turned out," she said. "You read that to me once, but I didn't dream my own happiness would someday consist of recollection."

"Why should it, Gloria? Hope is ready to welcome you. Your home stands open; my arms are outstretched."

"No!" she exclaimed, with a shake of her dark head. "There is someone besides me to consider. Natalie is happy here; no one seems to know or to care what I have done."

"But surely you are not satisfied with this."

CURTIS GORDON FAILS

He ran his eye critically over the garish newness of the little hotel parlor. It was flimsy, cheap, fresh with paint, very different from the surroundings he had given her at Hope. "I wonder that he presumed to offer you this after what you have had. A hotel keeper! A landlady!"

"I was glad to get even this, for I have no pride now," she replied, coldly. "At least the house is honest, and the men who come here are the same. Mr. O'Neil is especially kind to Natalie, and she thinks a great deal of him."

"I presume he wants to marry her."

"I pray that he will. I don't intend her to make the mistake I did."

Gordon received this announcement with grim satisfaction. It was what he had suspected, and it fitted perfectly into his plans.

"I shan't allow this to continue, Gloria," he said. "Our difference has gone far enough, and I shan't permit O'Neil to put me in his debt. We have come to a final understanding, he and I. While my views on the holiness of the marriage relation have not changed in the least, still I am ready to follow your wishes."

"You—mean it?" she asked, breathlessly.

"I do. Come home, Gloria."

"Wait! I must tell Natalie." She rose unsteadily and left the room, while he reflected with mingled scorn and amusement upon the weakness of human nature and the gullibility of women.

A moment later mother and daughter appeared, arm in arm, both pale.

"Is this true?" Natalie demanded.

"Quite true. You and Gloria seem to think I owe something; I never shirk a debt." Mrs. Gerard's fingers tightened painfully on her daughter's arm as he continued. "There is only one condition upon which I insist: you must both return to Hope at once and have done with this—this man."

Natalie hesitated, but the look in her mother's eyes decided her. With some difficulty she forced herself to acquiesce and felt the grip on her arm suddenly relax. "When will the wedding take place?" she asked.

"At the earliest possible moment," Gordon declared, with well-feigned seriousness. "Once we return to God's country...."

"No!" cried Natalie. "We can't go back to Hope until she is married; it would be scandalous."

"Why more scandalous to accept my protection than that of a stranger? Do you care what these people think?" he demanded, with an air of fine scorn.

"Yes! I care very much."

"Is there any reason for waiting?" Mrs. Gerard inquired.

"Many! Too many to enumerate. It is my condition that you both leave Omar at once."

Gloria Gerard looked at her daughter in troubled indecision, but Natalie answered firmly.

"We can't do that."

"So! You have your own plans, no doubt, and it doesn't trouble you that you are standing in the way of your mother's respectability?" His voice was harsh, his sneer open. "Bless my soul! Is the generosity to be all on my side? Or has this man O'Neil forbidden you to associate with me?"

"I don't trust you," Natalie flared up. "I'm afraid you are trying...."

"It is my condition, and I am adamant. Believe me, O'Neil knows of your disgrace, or will learn of it in time. It would be well to protect your name while you can." He then turned to the other woman.

"Gloria, the girl is ready to sacrifice you to her own ends," he said.

"Wait!" Natalie's nerves were tingling with dislike of the man, but she had made a decision. "I shall do exactly as mother wishes."

Be it said to the credit of Gloria Gerard she did not hesitate.

"I shall be here when you are ready," she told him.

With an exclamation of rage Gordon rose and strode out of the room.

13

JOURNEY TO A PLACE OF MANY WONDERS

Curtis Gordon's men broke camp upon his return from Omar, and by taking the east bank of the Salmon River pressed through to the upper valley. Here they recrossed to the west side and completed their survey, except for the three-mile gap Dan Appleton held.

Gordon continued to smart under the sting of his defeat, however. O'Neil had gotten the better of him in argument, and Natalie's simplicity had proved more than a match for his powers of persuasion. At no time had he seriously considered making Mrs. Gerard his wife, but he had thought to entice the two women back under his own roof to humble them and their self-appointed protector. He felt sure Natalie's return to Hope and her residence there would injure her seriously in the eyes of the community, and this would be a stab to O'Neil. Although he had failed for the moment, he did not abandon the idea. His display of anger upon leaving the hotel had been due mainly to disappointment at the checkmate. But knowing well the hold he possessed upon the older woman, he laid it away for later use when the fight grew hot, and meanwhile devoted himself to devising further measures by which to harass his enemy and advance his own fortunes.

Gordon's business career had consisted of a series of brilliant manipulations whereby, with little to go on, he had forced financial recognition for himself. No one knew better than he the unstable foundation beneath his Alaska enterprises; yet more than once he had turned desperate ventures into success. By his present operations he sought not only to hamper O'Neil, but to create an appearance of opposition to both him and the Trust that could be coined into dollars and cents.

There are in the commercial world money wolves who prey upon the weak and depend on the spirit of compromise in their adversaries. Gordon was one of these. He had the faculty of snatching at least half a victory from apparent defeat, and for this reason he had been able to show a record sufficiently impressive to convince the average investor of his ability.

By purchasing for a song the McDermott rights at Kyak, he had placed himself in position to share in the benefits of the Heidlemann breakwater, and by rapidly pushing his tracks ahead, he made his rivalry seem formidable. As a means of attack on O'Neil, he adopted a procedure common in railroad building. He amended his original survey, so it crossed that of the S. R. & N. midway between the lower bridge over the Salmon River and the glaciers, and at that point began the hasty erection of a grade.

He rushed forward a large body of men and supplies and began to lay track across the S. R. & N. right-of-way. If Appleton could hold a hillside, he reasoned, he himself could hold a crossing, if not permanently, at least for a sufficient length of time to serve his purpose.

His action came as a disagreeable surprise to Omar. These battles for crossings have been common in the history of railroading, and they have not infrequently resulted in bloody fights. Long after the ties are spiked and the heads are healed, the legal rights involved have been determined. But usually amid such a tangle of conflicting testimony and such a confusion of technicalities as to leave the justice of the final decision in doubt. In the unsettled conditions that prevailed in the Salmon River valley physical possession of a right-of-way was at least nine-tenths of the law, and O'Neil realized he must choose between violence and a compromise. Not being given to compromise, he continued his construction work, and drew closer, day by day, to the point of contact.

Reports came from the front of his opponent's preparations for resistance. Gordon had laid several hundred yards of light rails on his grade, and on these he had mounted a device called a "go-devil" or skip, which he shunted back and forth by means of a donkey engine and steel cable. With this in operation across the point of intersection like a shuttle, interference would be extremely dangerous. In addition, he had built blockhouses and breastworks of ties, and in these, it was reported, he had stationed the pick of his hired helpers, armed and well provisioned.

Toward this stronghold Murray O'Neil's men worked, laying his roadbed as straight as an arrow, and as the intervening distance decreased anxiety and speculation at Omar increased.

Among those who hung on the rumors of the approaching clash with greatest interest was Eliza Appleton. Since Dan's departure for the front she had done her modest best to act the part he had forced upon her, and in furtherance of their conspiracy she had urged O'Neil to fulfil his promise of taking her over the work. She felt an ever-growing curiosity to see those glaciers, about which she had heard so much. And she reflected, though not without a degree of self-contempt, nothing could be more favorable to her design than the intimacy of several days together on the trail. Nothing breeds a closer relationship than the open life, nothing brings people more quickly into accord or hopeless disagreement. Although she had no idea Murray could or would ever care seriously for her, she felt there was a bare possibility of winning his transient interest and in that way, perhaps, affording her brother time in which to attain his heart's desire. Of course, it was all utterly absurd, yet it was serious enough to Dan; and her own feelings — well, they didn't matter.

She was greatly excited when O'Neil made an announcement one evening.

"I'm ready to make that trip to the front if you are. I have business at Kyak. So after we've seen the glaciers, we will go down there and you can take in the coalfields."

"How long shall we be gone?"

"Ten days, perhaps. We'll start in the morning."

"I'm ready to leave at a moment's notice."

"Then perhaps you'd better help Natalie."

"Natalie!" exclaimed Eliza, seeing all her well-laid plans tottering. "Is she going?"

"Oh yes. It's an opportunity she shouldn't miss, and I thought it would be more pleasant for you if she went with us."

Eliza was forced to acknowledge his thoughtfulness, although it angered her to be sacrificed to the proprieties. Her newspaper training had made her feel superior to such things, and this of all occasions was one upon which she would have liked to be free of mere conventions. But of course she professed the greatest delight.

O'Neil had puzzled her greatly of late; for at times he seemed wrapped up in Natalie, and at other times he showed a preference for Eliza's own company. He was so impartial in his attentions that at one moment the girl would waver in her determination and in the next would believe herself succeeding beyond her hope. The game confused her emotions curiously. She accused herself of being overbold, and then she noted with horror she was growing as sensitive to his apparent coldness as if she were really in earnest. She had not supposed the mere acting of a sentimental role could so obsess her.

To counteract this tendency she assumed a professional air when they set out the following morning. She was once more Eliza Appleton the reporter, and O'Neil, in recognition of this fact, explained rapidly the difficulties of construction he had met and overcome. As she began to understand there came to her a fuller appreciation of the man and the work he was doing. Natalie, however, could not seem to grasp the significance of the enterprise. She saw nothing beyond the even gravel roadbed, the uninteresting trestles and bridges and cuts and fills, the like of which she had seen many times before, and her comment was childlike. O'Neil, however, appeared to find her naivete charming, and Eliza thought bitterly:

If my nose was perfectly chiseled and my eyebrows nice, he wouldn't care if my brain was the size of a rabbit's. Here am I, talking like a human being and really understanding him, while she sits like a Greek goddess, wondering if her hat is on straight. If ever I find a girl uglier than me, I'll make her my bosom friend.

She jabbed her pencil viciously at her notebook.

The track now extended considerably beyond the lower crossing, which rendered their boat journey to the glaciers much shorter than the one Dan had taken with his cargo of dynamite. When the engine finally stopped, it was near a tent village beside which flowed one of the smaller branches of the Salmon. In the distance, the grade stretched out across the level swamps like a thin, lately healed scar, and along its crest, gravel trains were slowly creeping. An army of men were toiling on it, and still farther away shone the white sides of another encampment.

"Oh! That's Gordon's track," Eliza said. "Why, you're nearly up to him. How do you intend to get across?"

O'Neil nodded at the long thin line of moiling men in the distance.

"There's a loose handle in each one of those picks," he said.

"Somebody will be killed in that kind of a racket."

"That rests with Gordon. I'm going through."

"Suppose he had said that when Dan stopped him at the canyon?"

"If he'd said it and meant it, he'd probably have done it. He bluffs; I don't. I must go on; he didn't. Now lunch is served, and since this is our last glimpse of civilization, I advise you to fortify yourselves. From here on we shall see nothing but the wilderness."

He led them to a spotless tent that had been newly erected at the edge of the spruce. It was smoothly stretched on a framework of timber, its walls and floor were of dressed lumber, and inside were two cots all in clean linen. There were twin washstands, also, and dressers and rocking-chairs, a table, and a stove. On the floor beside the beds lay several deep, soft bear rugs. A meal was spread amid glass and figured china and fresh napkins.

"How cozy – why, it's a perfect dear of a house!" Natalie said.

"You will leave everything but your necessaries here, for we are going light," Murray told them. "You will stop here on our way back to Kyak, and I'll warrant you'll be glad to see the place by that time."

"You built this just for us?" Eliza asked.

"Yes. But it didn't take long. I phoned this morning you were coming." He ran a critical eye over the place to see that its equipment was complete, then pulled out chairs for them.

A white-coated boy served a luncheon in courses, the quality of which astonished the visitors, for there was soup, a roast, delicious vegetables, crisp salad, a camembert O'Neil had imported for his private use, and his own blend of coffee.

The girls ate with appetites that rivaled those of the men in the mess tent nearby. Their presence in the heart of great activity, the anticipation of adventure to come, the electric atmosphere of haste and straining effort on every hand excited them. Eliza began to be less conscious of her secret intention, and Natalie showed a gaiety rare in her since the shadow of her mother's shame had fallen upon her life.

The boat crews were waiting when they had finished, and they soon were underway. A mile of comparatively slack water brought them out into one of the larger estuaries of the river, and there the long, uphill pull began. O'Neil had equipped his two companions with high rubber boots, which they were only too eager to try. As soon as they got ashore, they began to romp and play and splash through the shallows quite like unruly children. They spattered him mischievously, tugged at the towing ropes with a great show of assistance, scampered ahead of the party, and kept him in a constant panic lest they meet with serious accident.

It was with no little relief he gave the order to pitch camp some hours later. After sending them off to pick wild currants, with a grave warning to beware of bears, he saw to the preparations for the night. They returned shortly with their hats filled and their lips stained; then, much to his disgust, they insisted on straightening out his tent with their own hands. Once inside its low shelter, they gleefully sifted sand between his blankets and replaced his pillow with a rock; then they induced the cook to coil a wet string in his flapjack. When supper was over and the campfires of driftwood were crackling merrily, they fixed themselves comfortably where their feet would toast, and made him tell them stories until his eyes drooped with weariness.

It was late summer, and O'Neil had expected to find the glaciers less active than usual, but heavy rains in the interior and hot thawing weather along the coast had swelled the Salmon until many bergs clogged it. The reverberations that rolled down the valley told him both Garfield and Jackson were caving badly. It was not the safest time to approach the place, he reflected, but the girls had shown themselves nimble of foot, and he put aside his uneasiness.

Short though the miles had been, and easy as the trip had proved, Eliza soon found herself wondering if it would be possible to penetrate this region at all. The snarling river, the charging icebergs, the caving banks, and the growing menace of that noisy gap ahead began to have their effect upon her and Natalie. When the party finally rounded the point where Murray and Dan had caught their first glimpse of the lower glacier, they paused with exclamations of amazement. They stood at the upper end of a gorge between low bluffs, and just across the hurrying flood lay the lower limit of the giant icefield. The edge, perhaps 600 feet away, was sloping and mud stained, for in its slow advance it had plowed a huge furrow, lifting boulders, trees, acres of soil on its back. The bluff through which the river had cut its bed was formed of the debris it had thrown off and constituted a bulwark protecting its flank.

Farther upstream the slope became steeper, then changed to a rugged perpendicular face showing marks of recent cleavage. This palisade extended on and on, around the nearest bend, following the contour of the Salmon as far as they could see. The sun was reflected from its myriad angles and facets in splendid iridescence. Mammoth caves and caverns gaped. In some spots the ice was white, opaque; in other places it was a light cerulean blue shaded into purple. Ribbons and faint striations meandered through it like the streaks in an agate.

But what struck the beholders with overwhelming force was the tremendous, the unbelievable bulk of the whole slowly moving mass. It reared itself 300 feet high, and along its foot the river hurried, dwarfed to an insignificant trickle. Here and there it leaned outward threateningly, bulging from the terrific weight behind; at other points the muddy flood recoiled from vast heaps that had slid downward and half dammed its current. Back of these piles the fresh cleavage showed dazzlingly. On, upward, back into the untracked mountains it ran through mile upon mile of undulations until it joined the icecap that weighted the plateau. As far as the eye could follow the river ahead it stood solidly. Across its entire face it was dripping; a thousand little rills and waterfalls ate into it, and over it swept a cool, dank breath.

The effect of the first view was overwhelming. Nothing upon the earth compares in majesty and menace to these dull-eyed monsters of bygone ages; nothing except the roots of mountains can serve to check them; nothing less than the ceaseless energy of mighty rivers can sweep away their shattered fragments.

Murray O'Neil had seen Jackson Glacier many times, but always he experienced the same feeling of awe, of personal insignificance, as when he first came stumbling up that gorge more than a year before.

For a long time the girls stood gazing without a word. They seemed to have forgotten his presence.

"Well?" he said at last.

"Isn't it *big*?" Natalie faltered, with round eyes. "Will it fall over on us?"

He shook his head. "The river is too wide for that, but when a particularly big mass drops it makes waves large enough to sweep everything before them. This bank on our right is 60 feet high, but I've seen it inundated."

He then turned to Eliza.

"What do you think of it?"

Her face as she met his was strangely glorified, her eyes were shining, her fingers tightly interlocked.

"I—I'd like to cry or—or swear," she said, uncertainly.

"Why, Eliza!" Natalie regarded her friend in shocked amazement, but Murray laughed.

"It affects people differently," he said. "I have men who refuse to make this trip. There's something about Jackson that frightens them— perhaps it is its nearness. You see, there's no other place on the globe where we pygmies dare come so close to a live glacier of this size."

"How can we go on?" Natalie asked.

"We must work our boats along this bank. If the ice begins to crack anywhere near us, I want you both to scamper up into the alders as fast as your rubber boots will carry you."

"What will you do?" Eliza asked as she eyed him curiously.

"Oh, I'll follow; never fear. If it's not too bad, I'll stay with the boats, of course. But we're not likely to have much difficulty at this season."

Eliza noted the intensity with which the boatmen were scanning the passage ahead, and something in O'Neil's tone told her he was speaking with an assurance he did not wholly feel.

"You have lost some men here, haven't you?" she asked.

"Yes. But the greater danger is in coming down. Then we must get out in the current and take our chances."

"I'd like to do that!" Her lips were parted, her eyes were glowing, but Natalie gave a little cry of dismay.

"It's an utterly new sensation," O'Neil admitted. "I've been thinking of sending you up across the moraine, but the trail is bad, and you might get lost among the alders."

"And miss any part of this? I wouldn't do it for worlds." Eliza's enthusiasm was irresistible, and the expedition was soon underway again.

Progress was more difficult now, for the river shore was paved with smooth, round stones that rolled under foot, and the boats required extreme attention in the swift current. The farther they proceeded, the more the ice wall opposite increased in height, until finally it shut off the mountains behind. Then as they rounded the first bend, a new prospect unfolded itself. The size of Jackson became even more apparent; the gravel bank under which they crept was steeper and higher also. In places it was undercut by the action of the waves that periodically surged across. At such points Murray sent his charges hurrying on ahead, while he and his men tracked the boats after them. In time they found themselves opposite the backbone of the glacier, where the Salmon gnawed at the foot of a frozen cliff of enormous height. And now, although there had been no cause for apprehension beyond an occasional rumble far back or a splitting crack from near at hand, the men assumed an attitude of strained watchfulness and kept their faces turned to the left. They walked quietly, as if they felt themselves in some appalling presence.

At last there came a sound like that of a cannon shot, and far ahead of them a fragment loosened itself and went plunging downward.

Although it appeared small, a ridge promptly leaped out from beneath the splash and came racing down the river's bosom toward them.

"Better go up a bit," O'Neil called to his charges.

The men at the ends of the tow lines scrambled part way up the shelving beach and braced themselves, then wrapped the ropes about their waists, like anchormen on a tug-of-war team. Their companions waded into the flood and fended the boats off the rocks.

The wave came swiftly, lifting the skiffs high upon the bank, then it sucked them back amid a tangle of arms and legs. A portion of the river bottom suddenly bared itself and as suddenly was submerged again. The boats plunged and rolled and beat themselves upon the shore, wrenching the anchormen from their posts. They were half filled with water, too, but the wave had passed and was scudding away downstream.

Eliza Appleton came stumbling back over the rock-strewn bank, for during that first mad plunge she had seen O'Neil go down beneath one of the rearing craft. A man was helping him out.

"Nothing but my ankle," he reassured her when she reached his side. "I was dragged a bit and jammed among the boulders." He sank down, and his lips were white with pain, but his gray eyes smiled bravely. The boatman removed his chief's boot and fell to rubbing the injury, while the girls looked on helplessly.

"Come, come – We can't stay here," Murray told them. He pulled on the boot again to check the swelling.

"Can you walk?" they asked him, anxiously.

"Certainly! Two feet are unnecessary. A man can get along nearly as well on one." He hurried his men back to their tasks, and managed to limp after them, although the effort brought beads of sweat to his lips and brow.

It was well he insisted upon haste, for they had not gone far when the glacier broke abreast of the spot they had just left. There came a rending crack, terrifying in its loudness; a tremendous tower of ice separated itself from the main body, leaned slowly outward, then roared downward, falling in a solid piece like a skyscraper undermined. Not until the arc described by its summit had reached

JOURNEY TO A PLACE OF MANY WONDERS

the river's surface did it shiver itself. Then there was a burst as of an exploded mine.

The saffron waters of the Salmon shot upward until they topped the main rampart, and there separated into a cloud of spray that rained down in a deluge. Out from the fallen mass rushed a billow that gushed across the channel, thrashed against the high bank, then inundated it until the alder thickets on its crest whipped their tips madly. A giant charge of fragments of every size flew far out across the flats or lashed the waters to further anger in its fall.

The prostrate column lay like a wing dam, half across the stream, and over it the Salmon piled itself. Disintegration followed; bergs heaved themselves into sight and went rolling and lunging after the billow that was rushing downstream with the speed of a locomotive. They ground and clashed together in furious confusion as the river spun them; the greater ones upended themselves, casting off muddy cascades. From the depths of the flood came a grinding and crunching as ice met rock.

Spellbound, the girls watched that first wave go tearing out of sight, filling the riverbank full. With exclamations of wonder, they saw the imprisoned waters break the huge dam to pieces. Finally the last shattered fragment hurried out of sight, the flood poured past unhampered, and overhead the glacier towered silent, unchanged, staring at them balefully like a blind man with filmed eyes. There remained nothing but a gleaming scar to show where the cataclysm had originated.

"If I'd known the river was so high, I'd never have brought you," O'Neil told them. "It's fortunate we happened to be above that break. You see, the waves can't run up against the current." He turned to his men and spurred them on.

It was not until the travelers had reached the camp at the bridge site that all the wonders of this region became apparent. Then the two girls, despite their fatigue, spent the late afternoon sightseeing. At this point, they were able to gain a comprehensive view; for at their backs lay Jackson Glacier, which they had just passed, and directly fronting them, across a placid lake, was Garfield, even larger and islands, and more impressive than its mate. Thirty, 40 miles it ran back, broadening into a frozen sea out of which scarred mountain peaks rose like bleak islands, and on beyond the range of vision was still more ice.

They were surrounded by ragged ramparts. The Salmon River ran through a broken chalice formed by the encircling hills, and over the rim of the bowl or through its cracks peered other and smaller ice bodies. The lake at its bottom was filled by as strange a navy as ever sailed the sea; for the ships were bergs, and they followed each other in senseless, ceaseless maneuvers, towed by currents swept through from the cataract at its upper end. They formed long battlelines, assembled into flotillas, and filed about the circumference of a devil's whirlpool at the foot of the rapids, gyrating, bobbing, bowing until crowded out by the pressure of their rivals. Some of them were grounded, like hulks defeated in previous encounters, and along the guardian bar that imprisoned them at the outlet of the lake others were huddled, a mass of slowly dissolving wreckage.

O'Neil was helped into camp, and when his boot had been cut away, he sent news of his arrival to Dan, who came like an eager bridegroom.

14

TRUTH COMES TO ELIZA

Dan Appleton found his employer with one foot in a tub of hot water and his lap full of blueprints. O'Neil explained the condition of affairs down river.

"I want someone to make that crossing," he said.

"A volunteer?" asked Dan, with quickened pulses.

"Yes."

"Will I do?"

"I sent for you to give you the first chance — you've been chafing so at your idleness. We must have steel laid to this point before snow flies. Every hour counts. I dare not risk Mellen or McKay, for they might be disabled. I intended to take charge myself, but I won't be able to walk now for some time." He swore a little, and Dan nodded sympathetically. "I wouldn't send anybody where I'd refuse to go myself. You understand?"

"Of course."

"If either McKay or Mellen were hurt I couldn't build the bridge, and the bridge must be built."

"If Gordon stands pat somebody may be hurt."

"I don't look for anything worse than a few broken heads, but of course I can't tell. I'll stand behind you with my last dollar, no matter what happens."

Dan laughed. "As I understand the situation you won't have a dollar unless we make the crossing."

"Right!" O'Neil said. "The life of the S. R. & N. depends upon it. I'd give $10,000 for your right ankle."

"You can have it for nothing, Chief. I'd amputate the whole leg and present it to you," Dan said.

Murray took his hand in a hearty grip. "Perhaps I'll be able to serve you some time," he said. "Anyhow, I'll look out for the chance. Now spend the evening with the girls and leave in the morning. I'll be down as soon as I can travel to watch the fight from the sidelines." O'Neil's voice was level, but his hands were clenched with rage at his disability.

Dan hurried away elated. But when he told Eliza of the job he had undertaken, she didn't share his enthusiasm.

"Why, the brute! He has no right to send you into danger. This isn't war."

"Sis, dear, it's my chance. He can't stand, and he dare not risk his righthand men."

"So he sacrifices you? I won't permit it. Your life and safety are worth more than all his dollars. Let his old railroad go to smash!"

"Wait! More than my safety depends on this. He said he'd wait for a chance to pay me back. If I do this, he'll owe me more than any man on the job, and when he learns that I love Natalie...."

"Dan!"

"Oh, he'll make good!"

"Why, you're worse than he! The idea of suggesting such a thing."

"Don't preach. I've had nothing to do lately but think of her. She's always in my mind. The loneliness up here has made me feel more than ever that I can't exist without her. The river whispers her name; her face looks at me from the campfire; the wind brings me her messages...."

"Fiddlesticks! She saves her messages for him. When a man reaches the poetical stage, he's positively sickening. You'll be writing verses next."

"I've written 'em," Dan confessed. "Oceans of mush."

TRUTH COMES TO ELIZA

"Fancy! Thank Heaven one of us is sane."

"Our dispositions were mixed when we were born, Eliza. You're unsentimental and hard-headed. I'm romantic. You'll never know what love means."

"If you are a sample, I hope not." Eliza's nose assumed an even higher tilt than usual.

"Well, if I knew I had no chance with Natalie I'd let Gordon's men put an end to me—that's how serious it is. But I have a chance—I know I have."

"Bosh! You've lived in railroad camps too long. I know a dozen girls prettier than her." She then eyed him with concern. "You wouldn't really take advantage of a service to Murray O'Neil to—to tell him the nature of your insanity?"

"I might not actually tell him, but I'd manage it so he'd find out."

"Don't you think Natalie has something to say? Don't you think she is more than a piece of baggage waiting to be claimed by the first man who comes along?" sputtered Miss Appleton in fine disgust at this attitude. "She has more sense and determination than any girl, any pretty girl, I ever saw. That's one reason why I hate her so. There's no use trying to select a husband for her. When the time comes, she'll do the selecting herself. She'll knock over all our plans and walk blushingly up to the altar with O'Neil, leaving us out on the sidewalk to cheer. I'm sorry I ever tried to help you! I'm going to quit and get back my self-respect."

"You'll do no such thing. You'll continue to help your poor red-headed brother to the finish. When I'm alone I'm just bursting with optimism; when I'm with you I wither with despair; when I'm with Natalie I become as heavy and stupid as a frog full of buckshot—I just sit and blink and bask and revel in a sort of speechless bliss. If she ever saw how bright and engaging I am...."

"You?" Eliza sniffed. "You're as uninteresting as I."

"Now that you've pledged your undying support, here goes for some basking," Dan said, and then raced off in search of Miss Gerard.

Eliza made up her mind to wash her hands of the affair, but she wavered, and, as usual, she gave in. She did go to O'Neil to protest at

Dan's selection for the post of danger, but after talking with him she began to see the matter in a new light, and her opposition weakened. He showed her the S. R. & N. had an individuality of its own—an individuality greater than Murray O'Neil's, or Dan Appleton's, or of any man connected with it. She began to understand it was a living thing, and O'Neil was merely a small part of it—a person driven by a power outside himself, the head servant of a great undertaking, upon whom rested a heavy responsibility. She saw for the first time the millions invested in the project imposed upon those concerned with its management a sacred duty, and failure to defend the company's rights would be the worst sort of treachery. She began to appreciate also how men may be willing to lay down their lives, if necessary, to pave the way for the march of commerce.

"I never looked at it in this way," she told him when he had finished. "I don't like to take that view of it, even now, but I suppose I must."

"Try not to worry about Dan," he said. "We'll start back as soon as I'm able to move around, and I'll do my best to see he isn't hurt. It's tough to be laid up this way."

"There's another sick man in camp, by the way."

"Who?"

"The Native boy who helps the cook. He was hunting and shot himself in the arm."

"They told me he was doing well."

"Oh, he is, but the pain has kept the poor fellow awake until he's nearly out of his head. There are no drugs here."

"None this side of the end of the track."

"Can't we do something?"

"We can give Dan a note for Happy Tom in the morning and have whatever you want sent up. Tom will be there, and perhaps if you ask him, he'll send a man on foot at once."

Seizing pen and paper from the table, Eliza wrote a note.

"Dear Uncle Tom," she read aloud to O'Neil when she finished writing. "There is a sick Native boy here. Won't you please send up an opiate by special messenger and receive the blessing of your affectionate Eliza."

"Better change the word opiate," O'Neil advised. "I don't think Tom is equal to that. He might send overalls!"

So Eliza substituted "something to put him to sleep."

Dan promised to deliver the message.

Murray had expected to begin the return journey within 24 hours after his arrival. But his injury mended slowly, and when the time came, he still was unable to stand. The girls spent the time watching the glaciers, of which they never seemed to tire, and in spoiling many films.

It was late on the second day when a tired and sodden messenger bearing the marks of heavy travel appeared at O'Neil's tent and inquired for Miss Appleton. To her he handed a three-foot bundle and a note from Tom Slater.

"Dear Madam – Here is the best thing I know of to put a man to sleep. Thos. Slater"

"There's some mistake, surely," said the girl, as she unrolled the odd-looking package. She then cried out angrily, and O'Neil burst into laughter. Inside the many wrappings was a pick handle.

Eliza's resentment at Happy Tom's unsympathetic sense of humor was tempered in a measure because the patient had taken a turn for the better and really needed no further medical attention. But she was not accustomed to practical jokes, and she vowed to make Tom's life miserable if ever the occasion arose.

As the days wore on, and Murray remained helpless, his impatience became acute. And on the fourth morning, he decided to leave, no matter the cost in pain or danger to the injury. He gave orders to have a boat prepared and allowed himself to be carried to it. He delegated the foreman of the bridge crew to guide the girls down across the moraine, where he promised to pick them up. He sent the men who had come with him to the cataract where Dan had been.

"Aren't you coming with us?" asked Natalie when they found him seated in the skiff with an oarsman.

"It's rough going. I'd have to be carried, so I prefer this," he told them.

"Then we'll go with you," Eliza promptly declared.

Natalie paled and shook her dark head. "Is it safe?" she ventured.

"No, it isn't – run along now! I'll be down there waiting when you arrive."

"If it's safe enough for you, it's safe enough for us," Eliza said. Climbing into the boat, she plopped herself down with a look that seemed to defy any power to remove her. Her blue eyes met O'Neil's gray ones with an expression he had never seen in them until this moment.

"Nonsense, child!" he said. "Don't be silly."

"Don't you try to put me out. I'll hang on and – kick. Don't you say 'please,' either," she warned him.

"I must," he protested. "Please don't insist."

She scowled like an angry boy and seized the gunwales. Her expression made him smile despite his annoyance, and this provoked her the more.

"I'm going!" she said.

This outing had done wonders for both girls. The wind and the sunshine had tanned them, the coarse fare had lent them a hearty vigor, and they made charming pictures in their trim short skirts and sweaters and leather-banded hats.

"Very well. If you're going, take off your boots," O'Neil said.

"What for?"

"We may be swamped and forced to swim for it. You see the man has taken his off." Murray pointed to the raw-boned Norwegian oarsman who had stripped down as if for a footrace.

Eliza obeyed.

"Now your sweater."

Natalie had watched this scene with evident concern. She now seated herself on a boulder and began to tug at her rubber boots.

"Here! Here! You're not going, too." O'Neil exclaimed.

"Yes, I am. I'm frightened to death, but I won't be a coward." Her shaking hands and strained voice left no doubt of her seriousness.

"She can't swim," Eliza said.

O'Neil put an end to this display of heroism with a firm refusal.

"You'll think I'm afraid," Natalie said.

"Bless you, of course we will, because you are. So am I, and so is Eliza, for that matter. If you can't swim, you'd only be taking a foolish risk and adding to our danger. Besides, Eliza doesn't know the feel of cold water as we do."

Natalie smiled a little as she recalled their shipwreck experience.

"I'd much rather walk, of course," she said. She then looked at Eliza.

"It—it will be a lovely ramble for us," Natalie assured her.

But Eliza shook her head. "This is material for my book, and I'll make enough out of it to—to...."

"Buy another orchard?" Murray suggested.

Feeling more resigned now the adventure had taken on a purely financial color, Natalie at length allowed herself to be dissuaded, and Eliza settled herself in her seat with the disturbing consciousness she had made herself appear selfish and rude in O'Neil's eyes. Nevertheless, she had no notion of changing her mind.

When the other girl had gone, the oarsman completed his preparations by lashing fast the contents of the skiff—a proceeding Eliza watched with some uneasiness. O'Neil showed his resentment by a pointed silence, which nettled her, and she resolved to hold her seat even if the boat turned somersaults.

Word was finally given, and they swung out into the flood. O'Neil stood as best he could on his firm leg and steered by means of a sculling oar, while the Norwegian rowed lustily.

Bits of drift, patches of froth, fragments of ice accompanied them, bobbing alongside so persistently that Eliza fancied the boat must be stationary until, glancing at the riverbanks, she saw them racing past like the panoramic scenery in a melodrama. The same glance showed her they were rushing directly toward the upper ramparts of Jackson Glacier, as if for an assault. Out here in the current there were waves, and these increased in size as the bed of the Salmon grew steeper, until the poling boat began to rear and leap like a frightened horse.

The gleaming wall ahead rose higher with every instant. It overhung, a giant, crumbling cliff, imposing, treacherous. Then the stream turned at right angles. They were swept along parallel with the ice face, and ahead of them for three miles stretched the gauntlet. The tottering wall seemed almost within reaching distance, its breath cold, damp, and clammy.

O'Neil stood erect and powerful in the stern, swaying to the antics of the craft, his weight on the sweep, his eyes fixed on the thing overhead. The Norwegian strained at his oars while sweat ran down into his open shirt. The boat lunged and wallowed desperately, rising on end, falling with prodigious slaps, drenching the occupants with spray. It was splendid, terrifying. Eliza clung to her seat and felt her heartbeats smothering her. Occasionally the oarsman turned, staring past her with round, frightened eyes, affording her a glimpse of a face working with mingled fear and exultation.

Thus far the glacier had not disputed their passage. It maintained the silence and the immobility of marble; nothing but the snarl of the surging flood re-echoed from its face. But with the suddenness of a rifle shot there came a detonation, louder, sharper than any blast of powder. The Norwegian cursed. The helmsman dropped his eyes to the white face in the bow and smiled.

Half a mile ahead of them a mass of ice came rumbling down, and the whole valley rocked with the sound. Onward the little craft fled, a dancing speck beneath the majesty of that frozen giant, an atom threatened by the weight of mountains. At last through the opening of the gorge below came a glimpse of the flats that led to the sea. A moment later the boat swung into an eddy and came to rest, bumping against the boulders.

O'Neil sat down, wiping his wet face.

"Well, was it worth your trouble, Miss Kick-over the-traces?" he asked.

"Oh, it was glorious! I'll never forget it."

Eliza's cheeks were burning now, her aching hands relaxed their hold, and she drew a deep breath—the first of which she had been conscious since the start, 15 minutes before.

"Now, on with your boots and your sweater. We'll have an hour's wait for Natalie."

She gave a cry of surprise and offered him a glimpse of a trim ankle and a dripping foot.

"See? They're wet, and I wriggled my toes right through my stockings. I *never* was so excited."

The boatman fastened the painter and resumed his outer clothing.

"Tell me, why did you insist on coming?" O'Neil asked her as he lit a cigar.

"I was afraid something might happen to you."

He raised his brows, and she flushed.

"Don't you understand?" she continued. "Dan would never have forgiven me, and—and—I just *had* to come, that's all. It's corking material for me—I thought you might upset, and I—I don't know why I insisted." She bent over her stubborn boots, hiding her face. She was flaming to the ears, for suddenly she knew the reason that had prompted her. It rushed upon her like a sense of great shame. She recalled the desperate grip at her heart when she had seen him ready to leave, the wildness of her longing to share his danger, the black fear he might meet disaster alone. It had all come without warning, and there had been no time for self-consciousness, but now she realized the truth. The poignant pain of it made her fingers clumsy and sent that flood of scarlet to her neck and ears.

When Natalie arrived, they cast off, and the remaining miles were made in a few hours.

Appleton joined them for lunch in the tent they remembered so well and professed to be shocked at the report of his sister's foolhardiness. But whatever may have been Natalie's fear of ridicule, it promptly disappeared under his complete indorsement of her wisdom in refraining from such a mad adventure. As if to put her even more at ease, O'Neil was especially attentive to her. Eliza reflected gloomily that men, after all, dislike bravado in women, that a trapeze artist or a lady balloonist inspires only a qualified admiration.

Work had progressed steadily during O'Neil's absence. On his return he found the grade completed to within a few yards of Gordon's right-of-way. Although he was still unable to walk, he insisted on going to the front, helped by Appleton and Happy Tom.

Into the narrow space between the end of his embankment and that of his rival's a gravel train was spilling its burden, and a hundred pick-and-shovel men were busy. The opposing forces also seemed hard at work, but their activity was largely a pretense, and they showed plainly they were waiting for the clash. They were a hard-looking crew, and their employer had neglected no precaution. He had erected barricades for their protection until his grade looked like a military work.

"They haven't showed any guns yet, but I'm sure they're armed," Appleton told his chief.

"How is the place lighted by night?" O'Neil asked.

"Oil torches," Slater answered. "Ah! We've been recognized. That comes from being fat, I s'pose."

As he spoke a donkey engine at the right of the proposed crossing set up a noisy rattling, a thin steel cable whipped into view between the rails, and from the left there appeared a contrivance that O'Neil eyed curiously. It was a sort of drag and rode back and forth on the rails.

"Humph! They'd better not put much trust in that," Murray grunted.

"Don't fool yourself – it's no rubber-tired baby carriage," Slater said. "Our men are afraid of it."

"Post a notice at once, offering $1,000 for any man who cuts that cable," O'Neil said after watching the device scuttle back and forth for a few moments.

"1,000...,"Appleton gasped. "Why, I'll do it. Let me!"

"No, you won't," Slater broke in. "I'll take that on myself."

"I spoke first. It's my first chance," Dan cried.

"It's my job! I'm going...."

"Wait a minute!" O'Neil silenced the two, who were glaring at each other angrily. "No fighting. There will be enough of that later."

"I spoke first," Dan repeated, stubbornly.

"I had my mouth puckered to spit, that's why," the fat man explained. "A fellow has to spit."

"I'd rather you wouldn't volunteer, Dan," O'Neil said.

"Why?"

"You might get hurt."

Happy Tom nodded his agreement. "Certainly – never send a boy on a man's errand."

"And I don't want you to do it either, Tom, for the same reason."

Slater mumbled some sort of sour acquiescence, but Dan would not be denied.

"You made the offer, and I took it up," he told O'Neil. "Somebody must make the first move, and I have a particular need for exactly $1,000. If they start a rumpus, it will give us the excuse we're looking for. I've been studying that 'go-devil' through field glasses for two days now, and I'll guarantee to put it out of commission before Gordon's men know what I'm about. Just forget the reward, if you like, and give me a chance."

"What's your plan?" Slater asked.

But Appleton shook his head. "No you don't, Tommy," he said. "I'm wise to you."

Murray hesitated briefly, then gave his permission. "I'd rather you'd let one of the roughnecks take the chance, but if you insist...."

"I do."

"Then get your sister's consent."

Slater swore mournfully, as if from a heart filled with black despair.

"Ain't that my luck? One cud of gum cost me $1,000. Hell! It would take a millionaire to afford a habit like that." He expelled the gum violently and went grumbling up the track.

"Sis won't object," Dan said. "She'd offer to do the trick herself, for she's getting the spirit of the work."

When O'Neil had managed to reach the camp, he began using the telephone to make preparations for an attack that night. News of the coming fight quickly spread, and both the day and night shifts discussed it at suppertime.

The excitement did not lessen when a loaded gravel train rolled in, and Dr. Gray and two helpers from the hospital at Omar descended.

Up to this point, both Eliza and Natalie had hoped the affair might not, after all, turn out to be serious. But the presence of the grim-faced surgeon with his emergency kit, along with the significant preparations he set about making, boded otherwise. Eliza tried to reason with her brother, but her words refused to come. As a matter of fact, deep down in her heart was a great rebellion at the fate that had made her a woman and thus debarred her from an active part in the struggle. Natalie, on the other hand, was filled with dread, and she made a much more vigorous attempt to dissuade Dan from his purpose than did his sister. But he refused to heed even her, and soon hurried away to finish his preparations.

The camp settled itself to wait for darkness after supper. Night was slow in coming and speculation rife long before Appleton signified his readiness. With the approach of twilight, the torches along Gordon's grade began to glow brightly. Then Dan set his watch with Happy Tom's, kissed Eliza, and made off across the tundra. He left the S. R. & N. at right angles and continued in that direction for a mile or more before swinging about in a wide circle that brought him well to the rear of Gordon's encampment. The gloom now covered his movements, and by taking advantage of an alder thicket he managed to approach close to the enemy's position. But the footing was treacherous, the darkness caused him to fall several times. He was wet, muddy, and perspiring when he finally paused not more than 200 feet from the scene of the proposed crossing.

15

BATTLE AT GORDON'S CROSSING

C urtis Gordon was not in charge of his field forces, having left the command to his favorite jackal, Denny. Beneath his apparent contempt for the law there lurked a certain caution. He knew his rival's necessity, he appreciated his cunning, but wishing to guard against the possibility of a personal humiliation, he retired to Kyak, where he was prepared to admit or deny as much responsibility as suited him. Denny had not forgotten O'Neil's exposure of his dishonesty, and his zeal could be relied upon. He personally knew all the men under him, had coached them carefully, and assured Gordon of his ability to hold his ground.

From his hiding place, Dan Appleton measured the preparations for resistance with some uneasiness. He knew if Denny had the nerve to use firearms, he would undoubtedly rout O'Neil's men, who had not been permitted to carry guns. By the bright torchlight he could see figures coming and going like sentinels along the grade, and from within the barricades of ties he heard others talking. The camp itself, which lay farther to the left, was lighted, and black silhouettes were painted against the canvas walls and roofs. Someone was playing an accordion, and its wailing notes came to him intermittently. He saw steam was up in the boiler that operated the "go-devil," although the contrivance itself was stationary. It was on this he centered his attention, consulting his watch nervously.

At last 10 o'clock came, bringing with it a sound that startled the nearby camp into activity. It was a shrill blast from an S. R. & N. locomotive and the grinding of car wheels. The accordion ceased its complaint, men poured out of the lighted tents, Appleton moved cautiously out from cover.

He stumbled forward through the knee-deep mud and moss, bearing slightly to his right, counting on the confusion to mask his approach. He timed it to the gravel train, which came slowly creaking nearer, rocking over the uneven tracks, then down on the half-submerged rails that terminated near the opposing grade. It stopped finally, with headlight glaring into the faces of Denny and his troops, and from the high-heaped flat cars tumbled an army of pick-and-shovel men. During this hullabaloo Appleton slipped out of the marsh and climbed the gravel bed in time to see the steel cable of the skip tighten, carrying the drag swiftly along the track. The endless cable propelling the contrivance ran through a metal block that was secured to a deadhead sunk between the ties, and up to this post Dan hastened. He carried a cold chisel and hammer, but he found no use

Courtesy Richard Bell

Railroad companies often used a go-devil, like this one displayed at the Colorado Railroad Museum, to help with construction of railroad tracks.

for them, for the pulley was roped to the deadhead. Drawing his knife, he sawed at the manila strands. Men were all around him, but they took no notice of him in their excitement. Not until he had nearly completed his task was he discovered; then someone raised a shout. The next instant they charged on him. But his work had been done. With a snap, the ropes parted, the cable went writhing and twisting up the track, the unwieldy apparatus came to a stop.

Dan found himself beset by a half-dozen of the enemy, who, having singled him out of the general confusion as the cause of disaster, came at him headlong. But by this time, O'Neil's men were pouring out of the darkness and overrunning the grade so rapidly there was little opportunity for concerted action. Appleton had intended, as soon as he had cut the cable, to beat a hasty retreat into the marsh; but now, with the firm gravel roadbed under his feet and the battle breaking before his eyes, he changed his mind. He carried a light heart, and the love of trouble romped through his veins. He lowered his head, therefore, and ran toward his assailants.

He met the first one fairly and laid him out. He vanquished the second, then closed with a burly man who withstood him capably. They went down together, and Dan began to repent his haste, for blows rained upon him and he became the target, not only of blows of every kind, but of heavy hobnailed shoes that were more dangerous than horses' hoofs.

The engineer dearly loved a fair fight, even against odds, but this was entirely different. He was trampled, stamped upon, kicked. He felt himself being reduced to a pulp beneath the overpowering numbers of those savage heels. The fact his opponent received an equal share of the punishment was all that saved Dan. Over and over between the ties the two rolled, scorning no advantage, regarding no rules of combat, each striving to protect himself at the other's expense.

They were groveling there in a tangle of legs and arms when Happy Tom came down the grade, leading a charge that swept the embankment clean.

The boss packer had equipped his command with pick handles and now set a brilliant example in the use of this, his favorite weapon.

For once the apathetic Slater was fully roused, he was tremendous, irresistible. In his capable grasp, the oaken cudgel became both armor and flail. In defense it was as active as a fencing master's foil, in offense as deadly as the kick of a mule. Beneath his formless bulk were the muscles of a gladiator; his eye had all the quickness of a prizefighter. There was something primeval, appallingly ferocious about the fat man, too. He fought with a magnificent enthusiasm, a splendid abandon. And yet, despite his rage, he was clear headed, and his ears were sensitively strained for the sound of the first gunshot – something he dreaded beyond measure.

He was sobbing as much from anxiety as from the violence of his exertions when he tore Appleton from the clutch of Gordon's man and set him on his feet.

"Are you hurt, son?" he gasped.

"I'm hurt like hell." Dan spat out a mouthful of blood and sand. "Gimme a club."

"Go back yonder," Tom told him. "Nail Denny before he gets 'em to shooting. Kill him if you must. I'll take care of these fellers."

The younger man saw the engagement at this end of the line was no longer general, but had become a series of individual combats, so he made what haste he could toward the scene of the more serious encounter to the right of the crossing. He judged the issue was still in doubt there, although he could make out little in the confusion on account of the glaring headlight, which dazzled him.

As he ran, however, he discovered the S. R. & N. forces were in possession of the middle ground, having divided the enemy's ranks like a wedge, and this encouraged him. Out of the darkness to right and left came shouts, curses, the sounds of men wallowing about in the knee-deep tundra. They were Gordon's helpers who had been routed from their positions.

Now that Appleton had time to collect his wits, he, too, grew sick with suspense, for he knew arms had been stacked inside the barricades. Any instant might bring them into play. He began to wonder why Denny withheld the word to fire.

But the explanation was simple, although it did not appear until later. Mr. Denny at that moment was in no condition to issue orders of any kind. When preparations for the advance were made, Dr. Gray, who understood perhaps more fully than anyone else except O'Neil the gravity of the issue and the slender pivot upon which the outcome balanced, had taken his place in the vanguard of the attacking party instead of in the background, as befitted his calling. The first rush had carried him well into the fray, but once there he had shown his good judgment by refusing to participate in it.

Instead, he had selected Denny out of the opposing ranks and bored through the crowd in his direction, heedless of all efforts to stop him. His great strength had enabled him to gain ground. He had hurled his assailants aside, upsetting them, bursting through the press as a football player penetrates a line. And when the retreat had begun, he was close at the heels of his victim. He had overtaken Denny beside one of the barricades just as Denny seized a rifle and raised it. With one wrench Dr. Gray grabbed the weapon, and the next instant had bent the barrel over its owner's head.

Then, as the fight surged onward, he had gathered the limp figure in his arms and carried it into the light of a gasoline torch, where he could administer first aid. He was kneeling over the fellow when Appleton found him as he came stumbling along the grade.

But the decisive moment had come and gone now, and without a leader to command them, Gordon's men seemed loath to adopt a bloodier reprisal. They gave way, therefore, in a half-hearted hesitation that spelled ruin to their cause. They were forced back to their encampment over the ground where picks and shovels began to fly. Soon rails were torn up and gravel rained from the flat cars, the blockhouses were razed, and above the rabble the locomotive panted and wheezed, its great yellow eye glaring through the night. When it backed away, another took its place; the grade rose to the level of the intersection, then as morning approached it crept out beyond. By breakfast time, a long row of flats extended across the line Curtis Gordon had tried to hold in defiance of the law.

Dan Appleton – dirty, tired, but happy – found Natalie and Eliza awaiting him when he limped up to their tent in the early morning light. One of his eyes was black and nearly closed, his lips were cut and swollen, but he grinned cheerfully.

"Say! It was a great night, wasn't it?"

Eliza cried out in alarm at his appearance.

"You poor kid! You're a sight." She ran for hot water and soap.

"You were perfectly splendid, Dan," Natalie said. "I knew you'd do it."

"Did you?" He tried to smile his appreciation, but the effort resulted in a leer so repulsive the girl looked dismayed. "You ought to have seen the shindy."

"Seen it? Maybe we did!"

"Honestly?"

"Did you think we could stay behind? We sneaked along with the cookhouse gang, and one of them helped us up on the gravel cars. He smelled of dishwater, but he was a hero. We screamed and cried, and Eliza threw stones until Mr. O'Neil discovered us and made us get down. He was awfully mean."

"He's a mean man."

"He isn't! He was jumping around on one leg like a crippled grasshopper."

"I made $1,000," Dan said. "Guess what I'm going to do with it?"

"How can I guess?"

"I'm going to buy an engagement ring." Once more he leered repulsively.

"How nice." Natalie said, coolly. "Congratulations."

"Guess who it's for?"

"I couldn't, really."

"It's for you."

"Oh no, it isn't!" Natalie's voice was freezing. "You have made a mistake, a great mistake, Dan. I like you, but—we won't even mention such things, if you please."

Eliza's entrance saved her further embarrassment, and she quickly made her escape. Dan groaned so deeply as his sister bathed his injuries that she was really concerned.

"Goodness, Danny," she said, "are you as badly hurt as all that?"

"I'm worse," he confessed. "I've just been shot through the heart.

Slow music and flowers for me. Arrange for the services and put a rose in my hand, Sis."

"Nonsense! I'll put a beefsteak on your eye," she told him.

Under Dr. Gray's attention, O'Neil's ankle began to mend, and by the time the track had been laid far enough beyond the crossing to insure against further interference from Gordon, he declared himself ready to complete the journey to Kyak, which he and the girls had begun nearly three weeks before.

During the interval, Eliza had occupied herself in laying out her magazine stories, and now she was eager to complete her investigations so she could begin the final writing. Her experience in the north thus far had given her an altered outlook on the railroad situation, but still she knew little of the coal problem. That, after all, was the more important subject, and she expected it to afford her the basis for a sensational exposure. She had come to Alaska sharing her newspaper's views on questions of public policy, looking upon Murray O'Neil as a daring promoter bent upon seizing the means of transportation of a mighty realm for his own individual profit; on Gordon as an unscrupulous adventurer; and on the Copper Trust as a greedy corporation reaching out to strangle competition and absorb the riches of the northland. But she had found O'Neil an honorably ambitious man, busied, like others, in the struggle for success, and backing his judgment with his last dollar. She had learned, moreover, to sympathize with his aims, and his splendid determination awoke her admiration. Her idea of the Trust had changed, likewise, for it seemed to be a fair and dignified competitor. She had seen no signs of that conscienceless, grasping policy usually imputed to big business. Regarding Gordon, her first conviction had remained unchanged. He was, in truth, as evil as he had been reputed.

The readjustment of her ideas had been disappointing, in a way, since it robbed her of a large part of her ammunition; but she consoled herself with the thought she had not yet reached the big, vital story that most deeply concerned the welfare of the north.

She was a bit afraid to pursue her inquiries into the coal subject, for her ideas were fixed, and she feared that O'Neil's activities merited condemnation. In his railroad building, she believed, he was doing fine work, but the coal was another matter. Obviously, it belonged to the people, and he had no right to lay hands upon their heritage.

She wondered if it would not be possible to omit all mention of him in her coal stories and center attention upon the Trust. It was impossible for her to attack him now since she had come to understand her feelings toward him. Even so, she reflected with horror that if her articles created the comments she anticipated, their effect would be to rob him of his holdings. But she took her work seriously, and her sense of duty was unwavering. She was one of the few who guide themselves by the line of principle, straight through all other considerations. She would write what she found true, for that was her mission in life. If Murray proved culpable, she would grieve over his wrongdoing — and continue to love him.

O'Neil had recognized her sincerity, and on the broad subject of conservation he had done nothing to influence her views. He preferred to let her see the workings of the principle and, after meeting some of those who had suffered by it, form her own conclusions. This was the main reason he had arranged the trip to Kyak.

The journey in a small boat gave Eliza a longed-for opportunity to discuss with him the questions that troubled her. He was uncommunicative at first, but she persisted in her attempt, drawing him out in the hope of showing him the error of his ways. At last she provoked him to a vigorous defense of his views.

"Conservation is no more than economy," he said, "and no one opposes that. It's the misapplication of the principle that has retarded Alaska and ruined so many of us. The situation would be laughable if it weren't so tragic."

"Of course you blame your troubles on the government. That's one thing governments are for."

"Our ancestors blamed King George for their troubles, more than a hundred years ago, and a war resulted. But every abuse they suffered is suffered by the people of Alaska today, and a lot more besides. Certainly England never violated her contracts with the colonies half so flagrantly as our government has violated its contracts with us."

"Of course you exaggerate."

"I don't. Judge for yourself. The law offers every citizen the chance — in fact, it invites him — to go on the public domain and search for treasure. If he is successful, it permits him to locate the land in blocks, and it agrees to grant him a clear title after he does a certain amount of work and pays a fixed price. Further, it says in effect: 'Realizing that you may need financial assistance in this work, we will allow you to locate not only for yourself, but also for your friends, through their powers of attorney, and thus gain their cooperation for your mutual advantage. These are the rules, and they are binding upon all parties to this agreement; you keep your part, we will keep ours.'

Now then, some pioneers, at risk of life and health, came to Kyak and found coal. They located it; they did all the law required them to do — but did the government keep its word? Not at all. It was charged that some of them hadn't conformed strictly to the letter of the agreement, and therefore all the claims were blacklisted. Because one man was alleged to have broken his contract the government broke its contract with every man who had staked a coal claim, not only at Kyak, but anywhere else in Alaska. Guilty and innocent were treated alike. I was one of the latter. Was our money returned to us? No! The government had it and it kept it, along with the land. We've been holding on now for years, and the Interior Department has tried by various means to shake us off. The law has been changed repeatedly at the whim of every theorist who happened to be in power. It has been changed without notice to us even while we were out in the wilderness trying to comply with the regulations already imposed. You can see how it worked in the case of Natalie and her mother. The government succeeded in shaking them off."

"That's only one side of the question," Eliza said. "You lose sight of the fact this treasure never really belonged to you, but to the public. The coal lands were withdrawn from entry because men like you and the agents of the Heidlemanns were grabbing it all up."

O'Neil shook his head and frowned.

"That's what the papers say, but it isn't true. There are 20 million acres of coal in Alaska, and not more than 30,000 acres have been located. The law gave me the right to locate and buy coal claims, and I took advantage of it. Now it tells me I have money enough and takes back what it gave. If it did the right thing, it would grant patents to those who located under the law as it then existed and withdraw the rest of the land from entry if advisable. This country needs two things to make it prosper — transportation and fuel. We are doing our best to supply the first despite hindrance from Washington; but the fuel has been locked away from us as if behind stone walls. Rich men must be brave to risk their dollars here under existing conditions, for they are not permitted to utilize the mines, the timber, or the waterpower, except upon absurd and unreasonable terms. Why, I've seen timber lying four layers deep and rotting. The government won't save it, nor will it allow us to do so. That's been its policy throughout. It is strangling industry and dedicating Alaska to eternal solitude.

"Railroads are the keys by which this realm can be unlocked; coal is the strength by which those keys can be turned. The keys are fitted to the lock, but our fingers are paralyzed. For eight years Alaska's greatest wealth has lain exposed to view, but the government has posted the warning, 'Hands off! Someone among you is a crook!'

"Meanwhile the law has been suspended, the country has stagnated, men have left dispirited or broken, towns have been abandoned. The cost in dollars to me, for instance, has been tremendous. I'm laying my track alongside rich coalfields, but if I picked up a chunk from my own claim to throw at a chipmunk, I'd become a lawbreaker. I import from Canada the fuel to drive my locomotives past my own coalbeds — which I have paid for — and I pay five times the value of that fuel, 40 percent of which is duty. I haul it 2,000 miles, while there are a billion tons of better quality beneath my feet. Do you call that conservation? I call it waste."

"Fraud was practiced at the start, and of course it takes time to find out just where it lay," Eliza said.

"That's the excuse, but after all these years no fraud has been proved. In administering the criminal law there is an axiom to the effect that it is better for 99 guilty men to escape than for one innocent man to suffer, but the Land Office says 99 innocent Alaskans shall suffer rather than that one guilty man shall escape. The cry of fraud is only a pretense, raised to cover the main issue. There's something sinister back of it."

"What do you mean?"

"A conspiracy of the Eastern coal operators and the transcontinental freight lines."

"How ridiculous!" Eliza said.

"You think so? Listen! Since all the high-grade coal of the Pacific coast must come from the East, who, then, would discourage the opening of local fields but those very interests? Every ton we burn means a profit to the Eastern miner and the railroad man. Yes, and 20 percent of the heat units of every ton hauled are consumed in transportation. Isn't that waste? Every two years it costs our U.S. Navy the price of a battleship to bring coal to the Pacific fleet, while we have plenty of better fuel right here on the ground. Our coal is 2,500 miles nearer to the Philippines than San Francisco, and 12,000 miles nearer than its present source. If Alaska coalbeds were opened, we wouldn't have this yearly fight for battleship appropriations; we'd make ourselves a present of a first-class Navy for nothing. No, our claims were disputed, and the dispute was thrown into politics to keep us out of competition with our Eastern cousins. We Alaskans sat in a game with high stakes, but after the cards were dealt, the rules were changed."

"You argue very well," said Eliza, who was a bit dazed at this unexpected, forceful counterattack. "But you haven't convinced me this coal should be thrown open to the first person who comes along."

"I didn't expect to convince you. It's hard to convince a woman whose mind is made up. It would take hours to cover the subject; but I want to open your eyes to the effect of this new-fangled national policy. Any great principle may work evil if it isn't properly directed, and in Kyak you'll see the results of conservation ignorantly applied. You'll see how it has bound and gagged a wonderful country, and made loyal Americans into ragged, bitter traitors who would spit upon the flag they used to cherish."

"Is that the only reason why you came along—just to make sure I saw all this?"

"No. I want to look at the Heidlemann breakwater. My fortune hangs upon it."

"It's as serious as that?"

O'Neil shrugged. "I'm waiting for the wind. My coal is in the hands of the bureaucracy at Washington, my railroad is in the hands of the wind god. Incidentally, I'd much rather trust the god than the government."

Natalie, who had listened so far without the least sign of interest, now spoke up.

"If the storm doesn't come to your help, will you be ruined?" she asked.

Murray smiled cheerfully. "No man is ruined if he keeps his dreams. Money isn't much, after all, and failure is merely a schooling. But—I won't fail. Autumn is here. The tempest is my friend, and he won't be long in coming now. He'll arrive with the equinox, and when he does, he'll hold my fortune in his hand."

"Why, the equinoctial storm is due," Eliza said.

"Exactly! That's why I'm going to meet it and to bid it welcome."

The village of Kyak lay near the mouth of the most easterly outlet of the Salmon, and it was similar in most respects to Hope and to Omar, except it looked out across a shallow, unprotected bay to the open reaches of the north Pacific. The shores were low; a pair of rocky islets afforded the only shelter to its shipping, and it was from these as a starting point the Copper Trust had built its breakwater. A trestle across the tide flats connected the work with the mainland, and along this rock trains crawled, adding their burdens to the strength of the barrier. Protected by this arm of steel and stone and timber lay the terminal buildings of the Alaska Northern, as the Heidlemann line was called, and there also lay the terminus of the old McDermott enterprise into which Curtis Gordon had infused new life. Both places showed plenty of activity when O'Neil and his two companions arrived late one afternoon.

Kyak, they found, was inferior to Omar in its public accommodations, and Murray was at a loss to find shelter for the girls until his arrival was made known to the agents of the Alaska

Northern. Then Mr. Trevor, the engineer in charge, looked him up and insisted on sharing his quarters with the visitors. In Trevor's bearing was no suggestion of an enmity like Gordon's. He welcomed his rival warmly—and indeed the Trust had never been small in its opposition. O'Neil accepted the invitation gratefully.

After dinner he took Natalie with him to see the sights, while Eliza profited by the opportunity to interview Trevor. In her numerous tilts with O'Neil she had not been over successful from the point of view of her magazine articles, but here at her hand was the representative of the power best known and best hated for its activities in the northland, and he seemed perfectly willing to talk. Surely from him she would get information that would count.

"Understand, I'm on the side of your enemies," she warned him.

"So is everybody else," Mr. Trevor said with a laugh. "But that's because we're misunderstood."

"The intentions of any Trust warrant suspicion."

He shrugged. "The Heidlemanns are just ordinary businessmen, like O'Neil, looking for investment. They heard of a great big copper field hidden away back yonder in the mountains, and they bought what they considered to be the best group of claims. They knew the region was difficult to access, but they figured a railroad from tidewater would open not only their own properties, but the rest of the copper belt and the whole interior country. They began to build a road from Cortez, when some 'shoe-stringer' raised the cry that they had monopolized the world's greatest copper supply, and had double-cinched it by monopolizing transportation also. That started the fuss. They needed cheap coal, of course, just as everybody else needs it; but somebody discovered the danger of a monopoly of that and set up another shout. Ever since then the yellow press has been screaming. The government withdrew all coal lands from entry, and it now refuses to grant patents to that which had been properly located. We don't own a foot of Alaska coal land, Miss Appleton. On the contrary, we haul our fuel from British Columbia, just like O'Neil and Gordon. Those who would like to sell local coal to us are prevented from doing so."

"It sounds well to hear you tell it," Eliza said. "But the minute the coal patents are issued, you will buy what you want, then freeze out the other people. You expect to control the mines, the railroads, and the steamship lines, but public necessities like coal and oil and timber and waterpower should belong to the people. There has been an awakening of the public conscience, and the day of monopolized necessities is passing."

"As long as men own coal mines they will sell them. Here we are faced not by a question of what may happen, but of what has happened. If you agreed to buy a city lot from a real estate dealer, and after you paid him his price, he refused to give you a deed, you'd at least expect your money back, wouldn't you? Well, that's the case of Uncle Sam and the Alaskan miners. He not only refuses to deliver the lot, but keeps the money, and forces them to pay more every year. I represent a body of rich men who, because of their power, are regarded with suspicion; but if they did anything so dishonest as what our government has done to its own people they would be jailed."

"No doubt there has been some injustice, but the great truth remains that the nation should own its natural resources and should not allow favored individuals to profit by the public need."

"You mean railroads and coalfields and such things?"

"I do."

Trevor shook his head. "If the people of Alaska waited for a government railroad, they'd die of old age and be buried where they died for lack of transportation. The government owns telegraph lines here, but it charges us five times the rates of the Western Union. No, Miss Appleton, we're not ready for government ownership, and even if we were it wouldn't affect the legality of what has been done. Through fear that the Heidlemanns might profit, this whole country has been made to stagnate. Alaska is being depopulated; houses and stores are closed; people are leaving despondent. Alaskans are denied self-government in any form; theories are tried at their expense, but they are never consulted. Not only does Congress fail to enact new laws to meet their needs, but it refuses to proceed under the laws that already exist. If the same policy had been pursued in the settlement of the Middle West that applies to this country, the buffalo would still be king of the plains and Chicago would be a frontier town. You seem to think that coal is the most important issue up here, but it isn't. Transportation is what the country needs, for the main riches of Alaska are as useless today as if hidden away in the chasms of the moon. O'Neil had the right idea when he selected the Salmon River route, but he made an error of judgment, and he lost."

"He hasn't lost!" cried Eliza, in quick defense of her friend. "Your breakwater hasn't been tested yet."

"Oh, it will hold," Trevor said with a smile. "It has cost too much money not to hold."

"Wait until the storms come," the girl persisted.

"That's what we're doing, and from present indications, we won't have much longer to wait. Weather has been breeding for several days, and the equinox is here. Of course I'm anxious, but—I built that breakwater, and it can't go out."

When O'Neil and Natalie returned, they found the two still arguing. "Haven't you finished your tiresome discussions?" Natalie asked.

"Mr. Trevor has almost convinced me the octopus is a noble creature, filled with high ideals and writhing at the thrusts of the muckrakers," Eliza told them.

But at that the engineer protested.

"No, no!" he said. "I haven't half done justice to the subject. There are a dozen men in Kyak tonight who could put up a much stronger case than I. There's McCann, for instance. He was a prospector back in the States until he made a strike that netted him $100,000. He put nearly all of it into Kyak coal claims and borrowed $70,000 more. He got tired of the interminable delay and finally mined a few tons he sent out for a test in the Navy. It had better steaming qualities than the Eastern coal now being used, but six weeks later an agent of the Land Office ordered him to cease work until his title had been passed upon. That was two years ago, and nothing has been done since. No charges of irregularity of any sort have ever been filed against McCann or his property. The government has had his money for five years, and still he can't get a ruling. He's broke now and too old to make a living. He's selling pies on the street...."

"He borrowed a dollar from me just now," said O'Neil, who was staring out of a window. Suddenly he turned and addressed his host. "Trevor, it's going to storm." His voice was harsh, his eyes were eager; his tone brought the engineer to his side. Together they looked out across the bay.

The southern sky was leaden, the evening had been shortened by a rack of clouds that came hurrying in from the sea.

"Let it storm," said Trevor, after a moment. "I'm ready."

"Have you ever seen it blow here?"

"The old-timers tell me I haven't, but—I've seen some terrible storms. Of course the place is unusual...."

"In what way?" Eliza asked."

"The whole country back of here is ice capped. This coast for 100 miles to the east is glacial. The cold air inland and the warm air from the Japanese current are always at war."

"There is a peculiar difference in air pressures, too," O'Neil said. "Over the warm interior it is high, and over the coast range it is low; so every valley becomes a pathway for the wind. But that isn't where the hurricanes come from. They're born out yonder." He pointed out beyond the islands from which the breakwater flung its slender arm. "This may be only a little storm, Trevor, but some day the sea and the air will come together and wipe out all your work. Then you'll see I was right."

"You told me that more than a year ago, but I backed my skill against your prophecy."

"Men like you and me become overconfident of our powers," O'Neil told him. "We grow arrogant, but after all we're only pygmies."

"If Nature beats me here, I'm a ruined man," the engineer said.

"And if you defeat her, I'm ruined," O'Neil said as he smiled at him.

"Let's make medicine, the way the Indians did, and call upon the Spirit of the Wind to settle the question," Eliza suggested, with a woman's quick instinct for relieving a situation that threatened to become constrained. She and Natalie ran to Trevor's sideboard, and, seizing bottle and shaker, brewed a magic broth, while the two men looked on. They murmured incantations, they made mystic passes, then bore the glasses to their companions.

"To the wind!" Natalie cried as the men faced each other.

"Yes! More power to it!" Eliza echoed.

Trevor smiled. "I drink defiance."

"In my glass I see hope and confidence," O'Neil said. "May the storm profit him who most deserves help."

Despite their lightness, there was a certain gravity among the four, and as the night became more threatening, they felt a growing suspense. The men's restlessness communicated itself to the girls, who found themselves listening with almost painful intentness to the voice of the wind and the rumble of the surf, which grew louder with every hour. By bedtime, a torrent of rain was sweeping past, the roof strained, the windows were sheeted with water. Now and then the clamor ceased, only to begin with redoubled force. Trevor's guests were glad indeed of their snug shelter.

"It was fine of Mr. Trevor to treat Murray O'Neil so nicely," Natalie said as she prepared for bed. No one would dream they were rivals, or that one's success means the other's ruin. Now Gordon...." She turned to see her friend kneeling at the bedside and apologized quickly.

Eliza lifted her face and said simply, "I'm praying for the wind."

Natalie slipped down beside her and bowed her dark head close to the light one. They remained there for a long time, while outside the rain pelted, the surf roared, and the wind came shrieking in from the sea.

16

THE TEMPEST BEARS FRUIT

Neither O'Neil nor his host was in sight when the girls came to breakfast. The men had risen early and were somewhere out in the storm. A wilder day would be hard to imagine; a storm raged with rain whirling through the air like charges of shot. The mountains behind Kyak were invisible, and to seaward was nothing but a dimly discernible smother of foam and spray, for the crests of the breakers were snatched up and carried by the wind. The town was soaked as mud ran down the streets. Stovepipes were down, tents lay flattened in the mire, and the board houses were shaking as if they might fly to pieces at any moment. The darkness was uncanny, and the tempest seemed to be steadily growing in violence.

When an hour or two had passed with no word from the men, Eliza said she was going to look for them. She had spent most of her time since waking at a window, straining her eyes through the turbulence, while Natalie had curled up cozily with a book in one of Trevor's armchairs.

"But, dearie, you'll be drenched," Natalie said, as she looked up in surprise. "Mr. O'Neil is all right."

"Of course he is. I'm not going out to spank him and bring him in. I want to look at the storm."

"So do I, but it won't do any good. I can't make it blow any harder by getting my feet wet."

"You read your novel and talk to Mr. Trevor when he comes back. He knows we're to blame for this storm, so you must be nice to him. I can't."

She pulled on a raincoat, sou'wester, and boots, and hurried out. Walking was difficult enough, even in the shelter of the village, but not until she had reached the beach did she meet the full strength of the gale. Here it wrapped her garments about her limbs until she could scarcely move. The rain came horizontally and blinded her; the wind fairly snatched her breath away and oppressed her lungs like a heavy weight. She shielded herself as best she could, and by clinging to stationary objects and watching her chance she managed to work her way onward. At last she caught sight of O'Neil standing high above the surf, facing the wind defiantly, as if daring it to topple him. He saw her and came in answer to her signal. But to breast that wind was like stemming a rushing torrent, and when he reached her side, he was panting.

"Child! What are you doing here?" he demanded.

"I couldn't wait any longer," she shouted back. "You've been out since daylight. You must be wet through."

He nodded. "I lay awake all night listening. So did Trevor. He's beginning to worry already."

"Already? If the breakwater stands this...."

"The storm hasn't half started. Come! We'll watch it together."

He took her hand, and they lunged into the gale, battling their way back to his point of vantage. He paused at length, and with his arm about her pointed to the milk-white chaos that marked Trevor's handiwork. The rain pelted against their faces and streamed from their slickers.

The breakwater lay like a reef, and over it the sea was pounding in mighty wrath. High into the air the waters rose, only to disappear on the bosom of the gale. They engulfed the structure bodily, they raced along it with thunderous detonations, bursting in a lather of rage. Out beyond, the billows appeared to be sheared flat by the force of the wind, yet that ceaseless upheaval of spume showed the ocean was in furious tumult. For moments at a time the whole scene was blotted out by the scud, then the curtain would tear apart, and the wild scene would leap up again before their eyes.

Eliza screamed a question at her companion, but he did not seem to hear. His eyes roved back and forth along that lace-white ridge of rock on the weakness of which depended his salvation. She had never seen him so fierce, so hawklike, so impassive.

The gusts shook him, his garments slatted viciously, every rag beneath his outer covering was sodden, yet he continued to face the tempest as indifferently as he had faced it since dawn. The girl thrilled at thought of the issue these mighty forces were fighting out before her eyes, and of what it meant to the man beside her. His interests became hers. She shared his painful excitement. Her warm flesh chilled as the moisture embraced her limbs. But her heart was light, for O'Neil's strong arm encircled her, and her body lay against his.

After a long time he spoke.

"See? It's coming up!" he shouted.

She felt no increase in the wind, but she noted particles of sand and tiny pebbles from the beach were flying with the salt raindrops. Her muscles began to tremble from the constant effort at resistance, and she was relieved when Murray looked about for a place of refuge. She pointed to a pile of bridge timbers, but he shook his head.

"They'll go flying if this keeps up." He dragged her into the shelter of a little knoll. Here the blasts struck them with diminished force, the roaring in their ears grew less, and the labor of breathing was easier.

Rousing himself from his thoughts, the man looked at the girl.

"Poor kid – you must be cold," he said.

"I'm freezing. But – please don't send me back." The face that met his was supplicating; the eyes were bluer than a spring day. He patted her dripping shoulder.

"Not until you're ready."

"This is grander than our trip past the glacier. That was merely dangerous, but this – this means something."

"There may be danger here if we expose ourselves. Look at that!"

High up beyond reach of the surf a dory had been dragged and left bottom up. Under this the wind found a fingerhold and sent it flying. Over and over it rolled, until a stronger gust caught it and sent it in huge leaps, end over end. It brought up against the timber pile with a crash and was held there as if by a mighty suction. Then the beams began to tremble and lift. The pile was disintegrated bit by bit, although it would have required many hands to move any one of its parts.

Even where the man and woman crouched the wind harried them like a hound pack, but by clinging to the branches of a gnarled juniper bush they held their position and let the spray whine over their heads.

"Farther west I've seen houses chained to the earth with ships' cables," he shouted in her ear. "To think of building a harbor in a place like this...."

"I prayed for you last night. I prayed for the wind to come," the girl said after a time.

O'Neil looked at her, curiously startled, then he looked out at the sea once more. All in a moment he realized that Eliza was beautiful and that she had a heart. It seemed wonderful she should be interested in his fortunes. He was a lonely man. Beneath his open friendliness lay a deep reserve. A curiously warm feeling of gratitude flamed through him now, and he silently blessed her for bearing him company in the deciding hour of his life.

Noon came, and still the two crouched in their half-shelter, drenched, chilled, stiff with exposure, watching Kyak Bay lash itself into a boiling smother. The light grew dim, night was settling. The air seemed full of screaming furies. Then O'Neil noticed bits of driftwood racing in on the billows, and he rose with a loud cry.

"It's breaking up!" he shouted. "It's breaking up!"

Eliza lifted herself and clung to him, but she could see nothing except a misty confusion. In a few moments the flotsam came thicker. Splintered piling, huge square-hewn timbers with fragments of twisted iron or broken bolts came floating into sight. A confusion of wreckage began to clutter the shore, and into it the sea churned.

The spray broke apart at length, and the watchers caught a brief glimpse of the tumbling ocean. The breakwater was gone. Over the place where it had stood the billows raced unhindered.

"Poor Trevor," O'Neil said. "Poor Trevor. He did his best, but he didn't know." He looked down to find Eliza crying. "What's this? I've kept you here too long?"

"No, no! I'm just glad—so glad. Don't you understand?"

"I'll take you back. I must get ready to leave."

"Leave? Where—"

"For New York! I've made my fight, and I've won." His eyes kindled feverishly. "I've won despite them all. I hold the key to a kingdom. It's mine—mine! I hold the gateway to an empire, and those who pass through must pay." The girl had never seen such fierce triumph in a face. "I saw it in a dream, only it was more than a dream." The wind snatched O'Neil's words from his lips, but he ran on. "I saw a deserted fishing village become a thriving city. I saw glaciers part to let pass a great traffic in men and merchandise. I saw the unpeopled north grow into a land of homes, of farms, of mining camps, where people lived and bred children. I heard the mountain passes echo to steam whistles and the whir of flying wheels. It was a wonderful vision that I saw, but my eyes were true. They called me a fool, and it took the sea and the hurricane to show them I was right." He paused, ashamed of his outburst, and, taking the girl's hand in his, went stumbling ahead of the storm.

Their limbs were cramped, their teeth chattered, as they wallowed through mire, and more than once they fell. Nearing Trevor's house, they saw what the storm had done. Kyak was nearly razed. Roofs had been ripped off, chimneys were down, glass was out. None but the most substantial log cabins had withstood the assault, and men were busied in various quarters trying to repair the damage.

They found Natalie beside herself with anxiety for their safety, and an hour later Trevor came in, soaked to the skin. He was tired and his face haggard.

"Well – she went out!" he said. "I saw a million dollars swallowed up in that sea."

They tried to comfort him, but the collapse of his work had left him dazed.

"God! I didn't think it could blow like this—and it isn't over yet. The town is flat."

"I'm sorry. You understand I sympathize?" Murray asked.

The engineer nodded. "You told me it blew here, and I thought I knew what you meant, but nothing could withstand those rollers."

"Nothing."

"You'll go East and see our people, I suppose?"

"At once."

"Tell them what you saw. They'll never understand from my reports. They're good people. If there's anything I can do...."

O'Neil took his hand warmly.

Two days later Murray bade the girls goodbye, and left, traveling light. They remained in Kyak so Eliza might complete her investigations.

Of all those who suffered by the storm, Curtis Gordon took his misfortune hardest. This had been a black season for him, indeed. Beginning with O'Neil's rivalry, everything had gone against him. He had dropped his coal interests at Kyak in favor of the copper mine because they failed to yield quick profits. Then he had learned the mine was valueless and realized it could not serve him much longer as a means of raising funds. Still, he had trusted that by taking a vigorous part in the railroad struggle he would be able either to recoup his fortunes or at least to affect a compromise in the shadow of which his fiasco at Hope would be forgotten. The truth about Hope Consolidated was not generally known to his stockholders yet, but a certain restlessness among them had become troublesome. The stream of money had diminished alarmingly, and it was largely because of this he had bought the McDermott right-of-way and moved to Kyak. And now, just as he had his affairs in shape for another and greater campaign of stock flotation, the storm had come to ruin him.

The bitterest element in his defeat was the realization that O'Neil, who had bested him at every turn, was destined to profit by the blow that crushed him. Defeat at the hands of the Copper Trust he would have accepted with a bit of grace. But the mere thought that Murray O'Neil, whom he considered in every way his inferior, had gained the upper hand was intolerable. It was in keeping with Gordon's character that instead of blaming his own judgment, he became furiously angry at the Trust for the mistake of its engineers and held them responsible for his desperate situation. That it was truly desperate he soon realized, since disaster to his railroad project meant his stockholders would be around his ears like a swarm of hornets. And once they understood the true situation at Hope, the complete collapse of his fortunes would surely follow.

During the days succeeding the storm, he scarcely knew where to turn, so harassed was he. Yet he never for a moment wavered in his resolve to make O'Neil pay for his interference and to exact a reckoning from Gloria Gerard.

Natalie's presence in Kyak confirmed his belief that O'Neil was interested in her, and he began to plan a stroke by which he could take revenge upon all three. It did not promise in any way to help him out of his financial straits, but at least it would give him a certain satisfaction.

He sent word to the girl he would like to see her.

—

17

THE PRINCE BECOMES A MAN

Gordon found his erstwhile ward greatly improved by her recent life. She was brown, vigorous, healthy. Her physical charms quickened his pulses.

"You must have a good reason for coming to see me," she began. "I don't flatter myself it is from affection."

"There you wrong me," he assured her, with the warm earnestness he so easily assumed. "I have always regarded you as a daughter."

"I have no faith in you."

"Exactly, and the knowledge distresses me. You and Gloria were a large part of my life. I can't bear to lose you. I hope—and I believe—her regard for me has changed no more than mine for her. It remains for me to regain yours."

"That is impossible. You had the chance...."

"My dear, you can't know my reasons for acting as I did at Omar. But those reasons no longer exist."

"Just what do you mean by that?" Natalie asked.

"I mean what I say. I'm ready to marry your mother."

"When?"

"At once. You shall plead my cause for me. You shall add your voice to mine."

"That isn't necessary. You know mother is only waiting for you. It means so much to her that she couldn't refuse."

"Doesn't it mean anything to you?"

Natalie nodded. "It means more to me than to anyone else, perhaps. I have been carrying a great burden, almost more than I can bear. Sometimes I've wished I were a man—for just long enough to make you pay. Oh yes," she continued, as he started to protest. "Don't let us begin this new life with any false conceptions; you may as well know I shall always hate you. We shall see very little of each other."

"Nonsense! I can't let you feel like that. I shan't rest until I win back your love and confidence."

She eyed him searchingly for a moment, then opened her lips to speak, but closed them.

"Well?" he prompted her. "Let us be frank with each other."

"I'm merely wondering how greatly your decision has been influenced by the storm and the fight at the railroad crossing. I understand how you feel toward Mr. O'Neil, and I know he means to crush you."

"Oh!" Gordon's face lighted.

"Yes! He has never said so, but I can feel it. I wonder if you have snatched us up in your extremity as a defense."

"Ridiculous! Your suspicions are insulting. I have nothing to fear from him, for he is broken, his credit is gone, he is in desperate straits."

"Are you in any better condition? How long can you fool your people with that pretense of a mine?"

Gordon flushed but affected scorn. "So! Have you and Gloria begun to balance my wealth against my love? If so...."

"You know she would marry you if you were penniless."

"I hope so—and, indeed, I can't believe her mercenary. Well, I shall say goodbye to Kyak, without idle regret, and we three shall return to Hope, where I can attack my problems with fresh courage. I can well afford my loss here, if by doing so I gain the woman of my desires."

"You want me to go with you?"

"Of course. You can't stay in Omar, knowing what you do about O'Neil. Remember, I shall be in the position of a father to you."

"Very well. It is the least I can do. Miss Appleton and I are returning to Omar in a few days. Will you go with us?"

"I shall be delighted, my dear." He smiled upon her in his most fatherly fashion, but she was far from feeling the assurance he meant to convey.

The 18-hour train ride from Chicago bore Murray O'Neil into New York on time, and he hastened directly to the Holland House, where the clerk greeted him as if he had run in from Yonkers instead of from the wilderness of the far northwest. His arrival was always the forerunner of great prosperity for the bellboys, and there was the customary struggle for his baggage.

An hour later, having bathed and changed clothes, he was whizzing toward lower Broadway with the roar of the subway in his ears. New York looked good to O'Neil, for this time he came not as a suppliant, but as a conqueror, and a deep contentment rested in his heart. More than once during the last two years he had made this flying trip across an ocean and a continent, but heretofore he had been burdened with worries and responsibilities. Always he had needed to gather his wits for some supreme effort; always there had been the urgent necessity of raising money. As the S. R. & N. had grown, his obligations had increased. And, while he had never returned empty-handed, no one but he knew at what cost of time and strength he had succeeded in financing his venture. Invariably he had left New York mentally and physically exhausted, and his days in the open had barely served to replenish his store of nervous energy for the next campaign.

As he looked back upon it all, he was amazed at his daring in attempting to finance a railroad out of his own pocket. But he had won, and the Trust had met with a sharp reverse in attempting to beat him at his own game. He held the winning card, and he looked out upon the world through eyes that were strained and weary, but complacent.

Mr. Herman Heidlemann was expecting him.

"You have the most confident way of arranging appointments from the other side of the world," he began, as O'Neil entered his office. "Steamships and railroads appear to be your obedient servants."

"Not always. I find railroads very troublesome at times."

"Well, you're on time to the minute," Heidlemann said. "Now tell me about Kyak. Trevor cables you were there during the storm that ruined us." The head of the copper syndicate did not look like a man facing ruin; in fact, he seemed more curious to hear of the physical phenomena of that hurricane than of its effect upon his fortunes.

"Kyak was a great mistake," he admitted when O'Neil had given him the particulars. "We're all agreed on that point. Some of our associates feel the whole Alaska enterprise has been a mistake — mines and all."

"Your mines are as good as they ever were, but Kyak is a long way from Wall Street, and you relied too much on other people's judgment."

"We have to rely on our experts."

"Of course. But that country must have a railroad."

"Must?" Heidlemann lifted his brows. "It has done very well without one so far. Our friends call us crazy for trying to build one, and our enemies call us thieves."

"You can't afford to give up."

"No. There's an element of pride in the matter, and I really believe the country does need transportation."

"You can't understand how badly it needs it."

"Yet it's a heavy load to carry, for a road will lose money for many years," Heidlemann said with conviction. "We were willing to wait until the agriculture and mining developed, even though the profit came only to our children. But — we have been misunderstood, abused by the press and the public. Even Congress is down on us. However, I suppose you came to tell me once more that Omar is the gateway and we need it."

O'Neil smiled. "That's hardly necessary now, is it? I own every inch of waterfront at that point, and there's no other harbor. My track will be laid to the glaciers by the time snow flies."

"Trevor reports a bridge is possible, although expensive."

"It will cost $2 million."

"I don't see how it can be built to withstand the ice."

"I'll guarantee to build it so it will hold."

"What is your proposition?" Heidlemann asked.

"I'll sell the S.R.&N. for $5 million and contract to complete the road within two years on a 10 percent commission."

"It has cost you about $3 million, I believe. That would leave you a handsome profit."

"One million for me, $1 million for my associates."

"What will the remaining hundred miles cost?"

"About $10 million. That will give me another million profit as contractor. My force and equipment are on the ground. I can save you money and a year's time."

Mr. Heidlemann's fingers drummed on top of his desk for a moment.

"You're a high-priced man, O'Neil," he said, finally.

"You've had experience with the other kind."

"Counting the money we've already sunk into this venture, the road would stand us about $20 million completed."

"It will cost $30 million to build from Cortez and take two years longer."

Mr. Heidlemann seemed to consider this for a moment. "We've had this matter before us almost constantly since the report of the storm," he said, at length. "And after deliberation, our directors have voted to do nothing just yet."

O'Neil's eyes widened in amazement.

"I don't understand."

"It's this way. Our engineers first recommended Cortez as a starting point, and we spent a fortune there. Then you attacked the other route, and we sent Trevor up to find if you were right and we were wrong. He recommended the Salmon River valley and told us he could build a breakwater at Kyak. You know the result. We relied on him, for he seemed to be the best man in the country, but as a matter of precaution, we later sent other engineers. Their reports came in not three months ago, and, while all seemed confident the breakwater could be built, none of them were certain about the bridge. One, in fact, condemned it absolutely. Now on the heels of their statements comes the news the very work they united in declaring feasible has been undone. Naturally, we don't know where we are or whom to believe."

"They simply didn't know the conditions at Kyak," O'Neil said, "and they evidently haven't studied the bridge as I have. But you'll have to go at the breakwater again or build in from Cortez or give up."

"No, we have decided to mark time until that crossing is proved feasible. Understand, I voice the sentiment of the majority."

"If I build that bridge you may find it more difficult to buy me out," O'Neil said quietly.

"We'll have to take our medicine," Mr. Heidlemann replied, without heat. "We cannot afford another mistake."

"This is definite?"

"Oh, absolutely. We're going slow for a time."

A blow in the face could not have affected O'Neil more disagreeably than this statement. Fortune had seemed within his grasp when he entered the room; now ruin was more imminent than it had ever been before. The ground seemed to be slipping from beneath his feet. He felt dizzy. He thought himself utterly incapable of raising the $2 million necessary to carry his road to a point where the Trust would consider a purchase, yet to fail meant the loss of all he had put in. He knew also these men would never recede from a position once taken.

"Hasn't this public clamor had something to do with your determination?" he asked.

"A great deal. We had the best intentions when we started—we still have—but it's time to let the general sentiment cool. We thought we were doing a fine thing for the country in opening Alaska, but it seems we're regarded as thieves and grafters. One gets tired of abuse after a while."

"Will you take an option on the S. R. & N. conditional upon the building of the bridge?"

"We couldn't very well do that. Remember you are our rival." Heidlemann smiled in his recognition of the fact the rivalry was friendly. "To do so would fan excitement at Washington to a white heat. We'd then be in the position they now accuse us of occupying, and that would have a serious bearing on the coal situation. No, we can't help you, O'Neil, but rest assured we won't do anything to hinder you. You have treated us fairly; we will reciprocate. Once you have

THE PRINCE BECOMES A MAN

built your bridge, we can discuss a purchase and the abandonment of our original enterprise, but meanwhile we must proceed cautiously. It is unfortunate for us all."

"Especially for me."

"You need money badly, don't you?"

"I'm worse than broke," O'Neil admitted.

"I'd really be sorry to take over the wreck of your enterprise," Heidlemann said, earnestly, "for you have made a good fight, and your ideas were better than ours. I'd much prefer to pay your price than to profit by your misfortune. We don't feel that way about Gordon."

"There would be no uncertainty about the bridge if I had the money. With your means I could build a road to the moon, and double track it."

Although Murray felt further effort was useless, he continued to argue the matter from various angles, hoping against hope to sway Heidlemann's decision. But he gave up at last. Out in the marble hall that led to the elevators he discovered all his vigor of an hour ago had passed. The spring was out of his limbs; he walked slowly, like an old man. A glimpse of his image in the mirrors of the car as he shot downward showed him a face grave and haggard. The crowds jostled him, but he was hardly conscious of them. The knowledge his hardest fight was yet to come filled him with sickening apprehension. He was like a runner who toes the mark for a final heat knowing himself to be on the verge of collapse.

The magnitude of the deal narrowed his field of operations alarmingly, and he had already learned what a serious effect upon capital the agitation about Alaska had produced. More than once he had found men who were willing to invest but feared the effect of public sentiment. Popular magazines, newspapers like *The Review*, and writers like Eliza Appleton had been largely to blame for the wrong. They had misunderstood the problem and misinterpreted the spirit of commercial progress. But, strangely enough, he felt no bitterness at thought of Eliza. To the contrary, his heart softened in a sort of friendly yearning for her company. He would have liked to talk the matter over with her.

Looking the situation squarely in the face, he realized he must face a crash or raise $2 million within the next month. That meant $70 thousand a day. It was a man-size task.

He bought himself a cigar at the corner, hailed a taxicab, and was driven all the way up town to the Holland House. Once there, he established himself in that corner of the men's café that he always frequented.

The waiter who served him lingered to say:

"It's good to see you back in your 'office' again. You've been a long time away, sir."

O'Neil smiled as he left a silver dollar on the tray.

"It's good to be back, Joe," he said. "This time I may not leave."

18

THE MAN BECOMES A PRINCE AGAIN

Despite the most tormenting worries, O'Neil had the faculty of sleeping well. He arose on the morning after his interview with Mr. Heidlemann ready to begin the struggle with all his normal energy and confidence. But the day brought him only discouragement. He had a large acquaintance, the mention of his name in quarters where he was not personally known gained him respectful attention. But he found himself working in the shadow of the Copper Trust, and its silent influence overcame his strongest arguments. One banker expressed the general attitude by saying:

"If the Heidlemanns were not in the field we might help you, but it would be financial suicide to oppose them."

"There's no opposition about it," Murray assured him. "If I build that bridge, they'll buy us out."

At this his hearer naturally wished to know why, if the bridge were indeed feasible, the Heidlemanns delayed action. And O'Neil had to fall back on a recital of the facts, realizing perfectly they failed to carry conviction.

No one, it seemed, cared to risk even a semblance of rivalry with that monstrous aggregation of capital, for the interlacing of financial interests was amazingly intricate, and financiers were fearful of the least misstep. Everywhere O'Neil encountered the same disheartening timidity. His battle, it seemed, had been lost before it was begun.

Days passed in fruitless endeavors; evenings found O'Neil in his corner of the Holland House Cafe racking his brain for some way out of his perplexities. Usually he was surrounded by friends, for he continued to entertain in the lavish fashion for which he had gained a reputation. But sometimes he was alone, and then his solitude became more oppressive than it had ever been even in the farthest wastes of the northland. He was made to feel his responsibility with dreadful keenness, for his associates were in a panic and bombarded him with daily inquiries, vexatious and hard to answer. He had hoped in this extremity they might give him some practical help, and they did make a few half-hearted attempts, only to meet the same discouragements as he. At last they left him to carry the burden alone.

One week, two weeks went by. He was in constant cable communication with Omar, but not even the faithful Dr. Gray knew the dire straits in which his chief was struggling. Work on the S. R. & N. was going forward as usual. The organization was running at its highest efficiency. Rails were being laid, and gangs of rock workers were preparing the grade beyond the glaciers. Yet every day that passed, every paycheck drawn brought ruin closer. Nevertheless, O'Neil continued to joke and chat with the men who came to his table in the cafe and kept his business appointments with his customary cheerfulness. The waiters who attended him rejoiced in his usual princely tips.

One evening as he ran through his mail, he found a letter in a woman's handwriting and, glancing at the signature, started. It was signed "Gloria Gordon." Briefly it apprised him of her marriage and of her and Natalie's return to Hope. Gloria thanked him perfunctorily for his many kindnesses, but she neither expressed nor implied an invitation for him to visit them. He smiled a little grimly — already her loyalty had veered to Gordon's side, and Natalie no doubt shared her feeling. Well, it was but natural, perhaps. It would be unreasonable to expect them to sacrifice their desires, and what they now seemed to consider their interests, to a business quarrel they could hardly be

THE MAN BECOMES A PRINCE AGAIN

expected to understand. He could not help feeling hurt the women should so readily exchange his friendship for the protection of his bitterest enemy, but—they were helpless, and he had helped them. Let it rest at that. He was really troubled, however, they had been so easily deceived. If they had only waited - if only he had been able to advise them! For Gordon's intention was plain.

He was aroused from his train of thought by a stranger standing beside his table and looking down at him with wavering eye.

"Misser O'Neil, ain't it?" the fellow inquired. "Sure! Thought I knew you. I'm Bulker, of the old North Pass. Remember me?"

Mr. Bulker had been imbibing freely. He showed evidence of a protracted spree not only in his speech, but in the trembling hand he extended. His eyes were bloodshot, and his good-natured face was purple.

O'Neil greeted him pleasantly, and, considering himself enthusiastically welcomed, the newcomer sat down suddenly, as if someone had tripped him.

"Been washing you for 10 minutes."

"Washing me?"

"No! *Washing* you. Couldn't make you out—eyesight's getting bad. Too many bright lights in this town. Ha! Joke! Let's have a gill."

"Thank you, no."

"Must have a little dram for old time's sake. You're the only one of the North Pass crowd I'll drink with." Mr. Bulker gestured comprehensively at a group of waiters, and Murray yielded. "You were my friend, O'Neil. You always treated me right."

"What are you doing now?" asked O'Neil, with the interest he could not refuse to anyone who had ever worked with him. He remembered the fellow perfectly. He had come on from the East as auditor, and had appeared to be capable, although somewhat given to drink.

"I'm a broker. Wall Street's my habitat. Fine time to buy stocks, Misser O'Neil." Bulker assumed an expression of great wisdom. "Like to have a tip? No? Good! You're a wise man. They fired me from the North Pass. Wha'd you know about that? Fired me for drinking! Greatest injustice I ever heard of, but I hit running, like a turkey. That wasn't the reason they let me go, though. Not on your life!" He winked portentously, and strangely enough his eyelid failed to resume its normal position. It continued to droop, giving the appearance of a waggish leer. "I knew too mush! Isn't healthy to know too mush, is it?"

"I've never had a chance to find out," O'Neil said with a smile.

"Oh, don't be an ingenue; you savvied more than anybody on the job. I'll admit I took a nip now and then, but I never got pickled. Say! Who d'you s'pose I saw today? Old man Illis!"

O'Neil became suddenly intent. He had been trying to get in touch with Poultney Illis for more than a fortnight, but his cables to London had brought no response.

"When did he arrive?"

"Just lately. He's a game old rooster, ain't he? Gee, he's sore!"

"Sore about what?"

Bulker winked again, with the same lack of muscular control.

"About that North Pass deal, of course. He was blackmailed out of a cold million. The agreement's about up now, and I figure he's over here to renew it."

"You're talking Greek," said O'Neil. But his eagerness was manifest.

"I s'posed you knew. The North Pass has been paying blackmail to the Yukon steamboat companies for three years. When you built the line, it practically put 'em out of the Dawson market, understand?"

"Of course."

Now that Mr. Bulker's mind was running along well-worn grooves, his intoxication became less apparent.

"Those Frisco steamboat men got together and started a rate war against the railroad. They hauled freight to Dawson by way of St. Michaels at a loss. Of course, Illis and his crowd had to meet competition, and it nearly broke 'em the first two seasons. Gee, they were the mad ones! Finally they fixed up an agreement—had to or go bust—and of course the Native Sons put it over our English cousins. They agreed to restore the old rate, and each side promised to pay the other a royalty of $10 a ton on all the freight it hauled to Dawson and upriver points. You can guess the result, can't you? The steamboat companies let Illis haul all the freight and sat back on their haunches and took their profit. For every ton he hauled he slipped 'em ten round American dollars, stamped with the Goddess of Liberty. Oh, it was soft! When they had him fairly tied up, they drydocked their steamboats to save wear and tear. He paid 'em $1,000 a day for three years. If that ain't blackmail, it's a first cousin to it by marriage."

"Didn't the Interstate Commerce Commission get wise?"

"Certainly not. It looks wise, but it never *gets* wise. Oh, believe me, Poultney Illis is hopping mad. I s'pose he's over here now to renew the arrangement for another three years on behalf of his stockholders. Let's have a dram." Bulker sat back and stared as through a mist at his companion, enjoying the effect of his disclosure.

O'Neil was indeed impressed—more deeply than his informant dreamed. Out of the lips of a drunken man had come a hint that set his nerves to tingling. He knew Illis well, he knew the caliber of the Englishman, and a plan was already leaping in his brain whereby he might save his railroad.

It lacked an hour of midnight when O'Neil escaped from Bulker and reached his room. Once inside, he seized the telephone and rang up hotel after hotel, inquiring for the English capitalist, but without result. After a moment's consideration he took his hat and gloves and went out. The matter did not permit any delay. Not only were his own needs imperative, but if Poultney Illis had come from London to confer with his rivals there was little time to spare.

Remembering the Englishman's habits, O'Neil turned up the avenue to the Waldorf, where he asked for the manager, whom he well knew.

"Yes, Mr. Illis is here," he was informed, "but he's registered under a different name. No doubt he'll be glad to see you, however."

A moment later O'Neil recognized the voice of Illis' valet over the wire and greeted him by name. Another brief delay, and the capitalist himself was at the phone.

"Come right up," he said. O'Neil replaced the receiver with a sigh of relief.

Illis greeted him warmly, for their relations had been close.

"Lucky you found me," he said. "I'm going back on the next sailing."

"Have you signed up with the Arctic Navigation Company?" O'Neil asked.

"Bless me!" Illis said with a start. "What do you mean?"

His caller laughed. "I see you haven't. I don't think you will, either, after you've talked with me."

"My word!" Illis exclaimed without the tremor of an eyelash. "What are you driving at?"

"That agreement over freight rates, of course."

The Briton eyed him for a moment, then carefully closed the door leading from his sitting room. After seating himself, he lit a cigar.

"What do you know about that matter?" he asked, quietly.

"About all there is to know — enough, at least, to appreciate your feelings."

"I flattered myself that my affairs were private. Where did you get your information?"

"I'll tell you if you insist, although I'd rather not. There's no danger of it becoming public."

Illis showed his relief. "I'm glad. You gave me a start. Rotten fix for a man to be in. Why, I'm here under an assumed name. Fancy! But...," he waved his hand in a gesture that showed his acceptance of the inevitable.

"You haven't made your new agreement?"

"I'm to meet Blum and Capron tomorrow."

"Why didn't you take the S. R. & N. when I cabled you last month?"

"I couldn't. But what has that to do with the matter?"

"Don't you see? It's so plain to me I can't understand how you failed to realize the value — the necessity of buying my road."

"Explain, please."

"Gladly. The North Pass & Yukon is paying a fabulous blackmail to the river lines to escape a ruinous rate war."

"Right! It's blackmail, as you say."

"Under the present agreement, you handle the Dawson freight

THE MAN BECOMES A PRINCE AGAIN

and keep out of the lower river; they take the whole Tanana valley and lower Yukon."

"Correct."

"Didn't it occur to you the S.R.& N., which starts 400 hundred miles west of the North Pass and taps the Tanana valley, can be used to put the river steamers of that section out of business?"

"Let's have a look at the map." Mr. Illis hurried into an adjoining room and returned with a huge chart he unrolled on the table. "To tell you the truth, I never looked at the proposition from that angle. Our people were afraid of those glaciers and the competition of the Copper Trust. They're disgusted, too, with our treatment."

"The Trust is eliminated. Kyak harbor is wiped off the map, and I'm alone in the field."

"How about this fellow Gordon?"

"He'll be broke in a year. Incidentally, that's my trouble."

"But I'm told you can't pass the glaciers."

"I can. Parker says he'll have the bridge done by spring."

"Then I'd bank on it. I'd believe Parker if I knew he was lying. If you both agree, I haven't the slightest doubt."

"This is a bigger proposition than the North Pass, Mr. Illis. You made money out of that road, but this one will make more." He swiftly outlined the condition of affairs, even to the attitude assumed by the Heidlemanns. Illis, knowing the speaker as he did, had no doubt he was hearing the exact truth. "But that's not all," continued O'Neil. "The S. R. & N. is the club that will hammer your enemies into line. That's what I came to see you about. With a voice in it, you can control the traffic of all central Alaska and force the San Francisco crowd to treat the N. P. & Y. fairly, thereby saving half a million a year."

"It's a big undertaking. I'm not sure our crowd could swing it."

"They don't have to. There's a quick profit of $2 million to be had by selling to the Trust next spring. You can dictate your own terms to those blackmailers tomorrow, and then make a turn-over in nine months. It doesn't matter who owns the S. R. & N. after it's completed. The steamboat men will see their profits cut. As it is now, they can make enough out of their own territory to haul freight into yours for nothing."

"I dare say you'll go to them if we don't take you up, eh?"

"My road has its strategic value. I must have help. If you don't come to my rescue, it will mean war with your line, I dare say."

Mr. Illis sat back, staring at the ceiling for a long time. From the street below came the whir and clatter of taxicabs as the midnight crowd came and went. The city's nocturnal life was at its height; men had put aside the worries of the day and were devoting themselves to the more serious and exhausting pastimes of relaxation. Still the white-haired Briton weighed in his mind the matter of millions, while the fortunes of Murray O'Neil hung in the balance.

"My people won't buy the S. R. & N.," Illis finally announced. "But I'll put it up to them."

"I can't delay action if there's a chance of a refusal. I'll have to see Blum and Capron," O'Neil said.

"I'll cable full details within the hour. We'll have an answer by tomorrow night."

"And if they refuse?" O'Neil lit a cigar with steady fingers.

"Oh, if they refuse, I'll join you. We'll go over the matter carefully in the meantime. Two million you said, didn't you?"

"Yes. There's $2 million profit for you in nine months." His voice was husky and a bit uneven, for he had been under a great strain.

"Good! You don't know how resentful I feel toward Blum and his crowd. I—I'm downright angry. I am that."

Illis took the hand his caller extended with an expressionless face.

"I'm glad I found you," O'Neil said. "I was on my last legs. Herman Heidlemann will pay our price when the last bridge bolt is driven home, and he'll pay with a smile on his face—that's the sort of man he is."

"He won't pay if he knows I'm interested. We're not exactly friendly since I sold out my smelter interests. But he needn't know—nobody need know."

Illis called his valet and instructed him to rouse his secretary and ring for some cable blanks.

"I think I'll cable, too," O'Neil told him. "I have some boys up there who are working in the dark with their teeth shut. They're waiting for the crash, and they'd like to hear the good news."

His fingers shook as he scrawled the name of Doctor Gray, but his eyes were bright, and youth was singing in his heart once more.

"Now let's get down to business," Mr. Illis said. "We'll have to talk fast."

It was growing light in the east when O'Neil returned to the Holland House – but he felt no fatigue, and he laughed from the pure joy of living, for his dream seemed to be coming true.

19

MISS APPLETON MAKES A SACRIFICE

Tom Slater came puffing up the hill to the Appleton bungalow, plopped himself into a chair, and sighed deeply. "What's the matter? Are you played out?" Eliza asked.

"No. I'm feeling like a colt."

"Any news from Omar Khayyam?"

"Not a word."

Eliza's brows drew together in a worried frown, for none of Murray's boys had awaited tidings from him with greater anxiety than she.

It had been a trying month for them all. Dr. Gray, upon whom the heaviest responsibility rested, had aged visibly under the strain. Parker, Mellen and McKay had likewise become worn and grave as the days passed and they saw disaster approaching. Even Dan was blue. And Sheldon, the light-hearted, had begun to lose interest in his commissary duties.

After the storm at Kyak, there had been a period of fierce rejoicing, which had ended abruptly with the receipt of O'Neil's curt cablegram announcing the attitude of the Trust. Gloom had succeeded the first surprise, deepening to hopeless despondency through the days that followed. Oddly enough, Slater had been the only one to bear up; under adversity he blossomed into a peculiar and almost offensive cheerfulness. It was characteristic of his crooked temperament that misfortune awoke in him a lofty and unshakable optimism.

"You're great on nicknames, ain't you?" he said to Eliza, regarding her with his never-failing curiosity. "Who's this Homer Keim you're always talking about?"

"He isn't any more: he *was* a cheerful old Persian poet."

"I thought he was Dutch, from the name. Well! Murray's cheerful, too. Him and me are alike in that. I'll bet he isn't worrying half so much as Doc and the others."

"You think he'll make good?"

"He never fails."

"But—we can't hold on much longer. Dan says some of the men are getting uneasy and want their money."

Tom nodded. "The men are all right—Doc has kept them paid up. It's the shift bosses. I say let 'em quit."

"Has it gone as far as that?"

"Somebody keeps spreading the story that we're busted, and Murray has skipped out. More of Gordon's work, I s'pose. Some of the sore heads are coming in this evening to demand their wages."

"Can we pay them?"

"Doc says he dare not. So I s'pose they'll quit. He should have fired 'em a week ago. Never let a man quit—always beat him to it. We could hold the roughnecks for another two weeks if it wasn't for these fellows, but they'll go back and start a stampede."

"How many are there?"

"About a dozen."

"I was afraid it was worse. There can't be much owing to them."

"Oh, it's bad enough! They've been letting their wages ride, that's why they got scared. We owe them about $4,000."

"They must be paid," Eliza said. "It will give Mr. O'Neil another two weeks—a month, perhaps."

"Doc's got his back up, and he's told the cashier to make 'em wait."

Eliza hesitated and flushed a little. "I suppose it's none of my business," she said, "but—couldn't you boys pay them out of your own salaries?"

Mr. Slater grinned—an unprecedented proceeding that lent his face an altogether strange and unnatural expression.

"Salary! We ain't had any salary," he said, cheerfully. "Not for months."

"Dan has drawn his regularly."

"Oh, sure! But he ain't one of us. He's an outsider."

"I see." Eliza's eyes were bright with a wistful admiration. "That's very nice of you men. You have a family, haven't you, Uncle Tom?"

"I have! Seven head, and they eat like a herd of stock. It looks like a lean winter for 'em if Murray don't make a sale—but he will. That isn't what I came to see you about, though. I've got my asking clothes on, and I want a favor."

"You shall have it, of course."

"I want a certificate."

"Of what?"

"Ill health. Nobody believes I had the smallpox."

"You didn't."

"Wh-what?" Tom's eyes opened wide. He stared at the girl in hurt surprise.

"It was nothing but pimples, Tom."

"Pimples!" He spat the word out indignantly, and his round cheeks grew purple. "I—I s'pose pimples gave me cramps and chills and backache and palpitation and swellings? Hunh! I had a narrow escape—narrow's the word. It was narrower than a knife edge! Anything I get out of life from now on is 'velvet,' for I was knocking at death's door. The grave yawned, but I jumped it. It's the first sick spell I ever had, and I won't be cheated out of it. Understand?"

"What do you want me to do?" the girl said as a smile spread across her face.

"You're a writer – write me an affidavit."

"I can't do that."

"Then put it in your paper. Put it on the front page, where folks can see it."

"I've quit *The Review*. I'm doing magazine stories."

"Well, that'll do. I'm not particular where it's printed so long as...."

Eliza shook her head. "You weren't really sick, Uncle Tom."

Mr. Slater rose to his feet.

"Don't call me 'Uncle!'" he shouted at her. "You're in with the others."

"It wouldn't be published if I wrote it."

"Then you can't be much of a writer." He glared at her, and slowly, distinctly, with all the emphasis at his command, continued his plea.

"I had smallpox—and a dam' bad case, understand? I was sick. I had miseries in every joint and cartage of my body. I'm going to use a pick handle for a cane, and anybody that laughs will get a hickory massage that'll take a crooked needle and a pair of pinchers to fix. Thank God I've got my strength back! You get me?"

"I do."

He snorted irately and turned to go, but Eliza checked him.

"What about those shift bosses?" she asked.

Slater rolled his eyes balefully. "Just let one of 'em mention smallpox," he said, "and I'll fill the hospital till it bulges."

"No, no! Are you going to pay them?"

"Certainly not."

Eliza considered for a moment. "Don't let them see Dr. Gray," she said, at length. "He has enough to worry him. Meet them at the train and bring them here."

"What for? Tea?"

"You boys have done all you can; I think it's time Dan and I did something."

Tom stared. "Are *you* going to pay 'em?" he asked.

"Yes. Mr. O'Neil needs time. Dan and I have saved $4,000. I'd offer it to Dr. Gray...."

"He wouldn't take it."

"Exactly. Send Dan up here when you see him."

"It doesn't seem exactly right." Tom was obviously embarrassed. "You see, we sort of belong to Murray, and you don't, but...." He shook his head as if to rid himself of unwelcome emotion. "Women are funny things! You're willing to do that for the chief, and yet you won't write me a little affidavit!" He grunted and went away, still shaking his head.

When Eliza explained her plan to Dan, she encountered an opposition that shocked and hurt her.

"I won't do it!" he said.

"What? We can't build the S. R...."

"Yes, and made you love him, too," Dan said. "I can see that."

Eliza lifted her head and met his eyes squarely.

"That's true! But why not? Can't I love him? Isn't it my privilege to help him if I want to? If I had $2 million instead of $2,000, I'd give it to him, and — and I wouldn't expect him to care for me, either. He'll never do that. He couldn't! But — oh, Danny, I've been miserable...."

Dan felt a certain dryness in his throat that made speech oddly difficult. "I don't see why he couldn't care for you," he said.

Eliza shook her head hopelessly. "I'm glad it happened," she said. "Glad. In writing these articles, I've tried to make him understood; I've tried to put my whole soul into them so the people will see that he isn't, wouldn't be, a thief nor a grafter. I've described him as he is — big, honorable, gentle...."

"I didn't know you were writing fiction," her brother said.

"I'm not. It's all true. I've cried over those articles, Dan. I've petted them, and I've kissed his name — oh, I've been silly!" She smiled at him through a sudden glimmer of tears.

Dan began to wonder if his sister, despite her exemplary conduct in the past, was after all going to have hysterics. Women were especially likely to, he reflected, when they demanded the impossible.

"Gee, I thought I was the dippy member of the family!" he said.

"It's our chance to help him," she urged. "Will you....?"

"No! I'm sorry, Sis, but my little bit wouldn't mean anything to him. It means everything to me. Maybe that's selfish — I don't care. I'm as mad over Natalie as you seem to be over him. A week's delay can't make any difference now — he played and lost. But I can't afford to lose. He'll make another fortune, that's sure — but do you think I'll ever find another Natalie? No! Don't argue, for I won't listen."

He left the house abruptly, and Eliza went into the white bedroom O'Neil had fitted up for her. From the remotest corner of her lowest bureau drawer she drew a battered tin box, and, dividing the money it contained into two equal parts, placed one in the pockets of her mannish jacket.

It was dark when Tom Slater arrived, at the head of a group of soiled workmen he ushered into the parlor of the bungalow.

"Here's the bunch!" he announced.

As the newcomers arranged themselves uncomfortably about the wall, Dan Appleton entered and greeted them with his customary breeziness.

"The pay-master is busy, and Doc Gray has a surgical case," he said. "So I'll cash your time checks. Get me the box, will you, Sis?"

He had avoided Eliza's eyes upon entering, and he avoided them now, but the girl's throat was aching as she hurried into her bedroom and hastily replaced the rolls of greenbacks she had removed from the tin box.

"Now we mustn't have any loafing around town, understand?" Dan said when he had finished paying off the men.

"We can't get back tonight," one of the men said.

"Oh yes, you can. I ordered an engine out."

"We hear — there's talk about quitting work," another ventured. "Where's O'Neil?"

"He's in the States buying a steamship," Dan said. "We can't get stuff fast enough by the regular boats."

"Good! That sounds like business. We don't want to quit."

"Now hurry! Your parlor car is waiting."

When he and Eliza were alone, he turned to her with a flush of embarrassment. "Aren't we the darnedest fools, Sis? I wouldn't mind if we had done the chief any good, but we haven't." He closed the lid of the tin box, which was nearly empty now, and pushed it away from him, laughing mirthlessly. "Hide that sarcophagus where I can't see it," he commanded. "It makes me sick."

Eliza flung her arm about his neck and laid her cheek against his. "Poor Danny! You're a brick!"

"It's the bread line for us," he told her.

"Never mind. We're used to it now." She laughed contentedly and snuggled her face closer to his.

It was on the following morning O'Neil's cablegram announcing the result of his interview with Illis reached Omar. Dr. Gray brought the news to the Appleton bungalow while Dan and his sister were still at breakfast. Happy Tom came puffing and blowing at his heels with a highly satisfied I-told-you-so expression on his round features.

"He made it! The tide has turned," cried the doctor as he burst in waving the message on high. "Yes!" he explained, in answer to their excited questions. "Murray got the money, and our troubles are over. Now give me some coffee, Eliza. I'm all shaky."

"English money!" Slater said. "The same as we used on the North Pass."

"Then he interested Illis!" Dan cried.

"Yep! He's the white-winged messenger of hope. I wasn't worried for a minute," Tom said.

The breakfast that followed was of a somewhat hysterical and fragmentary nature, for Eliza felt her heart swelling, and the faithful Gray was all but undone by the strain he had endured

"That's the first food I've tasted for weeks," Doc Gray confessed. "I've eaten, but I haven't tasted. And now—I'm not hungry." He sighed, stretched his long limbs gratefully, and eyed the Appletons with a kindly twinkle. "You were up in the air, too, weren't you? The chief will appreciate last night's affair."

Eliza colored faintly. "It was nothing. Please don't tell him." At the incredulous lift of his brows she hastened to explain: "Tom said you men 'belonged' to Mr. O'Neil and Dan was an outsider. That hurt me dreadfully."

"Well, he can't say that now. Dan is one of Murray's boys, all right, and you—you must be his girl."

At that moment Mellen and McKay burst into the bungalow, demanding the truth behind the rumor that had just come to their ears. There followed fresh explanations and rejoicings, through which Eliza sat quietly, thrilled by the note of genuine affection and loyalty that pervaded it all. But now that the general despondency had vanished and joy reigned in its place, Tom Slater relapsed into his habitual gloom and spoke forebodingly of the difficulties yet to be encountered.

"Murray don't say how *much* he's raised," he said. "It may be only a drop in the bucket. We'll have to go through all this again, probably, and the next time he won't find it so easy to sting a millionaire."

"We'll last through the winter anyhow...."

"Winter!" Slater shook his bald head. "Winter is hard on old men like me."

"We'll have the bridge built by spring, sure!" Mellen said.

"Maybe – I hope so. I wish I could last to see it, but the smallpox undermined me. Perhaps it's a mercy I'm so far gone; nobody knows yet whether the bridge will stand, and – I'd hate to see it go out."

"It won't go out," said the confident engineer.

"Maybe you're right. But that's what Trevor said about his breakwater. His work was done, and ours isn't hardly begun. By the way, Murray didn't say he *had* the money – he just said he expected to get it."

"Go out and hang your crepe on the roundhouse," Dan told him. "This is a jubilee. If you keep on rejoicing, you'll have us all in tears." When the others had gone, he turned to Eliza. "Why don't you want O'Neil to know about that money, Sis?" he asked, curiously. "When I'm a hero I like to be billed as one."

"Please!" She hesitated and turned her face away. "You – you are so stupid about some things."

That same afternoon Curtis Gordon found Natalie at a window staring out across the sound in the direction of Omar. He laid a warm hand on her shoulder.

"My dear, confess," he said. "You are lonesome."

She nodded silently.

"Well, well! We mustn't allow that. Why don't you run over to Omar and see your friend Miss Appleton? She has a cheerful way with her."

"I'm afraid things aren't very gay over there," Natalie said.

"Quite probably. But the fact O'Neil is on his last legs needn't interfere with your pleasure. A change will do you good."

"You are very kind," she murmured. "You have done everything to make me happy, but – it's autumn. Winter is coming. I feel dull and lonely and gray, like the sky. Are you sure Mr. O'Neil has failed?"

"Certainly. He tried to sell his holdings to the Trust, but they refused to consider it. Poor fellow!" he said. "Now that he's down, I pity him. One can't dislike a person who has lost the power of working harm. His men are quitting. I doubt if he'll dare show his face in this country again. But never mind all that. There's a boat leaving for Omar in the morning. Go – have a good time, return when you will, and tell us how they bear up under their adversity." He patted her shoulder affectionately and went up to his room.

It was true enough Natalie had been unhappy since returning to Hope—not even her mother dreamed how she rebelled at remaining here. She was lonely, uninterested, vaguely homesick. She missed the intimate companionship of Eliza. She missed Dan's extravagant courting and O'Neil's grave, respectful attentions. She also felt the loss of the honest, good fellowship of all those people at Omar whom she had learned to like and to admire. Life here was colorless and was still haunted by the shadow of that thing from which she and her mother had fled.

Gordon, indeed, had been generous to them both. Since his marriage his attitude had changed entirely. He was polite, agreeable, charmingly devoted. No ship arrived without some tangible and expensive evidence of his often-expressed desire to make his wife and stepdaughter happy. He anticipated their slightest wish. Under his assiduous attentions Natalie's distrust and dislike had slowly melted, and she came to believe she had misjudged him. There were times when he seemed to be overdoing the matter a bit, times when she wondered if his courtesy could be altogether disinterested. But these occasions were rare, and always she scornfully accused herself of disloyalty. As for Gloria, she was deeply content—as nearly happy, in fact, as a woman of her temperament could be, and in this the daughter took her reward.

Natalie arrived at Omar in time to see the full effect of the good news from New York and joined sincerely in the general rejoicing. She returned after a few days, bursting with the tidings of O'Neil's victory.

Gordon listened to her with keenest attention; he drew her out artfully, and when he knew what he had sent her to learn, he gave voice to his unwelcome surprise.

"Jove!" he snarled. "That beggar hoodwinked the Heidlemanns, after all. It's their money. What fools! What fools!"

Natalie looked up quickly.

"Does it affect your plans?" she asked.

"Yes — in a way. It consolidates my enemies."

"You said you no longer had any ill feeling toward Mr. O'Neil."

Gordon had resumed his usual suavity. "When I say enemies," he qualified, "of course, I mean it only in a business sense. I heard the Trust had withdrawn, discouraged by their losses, but now that they re-enter the field, I shall have to fight them. They would have done well to consult me — to buy me off, rather than be bled by O'Neil. They shall pay well for their mistake, but — it's incredible! That man has the luck of the devil."

That evening he and Denny sat with their heads together until a late hour, and when they retired, Gordon had begun to whip new plans into shape.

20

GORDON CHANGES HIS ATTACK

Murry O'Neil's return to Omar was triumphal. All his lieutenants gathered to meet him at the pier and the sincerity of their welcome stirred him deeply. His arrangements with Illis had taken time; he had been delayed at Seattle by bridge details and the placing of steel contracts. He had worked swiftly, and with such absorption he had paid little heed to the rumors of Gordon's latest activities. Of the new venture his own success had inspired he knew only the bare outline. He had learned enough, however, to arouse his curiosity, and as soon as the first confusion of his arrival at the front ended, he asked for news.

"Haven't you read the papers?" Happy Tom asked. He had attached himself to O'Neil from the moment he stepped ashore, and now followed him to headquarters, with an air of melancholy satisfaction in mere physical nearness to his chief.

"Barely," O'Neil confessed. "I've been working 20 hours a day getting that steel under motion."

"Gordon is a remarkable man. It's a pity he's crooked," Dr. Gray said.

"I think it's dam' lucky," Tom said. "He's smarter than us, and if he wasn't handicapped by a total lack of decency, he'd beat us."

"After the storm, he moved back to Hope," Gray said. "And we thought he'd made his last bow. But somehow, he got the idea the Trust was back of us."

"So I judged from the little I read."

"Well, we didn't undeceive him, of course. His first move was an attack through the press in the shape of a broadside against the Heidlemanns. It fairly took our breaths. It appeared in the *Cortez Courier* and all over the States, we hear—a letter of defiance to Herman Heidlemann. It declared the Trust was up to its old tricks here in Alaska had gobbled the copper, had the coal tied up under secret agreements, and was trying to get possession of all the coast range passes and defiles—the old story. But the man can write. That article caused a stir."

"I saw it."

"Naturally, the Cortez people ate it up. They're sore at the Trust for leaving their town, and at us for building Omar. Then Gordon called a mass meeting, and some of us went up to watch the fireworks. I've never seen anything quite like that meeting; every man, woman, and child in the city was there, and they hissed us when we came in. Gordon knew what he was about, and he was in fine voice. He told them Cortez was the logical point of entry to the interior of Alaska and ought to have all the traffic. He fired their animosity toward the Trust and accused us of basely selling out to it. Then he broached a project to build, by local subscription, a narrow-gauge electric line from Cortez, utilizing the waterfalls for power. The idea caught on and went like wildfire. The people cheered themselves hoarse and pledged him over $100,000 that night. Since then they have subscribed as much more, and the town is crazy. Work has begun – they hope to reach the first summit by Christmas."

Slater broke in.

"He's a spellbinder, all right. He made me hate the Heidlemanns and detest myself for five minutes. I wasn't even sure I liked *you*, Murray."

"It's a wild scheme, of course," continued the doctor. "But he's putting it over. The town council has granted him a 99-year lease covering every street. The roadbed is started, and things are booming. Lots have been staked all over the flats, property values are somersaulting, everybody is out of his head, and Gordon is a god. All he does is organize new companies. He has bought a sawmill, a wharf, a machine shop, acres of real estate. He has started a bank and a new hotel; he has consolidated the barber shops; and he talks about roofing in the streets with glass and making the town a series of arcades."

Slater half smiled—evidence of a convulsive mirth within.

"They've even picked out a site for a university!" he said. "Cortez is going to be a seat of learning and culture. They're planning a park and a place for an Alaska World's Fair and a museum and a library. I've always wondered who starts public libraries—it's nuts. But I didn't s'pose more than one or two people got foolish that way."

O'Neil drew from his pocket a newspaper five days old, which he unfolded and opened at a full-page advertisement.

"This is running in all the coast papers," he said and then read it to his men.

CORTEZ HOME RAILWAY

OUR PLATFORM:

- No promotion shares. No construction profits.
- No bonds. No incompetence.
- No high-salaried officials. No monopoly.
- No passes or rebates. No graft.

OF ALASKA, BY ALASKA, FOR ALASKA

There was much more of a similar kind, written to appeal to the quick-profit-loving public, and it was followed by a violent attack on the Trust and an appeal to the people of Seattle for assistance at $1 per share.

"Listen to this," O'Neil said, and then continued reading.

Among the original subscribers are the following:

Hotels and saloons of Cortez $17,000
City Council $15,000
Prospectors.................................... $7,000
Ladies' Guild of Cortez $740
Schoolchildren of Cortez................. $420

Tom grew red in the face and gave his characteristic snort. "I don't mind his stringing the City Council and the saloons, and even the Ladies' Guild," he growled. "But when he steals licorice and slate pencils from the kids it's time he was stopped."

Murray agreed. "I think we are about done with Gordon. He has led his ace."

"I'm not sure. This is a kind of popular uprising, like a camp meeting. If I went to Cortez now, some prattling schoolgirl would wallop me with her dinner bucket. We can't shake Gordon loose – he's a regular splavvus."

"What is a splavvus, Tom?" Dr. Gray asked.

"It's a real peculiar animal, being a cross between a bulldog and a skunk. We have lots of 'em in Maine!"

O'Neil soon found the accounts he had received of Gordon's last attempt to recoup his fortunes were in no way exaggerated. Cortez,

Courtesy Alaska State Library

THE FIRST RAIL FOR THE ALASKA HOME RY. SEPT. 16-07.

The first track for the Home Railway, seen here, was laid on Sept. 16, 1907 in Valdez.

long the plaything of the railroad builders, had been ripe for his touch. It rose in its wounded civic pride and greeted his appeal with frantic delight. It was quite true the schoolchildren had taken stock in the enterprise, their parents turned their own pockets inside out, and subscriptions came in a deluge. The price of real estate doubled, quadrupled, and Gordon bought just enough to establish the price firmly. The money he paid was deposited again in his new bank, and he proceeded to use it over and over in maintaining exorbitant prices and in advancing his grandiose schemes.

His business took him often to Seattle, whereby his whirlwind methods allowed him to duplicate his success. His sensational attack on the money powers got a wide hearing, and he finally secured an indorsement of his scheme by the Businessmen's Association. This done, he opened splendid offices and began a widespread stock flotation campaign. Soon the Cortez Home Railway became known as a mighty, patriotic effort of Alaskans to throw off the shackles of oppression.

Gordon perfectly understood that something more than vague accusations would be necessary to bring the public to his support in sufficient numbers to sweep him on to victory. He laid crafty plans to seize the Heidlemann grade. The Trust had ceased active work on its old right-of-way and moved to Kyak, to be sure, but it had not abandoned its original route. It had maintained a small crew at the first defile outside of Cortez, known as Beaver Canyon. Gordon reasoned shrewdly a struggle between the agents of the Trust and the patriotic citizens of the town would afford him precisely the advertising he needed and give point to his charge of unfair play against the Heidlemanns.

It was not difficult to incite his victims to this act of robbery. On the contrary, once he suggested it, he had hard work to restrain them, until he had completed his preparations. These preparations were simple. They consisted in writing and mailing to every newspaper of consequence a highly colored account of the railroad struggle. These mimeographed stories were posted from Seattle in time for them to reach their destinations on the date set for the seizure of the grade.

It was an ingenious publicity move, worthy of a theatrical press agent, and it succeeded beyond the promoter's expectations—too well, in fact, for it drove the Trust in desperation to an alliance with the S. R. & N.

When the day set for the demonstration came, the citizens of Cortez boldly marched into Beaver Canyon to take possession of the old Heidlemann workings. But it appeared they had reckoned prematurely. A handful of grim-faced Trust employees warned them back.

There was a rush, some rough work on the part of the aggressors, and then the guards brought their weapons into play. The result afforded Gordon far more sensational material than he had hoped for. One citizen died and five others were badly wounded. Cortez, dazed and horror-stricken, arose in her wrath and descended upon the assassins. Mobs planned to lynch those involved and threatened the local jail until soldiers arrived and martial law declared.

Of course, the wires buzzed with the accounts. The reading public of the States awoke to news that a bitter strife was waging in the north between honest miners and the soulless Heidlemann syndicate. Gordon's previously written and carefully colored stories of the clash were printed far and wide. Editorials breathed indignation at such lawlessness and pointed to the Cortez Home Railway as a commendable effort to destroy the Heidlemann throttlehold on the northland. Stock subscriptions came in a deluge that engulfed Gordon's Seattle office force.

During this brief white-hot campaign, the promoter had been motivated as much by his senseless hatred of O'Neil as by lust for glory and gain, and it was with no little satisfaction that he returned to Alaska conscious of having dealt a telling blow to his enemy. He sent Natalie to Omar on another visit in order that he might hear firsthand how O'Neil took the matter. But his complacency received a shock when the girl returned. He had no need to question her.

"Uncle Curtis," she began, excitedly, "you ought to stop these terrible newspaper stories about Mr. O'Neil and the Trust."

"Stop them? My dear, what do you mean?"

"He didn't sell out to the Trust. He has nothing to do with it."

"What?" Gordon's incredulity was a challenge.

"He sold to an Englishman named Illis. They seem to be amused by your mistake over there at Omar, but I think some of the things printed are positively criminal. I knew you'd want the truth...."

"The truth, yes! But this can't be true," Gordon stammered.

"It is. Mr. O'Neil did try to interest the Heidlemanns, but they wouldn't have anything to do with him, and the S. R. & N. was going to smash when Mr. Illis came along, barely in time. It was too exiting and dramatic for anything the way Mr. O'Neil found him when he was in hiding."

"Hiding?"

"Yes. There was something about blackmail, or a secret arrangement between Mr. Illis and the Yukon River lines — I couldn't understand just what it was — but, anyhow, Murray took advantage of it and saved the North Pass and the S. R. & N. at the same time. It was really a perfectly wonderful stroke of genius. I determined at once that you should stop these lies and correct the general idea he is in the pay of the Trust. Why, he went to Cortez last week and they threatened his life!"

Mrs. Gordon had been listening.

"Don't blame Curtis for that," she told her daughter. "That bloody battle at Beaver Canyon has made Cortez bitter against everyone connected with the Heidlemanns."

"What about this blackmail?" asked her husband, upon whose ear the word had made a welcome impression. "I don't understand what you mean by O'Neil's saving the North Pass and his own road at the same time — nor Illis's being in hiding."

"Neither do I." Natalie confessed. "But I know you have made a mistake that ought to be set right."

"Why doesn't he come out with the truth?"

"The whole thing is secret."

"Why?"

Natalie shrugged hopelessly, and Gordon lost himself in frowning thought.

"This is amazing," he said, brusquely, after a moment. "It's vital. It affects all my plans. I must know everything at once."

"I'm sorry I paid so little attention."

"Never mind. Try it again and be diplomatic. If O'Neil won't tell you, question Appleton—you can wind him around your fingers easily enough."

The girl eyed him with a quick change of expression.

"Isn't it enough to know the Trust has nothing to do with the S. R. & N.?"

"No!" he shouted. "I must know the whole inside of this secret understanding—this blackmail, or whatever it is."

"Then—I'm sorry."

"Come! Don't be silly. You can do me a great service."

"You said you no longer disliked Mr. O'Neil and he couldn't harm you."

"Well, well! Must I explain the whys and wherefores of every move I make?"

"It would be spying if I went back. The matter is confidential—I know that."

"Will you do as I ask?"

"No!" Natilie said. "I told you what I did tell you only so that you might correct...."

"You rebel, eh?" Gordon said.

It was their first clash since the marriage. Mrs. Gordon looked on, torn between loyalty to her husband and a desire to protect her daughter. She searched her mind painfully for a compromise, the half-truth was her remedy for every moral distress.

"I'm sure Natalie will help you in any way she can, Curtis. She isn't rebellious, she merely doesn't understand."

"She doesn't need to understand. It is enough I direct her...." As Natalie turned and walked silently to the window, he stifled an oath.

"Have I no authority?" he stormed. "Do you mean to obey?"

"Wait!" Gloria laid a restraining hand on his arm. "Perhaps I can learn what you want to know. Mr. O'Neil was very kind...."

Her daughter whirled, with white face and flashing eyes.

"Mother!" she gasped.

"Our loyalty begins at home," Gloria whispered.

"Oh-h! I can't conceive of your — of such a thing. If you have no decency, I have. I'm sorry I spoke, but — if you dare to do such a thing, I shall warn Mr. O'Neil you are a spy." She turned a glance of loathing on Gordon. "I see," she said, quietly. "You used me as a tool. You lied about your feeling toward him. You meant harm to him all the time." She faced the window again.

"Lied!" he shouted. "Be careful — that's strong language. Don't try me too far, or you may find yourself adrift once more. I have been too patient. But I have other ways of finding out what I wish to know, and I shall verify what you have told me."

He strode angrily from the room, leaving Natalie staring out on the bleak fall scene, her shoulders straight, her breast heaving. Gloria did not venture to address her.

Fortunately for the peace of all concerned, Gordon left for Seattle on the next steamer. Neither of the women believed Natalie's fragmentary revelation was the cause of his departure. But, once in touch with outside affairs, he lost no time in running down the clues he had gathered, and it was not long before he had learned enough to piece the truth together. Then he once more brought his mimeograph into use.

21

DAN APPLETON SLIPS THE LEASH

The first winter snows found O'Neil's track laid to the bridge site and the structure itself well begun. He had moved his office out to the front, and now saw little of Eliza, who was busy writing her book. She had finished her magazine articles, and they had been accepted, but she had given him no hint as to their contents.

One afternoon Happy Tom burst in on his chief, having hastened out from Omar on a construction train. Drawing a Seattle paper from his pocket, he began excitedly to share its contents.

"Well, the fat's in the fire, Murray! Somebody has belched up the whole North Pass story."

O'Neil seized the newspaper and scanned it hurriedly. He looked up, scowling.

"Who gave this out?" he asked.

Slater shrugged. "It's in the *Cortez Courier* too, so I s'pose it came from Gordon. Blessings come from one source, and Gordon's the fountain of all evil. I'm getting so I blame him for everything unpleasant. Sometimes I think he gave me the smallpox."

"Where did he learn the inside of Illis' deal? By God! There's a leak somewhere!"

"Maybe he uncovered it back there in the States."

Murray shook his head. "Nobody knows anything about it except you boys." He seized the telephone at his elbow and called Dr. Gray, while Tom listened with his shining forehead puckered anxiously. O'Neil hung up with a black face.

"Appleton!" he said.

Tom looked, if possible, a shade gloomier than usual. "I wouldn't be too sure it was Dan if I was you," he ventured, doubtfully.

"Where is he?" O'Neil ground out the words between his teeth.

"Surveying the townsite addition. If he let anything slip it was by mistake...."

"Mistake! I won't employ people who make mistakes of that kind. This story may bring the Canadian Government down on Illis and forfeit his North Pass charter—to say nothing of our authorities. That would finish us." He rose, went to the door, and ordered the recently arrived engine uncoupled.

"I'd rather have a crook under me than a fool," he growled, as he flung himself into his fur coat. "Appleton told us he talked too much."

Tom pursed his lips thoughtfully. "Gordon got it through the Gerard girl, I s'pose."

"Gordon! Gordon! Will there never be an end to Gordon?" His frown deepened. "He's in the way, Tom. If he balks this deal, I'm afraid I'll...have to change ghosts."

"It would be a pious act," Slater said. "And his ghost wouldn't haunt you none, either. It would put on its asbestos overshoes and go out among the other shades selling stock in electric fans or 'Gordon's Arctic Toboggan Slide.' He'd promote a Purgatory Development Company and underwrite the Bottomless Pit for its Sulphur. I—I'd hate to think this came from Dan."

The locomotive had been switched out by this time, and O'Neil hurried to board it. On his way to Omar he had time thoroughly to weigh the results of this unexpected complication. His present desire was merely to verify his suspicion that Appleton had told his secret to Natalie; beyond that he did not care to think, for there was but one course open.

His anger reached the blazing point after his arrival. As he stepped down from the engine cab, Gray silently handed him a coded message from London that had arrived a few moments before. When its contents had been deciphered, O'Neil cursed and was furious as he stumbled through the dark toward the green bungalow on the hill.

Swinging round the corner of the house, he came into a bright radiance that streamed forth from Eliza's window, and he could not help seeing the interior of the room. She was there, writing busily, and he saw she was clad in the elaborate kimono he had given her. Yet it was not her personal appearance that arrested his angry eyes and caused his step to halt; it was, instead, her surroundings.

He had grown to accept her prim simplicity as a matter of course and never associated her in his thoughts with anything feminine. But the room as it lay before him now was a revelation of daintiness and artful decoration. Tasteful watercolors hung on the walls, a warm rug lay on the floor, and everywhere were rosy touches of color. The plain white bed had been transformed into a couch of Oriental luxury. A lace spread of weblike texture covered it, the pillows were hidden beneath billowing masses of ruffles and ribbons. He saw a typical woman's cozy corner piled high with cushions; there was a jar of burning incense sticks near it—everything, in fact, was utterly at variance with his notions of the owner. Even the girl herself seemed transfigured for her hair was brought forward around her face in some loose mysterious fashion that gave her a bewilderingly girlish appearance. As he looked in, she raised her face and the light shone full upon it. Her brows were puckered, and she nibbled at the end of her pencil, as if contemplating some creative puzzle.

O'Neil's eyes photographed all this in a single surprised glance as he passed; the next moment he was mounting the steps to the porch.

Dan flung open the door, but his words of greeting froze, his smile of welcome vanished at the sight of his chief's forbidding visage.

Murray was in no mood to waste words.

"Did you tell Miss Gerard that Poultney Illis is backing me?"

Dan stammered. "I—perhaps—I—What has gone wrong, Chief?"

"Did you tell her the inside—the story of his agreement with the steamboat people?"

Dan paled beneath his tan, but his eyes met Murray's without flinching. "I think I did—tell her something. I don't quite remember. But anything I may have said was in confidence...."

"I thought so. I merely wished to make certain. Well, the whole thing is in the papers."

Appleton laid his hand on the table to steady himself.

"Then it—didn't come from her. She wouldn't...."

"Gordon has spread the story. It couldn't have come from any other source. It couldn't have reached him in any other way, for none of my boys has breathed a word." His voice rose despite his effort at self-control. "Illis' agreement was *illegal*," he said. "It will probably forfeit the charter of the North Pass or land him in court. I suppose you realize that! I discovered his secret and assured him it was safe with me; now you peddle it to Gordon, and the whole thing is public. Here's the first result."

He shook the London cablegram in Dan's face, and his own was distorted with rage. There was a stir in Eliza's room that neither noticed. Appleton wiped his face with uncertain hand; he moistened his lips.

"I—I'm terribly sorry! But I'm sure Natalie wouldn't spy—I don't remember what I told her, or how I came to know about the affair. Doc Gray told me, I think, in the first excitement, but—God! She—wouldn't knowingly...."

"Gordon fired you for talking too much. I thought you had learned your lesson, but it seems you haven't. Don't blame Miss Gerard for pumping you—her loyalty belongs to Gordon now. But I require loyalty, too. Since you lack it, you can go."

O'Neil turned as Eliza's door opened. She stood before him, pale, frightened, trembling.

"I couldn't help hearing," she said. "You discharge us?"

He nodded. "I'm sorry! I've trusted my boys so implicitly that the thought of betrayal by them never occurred to me. I can't have men close to me who make such mistakes as this."

"Perhaps there was—an excuse, or the shadow of one, at least. When a man is in love, you know...."

Murray wheeled upon Dan.

"What's this?" Then in a noticeably altered tone he asked, "Do you love Natalie?"

"Yes."

"Does she love you?"

"No, sir!"

O'Neil turned back to the girl.

"I told Dan, when I hired him, that he would be called upon to dare much, to suffer much, and my interests must be his. He has disregarded them, and he must go. That's all. There's little difference between treachery and carelessness."

"It's—too bad," the girl said. Dan stood stiff and silent, wholly dazed by the collapse of his fortunes.

"I'm not ungrateful for what you've done, Appleton," O'Neil went on. "I intend to pay you well for the help you gave me. You took a chance at the canyon and at Gordon's Crossing. You'll get a check."

"I don't want your damned money," the other gulped. "I've drawn my wages."

"Nevertheless, I shall pay you well. It's highly probable you've wrecked the S. R. & N. and ruined me, but I don't intend to forget my obligations to you. It's unfortunate. Call on the cashier in the morning. Goodnight."

He left them standing there unhappy, dumb, and stiff with shame. Once outside the house, he plunged down the hill as if fleeing from the scene of some crime. He rushed through the night blindly, for he had loved his assistant engineer, and the memory of that chalk-faced, startled girl hurt him abominably.

When he came to the company office he was walking slowly, heavily. He found Doc Gray inside and dropped into a chair. His face was grimly set, and he listened dully to the physician's rambling talk.

"I fired Appleton!" he broke out, at last. Gray looked up quickly. "He acknowledged that he—did it. I had no choice. It came hard, though. He's a good boy."

"He did some great work, Chief!"

"I know! That affair at the Crossing—I intend to pay him well if he'll accept. It's not that—I like those kids, Stanley. Eliza took it harder than he. It wasn't easy for me, either," he sighed, wearily. "I'd give $10,000 if it hadn't happened. She looked as if I'd struck her."

"What did they say?"

"Nothing. He has been careless, disloyal."

"You told them so?"

O'Neil nodded.

"And they said nothing?"

"Nothing! What could they say?"

"They might have said a good deal," Gray answered. "They might have told you how they paid off your men and saved a walkout when I had no money."

O'Neil stared incredulously. "What are you talking about?" he demanded.

When he had the facts, he rose with an exclamation of dismay.

"God! Why didn't you tell me? Why didn't they speak out? I—I—why, that's loyalty of the finest kind. All the money they had saved, too—when they thought I had failed! Jove! That was fine. Oh, I'm sorry! I wonder what they think of me? I can't let Dan go after that. I...." He seized his cap and hurried out of the building.

Back at the cabin, the Appletons were trying to absorb what had just happened.

"It's hardly right—when things were going so well, too!" Dan said. He was sitting crumpled up in a chair, Eliza's arm encircling his shoulders. "I didn't mean to give up any secrets, but—I'm not myself when I'm with Natalie."

"We must take our medicine," his sister told him. "We deserve it, for this story may spoil all he's done. I didn't think it of her, though."

Dan groaned and bowed his head in his hands. "I don't know which hurts worse," he said. "His anger or her action. She couldn't do such a thing, Sis; she just couldn't!"

"She probably didn't realize—she hasn't much sense, you know. But after all he's suffered, to think we should injure him! I could cry. I think I shall."

The door opened before a rough hand, and O'Neil strode into the room, huge, shaggy in his coonskin coat. They rose, startled, but he came to them swiftly, a look of mingled shame and gladness in his face.

"I've come back to apologize," he cried. "I couldn't wait. I've learned what you children did while I was gone, and I've come to beg forgiveness. It's all right — it's all right."

"I don't know what you mean," Dan gasped.

"Doc told me how you paid those men. That was real friendship. It was splendid. It touched me, and I — I want to apologize. You see, I hurried right back."

They saw his eyes were moist, and at the sight Eliza gave a quivering cry, then turned swiftly to hide her face. She felt O'Neil's fur-clad arm about her shoulder; his hand was patting her, and he was saying gently: "You are a dear child. It was tremendously good of you both, and I — ought to be shot for acting as I did. I wonder if you can accept a wretched apology as bravely as you accepted a wrong accusation."

"It wasn't wrong, it was right," she sobbed. "Dan told her, and she told Gordon."

"There, there! I was to blame, after all, for letting anyone know, and if Dan made a mistake, he has more than offset it by his unselfishness — his sacrifices. It seems I forgot how much I really owe him."

"That affair with the shift bosses wasn't anything," Dan said. "And it was all Eliza's idea. I refused at first, but when she started to pay them herself, I weakened." He stuttered awkwardly, for his sister was motioning him desperately to be silent, but he ran on. "Oh, he ought to know the whole truth and how rotten I acted, Sis. I deserve to be discharged."

"Please don't make this any harder for me than it is," Murray said with a smile. "I'm terribly embarrassed, for I'm not used to apologies. I can't afford to be unjust. I — have so few friends that I want to cherish them. I'm sorry you saw me in such a temper. Anger is a treacherous thing, and it always betrays me. Let's forget I was here before and pretend I just came to thank you for what you did." He drew Dan into the shelter of his other arm and pressed the two young people to him.

"I didn't realize how deeply you kids care for each other and for me."

"Then I'm not fired?" Dan asked.

"Of course not. When I take time to think about discharging a man, I invariably end by raising his salary."

"Dan isn't worth half what you're paying him," came Eliza's muffled voice. She freed herself from Murray's embrace and rearranged her hair with tremulous fingers. Surreptitiously she wiped her eyes. "You gave us an awful fright. It's terrible to be evicted in wintertime." She tried to laugh, but the attempt failed miserably.

"Just the same, when a man contemplates marriage, he must have money."

"I don't want your blamed money." Dan blurted. "And it doesn't cost anything to contemplate marriage. That's all I'm doing—just looking at it from a distance."

"Perhaps I can help you to prevail on Miss Natalie to change her mind. That would be a real service, wouldn't it?" Under his grave glance, Dan's heart leaped. "I can't believe she's indifferent to you, my boy. You're suited to each other, and there's no reason on earth why you shouldn't marry. Perhaps she doesn't know her own mind."

"You're mighty good, but...." The lover shook his head.

Murray smiled again. "I think you're too timid. Don't plead and beg—just carry her off. Be firm and masterful. Be rough."

"The idea!" Eliza said. "She's no cavewoman!"

"Exactly. If she were, Dan would need to court her and send her bouquets of wild violets. She's over-civilized, and therefore he needs to be primitive."

Dan blushed and faltered. "I can't be firm with her, Murray. I turn to jelly whenever she looks at me." There was something so friendly and kind in his employer's attitude that the young fellow was tempted to pour out all his vexations. He had never felt so close to O'Neil as now – but his masculine reserve could not be overcome all in a moment, and he held his tongue.

When Murray had put the two young people fully at their ease he rose to go, but Eliza's eager voice made him turn with his hand on the doorknob.

"What can we do about this unfortunate Illis affair?" she asked. "Dan must try to...."

"Leave that to me. I'll straighten it out somehow. It is all my fault, and I'll have to meet it." He pressed their hands warmly.

When he had gone, Dan heaved a great sigh of relief.

"I'm glad it happened just as it did, Sis," he announced. "He knows my secret now, and I can see he never cared for Natalie. It's a load off my mind to know the track is clear."

"What a simpleton you are!" she told him. "Don't you see he's merely paying his debt?"

"I wonder...." Dan eyed her in amazement.

"Gee! If that's so, he is a prince, isn't he?"

The same ship that brought the ominous news to O'Neil also brought Curtis Gordon north. He had remained in Seattle only long enough to see the Illis story in print, and then had hastened back to the front. But his satisfaction over the mischief he had done received a rude jolt when at his first moment of leisure he looked over the late magazines he had bought before taking leave. In one that had appeared on the newsstands that very day he found, to his amazement, an article by Miss Eliza Appleton, in which his own picture appeared.

He pounced upon it eagerly; and then, as he read, his eyes narrowed, and his jaw stiffened. There, spread out to the public gaze, was his own record in full, including his initial venture into the Kyak coalfields, his abandonment of that project in favor of Hope Consolidated, and an account of his connection with the latter enterprise. Eliza had not hesitated to call the mine worthless, and she showed how he, knowing its worthlessness from the first, had used it as a lure to investors.

Then followed the story of his efforts to gain a foothold in the railroad struggle, his defeat at the Salmon River Canyon, his rout at the delta crossing, and his final death blow at Kyak. His career stood out boldly in all its fraudulent colors; failure was written across every one of his undertakings. The naked facts showed him visionary, incompetent, unscrupulous.

Thus far he had succeeded in keeping a large part of his stockholders in ignorance of the true condition of Hope Consolidated, but he recoiled at the inevitable result of this article, which had been flung far and wide into every city and village in the land. He dared not think of its effect upon his present enterprise, now so auspiciously launched. He had made a ringing appeal to the public, and its support would hinge upon its confidence in him as a man of affairs. Once that trust was destroyed, the Cortez Home Railway would crumble as swiftly as had all his other schemes.

The worst of it was he knew himself shut off from the world for five days as effectually as if he were locked in a dungeon. There was no wireless equipment on the ship, he could not start the machinery of his press bureau, and with every hour this damnable story was bound to gain momentum. He cursed the luck that had set him on this quest for vengeance and bound his hands.

Once he had gathered his wits, he occupied himself in the only possible way — by preparing a story of his own for the wire. But for the first time in his experience he found himself on the defensive and opposing a force against which no bland persuasiveness, no personal magnetism could prevail. In the scattered nature of his support lay his greatest weakness, for it made the task of self-justification extremely difficult. Perhaps it was well for his peace of mind he could not measure the full effect of those forces Eliza Appleton's pen had set in motion.

In Omar, of course, the article excited lively interest. O'Neil felt a warm thrill of satisfaction as he read it on the morning after his scene with Eliza and Dan. But it deepened his feeling of obligation almost painfully; for, like all who are thoughtlessly prodigal of their own favors, he was deeply sensible of any kindness done himself. Eliza's dignified exposition of Alaska affairs, and particularly the agreeable things she had written about him, were sure to be of great practical assistance, he knew, and he longed to make some real return. But so far as she was concerned there seemed to be nothing he could do. With Dan, of course, it was quite different. Mere money or advancement, he admitted seemed paltry, but there was a possibility of another kind of service.

Meanwhile Dan was struggling with his problem in his own way. The possibility Natalie had voluntarily betrayed him was a racking torture, and the remembrance of Eliza's words added to his suffering. He tried to gain some hint of his chief's feeling, but Murray's frank and friendly attitude baffled him.

When at last he received a brief note from Natalie asking him to call, he raced to Hope afraid, yet eager to hear what she might say. She met him on the dock as he left the S. R. & N. motorboat and led him directly to the house.

Natalie went straight to the point. "I'm in dreadful trouble," she said. "I sent for you to tell you I had no idea of betraying confidences."

Dan uttered some inane platitude, but his eyes lighted with relief.

"When I saw in the papers what a stir that North Pass & Yukon story had made, I was afraid I had done something dreadful. Tell me, is it so? Did I make trouble?"

"You certainly did. O'Neil was furious, and nobody knows yet what the result will be. It—it nearly cost me my head."

"Does he blame me?"

"No – he says you're on Gordon's side now. He blames me, or did, until he generously took it on himself."

"What does it all mean? I'm nearly distracted." Natalie's eyes were pleading. "Did you think I spied on you?"

Dan glowed with embarrassment and something more. "I didn't know what to think," he said. "I was wretchedly miserable, for I was afraid. And yet I knew you couldn't do such a thing. I told O'Neil I wasn't responsible for what I did or said when with you."

"Mr. Gordon sent me to Omar purposely. He sent me twice. It was I who brought him word the road was saved. I told all I'd learned because I believed he no longer hated Mr. O'Neil. I was happy to tell all I knew, for he deceived me as he deceives everyone. I learned the truth too late."

"Why do you stay here?" Dan asked.

"Why? I—don't know. Perhaps because I'm afraid to leave. I'm alone—you see mother believes in him. She's completely under his sway, and I can't tell her the sort of man he is. She's happy, and her happiness is worth more to me than my own. But—I *shall* go away. I can't stand it here much longer."

"Where will you go?"

"Back to my old home, perhaps. Somewhere—anywhere away from Alaska."

"I suppose you know I can't get along without you."

"Please don't! You have been very good and sweet to me, but...." She shook her dark head. "You couldn't marry me—even if I cared for you in that way."

"Why? I intend to marry you whether you want to or not."

"Oh, Dan, it wouldn't do. You know—about—mother. I've nearly died of shame, and—it would be sure to come up. Somebody would speak of it, sometime."

Dan's blue eyes went cold and smoky.

"It would take a brave person to mention the subject in my presence. I don't care a whoop for anything Gordon or your family may say or do. I...."

There was a stir in the hall outside. Dan turned and saw Curtis Gordon in the doorway. He'd been drawn by the sound of voices and peered into the library. Recognizing Natalie's caller, he frowned.

"What is this?" he asked. "A proposal? Do I interrupt?"

"You do," Dan said. Then, after a pause, he added, "I'll finish it when you leave."

Gordon entered and spoke to his stepdaughter.

"What is this man doing in my house?"

"He is here at my invitation," she said.

"Tell him to leave. I won't have him here."

"Why don't *you* tell me?" Dan challenged. "I don't need an interpreter."

"Don't be rash young man. There is a limit to my patience. If you have the indecency to come here after what you have done, and after what your sister has said about me, I shall certainly...."

"I didn't come to see you, Gordon," Dan interrupted. "You may be an agreeable sight to some people, but you're no golden sunset in my eyes. Eliza flattered you."

Natalie gave a little terrified cry, for the men were glaring at each other savagely. Neither seemed to hear her.

"Did you read that article?"

"Read it? I wrote it!"

Gordon's face flamed suddenly with rage. He pointed to the door with trembling fingers.

"Get out! I'll not have you here," he shouted as his face turned red. "I discharged you once. Get out!"

Dan smiled mirthlessly, dangerously.

"I haven't finished proposing," he said. "I expect to be accepted. You'll pardon me, I know."

"Will you go, you...."

Dan turned to the girl, who, after that first outcry, had stood as if spellbound, her face pale, her eyes shining.

"Natalie dear," he said. "You can't live in the same house with this beast. He's a cheat and a scoundrel. He's done his best to spoil your life, and he'll succeed if you stay, so come with me now. Eliza loves you and wants you, and I'll never cease loving you with all my heart. Marry me, and we'll go...."

Gordon uttered an inarticulate sound and came forward with his hands working hungrily.

"Don't interrupt!" Dan warned over his shoulder. His white teeth gleamed in sudden contrast with his tan. "No man could love you as I do, dear...." Gordon's clutch fell upon him and tightened. Dan stiffened, and his words ceased. Then the touch upon his flesh became unbearable. Whirling, he wrenched himself free. He was like a wild animal now. Body and spirit had leaped into rebellion at contact with Gordon. His long resentment burst its bounds and his lean muscles quivered. His frame trembled as if it restrained some tremendous pressure from within.

"Don't do that!" he cried, hoarsely, and brushed the sleeve where his enemy's fingers had rested, as if it had been soiled.

Gordon snarled and stretched out his hand a second time. But the younger man raised his fist and struck. Once, twice, again and again he flung his bony knuckles into that purple, distorted face, which he loathed as a thing unclean. He battered down the big man's guard. Right and left he rained blows, stepping forward as his victim fell back. Gordon reeled, he pawed wildly, he swung his arms, but they encountered nothing. Yet he was a heavy man, and, although half stunned by the sudden onslaught, he managed to retain his feet until he landed against the heavy mahogany reading table in the center of the room. His retreat ended there. Another blow and his knees buckled; his arms sagged. Then Dan summoned all his strength and swung. Gordon groaned, lurched forward, and sprawled on the warm red velvet carpet, face down, with his limbs twisted under him.

His vanquisher stood over him for an instant, then turned on Natalie a face now keen and cruel and predatory.

"Come! We'll be married today," he said as he crossed swiftly and took her two hands in his. "He's down and out, so don't be frightened. Now hurry! I've had enough of this nonsense."

"I—I'm not frightened," she said. "But—I...." Her eyes roved past him as if in quest of something.

"Here! This'll do for a wrap." Dan whipped his fur overcoat from a chair and flung it about her. "My hat, too!" He crushed his gray Stetson over her dark hair and, slipping his arm about her shoulders, urged her toward the hall.

"Mother! She'll never...."

"We'll call on her together. I'll do the talking for both of us." He jerked the front door open with a force that threatened to wrench it from its hinges and thrust his companion out into the bracing cold. Then, as Gordon's Japanese butler came running from the rear of the house, he turned.

"Hey, you!" he said. "The boss has gone on a little visit. Don't stumble over him. And tell Mrs. Gordon that Mr. and Mrs. Appleton will call on her in a few days—Mr. and Mrs. Dan Appleton of Omar!"

It was but a few steps to the pier. Dan felt he was treading on air, for the fierce, unreasoning joy of possession was surging through his veins. His old indecision and doubt had vanished, and the men he met recoiled before his hostile glance, staring after him in bewilderment.

But as he lifted Natalie down into the launch, he felt her shaking violently, and suddenly his selfish exultation gave way to a tender solicitude.

"There, there," he said. "Don't cry, honey. It's all right. It's all right!"

She raised her face to his, and his head swam, for he saw she was radiant.

"I'm not crying. I'm laughing. I—I'm mad—insane with happiness."

He crushed her to him, he buried his face in her neck, mumbling her name over and over. And neither of them knew he was rapturously kissing the coonskin collar of his own greatcoat. The launchman, motor crank in hand, paused, staring; he was still open-mouthed when Dan, catching sight of him, shouted:

"What's the matter? Is your back broken?"

"Yes—No, sir!" The fellow spun the flywheel vigorously. The little craft began to vibrate and quiver and then swung out from shore.

A moment later and the engineman yelled. He came stumbling forward and seized the steering wheel as the boat grazed a buoy.

"That's right, you steer," Dan said with a laugh, relaxing his hold. He then turned to Natalie.

"There's a preacher in Omar," he said as he pressed her to him.

"It's a long way to Omar," she answered, then hid her face against his breast. "There's one in Cortez, too, and he's much nearer."

22

O'Neil Deftly Plays The Hazzard

Eliza's greeting to the runaways was as warm as their hearts could wish. She divined the truth before they could speak and took Natalie in her arms with a glad cry of welcome. The two girls kissed each other, wept, laughed, wept a little more, kissed again, and then the story came out.

Dan was plainly swollen with pride.

"I walloped him, Sis!" he told her. "I got even for the whole family, and I believe his eyes are closed even to the beauties of nature. He won't be able to read the wedding notice."

Eliza hugged his arm and looked at him adoringly.

"It must have been perfectly splendid!"

Natalie nodded. "I was asleep," she said. "But Dan shocked me wide awake. Can you imagine it? I didn't know my own feelings until he went for that brute. Then I knew all at once I had loved him all the time. Isn't it funny? It came over me so suddenly! I—I can't realize he's mine." She turned her eyes on him with an expression that made his chest swell proudly.

"Gee!" he exclaimed. "If I'd known how she felt I'd have pitched into the first fellow I met. A man's an awful fool till he gets married."

There followed a recital of the day's incidents, zestful, full of happy digressions, endless. The couple, after the manner of lovers, took it for granted that Eliza was caught up into the seventh heaven along with them. Dan was drunk with delight, and his bride seemed dizzied by the change that had overtaken her. She looked as if it was miraculous, almost unbelievable, and under the spell of her happiness her real self asserted itself. Those cares and humiliations that had reacted to make her cold and self-contained disappeared, giving place to an impetuous girlishness that distracted her newly made husband and delighted Eliza. The last lingering doubts Dan's sister had cherished were cleared away.

It was not until the bride had been banished to prepare for dinner that Eliza thought to ask her brother:

"Have you told Mr. O'Neil?"

The triumph faded suddenly out of his face.

"Gee, no! I haven't told anybody."

They stared at each other, reading the thoughts they had no need to voice. "Well, I've done it! It's too late now," Dan said.

"Maybe he'll fire us again. I would if I were he. You must tell him this very minute."

"I suppose so," he agreed, reluctantly, and picked up his hat. "And yet—I—I wonder if I'd better, after all. Don't you think it would sound nicer coming from someone else?"

"Why?"

"Wouldn't it seem like crowing for me to…to…for instance, now, if you…."

"Coward!" the girl said.

He nodded. "But, Sis, you *do* have a nicer way of putting things than I have."

"Why, I wouldn't tell him for worlds. I couldn't. Poor man! We've brought him nothing but sorrow and bad luck."

"It's fierce!"

"Well, don't hesitate. That's what Gordon did, and he got licked."

Dan scowled and set his features in a brave show of moral courage. "She's mine, and he can't take her away," he said. "So I don't care what happens. But I'd just as soon slap a baby in the face." He left the house like a man under sentence.

When he returned, a half-hour later, Eliza was awaiting him on the porch. She had been standing there with chattering teeth and limbs shaking from the cold while the minutes dragged.

"What did he say?" she asked.

"It went off fine. Thank Heaven, he was out at the front, so I could break it to him over the phone!"

"Did he—curse you?"

"No. I opened right up by saying I had bad news for him."

"Oh, Dan!"

"Yes! I dare say I wasn't very tactful, now that I think it over, but, you see, I was rattled. I spilled out the whole story at once. 'Bad news?' said he. 'My dear boy, I'm delighted. God bless you both.' Then he made me tell him how it all happened and listened without a word. I thought I'd faint. He pulled some gag about Daniel and the lion; then his voice got far away, and the blamed wire began to buzz, so I hung up and beat it back here. I'm glad it's over."

"He'll probably send you a solid-silver dinner set or raise your pay. That's the kind of man he is." Eliza's voice broke. "Oh, Danny," she cried. "He's the dearest, sweetest thing." She turned away, and he kissed her sympathetically before going inside to the waiting Natalie.

Instead of following, Eliza remained on the porch, gazing down at the lights of the little city. An engine with its row of empty flats rolled into the yard, panting from its exertions; the notes of a piano came to her faintly from the street below. The lights of an incoming steamer showed far down the Sound. O'Neil had made all this, she reflected. The busy town and the hopeful thousands who came and went daily owed their prosperity to him. He had made the wilderness fruitful, but what of his own life? She suspected it was as bleak and barren as the mountain slopes above Omar.

He, too, looked down upon this thriving intimate little community, but from a distance. Beneath his unfailing cheerfulness she felt sure there lurked a hunger the mere affection of his boys could never satisfy. And now the thought that Dan had come between him and his heart's desire filled her with pity. He seemed suddenly a very lonely figure of a man, despite his material success. When his enemies were doing, had already done, so much to defeat him, it seemed unfair his trusted friend should step between him and the fulfilment of his dearest ambition—ambition common to all men, failure in which brings a sense of failure to a man's whole life, no matter what other ends are achieved. Of course, he would smile and swallow his bitterness—that was his nature—but she would know the truth.

"Poor Omar Khayyam," she thought. "I wish there were love enough in the world for you. I wish there were two Natalies, or that...." Then she shook the dream from her mind and went into the house, for the night was cold and she was shaking.

O'Neil behaved more handsomely even than Eliza had anticipated. He hurried into town on the following morning, and his congratulations were so sincere, his manner so hearty Dan forgot his embarrassment and took a shameless delight in advertising his happiness. Nor did Murray stop with mere words. He summoned all his lieutenants, and Omar rang that night with a celebration such as it had never known. The company chef had been busy all day, the commissary had been ransacked, and the wedding supper was of a nature to interfere with office duties for many days thereafter.

Tom Slater made a congratulatory speech—in reality, a mournful adjuration to avoid the pitfalls of matrimonial inharmony—and openly confessed his digestion was now impaired beyond relief. Others followed him. There was music, laughter, a riotous popping of corks; and over it all O'Neil presided with grace and mellowness. Then, after the two young people had been made thoroughly to feel his good will, he went back to the front, and Omar saw him but seldom in the weeks that followed.

To romantic Eliza, this self-sought seclusion had but one meaning—the man was broken hearted. She did not consider there might be other reasons for his constant presence at the glaciers.

Of course, since the unwelcome publication of the North Pass & Yukon story, O'Neil had been in close touch with Illis, and by force of strong argument had convinced the Englishman of his own innocence in the affair. A vigorous investigation might have proved disastrous, but, fortunately, Curtis Gordon lacked leisure in which to follow the matter up. The truth was, after his public exposure at Eliza's hands, he was far too busy mending his own fences to spare time for attempts on his rival. Consequently, the story was allowed to die out, and O'Neil was finally relieved to learn its effect had been killed. Precisely how Illis had affected this he did not know, nor did he care to inquire. Illis had been forced into an iniquitous bargain; and, since he had taken the first chance to free himself from it, the question of abstract right or wrong was not a subject for squeamish consideration.

It was at about this time the bloody battle at Beaver Canyon began to bear fruit. One day a keen-faced, quiet stranger presented a card ,bearing the name Henry T. Blaine, at Murray's office.

Beneath was only the address of the Heidlemann building in New York, but otherwise the card told nothing. Something in Mr. Blaine's manner, however, led Murray to treat him with more than ordinary consideration.

"I should like to go over your work," the stranger announced.

O'Neil himself acted as guide. Together they inspected the huge concrete abutments, then were lowered into the heart of the giant caissons that protruded from the frozen stream. The Salmon lay locked in its winter slumber now, the glaciers stood as silent and inactive as the snow-mantled mountains that hemmed them in. Down into the bowels of the river the men descended, while O'Neil described the nature of the bottom, the depth and character of his foundations, and the measure of his progress. He explained the character of the bar that lay above the bridge site and pointed out the heavy layers of railroad iron with which his cement work was reinforced.

"I spent nearly two seasons studying this spot before I began the bridge," he told his visitor. "I had men here, night and day, observing the currents and the action of the ice. Then I laid my piers accordingly. They are armored and reinforced to withstand any shock."

"The river is subject to quick rises, I believe?" Blaine said.

"Twenty feet in a few hours."

"The volley of ice must be almost irresistible."

"Almost," Murray said and smiled. "Not quite. Our icebreakers were especially designed by Parker to withstand any weight. There's nothing like them anywhere. In fact, there will be nothing like this bridge when it's completed."

Blaine offered no comment, but his questions searched to the depths of the builder's knowledge.

"Of course you know why I'm here?" Blaine said back in camp.

"Your card told me that, but I don't need the Heidlemanns now."

"We are prepared to reopen negotiations."

"Why?"

"My people are human. They have feelings. You read Gordon's lies about us and about that fight at Beaver Canyon? Well, we're used to abuse, and opposition of a kind we respect. But that man stirred public opinion to such a point there's no further use of heeding it. We're ready to proceed with our plans now, and the public can go to the devil till it understands us better. We have several men in jail at Cortez, charged with murder – it will cost us a fortune to free the poor fellows. First the Heidlemanns were thieves and grafters and looters of the public domain, and now they have become assassins! If this route to the interior proves feasible, well and good. If not, we'll resume work at Cortez next spring. Kyak, of course, is out of the question."

"This route depends on the bridge."

"Exactly."

"It's a two years' job."

"You offered to complete it this winter, when you talked with Mr. Herman Heidlemann."

"And — I can."

"Then we'll consider a reasonable price. But we must know where we stand by next spring. We have a great deal of capital tied up in the interior – we can't wait."

"This delay will cost you something."

Mr. Blaine shrugged. "You made that point plain when you were in New York. We're accustomed to pay for our mistakes."

"Will you cover this in the shape of an option?"

"That's what I'm here for. If you finish your bridge, and it stands the spring breakup, we'll be satisfied. I shall expect to stay here and watch the work."

O'Neil agreed heartily. "You're very welcome, Mr. Blaine. I like your brand of conversation. I build railroads; I don't run them. Now let's get down to figures."

The closing of the option required several weeks, of course, but the outcome was that even before mid-winter arrived O'Neil found himself in the position he had longed to occupy. In effect the sale was made, and on terms that netted him and his backers 100 percent profit. There was but one proviso: the bridge should be built by spring. The Heidlemanns were impatient, their investment up to date had been heavy, and they frankly declared failure to bridge the chasm on time would convince them the task was hopeless.

In a way this was unreasonable, but O'Neil was aware they could not permit delay—or a third failure. Unless his route was proved feasible, without loss of time, they would abandon it for one they knew to be certain, even though more expensive. He did not argue the task was of unprecedented difficulty, for he had made his promise and was ready to stand or fall by it. It is doubtful, however, if any other contractor would have undertaken the work on such time; in fact, had it been a public bridge it would have required four years in the building. Yet O'Neil cheerfully staked his fortune on completing it in eight months.

With his option signed and the task squarely confronting him, he realized with fresh force its bigness and the weight of responsibility that rested on his shoulders. He began the most dramatic struggle of his career, a fight against untried conditions, a desperate race against the seasons, with ruin as the penalty of defeat.

The channel of the Salmon at this point is 1,500 feet wide and 30 feet deep. Through it boils a 10-mile current. In other words, the waters race by with the speed of a running man. Over this O'Neil expected to suspend a structure capable of withstanding the mightiest strains to which any bridge had ever been subjected.

Parker's plans called for 17,000 yards of cement work and nine million pounds of steel, every part of which had to be fabricated to a careful pattern. It was a man-size job, and O'Neil was thankful he had prepared so systematically for the work. He had gathered his materials with extraordinary care. Supplies were arriving now in carloads, in trainloads, in shiploads from Seattle, Vancouver, and as far as Pittsburg. They came in a thin continuous stream, any interruption of which meant confusion and serious loss of time. The movement of this vast tonnage required the ceaseless attention of a corps of skilled men.

He had personally directed affairs up to this point, but he now obliterated himself, and the leadership devolved on two others — Parker, small, smiling, gentle-mannered, and Mellen, tall, angular, gloomy. Upon them, engineer and bridge builder, O'Neil rested his confidence, serene in the knowledge that of all men they were the ablest in their lines.

As for himself, he had all he could do to bring materials to them and to keep the long supply trail open. Long it was, indeed; for the shortest haul was from Seattle, 1,200 miles away, and the steel bridge members came from Pennsylvania.

The piers at Omar groaned beneath the cargoes that belched from the big freighters. Incidentally, Happy Tom Slater likewise groaned beneath his burdens as superintendent of transportation. A city as large as Omar sprang up at the glaciers. A city with electric lights, powerhouses, machine shops, freight yards, and long rows of winter quarters. It lay behind ramparts of coal, grillage timbers and piling, shelters with cement barrels, and tons of steel. Over it the winter snows sifted, the north winds howled, and the arctic cold deepened.

Here, locked in a mountain fastness more than 1,000 miles from his base of supplies, O'Neil began the decisive struggle of his life. Here, at the focusing point of his enterprise, in the white heat of the battle, he spent his time, heedless of every other interest or consideration. The shifts were lengthened, wages increased, a system of bonuses adopted. Only picked men were given places, but of these there were hundreds: over them the grim-faced Mellen brooded, with the fevered eye of a fanatic and a tongue of flame.

Wherever possible the men were sheltered, and steam pipes were run to guard against the cold; but most of the labor was, of necessity, performed in the open and under trying conditions. At times the wind blew a hurricane; always there was the bitter cold. Men toiled until their flesh froze and their tools slipped from their fingers, then dragged themselves stiffly into huts and warmed themselves for further effort. They worked amid a boiling snow-smother that hid them from view, while gravel and fine ice cut their faces like knives; or again, on still, sharp days, when the touch of metal was like the bite of fangs and echoes filled the valley to the brim with an empty clanging.

But they were no ordinary fellows — no chaff, to drift with the wind: they were men toughened by exposure to the breath of the north, men winnowed out from many thousands of their kind. Nor were they driven – they were led. Mellen was among them constantly; so was the soft-voiced smiling Parker, not to mention O'Neil with his cheery laugh and his words of praise. Yet often it was hard to keep the work moving at all; for steam condensed in the cylinders, valves froze unless constantly operated, pipes were kept open only by using hot cloths. Then, too, the snow crept upward steadily, stealthily, until it lay in heavy drifts that nearly hid the little town and changed the streets to miniature canyons.

Out of this snow-smothered, frost-bound valley there was but one trail. The army lay encamped in a cul-de-sac; all that connected it with the outside world were two slender threads of steel. To keep them clear of snow was a giant's task, for there were no snowsheds yet, and in many places the construction trains passed through deep cuts between solid walls of white. Every wind filled these and threatened to seal the place fast. But furiously the "rotaries" attacked the choking mass, slowly it was whirled aside, and onward flowed that steady stream of supplies. No army of investment was ever in such constant peril of being cut off. For every man engaged in the attack there was another behind him fighting back the allied forces that swept down from either hand.

Only those who know that far land in her sterner moods can form any conception of the stupefying effect of continuous, unbroken cold. There is a point beyond which the power of reaction ceases: where the human mind and body recoils uncontrollably from exposure, and where the most robust effort results in spiritless inactivity. It is then that efficiency is cut in half, then cut again. And of all the terrors of the Arctic there is none so compelling as the wind. It is a monstrous, deathly thing, a creature that has life and preys upon the agony of men. There are regions sheltered from it, of course; but in the gutters that penetrate the mountain ranges it lurks with constant menace, and of all the coast from Sitka westward the valley of the Salmon, is the most evil.

In the throat of this mighty-mouthed funnel, joining the still, abysmal cold of the interior with the widely varying temperatures of the open sea, O'Neil's band was camped, and there the great hazard was played. Under such conditions it was fortunate indeed he had field marshals like Parker and Mellen, for no single man could have triumphed. Parker was cautious, brilliant, far-sighted; he reduced the battle to paper, he blueprinted it; with sliding rule he analyzed it into inches and pounds and stresses and strains. Mellen was like a grim Hannibal, tireless, cunning, cold, and he wove steel in his fingers as a woman weaves her thread.

It was a remarkable alliance, a triumvirate of its kind unsurpassed. As the weeks crept into months it worked an engineering marvel.

23

A NEW CRISIS EMERGES

Travel, consisting mainly of prospectors bound to and from the interior, increased with the completion of the railroad to the glacier crossing. The Cortez winter trail was open, and over it passed most of the traffic from the northward mining camps, but now and then a frost-rimed stranger emerged from the canyon above O'Neil's terminus with tales of the gold country, or a venturesome sledge party snowshoed its way inland from the end of the track. Murray made a point of hauling these trailers on his construction trains and feeding them in his camps as freely as he did his own men. In time the wavering line of sled tracks became well broken, and scarcely a week passed without bringing several mushers.

As O'Neil was picking his way through the outskirts of the camp one day, he encountered one of his night foremen and was surprised to see the fellow was leading a trail dog by a chain. Now these malamutes are as much a part of the northland as the winter snows, and they are a common sight in every community. But the man's patent embarrassment challenged Murray's attention – he acted as if he had been detected in a theft or a breach of duty.

"Hello, Walsh. Been buying some livestock?" O'Neil asked.

"Yes, sir. I picked up this dog cheap."

"Harness too, eh?" Murray noted Walsh's arms were full of gear — enough, indeed, for a full team. He knew the foreman owned no dogs.

"You're not getting ready for a trip, I hope?"

"No, sir. Not exactly, sir. The dog was cheap, so I—I just bought him."

As a matter of fact, dogs were not cheap, and Walsh should have been in bed at this hour. Murray walked on wondering what the fellow could be up to.

Later he came upon a laborer dickering with a Kyak Native over the price of a fur robe, and in front of a bunkhouse he found other members of the night crew talking with two strangers. They fell silent as he approached and responded to his greeting with a peculiar nervous eagerness, staring after him curiously as he passed on.

He expected Dr. Gray out from Omar, but as he neared the track, he met Mellen. The bridge superintendent engaged him briefly about some detail then changed the subject.

"I don't know what's the matter with the men this morning. They're loafing."

"Loafing? Nonsense! You expect too much," O'Neil said.

Mellen shook his head. "The minute my back is turned they begin to gossip. I've had to call them down."

"Perhaps they want a holiday."

"They're not that kind. There's something in the air."

The morning train pulled in while they were speaking, and O'Neil was surprised to see at least a dozen townspeople descending from it. They were loafers, saloon-frequenters, for the most part, and oddly enough, they had with them dogs and sleds and all the equipment for travel. He was prevented from making inquiry, however, by a shout from Dr. Gray.

"Hey, Chief! Look who's here!"

O'Neil hastened forward with a greeting on his lips, for Stanley was helping Eliza and Natalie down from the caboose that served as a passenger coach.

The young women, becomingly clad in their warm winter furs, made a picture good to look upon. Natalie had ripened wonderfully since her marriage and added to her rich dark beauty there was now an elusive sweetness, a warmth and womanliness that had been lacking before. As for Eliza, she had never appeared more sparkling, more freshly wholesome, and saucy than on this morning.

"We came to take pictures," she announced. "We want to see if the bridge suits us."

"Don't you believe her, Mr. O'Neil," Natalie said. "Dan told us you were working too hard, so Eliza insisted on taking you in hand. I'm here merely in the office of chaperon and common scold. You *have* been overdoing. You're positively haggard."

Gray nodded. "He won't mind me. I hope you'll abuse him well. Go at him hammer and tongs."

Ignoring Murray's smiling assertion he was the only man in camp who really suffered from idleness, the girls pulled him about and examined him critically, then fell to discussing him as if he were not present.

"He's worn to the bone," Eliza said.

"Did you ever see anything like his wrinkles? He looks like a dried apple," Natalie declared.

"Dan says he doesn't eat."

"Probably he's too busy to chew his food. We'll make him chew more thoroughly...."

"And eat soup. Then we'll mend his underclothes. I'll warrant he doesn't dress properly."

"How much sleep does he get?" Natalie asked of the physician.

"About half as much as he needs."

"Leave him to us," Eliza said. "Now where does he live? We'll start in there."

O'Neil protested. "Please don't! I hate soup, and I can't allow anybody to pry into my wardrobe. It won't stand inspection."

Miss Appleton pointed to his feet.

"How many pairs of socks do you wear?" she asked.

"One."

"Any holes?"

"Sometimes."

Natalie was shocked. "One pair of socks in this cold? It's time we took a hand. Now lead us to this rabbit hole where you live."

Reluctantly, yet with an unaccustomed warmth about his heart, O'Neil escorted them to his headquarters. It was a sharp, clear morning. The sky was as empty and bright as an upturned saucepan; against it the soaring mountain peaks stood out as if carved from new ivory. The glaciers to right and left were mute and motionless in the grip of that force that alone had power to check them; the turbulent river was hidden beneath a case-hardened armor; the lake, with its weird flotilla of revolving bergs, was matted with a broad expanse of white, across which meandered dim sled and snowshoe trails. Underfoot the paths gave out a crisp complaint, the sunlight slanting up the valley held no warmth whatever, and their breath hung about their heads like vapor, crystallizing upon the fur of their caps and hoods.

O'Neil's living quarters consisted of a good-size room adjoining the office building.

"I'm sorry to disappoint you, but your zeal is utterly misplaced," he said as he paused by the door. "I live like a pasha, in the midst of debilitating luxuries, as you will see for yourselves." He waved them proudly inside.

The room was bare, damp, and chill. It was furnished plentifully, but it was in characteristically masculine disorder. The bed was tumbled, the stove half filled with cold ashes, the water pitcher on the washstand frozen. In one corner was a heap of damp clothing, now stiff with frost.

"Of course, it's a little upset," he apologized. "I wasn't expecting callers, you know."

"When was it made up last?" Eliza inquired, a little weakly.

"Yesterday, of course."

"Are you sure?"

"Now, see here," he said. "I haven't time to make beds, and everybody else is busier than I am. I'm not in here enough to make it worthwhile—I go to bed late, and I tumble out before dawn."

The girls exchanged meaningful glances. Eliza began to take off her furs.

"Not bad, is it?" he said.

Natalie picked up the discarded clothing, which crackled stiffly under her touch and parted from the bare boards with a tearing sound.

"Frozen! The idea!" she said.

Eliza poked among the other garments that hung against the wall and found them also rigid. The nail heads behind them were coated with ice. Turning to the table, with its litter of papers and the various unclassified accumulation of a bachelor's house, she sighed.

"I suppose we'll have to leave this as it is."

"Just leave everything. I'll get a man to clean up while you take pictures of the bridge." As Natalie began preparing for action, he asked, in surprise, "Don't you like my little home?"

"It's awful," the bride answered.

"A perfect bear's den," Eliza agreed. "It will take us all day."

"It's just the way I like it," he told them. But the girls resolutely banished him and locked the door in his face.

"Hey! I don't want my things all mussed up," he called, pounding for re-admittance. "I know right where everything is, and...."

The door opened, out came an armful of papers, a shower of burnt matches, and a litter of trash from his worktable. He groaned.

"Now, run away, little boy," Eliza said. "You're going to have your face washed, no matter how you cry. When we've finished in here, we'll attend to you." The door slammed once more, and he went away shaking his head.

They grudgingly admitted him at lunchtime, and, although they protested they were not half through, he was naively astonished at the change they had brought to pass. For the first time in many days the place was thoroughly warm and dry; it likewise displayed an orderliness and comfort to which it had been a stranger. From some obscure source the girls had gathered pictures for the bare walls; hung figured curtains at the windows; and fresh white covers for bed, bureau, and washstand. His clothes had been rearranged and posted in conspicuous places were written directions telling him of their whereabouts. One of the cards bore these words: "Your soup! Take one in cup of hot brandy and water before retiring." Beneath were a bottle and a box of bouillon tablets. A shining teakettle was humming on the stove.

"This is splendid," he said when they had completed a tour of inspection. "But where are my blueprints?"

"In the drafting room where they belong. This room is for rest and sleep. We want to see it in this condition when we come back."

"Where did you find the fur rug?" he asked as he pointed to a thick bearskin beside the bed.

"We stole it from Mr. Parker," they confessed, shamelessly. "He had two."

"We nearly came to blows with the chef when we kidnapped his best boy," Eliza said. We've ordered him to keep this place warm and look after your clothes and clean up every morning. He's to be your valet and take care of you."

"But—we're dreadfully short-handed in the mess house," O'Neil protested.

"We've given the chef your bill of fare, and your man Ben will see that you eat it."

"I won't stand for soup. It...."

"Hush! Do you want us to come again?" Natalie asked.

"Yes – again and again!" he said. "I dare say I was getting careless. I pay more attention to the men's quarters than to my own. Do you know—this is the first hint of home I've had since I was a boy? And—it's mighty agreeable." He stared wistfully at the feminine touches on all sides.

The bride settled herself with needle and thread.

"Now take Eliza to the bridge while the light is good," Natalie said. "She wants to take photos of it. I'm going to sew on buttons and enjoy myself."

O'Neil read agreement in Eliza's eyes, and obeyed. As they neared the riverbank, the girl exclaimed in surprise; for up out of the frozen Salmon two giant towers of concrete thrust themselves, on each bank were massive abutments, and connecting them were the beginnings of a complicated "false-work" structure by means of which the steel was to be laid in place. It consisted of rows upon rows of piling, laced together with an intricate pattern of squared timbers. Tracks were being laid on it, and along the rails ran a towering movable crane, or "traveler," somewhat like a tremendous cradle. This too was nearing completion.

Piledrivers were piercing the ice with long slender needles of spruce; across the whole river was weaving a gigantic fretwork of wood that appeared to be geometrically regular in design. The air was noisy with the cries of men, and a rhythmic thudding, through which came the rattle of winches and the hiss of steam. Over the whole vast structure swarmed an army of human ants, feeble pygmy figures that crept slowly here and there, regardless of their dizzy height.

"Isn't it beautiful?" said the builder, gazing at the scene with kindling eyes. "We're breaking records every day despite the weather. Those fellows are heroes. I feel guilty and mean when I see them risking life and limb while I just walk about and look on."

"Will it really stand the breakup?" Eliza asked. "When that ice goes out, it will be as if the solid earth were sliding down the channel. It frightens me to think of it."

"We've built solid rock; in fact, those piers are stronger than rock, for they are laced with veins of steel and anchored beneath the riverbed."

But Eliza doubted it was enough. "I've seen rivers break, and it's frightful; but of course I've never seen anything to compare with the Salmon. Suppose—just suppose there should be some weak spot...."

O'Neil settled his shoulders a little under his coat. "It would nearly kill Mellen—and Parker, too, for that matter."

"And you?"

He hesitated. "It means a great deal to me. Sometimes I think I could pull myself together and begin again, but—I'm getting old, and I'm not sure I'd care to try." After a pause he added a little stiffly, as if not quite sure of the effect of his words: "That's the penalty of being alone in life, I suppose. We men are grandstand players. We need an audience, some one person who really cares whether we succeed or fail. Your brother, for instance, has won more in the building of the S. R. & N. than I can ever hope to win."

Eliza felt a trifle conscious, too, and she did not look at him when she said: "Poor, lonely old Omar Khayyam! You deserve all Dan has. I think I understand why you haven't been to see us."

"I've been too busy; this thing has kept me here every hour. It's my child, and one can't neglect his own child, you know — even if it isn't a real one." He laughed apologetically. "See - there's where we took the skiff that day we ran Jackson Glacier. He's harmless enough now. You annoyed me dreadfully that morning, Eliza, and — I've never quite understood why you were so reckless."

"I wanted the sensation. Writers must live before they can write. I've worked the experience into my novel."

"Indeed? What is your book about?"

"Well — it's the story of a railroad builder, of a fellow who risked everything he had on his own judgment. It's — you!"

"Why, my dear!" cried O'Neil, turning upon her a look of almost comic surprise. "I'm flattered, of course, but there's nothing romantic or uncommon about me."

"You don't mind?"

"Of course not. But there ought to be a hero, and love, and — such things — in a novel. You must have a tremendous imagination."

"Perhaps. I'm not writing a biography, you know. However, you needn't be alarmed; it will never be accepted."

"It should be, for you write well. Your magazine articles are bully."

Eliza smiled. "If the novel would only go as well as those stories, I'd be happy. They put Gordon on the defensive."

"I knew they would."

"Yes. I built a nice fire under him, and now he's squirming. I think I helped you a little bit, too."

"Indeed you did — a great deal! When you came to Omar, I never thought you'd turn out to be my champion. I...." He turned as Dr. Gray came hurrying toward them, panting in his haste.

"I've been looking for you, Murray," he said. "The men are all quitting."

O'Neil started. "All quitting? What are you talking about?"

"There's a stampede — a gold stampede!"

Murray stared at the speaker as if doubting his own senses.

"There's no gold around here," he finally said.

"Two men came in last night. They've been prospecting over in the White River and report rich quartz. They've got samples with 'em and say there are placer indications everywhere. They were on their way to Omar to tell their friends and telephoned in from here. Somebody overheard and it leaked. The whole camp is up in the air. That's what brought out that gang from town this morning."

The significance of the incidents that had troubled him earlier in the day flashed on O'Neil; it was plain enough now why his men had been gossiping and buying dogs and fur robes. He understood only too well what a general stampede would mean to his plans, for it would take months to replace these skilled ironworkers.

"Who are these prospectors?" he asked.

"Nobody seems to know. Their names are Thorn and Baker. That gang from Omar has gone on, and our people will follow in the morning. Those who can't scrape up an outfit here are going into town to equip. We won't have 50 men on the job by tomorrow night."

"What made Baker and Thorn stop here?"

Gray shrugged. "Tired out, perhaps. We've got to do something quick, Murray. Thank God, we don't have to sell 'em grub or haul 'em to Omar. That will check things for a day or two. If they ever start for the interior we're lost, but the cataract isn't frozen over, and there's only one sled trail past it. We don't need more than six good men to do the trick."

"We can't stop a stampede that way."

Dr. Gray's face fell into harsh lines. "I'll bend a Winchester over the first man who tries to pass. Appleton held the place last summer; I'll guarantee to do it now."

"No. The men have a right to quit, Stanley. We can't force them to work. We can't build this bridge with a chain gang."

"Humph! I can beat up these two prospectors and ship 'em to the hospital until things cool down."

"That won't do, either. I'll talk with them, and if their story is right — well, I'll throw open the commissary and outfit everyone."

Eliza gasped; Gray stammered.

"You're crazy!" the doctor cried.

"If it's a real stampede, they'll go anyhow, so we may as well take our medicine with good grace. The loss of even 100 men would cripple us."

"The camp is seething. It's all Mellen can do to keep the day shift at work. If you talk to 'em, maybe they'll listen to you."

"Argument won't sway them. This isn't a strike; it's a gold rush." He turned toward the town.

Eliza was speechless with dismay as she hurried along beside him; Gray was scowling darkly and cursing; O'Neil himself was lost in thought. The gravity of this final catastrophe left nothing to be said.

Stanley lost little time in bringing the two miners to the office, and there, for a half-hour, Murray talked with them. When they perceived he was disposed to treat them courteously, they told their story in detail and answered his questions with apparent honesty. They willingly showed him their quartz samples and told of the hardships they had suffered.

Gray listened impatiently and once or twice undertook to interpolate some question, but after one glance from his chief, he desisted. Nevertheless, his long fingers itched to lay hold of the strangers and put an end to this tale that threatened ruin. His anger grew when Murray dismissed them with every evidence of a full belief in their words.

"Now that the news is out and my men are determined to quit, I want everybody to have an equal chance," O'Neil said, as they rose to go. "There's bound to be a great rush and a lot of suffering—maybe some deaths—so I'm going to call the boys together and have you talk to them."

Thorn and Baker agreed and departed. As the door closed behind them Gray exploded, but Murray checked him quickly, saying with an abrupt change of manner: "Wait! Those fellows are lying."

Seizing the telephone, he rang up Dan Appleton and swiftly made known the situation. Stanley could hear the engineer's startled exclamation.

"Get the cable to Cortez as quickly as you can," O'Neil said. "You have friends there, haven't you? Good! He's just the man, for he'll have Gordon's payroll. Find out if Joe Thorn and Henry Baker are known, and, if so, who they are and what they've been doing lately. Get it quick, understand? Then phone me." He slammed the receiver on its hook. "That's not Alaska quartz," he said. "It came from Nevada, or I'm greatly mistaken. Every hard rock miner carries specimens like those in his kit."

"You think Gordon...."

"I don't know. But we've got rock men on this job who'll recognize ore out of any mine they ever worked in. Go find them, then come back here and hold the line open for Dan."

"Suppose he can't locate these fellows in Cortez?"

"Then — let's not think about that."

24

GORDON FALLS

The news of O'Neil's attitude spread quickly, and excitement grew among the workmen. Up through the chill darkness of early evening they came charging. They were noisy and eager, and when the gong summoned them to supper, they rushed the mess house in boisterous good humor. No attempt was made to call out the night crew. By tacit consent its members were allowed to mingle freely with their fellows and plan for the morrow's departure. Some, envious of the crowd from Omar that had profited by an early start, were anxious to be gone at once, but the more sober minded argued the road to White River was so long that a day's advantage would mean little in the end, and the advance party would merely serve to break trail for those behind.

These men were not those who had struck earlier in the season at the behest of Gordon's emissary, Linn, but fellows whose loyalty and industry were unquestioned. Their refusal to stampede at the first news was proof of their devotion, yet anyone who has lived in a mining community knows that no loyalty of employee to employer is strong enough to withstand for long the feverish excitement of a gold rush. These bridge workers were the aristocracy of the whole force, men inured to hardship and capable of extreme sacrifice in the course of their work; but they were also independent Americans who believed themselves entitled to every reward that fortune laid in their paths. For this reason they were even harder to handle than the unskilled, unimaginative men farther down the line.

The low-roofed mess house was crowded long before the hour when O'Neil appeared.

Natalie and Eliza, knowing the importance of this crisis, refused to go home, and begged Murray to let them attend the meeting. Mr. Blaine, who also felt the keenest concern in the outcome, offered to escort them, and at last with some difficulty he managed to wedge them inside the door, where they apprehensively scanned the gathering.

It was not an ideal place for a meeting of this size, but tables and benches had been pushed aside, and into the space thus cleared the men were packed. Their appearance was hardly reassuring. It was a brawny, heavy-muscled army with which O'Neil had to deal — an army of loud-voiced toilers whose ways were violent and whose passions were quick. Nevertheless, the two girls were treated with the greatest respect, and when O'Neil stepped to a bench and raised himself above their heads, his welcome was not unduly boisterous. Outside, the night was clear and cold; inside the cramped quarters the air was hot and close and fetid.

Murray had no skill as a public speaker in the ordinary sense; he attempted no oratorical tricks and addressed his workmen in a matter-of-fact tone.

"Boys," he began, "there has been a gold strike at the head of the White River, and you want to go. I don't blame you. I'd like to go myself if there's any chance to make money."

"You're all right, boss!" shouted someone. And a general laugh attested the crowd's relief at this acceptance of the inevitable. They had expected argument, despite the contrary assurances they had received.

"Now we all want an even break. We want to know all there is to know, so that a few fellows won't have the advantage of the rest. The strike is 300 miles away. It's winter, and — you know what that means. I talked with Baker and Thorn this afternoon. I want them to tell you just what they told me. That's why I called this meeting. If you decide to go you won't have to waste time going to Omar after your outfits, for I'll sell you what you want from my supplies. And I'll sell at cost."

There was a yell of approval, a cheer for the speaker; then came calls for Baker and Thorn.

The two miners were thrust forward, and the embarrassed Thorn, who had acted as spokesman, was boosted to a table. Under Murray's encouragement he stammered out the story of his good fortune, the tale running straight enough to fan excitement into a blaze. There was no disposition to doubt, for news of this sort is only too sure of credence.

When the speaker had finished, O'Neil asked him a question.

"Are you an experienced quartz miner? Do you know ore when you see it?"

"Sure! I worked in the Jumbo, at Goldfield, Nevada, up to last year. So did Baker."

"When did you go into the White River country?"

"August."

"How did you go in?"

"We packed in. When our grub ran out, we killed our horses and cached the meat for dog feed."

"Is there any other dog feed there?"

"No, sir."

"Any people?"

"Not a soul. The country is open to the first comers. It's a fine-looking country, too: we seen quartz indications everywhere. I reckon this speaks for itself." Thorn significantly held up his ore samples. "We've made our locations. You fellows is welcome to the rest. First come, first served."

There was an eager scramble for the specimens on the part of those nearest the speaker.

"Did you fellows ever see any rock like that?" Murray asked them after a minute.

"I have," one of his workmen answered.

"Where?"

"In the Jumbo, at Goldfield. I high-graded there in the early days."

There was a laugh at this. Thorn flushed angrily. "Well," he said, "we've got the same formation over there in the White River. It's just like Goldfield. It'll be the same kind of a camp, too, when the news gets out."

O'Neil broke in smoothly.

"Most of our fellows have no dogs," he said. "It will take them three weeks to cover the trail. They'll have to spend three weeks in there, then three weeks more coming out—over two months altogether. They can't haul enough grub to do them." He turned to his employees. "You'd better think it over, boys. Those who have teams can make it, but the rest of you will get left. Do you think the chance is worth all that work and suffering?"

The bridge workers shifted uncomfortably on their feet. Then a voice called out.

"Don't worry, boss. We'll make it somehow."

"Thorn says there's nobody over there," Murray continued. "But that seems strange, for I happen to know of half a dozen outfits at the head of the White River. Jack Dalton has had a gang working there for four years."

Dalton was a famous character in the north—one of the most intrepid of the early pioneers—and the mention of his name brought a hush. A large part of the audience realized the truth of O'Neil's last statement yet resented having it thrust upon them. Thorn and Baker were scowling. Gray had just entered the room and was signaling to his chief. O'Neil realized he must score a triumph quickly if he wished to hold the attention of his men.

"If this strike was genuine, I wouldn't argue, but—it isn't," he told the men. A confusion of startled protests rose, the two miners burst out indignantly. But O'Neil, raising his voice for the first time, managed to make himself heard. "Those jewelry samples came from Nevada," he said. "I recognized them myself this afternoon, and here's another fellow who can't be fooled. Thorn told you he used to work in Goldfield. You can draw your own conclusions."

The temper of the crowd changed instantly. Jeers, groans, hisses arose. The men were on their feet now and growing noisier every moment; Baker and Thorn were glaring balefully at their accuser. But Gray succeeded in shouldering his way forward, and whispered to O'Neil, who turned suddenly and faced the men again.

"Just a minute!" he shouted. "You heard Thorn say he and Baker went prospecting in August. Well, we've just had Cortez on the cable and learned they were working for Gordon until two weeks ago." A sudden silence fell. Murray smiled down at the two strangers. "What do you say to that?"

Thorn flew into a purple rage.

"It's a damned lie! He's afraid you'll quit work, fellows." Viciously he flung himself toward the door, only to feel the grasp of the muscular physician upon his arm.

"Listen to this message from the cashier of the Cortez Home Bank!" bellowed Gray, his big voice dominating the uproar. Undisturbed by his prisoner's struggles, he read the cable to the crowd.

"Joe Thorn and Henry Baker quit work fifteenth, leaving for Fairbanks over winter trail, with five dogs—four gray and white malamutes, black shepherd leader. Thorn medium size, 35, red hair. Baker dark, scar on cheek. WILSON, Cashier."

The doctor's features spread into a broad grin. "You've all seen the dog team, and here's the red hair." His fingers sunk into his prisoner's fiery locks with a grip that threatened to leave him a scalp for a trophy. Thorn cursed and twisted.

The crowd's allegiance had been quick to shift, but it veered back to O'Neil with equal suddenness.

"Bunco!" yelled a hoarse voice, after a brief hush.

"Lynch 'em!" cried another; and the angry clamor burst forth anew.

"Don't be foolish," Murray shouted. "Nobody has been hurt."

"We'd have been on the trail tomorrow. Send 'em down the river barefoot!"

"Yes! What about that gang from Omar?"

"I'm afraid they'll have to take care of themselves," O'Neil said. "But these two men aren't altogether to blame. They're acting under orders. Isn't that right?" he asked Thorn.

The miner hesitated, until the grip in his hair tightened; then, evidently fearing the menace in the faces on every side, he decided to seek protection in a complete confession.

"Yes!" he admitted. "Gordon cooked it up. It's all a fake."

O'Neil nodded with satisfaction. "This is the second time he's tried to get my men away from me. The other time he failed because Tom Slater happened to come down with smallpox. Thank God, he recovered!"

A ripple of laughter spread, then grew into a bellow, for the nature of Happy Tom's illness had long since become a source of general merriment, and O'Neil's timely reference served to divert the crowd. It also destroyed most of its resentment.

"You fellows don't seem able to protect yourselves; so Doc and I will have to do it for you. Now listen," he continued, more gravely. "I meant it when I said I'd open the commissary and help you out if the strike were genuine, but, nevertheless, I want you to know just what it would have meant to me. I haven't enough money to complete the S. R. & N., and I can't raise enough, but I have signed an option to sell the road if the bridge is built by next spring. It's really a two year's job, and some engineers don't believe it can be built at all, but I know it can if you'll help. If we fail I'm ruined; if we succeed...." He waved his hands and smiled at them cheerfully. "Maybe we'll build another railroad somewhere. That's what this stampede meant. Now, will you stick to me?"

"You bet we'll stick!" the men roared.

At the rear of the room, where they had witnessed the rapid unfolding of this drama, the two girls joined in the shout. They were hugging each other and laughing hysterically.

"He handled them just right," said Blaine, with shining eyes. "Just right—but I was worried."

Walsh, the night foreman, raised his voice over the crowd.

"Does anybody want to buy a dog team cheap?"

"Who wants dogs now?" someone cried.

"Give 'em to Baker and Thorn!"

O'Neil was still speaking in all earnestness.

"Boys," he said, "we have a big job on our hands. It means fast work, long hours, and little sleep. We picked you fellows out because we knew you were the very best bridge workers in the world. Now the life of the S. R. & N. lies with you, and that bridge *must be built* on time. About these two men who tried to stampede us: I think it's enough punishment if we laugh at them. Don't you?" He smiled down at Thorn, who scowled, then grinned reluctantly and nodded his head.

When general good feeling was restored, Murray attempted to make his way out; but his men seemed determined to thank him one by one, and he was delayed through a long process of handshaking. It pleased him to see they understood from what hardships and disappointments he had saved them, and he was doubly grateful when Walsh rounded up his crew and announced the night shift would resume work at midnight.

He escaped at last, leaving the men grouped contentedly about huge pans of smoking doughnuts and pots of coffee the cook boys had brought in. Liquor was taboo in the camp, but he gave orders that unlimited cigars be distributed.

He was exhausted when he reached his quarters, for the crisis, coming on top of his many responsibilities, had taken all his vitality.

His found his once cheerless room was warm and cozy as he entered. He saw Natalie sleeping peacefully on his bed and Eliza curled up in his big chair waiting. She opened her eyes drowsily and smiled up at him.

"You were splendid, Omar Khayyam. I'm *so* glad," she said.

He laid a finger on his lips and glanced at the sleeping Natalie.

"Sh-h!"

"Where are you going to put us for the night?"

"Right here, of course."

"Those men will do anything for you now. I—I think I'd die, too, if anything happened to the bridge."

He took her hand in his and smiled wearily down into her earnest eyes. "Nothing will happen. Now go to bed—and thank you for making a home for me. It really is a home now. I'll appreciate it tomorrow."

Furnishings were sparse in railroad quarters during the early 1900s.

He tiptoed out and tramped over to Parker's quarters for the night.

The news of the White River fiasco reached Curtis Gordon in Seattle where he had gone in a final attempt to bolster up the tottering fortunes of the Cortez Home Railway. His disappointment was keen, yet O'Neil from the beginning had met his attacks with such uniform success that new failure did not really surprise him; it had been a forlorn hope at best. Strangely enough, he had begun to lose something of his assurance of late.

Although he maintained his outward appearance of confidence with all his old skill, within himself he felt a growing uneasiness, a lurking doubt of his abilities. Outwardly there was reason enough for discouragement, for, while his cooperative railroad scheme had begun brilliantly, its initial success had not been sustained. As time passed and Eliza Appleton's exposure remained unrefuted, he had found it ever more difficult to enlist support. His own denials and explanations seemed powerless to affect the public mind, and as he looked back, he dated his decline from the appearance of her first article. It had done all the mischief he had feared. Not only were his old stockholders dissatisfied, but wherever he went for aid he found a disconcerting lack of response, a half-veiled skepticism that was maddening.

Yet his immediate business worries were not all, nor the worst of his troubles: his physical powers were waning. To all appearances he was as strong as ever, but a strange bodily lassitude hampered him; he tired easily, and against this handicap he was forced to struggle continually. He had never rightly valued his amazing equipment of energy until now, when some subtle ailment had begun to sap it. The change was less in his muscular strength than in his nerves and his mental vigor. He found himself growing peculiarly irritable; his failures excited spasms of blind fury that left him weak and spent; he began to suffer the depressing tortures of insomnia. At times the nerves in his face and neck twitched unaccountably, and this distressing affection spread.

These symptoms had first manifested themselves after his unmerciful drubbing at the hands of Dan Appleton: but they were not the result of any injury; they were due to some deeper cause. When he had recovered his senses, after the departure of Dan and Natalie, he had fallen into a paroxysm of anger that lasted for days. He had raged and stormed like a madman, for, to say nothing of other humiliations, he prided himself extravagantly on his physical prowess. While the marks of the rough treatment he had suffered were disappearing he remained indoors, plunged in such abysmal fury that neither Gloria nor the fawning Denny dared approach him.

The very force of his emotions had permanently disturbed his poise, or perhaps affected some obscure lesion in his brain. Even when he showed himself again in public, he was still abnormally choleric. His fits of passion became almost apoplectic in their violence; they caused his associates to shun him as a man dangerous, and in his calmer moments he thought of them with alarm. He had tried to regain his nervous control, but without success, and his wife's anxiety only chafed him further.

Gradually he lost his mental buoyancy, and for the first time in his life he really yielded to pessimism. He found he could no longer attack a problem with his accustomed certainty of conquering it but was haunted by a foreboding of inevitable failure. All in all, when he reached the States on his critical mission, he knew he was far from being his old self, and he had deteriorated more than he knew.

A week or two of disappointments should have shown him the futility of further effort; at any other time it would have set him to putting his house in order for the final crash, but now it merely enraged him. He redoubled his activity, launching a new campaign of publicity so extravagant and ill-timed as to repel the assistance he needed. He had lost his finesse; his nicely adjusted financial sense had gone.

The outcome was not long delayed. It came in the form of a newspaper dispatch to the effect his Cortez bank had suspended payment because of a run started by the dissatisfied employees of the railroad. Through Gordon's flamboyant advertising his enterprises were so well known by this time that the story was featured despite his efforts to kill it. His frantic cables to Cortez for a denial only brought assurances the report was true and conditions would not mend unless a shipment of currency was immediately forthcoming.

Harassed by reporters, driven on by the need for a show of action, he set out to raise the money, but the support he had hoped for failed him when it transpired his bank's assets consisted mainly of real estate at boom prices and stock in his various companies had been inflated to the bursting point. Days passed, a week or more; then he was compelled to relinquish his option on the steamship line he had partly purchased, and to sacrifice all that had been paid in on the enterprise. This, too, made a big story for the newspapers, for it punctured one of the most imposing corporations in the famous "Gordon System." It likewise threatened to involve the others in the general crash. Hope Consolidated remained and Gordon's declaration the value of its shares was more than sufficient to protect his bank met with some credence until, swift upon the heels of the other disasters, came an application for a receiver by the stockholders, coupled with the promise of a rigorous investigation into his various financial manipulations. Then at last Gordon acknowledged defeat.

Ruin had come swiftly; the diversity of his interests made his situation the more hopeless, for so cunningly had he interlocked one with another that to separate them promised to be an endless task.

He kept up a successful pretense of confidence, and publicly promised to bring order out of chaos, but in secret he gave way to the blackest despair. Heretofore, failure had never affected him deeply, for he had always managed to escape with advantage to his pocket and without serious damage to his prestige, but out of the present difficulty he could find no way. His office force stopped work, frightened at his bearing; the bellboys of his hotel brought to the desk tales of such maniacal violence he was asked to move.

At last the citizens of Cortez, who up to this time had been like putty in his fingers, realized their betrayal and turned against him. Creditors attached the railway property, and certain violent tempered men prayed openly and earnestly to their gods for his return to Alaska in order they might exact satisfaction in frontier fashion. Eastern investors in Hope Consolidated appeared in Seattle: there was talk of criminal procedure.

Bewildered as he was, half crazed with anxiety, Gordon knew the avalanche had not only wrecked his fortunes but was bearing him swiftly toward the penitentiary. Its gates yawned to welcome him, and he felt a chilling terror such as he had never known.

One evening as Captain Johnny Brennan stood on the dock superintending the final loading of cargo for the S. R. & N., he was accosted by a tall, nervous man with shifting eyes and twitching lips. It was hard to recognize in this pitiable shaken creature the once resplendent Gordon, who had bent the whole northland to his ends. Some tantalizing demons inside the man's frame were jerking at his sinews. Fear was in his roving glance; he stammered; he plucked at the little captain's sleeve like a frightened woman. The open-hearted Irishman was touched.

"Yes," Johnny said after listening for a time. "I'll take you with me, and they won't catch you, either."

"I'll pay you well, handsomely. I'm a rich man," Gordon told him. "I have interests that demand attention, so — accept this money. Please! Keep it all, my good fellow."

Brennan stared at the bundle Gordon had thrust into his hand, then regarded the speaker curiously.

"Man dear," he said, "this isn't money. These are stock certificates."

"Eh? Stock? Well, there's money in stocks, big money if you know how to handle them." The promoter's wandering eye shifted to the line of stevedores trundling their trucks into the hold, then up to the crane with its straining burden of bridge material. Every package was stenciled with his rival's name.

"Bravo, Captain! We'll be up to the summit by Christmas," he said. "No graft! No incompetence! The utmost publicity in corporate affairs!' That's our platform. We're destined for a glorious success. Glorious success!"

"Go aboard and lie down," Brennan said. "You need a good sleep." Then, calling a steward, he ordered, "Show Mr. Gordon to my cabin and give him what he wants."

He watched the tall figure stumble up the gangplank.

"'The utmost publicity,' is it? Well, it's you that's getting it now," the captain thought as he shook his head. "And to think that you're the man with the mines and the railroads and the widow! I'm afraid you'll be in irons when she sees you, but — that's as good a finish as you deserve, after all."

25

PREPARATIONS TESTED

The building of the Salmon River bridge will not soon be forgotten by engineers and men of science. But, while the technical features of the undertaking are familiar to a few, the general public knows little about how the work was actually done; and since the building of the bridge was the pivotal point in Murray O'Neil's career, it may be well to describe in some detail its various phases—the steps that led up to that day when the Salmon burst her bonds and put the result of all his planning and labor to the final test.

Nowhere else in the history of bridge building had such conditions been encountered; nowhere on earth had work of this character been attended with greater hazards; never had circumstances created a situation of more dramatic interest. By many the whole venture was regarded as a reckless gamble; for more than a million dollars had been risked on the chance not alone that O'Neil could build supports the ice could not demolish, but that he could build them under the most serious difficulties in record-breaking time.

Far more than the mere cost of the structure hinged upon his success. Failure would mean his whole investment up to that point would be wiped out, to say nothing of the $20 million project of a trunkline up the valley of the Salmon. Had the government permitted the Kyak coalfields to be opened, the lower reaches of the Salmon

River and Northwestern Railway would have had a value, but all activity in that region had been throttled, and the policy of delay and indecision at headquarters promised no relief.

Careful as had been the plans, exhaustive and painstaking as had been the preparations, the bridge builders met with unpreventable delays, disappointments, and disasters. For man is but a feeble creature whose brain tires and whose dreams are brittle. It is with these hindrances and accidents and with their effect upon the outcome we must deal.

Of course, the greatest handicap, the one ever-present obstacle, was the cold, and this made itself most troublesome in the sinking of the caissons and the building of the concrete piers. It was necessary, for instance, to house in all cement work, and to raise the temperature not only of the air surrounding it, but of the materials themselves before they were mixed and laid. Huge windbreaks had to be built to protect the outside men from the gales that scoured the riverbed, and these were forever blowing down or suffering damage from the hurricane force winds. All this, however, had been anticipated. It was but the normal condition of work in the northland. And it was not until the middle of winter, shortly after Eliza's and Natalie's visit to the front, an unexpected danger threatened, a danger more appalling than any upon which O'Neil and his assistants had reckoned.

In laying his plans, Parker had proceeded on the assumption that, once the cold had gripped the glaciers, they would remain motionless until spring. All available evidence went to prove the correctness of this supposition. But Alaska is a land of surprises, of contrasts, of contradictions. Study of its phenomena is too recent to make practicable the laying down of hard and fast rules. During a season of cruelly low temperatures there came a thaw, unprecedented, inexplicable.

A tremendous warm breath from the Pacific rolled northward, bathing the frozen plains and mountain ranges. Blizzards turned to rains and weeping fogs, the dry and shifting snowfields melted, water ran in the courses. Winter loosened its hold. Its mantle slipped. Nothing like this had ever been known or imagined. It was impossible!

It was as if the unhallowed region were bent upon living up to its evil reputation.

In a short time the loosened waters that trickled through the sleeping icefields greased the foundations upon which they lay. Jackson Glacier roused itself, then began to glide forward like a ship upon its ways. First there came the usual premonitory explosions — the sound of subterranean blasts as the ice cracked, gave way, and shifted to the weight above; echoes filled the sodden valley with memories of the summer months. It was as if the seasons had changed, as if the zodiacal procession had been thrown into confusion. The frozen surface of the Salmon was inundated. Water four feet deep in some places ran over it.

The general wonder at this occurrence changed to consternation when it was seen that the glacier acted like a battering ram of stupendous size, buckling the river ice in front of it as if ice were made of paper. That seven-foot armor was crushed, broken into a thousand fragments, which threatened to choke the stream. A half-mile below the bridge site the Salmon was pinched as if between two jaws. Its smooth surface was rapidly turned into an indescribable jumble of upended cakes.

When a fortnight had passed, O'Neil began to fear this movement would go on until the channel had been closed as by a huge sliding door. In that case, the rising waters would quickly wipe out all traces of his work. Such a crumpling and shifting of the ice had never occurred before — at least, not within 50 years, as the alder and cottonwood growth on the east bank showed; but nothing seemed impossible, no prank too grimly grotesque for Nature to play in this solitude. O'Neil felt his own ingenuity was quite unequal to the task of combating this peril. Set against forces so tremendous and arbitrary, human invention seemed dwarfed to a pitiable insignificance.

Day after day he watched the progress of that white palisade; day after day he scanned the heavens for a sign of change, for out of the sky alone could come his deliverance. Hourly tests were made at the bridge site, lest the ice should give way before the pressure from below and by moving upstream destroy the intricate pattern of piling that was being driven to support the steelwork. But day after day the snows continued to melt and the rain to fall. Two rivers were now boiling past the camp, one hidden deep, the other a shallow torrent that ran on a bed of ice. Sounds of the glacier's snaillike progress filled the valley.

Then, without apparent cause, the seasons fell into order again, the mercury dropped, the surface water disappeared, the country was sheeted with a glittering crust over which men walked, leaving no trace of footprints. Jackson became silent. Once again, the wind blew cold from out of the funnel mouth and the bridge builders threshed their arms to start their blood. But the glacier face had advanced 400 feet from its position in August; it had narrowed the Salmon by fully one-half its width.

Fortunately, the bridge had suffered no damage. But no one foresaw the effect these altered conditions were to have.

The actual erection of steelwork was impossible during the coldest months. Parker had planned only to rush the piers, abutments, and falsework to completion so he could take advantage of mild spring weather preceding the breakup. The execution of this plan was an unparalleled undertaking, making it necessary to hire double crews of picked men. Yet, as weeks wore into months, the intricate details were wrought out one by one, and preparations were completed for the great race.

Dan Appleton went to the front late in March, taking with him his wife and sister, for whom O'Neil had thoughtfully prepared suitable living quarters. The girls were as hungry as Dan to have a part in the deciding struggle, or at least to see it close at hand, for the spirit of those engaged in the work had entered them also. Life at Omar of late had been rather uneventful, and they looked forward with pleasure to a renewal of those companionable relations that had made the summer months so full of interest and delight.

But they were disappointed. They found life at the end of the line to be a grim, earnest, and in some respects, extremely disagreeable affair. The feverish, unceasing activity of their friends left no time for companionship or recreation. More and more they, too, came to feel the sense of haste and strain pervading the whole army of workers, the weight of responsibility that bore upon the commander.

Dan became almost a stranger to them, and when they saw him, he was obsessed by vital issues. Mellen was gruff and irritable. Parker in his preoccupation ignored everything but his duties. Of all their former comrades, O'Neil alone seemed aware of their presence. But behind his smile they saw the lurking worries. In his eyes was an abstraction they could not penetrate, in his bearing the fatigue of a man tried to the breaking point.

To Eliza there was a certain joy merely in being near the man she loved, even though she could not help being hurt by his apparent indifference. The long weeks without sight of him had deepened her feeling, and she had turned for relief to the writing of her book—the natural outlet for her repressed emotions. Into its pages she had poured all her passion, all her yearning, and she had written with an intimate understanding of O'Neil's ambitions and aims that later gave the story its unique success as an epic of financial romance.

Hers was a nature that could not be content with idleness. She took up the work she and Natalie had begun, devoting herself unobtrusively yet effectively to making O'Neil comfortable. It was a labor of love, done with no expectation of reward. It thrilled her, filling her with mingled sadness and satisfaction. But if Murray noticed the improvement in his surroundings, which she sometimes doubted, he evidently attributed it to a sudden access of zeal on the part of Ben, for he made no comment. Whether or not she wished him to see and understand she could hardly tell. Somehow his unobservant, masculine acceptance of things better and worse appealed to the woman in her. She slipped into O'Neil's quarters during his absence and slipped out again quietly. She learned to know his ways, his peculiarities. She found herself caressing and talking to his personal belongings as if they could hear and understand. She conducted long conversations with the objects on his bureau. Ben entered unexpectedly one morning and caught her in the act of kissing Murray's shaving mirror as if it still preserved the image of its owner's face. She banished the cook boy from O'Neil's room and performed his duties herself.

Of course, discovery was inevitable. At last O'Neil stumbled in upon her during her task, and, questioning her, read the truth from her blushes and her incoherent attempts at explanation.

'So – you're the one who has been doing this!" he exclaimed, in frank astonishment. "And I've been tipping Benny for his thoughtfulness all this time. The rascal has made enough to retire rich."

"He seemed not to understand his duties very well, so I took charge. But you had no business to catch me!" The flush died from Eliza's cheeks, and she faced him with thoroughly feminine indignation.

"I can't let you go on with this," Murray said. "I ought to be doing something for *you.*"

But the girl flared up defiantly. "I love it. I'll do it, no matter if you lock me out. I'm not on the payroll, you know, so you have no authority over me – none at all!"

His eyes roved around the room, and for the first time he fully took in the changes her hands had wrought.

"My dear child, it's very nice to be spoiled this way and have everything neat and clean, but – it embarrasses me dreadfully to have you saddled with the sordid work."

"It isn't sordid, and – what brought you home at this hour, anyhow?" she asked.

O'Neil's smile gave place to an anxious frown.

"The ice is rising, and…."

"Rising?"

"Yes. Our old enemy Jackson Glacier is causing us trouble again. That jam of broken ice in front of it is backing up the water – there's more running now, and the ice is lifting. It's lifting the falsework with it, pulling the piles out of the river bottom like splinters out of a sore hand."

"That's pretty bad, isn't it?"

"It certainly is. It threatens to throw everything out of alignment and prevent us from laying the steel if we don't check it."

"Check it!" Eliza said. "How can you check a thing like that?"

"Easily enough, if we can spare the hands, by cutting away the ice where it is frozen to the piles, so it won't lift them with it. The trouble is to get men enough—you see, the ice is nine feet thick now. I've set every man to work with axes and chisels and steam points, and I came up to telephone Slater for more help. We'll have to work fast, night and day."

"There's nobody left in Omar," Eliza said.

"I know. Tom's going to gather all he can at Cortez and Hope and rush them out here. Our task is to keep the ice cut away until help arrives."

"I suppose it's too late in the season to repair any serious damage?"

"Exactly. If you care to go back with me, you can see what we're doing." As they set off for the bridge site, Murray looked down at Eliza, striding manlike beside him, with something of affectionate appreciation in his eyes.

"It was careless of me not to see what you have been doing for me all this time," he told her. "My only excuse is I've been driven half mad with other things. I haven't time to think of myself."

"All housekeepers have a thankless task," Eliza said with a laugh.

When they reached the riverbank, she saw everything apparently just as when she had last seen it. "Why, it's not as bad as I imagined!" she said. "I thought I'd find everything going to smash."

"Oh, there's nothing spectacular about it. There seldom is with serious mishaps in this business. The ice has risen only an inch or more so far, but the very slowness and sureness of it is what's alarming. It shows the water is backing up, and as the flow increases the rise of the ice will quicken. If it starts to move up or downstream, we're lost."

There was ample evidence the menace was thoroughly understood, for the whole day shift was toiling at the ice, chopping it, thawing it, shoveling it away, although its tremendous thickness made their efforts seem futile. Everywhere there was manifested a frantic haste, a grim, strained eagerness that was full of ominous meaning.

All that day Eliza watched the unequal struggle, and in the evening, Dan brought her reports that were far from reassuring. The relentless movement showed no sign of ceasing. When she retired that night, she sought ease from her anxiety in a prayer that was half a petition for O'Neil's success and half an exceedingly full and frank confession of her love for him. Outside, beneath the glare of torches and hastily strung lights, a weary army toiled stubbornly, digging, gouging, chopping at the foot of the towering wall of timbers that stretched across the Salmon. In the north the Aurora Borealis played brilliantly as if to light a council of the gods.

On the following day Happy Tom arrived with 50 men.

"I got the last mother's son I could find," he said, as he warmed himself at O'Neil's stove. "I did, and I saw the splavvus, himself."

"Gordon?"

"He's worse than we thought." Tom tapped his shining forehead significantly. "Loft to let!"

"What? Insane?"

"Nothing but echoes in his dome. The town's as empty as his bonnet, too, and the streets are full of snow. It's a sight!"

"Tell me about Mrs. Gordon."

"She's quite a person," Slater said. "She surprised me. She's there, alone with him and a watchman. She does all the work, even lugging in the wood and coal—he's too busy to help—but she won't leave him. She told me Dan and Natalie wanted her to come over here, but she couldn't bring herself to do it or to let them assist in any way. Gordon spends all his time at his desk, promoting, writing ads and prospectuses. He's got a grand scheme. He's found that Hope Consolidated is full of rich ore, but the trouble is in getting it out; so he's working on a new process of extraction. It's a wonderful process—you'd never guess what it is. He *smokes* it out! He says all he needs is plenty of smoke. That bothered him until he hit on the idea of burning feathers. Now he's planning to raise ducks because they've got so much down. Isn't that the limit? She'll have to fit him into a padded cell sooner or later."

"Poor devil!" O'Neil said. "I'm sorry. He had an unusual mind."

Slater sniffed. "I think it's pretty soft for him, myself. He's made better than a standoff—he lost his memory, but he saved his skin. It's funny how some men can't fall. If they slip on a banana peel, somebody shoves a cushion under 'em before they 'light. I never got the best of anything. If I dropped asleep in church my wife would divorce me and I'd go to the electric chair. Gordon robs widows and orphans, right and left, then ends up with a loving woman to take care of him in his old age. Why, if I even robbed a blind puppy of a biscuit I'd leave a thumbprint on his ear, or the dog's mother would turn out to be a bloodhound.

"Anyhow, I'd spend *my* declining years nestled up to a rock pile, with a mallet in my mitt, and a low-browed gentleman scowling at me from the top of a wall. He'd lean on his shotgun and say, 'Hurry up, Fatty, it's getting late and there's a ton of oakum to pick.' It just goes to show that some of us is born behind the game and never get even, while others, like Gordon, quit winners no matter how much they lose." Having relieved himself of this fervid homily, Happy Tom unrolled a package of gum and thrust three sticks into his mouth. "Speaking of bad luck," he continued, "when are you going to get married, Murray?"

O'Neil started. "Why — never. It isn't the same kind of proposition as building a bridge, you know. There's a little matter of youth and good looks that counts considerably in the marriage business. No woman would have an old chap like me."

Slater took a mournful inventory of his chief's person. "You *might* put it over, Murray. I ain't strictly handsome, myself, but I did."

As O'Neil slipped into his fur coat, after the fat man had slouched out, he caught sight of himself in the glass of his bureau and paused. He leaned forward and studied the care-worn countenance that peered forth at him, then shook his head. He saw the hair was growing grayer, the face was plain, and — yes, unquestionably – it was no longer youthful. Of course, he didn't feel old, but the evidence that he was so admitted of no disproof, and it was evidence of a sort that no woman could disregard. He turned from the glass with a qualm of disgust at his weakness in allowing himself to be influenced in the slightest by Tom's suggestion.

The ice rose slowly for a week, a foot a day, and despite the greatest watchfulness it took the falsework with it here and there. But concentrated effort at the critical points saved the structure from serious injury.

Then the jam in front of Jackson Glacier went out, at least in part, and the ice began to fall. Down the falsework settled, smoothly, swiftly, until it rested once more upon the shores. It was still as firm as in midwinter and showed no sign of breaking; nor had it moved downstream a hair's breadth. O'Neil gathered his forces for the final onslaught.

26

THE RACE IS ON

The last of the steel for Span Number One reached the front on April 5, and erection began. The men fell to with a vim and enthusiasm impossible to describe. With incredible rapidity the heavy sections were laid in place. The riveters began their metallic song, the towering three bent traveler ran smoothly on its track, and under it grew a web work of metal braced and reinforced to withstand, in addition to ordinary strains, the pressure of 100-mile-an-hour winds. To those who looked on, the structure appeared to build itself, like some dream edifice. It seemed a miracle that human hands could work that stubborn metal so swiftly and with so little effort. But every piece had been cut and fitted carefully, then checked and placed where it was accessible.

Spring came with a rush now that winter had broken. The snows began to shrink, and the drifts settle. The air grew balmier with every day. The drip from eaves was answered by gurgling laughter of hidden waters. Here and there the boldest mountainsides began to show, and the tops of alder thickets thrust themselves into sight. Where wood or metal caught the sunrays, the snow retreated; pools of ice water began to form at noon.

The days were long, too, and no frozen winds charged out of the north. As the daylight lengthened, so did the working hours of the toilers.

On April 18, the span was completed. In 13 days, Mellen's crew had laid 400 feet of the heaviest steel ever used in a bridge of this type. But there was no halt. The material for the second section had been assembled, meanwhile, and the traveler began to swing it into place.

The din was unceasing. The clash of riveters, the creak and rattle of hoists, the shouts of men mingled in a persistent, ear-splitting clamor, and foot by foot the girders reached out toward the second monolith that rose from the riverbed. The well-adjusted human machine was running smoothly. Every man knew his place and the duties that went with it; the hands of each worker were capable and skilled.

Hillsides were growing bare, rills gashed the sloping snowfields, the upper gullies began to rumble to avalanches — forerunners of the process that would strip the earth of snow and ice and free the river in all its fury. In six days, 300 feet more of steel had been bolted fast to the complete section, and Span Two was in place. But the surface of the Salmon was no longer white and pure; it was dirty and discolored now, for the debris that had collected during the past winter was exposing itself. The icy covering was partially inundated also. Shallow ponds formed upon it and were rippled by the south breeze. Running waters on every side sang a menace to the workers.

Then progress ceased abruptly. A part for the third span had gone astray in its journey across the continent – a delay at the Pittsburg mills, then a blockade in the Sierras. O'Neil was in Omar at the end of the cable straining every nerve to have the shipment rushed through. Mellen brooded over his uncompleted work. Parker studied the dripping hills and measured the melting snows. He still smiled, but showed his anxiety in constant nervous unrest and could not sleep.

At length news came that Johnny Brennan had the steel aboard his ship and had sailed. A record run was predicted, but meanwhile the south wind brought havoc on its breath. The sun shone hotly into the valley of the Salmon, and instead of warmth it brought a chill to the hearts of those who watched and waited.

Twelve endless, idle days crawled by. Winter no longer gave battle. She was routed, and in her mad retreat she threatened to overwhelm O'Neil's fortunes.

THE RACE IS ON

On May 6, the needed bridge parts were assembled, and the erection of Span Three began. The original plan had been to build this section on the cantilever principle to gain independence of the river ice, but to do so would have meant slow work and delay — an expenditure of time the terms of the option made impossible. Arrangements had been made, therefore, to lay it on falsework as the other spans had been laid, risking everything upon the weather.

As a matter of precaution, the southern half of the span was connected to the completed portion; but before the connection could be fully made, the remainder of the jam in front of Jackson Glacier, which had caused so much trouble heretofore, went out suddenly, and the river ice moved downstream about a foot, carrying with it the whole intricate system of supporting timbers beneath the uncompleted span. Hasty measurements showed the north end of the steel then on the falsework was 13 inches out of line.

It was Mr. Blaine who brought the tidings of this last calamity to Eliza Appleton. From his evident anxiety, she gathered the matter was of graver consequence than she could understand.

"Thirteen inches in 1,500 feet can't amount to much," she said.

Blaine smiled despite himself. "You don't understand. It's as bad as 13 feet, for the work can't go on until everything is in perfect alignment. That whole forest of piles must be straightened."

"Impossible!" she gasped. "Why, there are thousands of them."

He shook his head, still smiling doubtfully. "Nothing is impossible to Mellen and Parker. They've begun clearing away the ice on the upstream side and driving new anchor piles above. They're going to fit tackle to them and yank the whole thing upstream. I never heard of such a thing, but there's no time to do anything else." He cast a worried look at the smiling sky. "I wonder what will happen next. This is getting on my nerves."

Out on the river, swift work was going on. Steam from every available boiler was carried across the ice in feedpipes, the night shift had been roused from sleep, and every available man was busied in relieving the pressure. Pile drivers hammered long timbers into the riverbed above the threatened point, hydraulic jacks were put in place, and steel cables were run to drum and pulley. The men worked sometimes knee-deep in ice water; but they did not walk, they ran. In an incredibly short time, the preparations were completed, a strain was put upon the tackle, and when night came the massive falsework had been pulled back into line and the traveler was once more swinging steel into place. It was a magnificent feat, yet not one of those concerned in it could feel confident the work had not been done in vain; for the time was growing terribly short, and, although the ice seemed solid, it was rotting fast.

After the southern half of the span had been completed, the warmth increased rapidly, therefore the steel crew lengthened its hours. The men worked from seven o'clock in the morning until eleven o'clock at night.

On the 13th, without warning of any sort, Garfield Glacier began moving forward. It had lain inactive even during the midwinter thaw that had started its smaller brother, but that warm spell had evidently had its effect upon the giant, for now he shook off his lethargy and awoke. He stirred, gradually at first and without sound, as if bent upon surprising the interlopers. Then his speed increased. As the glacier advanced, it thrust the nine-foot blanket of lake ice ahead of it, and this in turn crowded the river ice down upon the bridge. The movement at the camp site on the first day was only two inches, but that was sufficiently serious.

The onset of Garfield was unexpected. No forward motion had ever been reported prior to the spring breakup. The action of the ice heretofore had been alarming but now consternation spread, a panic swept the ranks of the builders, for this was no short-lived phenomenon, this was the annual march of the glacier itself that promised to continue indefinitely. A tremendous cutting-edge, nine feet in thickness, like the blade of a carpenter's plane, was being driven against the bridge by an irresistible force.

Once again, the endless thawing and chopping and gouging of ice began, but the more rapidly the encroaching edge was cut away the more swiftly did it bear down. The huge mass began to rumble; it calved, it split, it detonated, and, having finally loosened itself from its bed, it acquired increased momentum. As the men with chisels and steam points became exhausted, others took their places, but the structural gang clung to its perch above, augmenting the din of riveters and the groaning of blocks and tackle. Among the able-bodied men sleep now was out of the question, for the ice gained despite every effort. It was too late to remove the steel in the uncompleted span to a place of safety, for that would have required more time than to bridge the remaining gap.

Piling began to buckle and bend before that irresistible push; the whole nicely balanced mass of metal was in danger of being unseated. Mellen cursed the heavens in a black fury. Parker smiled through white lips. O'Neil ground his teeth and spurred his men on.

This feverish haste brought its penalty. On the evening of the 14th, when the span was more than three-quarters finished, a lower chord section fouled as it was lifted, and two loading beams at the top of the traveler snapped.

On that day victory had been in sight. The driving of the last bolt had been but a question of hours, a race with the sliding ice. But with the hoisting apparatus out of use work halted. Swiftly, desperately, without loss of a moment's time, repairs began. No regrets were voiced, no effort was made to place the blame, for that would have caused delay, and every minute counted. Eleven hours later the broken beams were replaced, and erection continued.

But now for those above there was danger to life and limb. During the pause, the ice had gained, and no effort could relieve the falsework of its strain. All knew if it gave way the workmen would be caught in a chaos of collapsing wood and steel.

From the morning of May 14 until midnight of the 16th, the ironworkers clung to their tasks. They dropped their tools and ran to their meals; they gulped their food and fled back to their posts. The weaker ones gave out and staggered away, cursed, and taunted by their companions. They were rough fellows, and in their deep-throated profanity was a prayer.

The strong ones struggled on, blind with weariness, but upheld by that desperate, unthinking courage that animates a bayonet charge.

It seemed every moment must see the beginning of slow work of demolition that would send them all scurrying to safety; but hour after hour the piling continued to hold and the fingers of steel to reach out, foot by foot, for the concrete pier that was their goal.

At midnight of the 16th, the last rivet was driven. But the ice had gained to such an extent the lower chord was buckled downstream about eight inches, and the distance was growing steadily. Quickly the traveler was shifted to the falsework beyond the pier, and the men under Mellen's direction fell to splitting out the blocking.

As the supports were chopped away, the mass began to crush the last few wedges. There was a great snapping and rending of wood. And someone, strained to the breaking point, shouted.

"Look out! There she goes!"

A cry of terror arose. The men fled, trampling one another in their panic. But Mellen charged them like a wild man, firing curses and orders at them until they rallied. The remaining supports were removed. The 1,500 tons of metal settled into place and rested securely on its foundations.

O'Neil was the last man ashore. As he walked the completed span from Pier Three, the barricade of piling beneath him was bending and tearing. But he issued no orders to remove it, for the river was doing that. In the general haste, pile drivers, hoists, boilers, and various odds and ends of machinery and material had been left where they stood. They were being inundated now, many of them submerged. There was no possibility of saving them at present, for the men were half dead from exhaustion.

As he lurched up the muddy, uneven street to his quarters, Murray felt his fatigue like a heavy burden, for he had been 60 hours without sleep. He saw Slater and Appleton and the rest of his boys. He also saw Natalie and Eliza but was too tired to speak to them, or to grasp what they said. He heard the workmen cheering Mellen and Parker and himself. It was foolish, he thought, to cheer, since the river had so nearly triumphed, and the final test was yet to come.

He fell upon his bed, fully clothed. An hour later the falsework beneath Span Three collapsed.

Although the bridge was not yet finished, the most critical point of its construction had passed, for the fourth and final portion would be built over shallow water, and no great difficulties were expected even though the ice went out before the work was finished. But Murray had made his promise and his boast to complete the structure within a stated time, and he was determined to live up to the letter of his agreement with the Trust. As to the result of the breakup, he had no fear whatever.

For once Nature aided him. She seemed to smile as if in approval of his steadfastness. The movement of the channel ice became irregular, spasmodic, but it remained firm until the last span had been put in place.

Of this dramatic struggle Eliza Appleton had watched every phase with intense interest. But when at last she knew the battle was won, she experienced a peculiar revulsion of feeling. So long as O'Neil had been working against odds, with the prospect of ruin and failure forever imminent, she had felt an almost painful sympathy, but now that he had conquered, she felt timid about congratulating him. He was no longer to be pitied and helped. He had attained his goal and the fame he longed for. His success would inevitably take him out of her life. She was sorry he needed her no longer.

She did not watch the last bridge member swung. Instead, she went to her room and tried to face the future. Spring was here, her book was finished, there was the need to take up her life again.

She was surprised when Murray came to find her.

"I missed you, Eliza," he said. "The others are all down at the riverbank. I want you to congratulate me."

She saw, with a jealous twinge, that exultation over his victory had overcome his weariness, that his face was alight with a fire she had never seen. He seemed young, vigorous, and masterful once more.

"Of course," he went on, "the credit belongs to Parker, who worked the bridge out in each detail—he's marvelous—and to Mellen, who built it, but I helped a little. Praise to me means praise to them."

"It is all over now, isn't it?"

"Practically. Blaine has cabled New York that we've won. Strictly speaking, we haven't yet, for there's still the breakup to face. But the bridge will come through it without a scratch. The ice may go out any minute now, and after that I can rest." He smiled at her. "It will feel good to get rid of all this responsibility, won't it? I think you've suffered under it as much as I have."

A little wistfully she answered: "You're going to realize that dream you told me about the day of the storm at Kyak. You have conquered this great country — just as you dreamed."

He acquiesced eagerly, boyishly. "Yes. Whirring wheels, a current of traffic, a broad highway of steel — that's the sort of monument I want to leave."

"I'll come back sometime and see it all completed and tell myself that I had a little part in making it."

"Come back?" he asked. "Why, you're going to stay till we're through, aren't you?"

"Oh no! I'm going south with the spring flight — on the next boat, perhaps."

His face fell. The exultant light gradually faded from his eyes.

"Why — I had no idea! Aren't you happy here?"

She nodded. "But I must try to make good in my work as you have in yours."

He was looking at her sorrowfully, almost as if she had deserted him.

"That's too bad, but — I suppose you must go. Yes, this is no place for you. I dare say other people need you to bring sunshine and joy to them just as we old fellows do, but — I've never thought about your leaving. It wouldn't be right to ask you to stay here among such people as we are when you have so much ahead of you. Still, it will leave a gap. Yes — it certainly will — leave a gap."

She longed desperately to tell him how willingly she would stay if he only asked her, but the very thought shocked her into a deeper reserve.

"I'm going East to sell my book," she said. "You've given me the climax of the story in this race with the seasons."

"Is it a—love story?" he asked.

Eliza flushed. "Yes. It's mostly love."

"You're not at all the girl I thought you when we first met. You're —different. I'm sure I won't recognize myself as the hero. Who—or what is the girl in the story?"

"Well, she's just the kind of girl that would appeal to a person like you. She's tall and dark and dashing, and—of course, she's remarkably beautiful. She's very feminine, too."

"What's her name?"

Miss Appleton stammered. "Why—I—called her Violet—until I could think of a better...."

"What's wrong with Violet? You couldn't think of a better name than that. I'm fond of it."

"Oh, it's a good book name, but for real life it's too—delicate." Eliza felt with vexation her face was burning. She was sure he was laughing at her.

"Can I read the manuscript?" he asked.

"Heavens! No! I...." She abruptly changed the subject. "I've left word to be called the minute the ice starts to go out. I want to see the last act of the drama."

When O'Neil left her, he was vaguely perplexed, for something in her bearing did not seem quite natural. He was forlorn, too, at the prospect of losing her. He wondered if fathers suffered thus, or if a lover could be more deeply pained at a parting than he. Somehow, he seemed to share the feelings of both.

27

A Dream Comes True

Early on the following morning, Eliza was awakened by a sound of shouting outside her window. She lay half dazed for a moment or two, until the significance of the uproar made itself apparent. Then she leaped from her bed.

"There she goes!" she heard men shout. "She's going out!"

Doors were slamming, there was the rustle and scuff of flying feet, and in the next room Dan was evidently throwing himself into his clothes like a fireman. Eliza called to him, but he did not answer. The next moment he had fled, upsetting some article of furniture in his haste. Drawing her curtains aside, the girl saw in the brightening dawn men pouring down the street, dressing as they went. They seemed half demented, yelling at one another, but she could not gather from their words whether it was the ice moving or—the bridge. The bridge! That possibility set her to dressing with tremulous fingers, her heart sick with fear. She called to Natalie, but scarcely recognized her own voice.

"I—don't know," came the muffled reply to her question. "It sounds like something—terrible. I'm afraid Dan will fall in or—get hurt." The confusion in the street was growing. "*Eliza!*" Natalie's voice was tragic.

"What is it, dear?"

"Help me, quick!"

"How?"

"I can't find my other shoe."

But Eliza was sitting on the floor, lacing up her own stout boots, and an instant later she followed her brother, pursued by a wail of dismay from the adjoining chamber. Through the chill morning light she hurried, asking many questions, but receiving no coherent reply from the racing men. Then after endless moments of suspense she saw with relief the massive superstructure of the bridge was still standing. Above the shouting she heard another sound, indistinct but insistent. It filled the air with a whispering movement. It was punctuated at intervals by a dull rumbling and grinding. She found the riverbank black with forms, but like a cat she wormed her way through the crowd until the whole panorama lay before her.

The bridge stood as she had seen it the day before — slender, strong, superb in the simplicity of its splendid outline. But beneath it and as far as her eyes could follow the river she saw, not the solid spread of white to which she had become accustomed, but a moving expanse of floes. At first the winter burden slipped past in huge masses, acres in extent, but soon these began to be pulled apart. Irregular black seams ran through them, opened, closed, and threw up ridges of ice shavings as they ground together. The floes were rubbing against the banks, they came sliding out over the dry shore like tremendous sheets of cardboard manipulated by unseen hands, and not until their nine-foot edges were exposed to view did the mind grasp the appalling significance of their movement. They swept down in phalanxes upon the wedge-like icebreakers that stood guard above the bridge piers, then they halted, separated, and the armored cutting edges sheared through them like blades.

A half-mile below, where the Salmon flung itself headlong against the upper wing of Jackson Glacier, the floating ice was checked by the narrowed passageway. There a jam was forming, and as the river heaved and tore at its growing burden, a spectacular struggle went on. The sound of it came faintly but impressively to the watchers — a grinding and crushing of bergs, a roar of escaping waters. Fragments were upended, masses were rearing themselves edgewise into the air, were overturning and collapsing. They were wedging themselves into every conceivable angle, and the crowding procession from above was adding to the barrier momentarily. As the passageway became blocked, the waters rose; the river piled itself up so swiftly that the eye could note its rise along the banks.

But the attention of the crowd was divided between the jam and something far out on the bridge itself. At first glance Eliza did not comprehend. Then she heard a man explain.

"He was going out when we got here, and now he won't come back."

The girl gasped, for she recognized the distant figure of a man, dwarfed to puny proportions by the bulk of the structure in the mazes of which he stood. The man was O'Neil. He was perched on one of the girders near the center of the longest span, where he could watch the attack upon the pyramidal icebreakers beneath him.

"He's a fool," said someone at Eliza's back. "That jam is getting bigger."

"He'd better let the damned bridge take care of itself."

She turned and began to force her way through the press of people between her and the south abutment. She arrived there, disheveled and panting, to find Slater, Mellen, and Parker standing in the approach. In front of them extended the long skeleton tunnel into which Murray had gone.

"Mr. O'Neil is out there!" she cried to Tom.

Slater turned and, reading the tragic appeal in her face, reassured her.

"Sure! But he's all right."

"They say — there's danger."

Happy Tom's round visage puckered into a doubtful smile. "Oh, he'll take care of himself."

Mellen turned to the girl.

"There's no danger whatever."

But Eliza's fear was not to be so easily quieted.

"Then why did he go out alone? What are you men doing here?"

"It's his orders," Tom told her.

Mellen was staring at the jam below, over which the Salmon was hurling a flood of ice and foaming waters. The stream was swelling and rising steadily. Already it had nearly reached the level of the timberline on the left bank. The blockade was extending upstream almost to the bridge. Mellen said something to Parker, who shook his head silently.

Dan Appleton shouldered his way out of the crowd with Natalie at his heels. She had dressed herself in haste: her hair was loose, her jacket was buttoned awry; on one foot was a shoe, on the other a bedroom slipper muddy and sodden. Her dark eyes were big with excitement.

"Why don't you make Murray come in?" Dan demanded sharply.

"He won't do it," Slater said.

"The jam is growing. Nobody knows what'll happen if it holds much longer. If the bridge should go...."

Mellen whirled. "It won't go!" he shouted. "All hell couldn't take it out."

From the ranks of the workmen came a bellow of triumph, as an unusually heavy icefloe was swept against the breakers and rent asunder. The tumult of the imprisoned waters below was growing louder every moment. Across the lake came a stentorian rumble as a huge mass was loosened from the front of Garfield. The channel of the Salmon, where the onlookers stood, was a heaving, churning caldron over which the slim bridge flung itself defiantly.

Eliza plucked at her brother's sleeve, and he saw her for the first time.

"Hello, Sis," he cried. "How did you get here?"

"Is he in danger, Danny?"

"Yes — no! Mellen says it's all right, so it must be, but — that dam...."

At that moment Natalie began to sob hysterically, and Dan turned his attention to her.

But his sister was not of the hysterical kind. Seizing Tom Slater by the arm, she tried to shake him, demanding information.

"Suppose the jam doesn't give way! What will happen?" Happy Tom stared at her uncomprehendingly. Her voice was shrill and insistent. "Suppose the water rises higher. Won't the ice sweep down on the bridge itself? Won't it wreck everything if it goes out suddenly? Tell me...."

"It can't hold. Mellen says so." Slater, like the others, found it impossible to keep his eyes from the river where those immeasurable forces were at play. Then in his peculiar irascible manner he complained, "I told 'em we was crazy to try this. It ain't a white man's country; it ain't a safe place for a bridge. There's just one God-awful thing after another...."

He broke into a shout, for Eliza had slipped past him and was speeding like a shadow out across the irregularly spaced ties upon which the bridge track was laid.

Mellen whirled at the cry and made after her, but he might as well have tried to catch the wind. As she ran, she heard her brother shout in sudden alarm and Natalie's voice pleading, but she sped on under an impulse as irresistible as panic fear. Down through the openings beneath her feet she saw, as in a nightmare, the sweeping flood, burdened with plunging ice chunks and flecked with foam. She seemed to be suspended above it, yet she was running at reckless speed, dimly aware of the consequences of a misjudged footstep, but fearful only of being overtaken.

Suddenly she hated her companions. Her mind was in a furious revolt at their cowardice, their indecision, or whatever it was that held them like a group of wooden figures safe on shore while the man whose life was worth all theirs put together exposed himself to needless peril. That he was really in danger she felt sure. She knew Murray was apt to lose himself in his dreams. Perhaps some visionary mood had blinded him to the menace of that mounting ice ridge in front of the glacier, or had he madly chosen to stand or fall with this structure that meant so much to him? She would make him yield to her own terror, drag him ashore, if necessary, with her own hands.

She stumbled, but saved herself from a fall, then gathered her skirts more closely and rushed on, measuring with instinctive accuracy the length of every stride. It was not an easy path over which she dashed, for the ties were unevenly spaced. Gaping apertures gave terrible glimpses of the river below, and across these ghastly abysses she had to leap.

The hoarse bursts of shouting from the shore ceased as the

workmen beheld her flitting out along the steel causeway. They watched her in dumb amazement.

All at once O'Neil saw her and hurried to meet her.

"Eliza!" he cried. "Be careful! What possessed you to do this?"

"Come away," she gasped. "It's dangerous. The jam—Look!" She pointed down the channel.

He shook his head impatiently.

"Yes!" she pleaded. "Yes! Please! They wouldn't come to warn you—they tried to stop me. You must go ashore." The frightened request in her clear, wide-open eyes, the disorder of her haste affected O'Neil strangely. He stared at her, bewildered, doubtful, then steadied her and grabbed with his free hand for support. He could feel her trembling.

"There's no danger, none whatever," he said. "Nothing can happen."

"You don't know. The bridge has never been tried. The ice is battering at it, and that jam—if it doesn't burst...."

"But it will. It can't last much longer."

"It's rising...."

"To be sure, but the river will overflow the bank."

"Please!" she urged. "You can do no good here. I'm afraid."

He stared at her in the same incredulous bewilderment. Some impulse deep within him was struggling for expression, but he could not find words to frame it. His eyes were oddly bright as he smiled at her.

"Won't you go ashore?" she begged.

"I'll take you back, of course, but I want to stay and see...."

"Then—I'll stay."

"Eliza!" Her name burst from his lips in a tone that thrilled her, but with it came a sudden uproar from the distant crowd, and the next instant they saw the ice barrier was giving way. The pressure had become irresistible. As the Salmon had risen, the ice had risen also, and now the narrow throat was belching its contents forth. The chaos of up-ended bergs was being torn apart; over it and through it burst a deluge that filled the valley with the roar of a mighty cataract. Clouds of spray were in the air; broken masses were leaping and somersaulting; high up on the shore were stranded floes and fragments, left in the wake of the moving body. Onward it coursed, clashing and grinding along the brittle face of the glacier. Over the alder tops beyond the bend they could see it moving faster and faster, like the crest of a tidal wave. The surface of the river lowered swiftly beneath the bridge. The huge white pans ground and milled, shouldered aside by the iron-sheathed pillars of concrete.

"See! It's gone already. Once it clears a passageway, we'll have no more gorges, for the freshets are coming. The bridge didn't even tremble—there wasn't a tremor, not a scratch!"

Eliza looked up to find O'Neil regarding her with an expression that set her heart throbbing and her thoughts scattering. She clasped a huge, cold bolthead and clung to it desperately, for the upheaval in her soul rivaled that which had just passed before her eyes. The bridge, the river, the valley itself were gyrating slowly, dizzily.

"Eliza!" She did not answer. "Child!" O'Neil's voice was shaking. "Why did you come to me? Why did you do this mad thing? I saw something in your face that I can't believe—that I—can't think possible. It—it gives me courage. If I don't speak quickly, I'll never dare. Is it—true? Dear girl, can it be? I'm so old—such a poor thing—you couldn't possibly care, and yet, *why did you come?*" The words were torn from him. He was gripped and shaken by a powerful emotion.

She tried to answer, but her lips were soundless. She closed her eyes, and Murray saw she was whiter than the foam far beneath. He stared into the colorless face upturned to his until her eyelids fluttered open, and she managed to voice the words that clung in her throat.

"I've always loved you like this."

He gave a cry, like that of a starving man. She felt herself drawn against him. But now he, too, was speechless. He could only press her close while his mind went groping for words to express joy that was unbelievable and stunning.

"Couldn't you see?" she asked.

He shook his head. "I'm such a dreamer. I'm afraid it—can't be true. I'm afraid you'll go away and—leave me. You won't ever—

will you, Eliza? I couldn't stand that." Then fresh realization of the truth swept over him. They clung to each other, drunk with ecstasy, senseless of their surroundings.

"I thought you cared for Natalie," she said, softly, after a while.

"It was always you."

"Always?"

"Always!"

She turned her lips to his and lifted her entwining arms.

The breakfast gong had called the men away before the two figures far out on the bridge picked their way slowly to the shore. The Salmon was still flooded with hurrying masses of ice, as it would continue to be for several days, but it was running free. The channel in front of the glacier was open.

Blaine was the first to shake O'Neil's hand, for the members of Murray's crew held aloof in some embarrassment.

"It's a perfect piece of work," Blaine said. "I congratulate you."

The others echoed his sentiments faintly, hesitatingly, for they were abashed at what they saw in their chief's face and realized that words were weak and meaningless.

Dan dared not trust himself to speak. He had many things to say to his sister, but his throat ached miserably. Natalie restrained herself only by the greatest effort.

It was Tom Slater who ended the awkward pause.

"If all the young lovers are safely ashore, maybe us old men who built the bridge can go and get something to eat."

Murray smiled at the girl beside him.

"I'm afraid they've guessed our secret, dear."

"Secret!" Slater rolled his eyes. "There ain't over a couple thousand people beside us that saw you pop the question. I s'pose she was out of breath and couldn't say no."

Eliza gasped and fled to her brother's arms.

"Sis! Poor—little Sis!" Dan cried, and two tears stole down his brown cheeks. "Isn't this—just great?" Then the others burst into a noisy expression of their gladness.

Happy Tom regarded them all pessimistically. "I feel bound to warn you," he said at length, "that marriage is an awful gamble. It ain't what it seems."

"It is!" Natalie said. "It's better, and you know it."

"It turned out all right for me," Tom acknowledged, "because I got the best woman in the world. But...." He eyed his chief accusingly. "I went about it in a modest way. I didn't humiliate her in public."

He turned impatiently on his companions, still pouring out their babble of congratulations.

"Come along, can't you," he cried, "and leave 'em alone. I'm a dyspeptic old married man, but I used to be young and affectionate, like Murray. After breakfast I'm going to cable Mrs. Slater to come and bring the kids with her and watch her bed-ridden, invalid husband build the rest of this railroad. I'm getting chuck full of romance."

"It has been a miraculous morning for me," Murray said after a time. "And the greatest miracle is — you, dear."

"This is just the way the story ended in my book," Eliza told him happily. "Our book."

He pressed her closer. "Yes! Our book — our bridge — our everything, Eliza."

She hid her blushing face against his shoulder, then with thumb and finger drew his ear down to her lips.

"Murray dear, won't you call me — Violet?" she whispered.

The End

A DREAM COMES TRUE

CORDOVA TO KENNECOTT RAILWAY

BY LAUREL DOWNING BILL

Blood. Sweat. Determination. These three factors played heavily in the construction of the Copper River and Northwestern Railway tracks and bridges that eventually reached the riches locked within Southcentral Alaska's rugged wilderness. Rex Beach's novel, *The Iron Trail*, mirrors railroad engineer Michael James Heney's struggle to build the railroad from Cordova to the copper-rich Kennecott fields. Building the Million Dollar Bridge at the Miles and Childs glaciers, completed in 1910, is the high point of the story. As you read the following pages, you will recognize several people and events upon which Beach based his tale.

The actual railroad's story began in July 1900 when two gold seekers stumbled across a patch of what they mistakenly believed to be silver. While Clarence Warner and Jack "Tarantula" Smith settled alongside a stream to eat lunch, and let Warner rest a sprained ankle, the pair spotted a green patch high up on a slope across the Chitina River Valley. Unbeknownst to them, the men had "discovered" the largest deposit of copper known in the world at that time, although others had known of the copper long before.

"The copper of that region had been known for more than one hundred years before the discovery was made," wrote historian Clarence L. Andrews in *The Story of Alaska* published in 1931. "(Alexander) Baranof knew of it and collected metal from the Indians to cast a bell (1795). The finding of the Mountains of Red Metal was one of the parts of the story of the *Trail of Ninety-Eight*, when the gold-seekers passed through the Copper River Valley in the effort to reach the Klondike, and some of them tarried and found copper. Not only were the rich deposits of copper glance and bornite discovered in those stupendous mountains threaded with glaciers, but pure copper in masses of tons in weight, silver in nuggets, and placer gold...."

Warner and Smith staked several claims, including Jumbo, Mammoth and Bonanza, for themselves and their backers. The pair then traveled to Valdez that fall and set about trying to find more investors.

Smith told a young mining engineer, Stephen Birch, about the discovery of Bonanza, according to historian Elizabeth A. Tower in her book, *Ghosts of Kennecott*.

"Mr. Birch, we've got a mountain of copper up there. There's so much of the stuff sticking out of the ground that it looks like a green sheep pasture in Ireland when the sun is shining at its best!"

Birch, convinced by Smith's account, bought a 1/11th share in the claim. He then investigated the mountain of copper himself, liked what he found, and by 1903 had bought 21 claims and consolidated them as the Alaska Copper and Coal Company.

In 1906 Birch, along with his friend Judge James Wickersham, met with Daniel Guggenheim who was in Alaska checking out mining opportunities. Impressed, Guggenheim returned to New York, joined with the House of Morgan to form the Alaska Syndicate, and brought Birch in as one of three managing directors. The Syndicate then provided capital for Birch's plan to develop a copper mine.

That insertion of capital allowed Birch to purchase and haul equipment and supplies to Kennecott for buildings and tramways. The goods were brought by pack train over Marshall Pass from Valdez to the Copper River and then loaded on boats to go up the Copper, Chitina and Nizina rivers. Birch also homesteaded a site at the junction of the Copper and Chitina rivers for what became the town of Chitina.

By late 1906, the Syndicate had consolidated most of the major mining claims in southcentral and had purchased the Alaska Steamship Company, too. Once they controlled the region's water transportation, they turned to the problem of transporting the resources hidden in their mining claims to tidewater. Others had discovered coal and oil in the Prince William Sound and Bering River regions, and only transportation – a railroad – was needed to bring the newly found copper, coal, and oil together to unlock the riches of Midas.

Five separate railroads were started from three different points on the coast. Then the fight was on – gun battles, political battles, court battles, fantastic rights-of-way battles – all a part of the history of Alaska's early railroad-building days.

At first the site of what later became Cordova was not even considered in choosing a railroad terminus. And there was a good reason. Up the Copper River Valley, 49 miles away, were two live mighty glaciers, the Miles and Childs, which most thought made that route insurmountable.

However, when Irish contractor Michael J. Heney surveyed the route, he found Mother Nature had made a slight concession. One of the glaciers was higher upstream than the other. By building a bridge and keeping the Copper River between the glaciers and the railroad, Heney was sure he could pass the huge ice barriers.

He was sure, too, this route was the best way into the Interior, for there was a "water grade" all the way and no mountains to cut through or climb over.

Before Heney began building the railroad over this route, however, he tried to persuade the Alaska Syndicate the route was feasible. The Syndicate already was trying to reach the Interior from Valdez.

Men gathered on December 19, 1905 to discuss the railway grade for the Valdez railway.

At the time, Valdez seemed a logical point from which to build a railroad to the Kennecott copper mines. Following the discovery of gold in the Klondike in the late 1890s, steamships dropped hopeful prospectors on its beaches who then headed north along Alaska Native trails in search of their fortunes. Some stampeders stayed on shore to set up shops and businesses. Valdez became a thriving supply center.

In late summer and fall 1898, U.S. Army Lt. William R. Abercrombie's men started cutting a rough trail through Keystone Canyon and over Thompson Pass following trails used by the Chugach and Ahtna people. The following spring, the Army approved that route as the new military trail to Eagle and built a fort to support the efforts to upgrade the road, as well as establish a telegraph line to the Alaska Interior.

The Keystone Canyon Trail became the Richardson Highway in 1919 and served as the only viable inland route to Fairbanks for several years. Valdez became the coastal port for most traffic going into and out of the Interior.

It wasn't long before prospectors turned their attention to the gold, copper and silver deposits on the islands and shores of Prince William Sound. The Cliff Gold Mine, which produced about 51,740 ounces of gold and 8,253 ounces of silver, and the Midas Mine, the fourth-largest producer of copper in the Sound, were the most profitable mines around Valdez. But Ellamar, near Tatitlek, and the Kennecott Mines, near McCarthy, both of which now were owned by the Morgan-Guggenheim Alaska Syndicate, produced far more copper than all the other mines combined. And nearly as much gold came out of Ellamar as a byproduct as came out of the Cliff Mine, according to the Valdez Museum and Historical Archive.

The Alaska Syndicate also had claims on rich Alaska coalfields. But in 1905, early conservationist Gifford Pinchot, first director of the U.S. Forest Service and close friend of U.S. President Theodore Roosevelt, ordered the withdrawal of vast coalfield holdings in the territory to protect them from the Guggenheim-Morgan Syndicate.

Despite Pinchot's closure of coalfield holdings, the Syndicate moved forward with plans to build a railway from the Kennecott copper mines to Valdez and was the subject of controversy from the beginning. Tensions escalated when a rival crew working on a railroad from Valdez was confronted by a rock barricade erected by the Guggenheims when they entered the Keystone Canyon, leading to Thompson Pass. Armed with tools, Valdez railroad men marched toward the Syndicate's obstruction and were met with gunfire backed by badges.

Local Syndicate officials had convinced the U.S. marshal in Fairbanks to issue temporary deputy marshal commissions to Syndicate employees, including a man named Edward C. Hasey. Sheltered behind the barricade, Hasey shot three marchers, killing one.

A grand jury was hastily convened. And even though Alaska's Governor Wilford B. Hoggatt, a well-known Syndicate supporter, hurried to Valdez to intervene on Hasey's behalf, the gunman was indicted for murder. His trial then was moved to Juneau since ill sentiments against the Syndicate abounded in Valdez.

It later was proven that Syndicate officials paid off witnesses to say the Valdez railroad men were armed, and after several weeks of testimony during a trial in spring 1908, jurors found Hasey's fear of bodily harm by the Valdez railroad crew justified his shooting in self-defense. The jury acquitted him of the murder charge. But in February 1909, Hasey was found guilty on a second charge of assault. He served 18 months at McNeil Island in Washington state, receiving full pay and benefits for his family during incarceration.

While the Guggenheim-Morgan Syndicate was influencing the outcome of its railroad worker's trial, it continued building its railroad from Valdez to Alaska's Interior. The Syndicate gave up the plan, however, when it found the going was expensive and difficult with rugged mountain grades. But it wasn't convinced that Heney's choice of Cordova was the right one and instead decided to build its railroad from a point several miles east of that new Prince William Sound town.

The Syndicate's decision meant some Valdez residents' ambitions would not be realized. But one man was determined to beat the Syndicate at its own game.

"When it appeared that Valdez would not be selected, H.D. Reynolds appeared on the scene touting his plan for the Alaska Home Railroad," according to the Valdez Museum and Historical Archive. "He convinced the people of Valdez that 'his railroad was their railroad.' Many Valdezans invested their entire savings or businesses into supporting his project. Reynolds bought up much of the town; he soon owned a newspaper, hotel, bank and even some of the streets.

"In 1907, a shootout erupted over the right of way through Keystone Canyon between the two rival railroad companies. The Alaska Home Railroad project fell apart ... Reynolds left town in a hurry, owing a great deal of money, and was last seen in an insane asylum. Valdezans were left with no railroad, 500 unemployed workers, and little money."

Following its decision to leave Valdez, the Syndicate settled on a route from Katalla, 40 miles east of Cordova, which was the site of the first discovery of commercial quantities of oil in Alaska in 1902. By spring 1907, when construction of the Syndicate's railroad began, the population had swelled to about 5,000.

Katalla had the advantage of being in the heart of the oil and coalfields. But other railroads were being built from there, also, and rival railroad gangs often clashed.

At one point, the Guggenheims had to cross the right-of-way of the Bruner outfit, which was trying to build tracks to the coalfields and then on to the Copper River. Once completed, they planned to sell it to the Alaska Syndicate. The Bruner crew would not allow the Syndicate workers to cross, posted no trespassing signs and blew up some of the Syndicate's equipment. The Bruner workers also constructed an immense "go devil" out of railroad ties. Its cable was operated by a machine that swung it back and forth over the disputed right-of-way, while armed men behind barriers guarded it.

"A $1,000 reward to any of you men with nerve enough to cut that cable," the Guggenheim boss promised.

One daring workman, under cover of protective fire, succeeded

Violence erupted when the Katalla Company tracks reached the Brunner Crossing, seen here in 1907. Note the giant "go-devil" on the tracks in the background.

and the Syndicate crew stormed the trestles. Many men were injured during the fierce gun battle, but the Syndicate prevailed and took over the right-of-way.

The Katalla route was abandoned as the terminus of the Guggenheim railroad a few months later, however, when an expensive breakwater failed to hold during early winter storms. The November storms were so savage they carried the jetty's huge boulders – weighing several tons and piled tens of feet deep – nearly 1,800 feet into the bay. Lack of a harbor proved an impossible handicap, as well, and after just five months, the Syndicate turned to Heney's choice. The Guggenheims bought Heney's right-of-way for $250,000 ($7.5 million today) and gave him the contract to build the railroad.

That intrepid Irishman was so sure it was the logical route, he'd already started building with his own resources. He'd secured the right-of-way up the Copper River in 1904 and began building the railroad at a spot he named Cordova (the original name given by explorer Don Salvador Fidalgo, who also named Valdez) on March 13,

1906. When the Alaska Syndicate purchased his right-of-way, Heney went to work for Daniel Guggenheim to complete the Copper River and Northwestern Railway – which some people called "Can't Run & Never Will." Heney was the right man for the job, as he had built the White Pass and Yukon Railway through rough terrain from Skagway to Whitehorse in the late 1890s.

The Copper River and Northwestern Railway was one of the most difficult railroad projects ever undertaken. Workers had to wind their way over and around steep canyons and rivers, endure hurricane-force winds and blood-thirsty mosquitoes, and slip in between two mighty glaciers under primitive conditions far from any supplies. Chief engineer Erastus Hawkins captured some of the difficulty Heney and his crew faced in such conditions while working on a 50-foot span of the Miles Glacier bridge the day they found the falsework displaced due to ice movement.

"The falsework under the third span of the bridge was moved out fifteen inches by the ice and had to be put back," Hawkins wrote in his diary on May 14, 1910.

Spring breakup had begun, and the flooding water had lifted the 7-foot-thick ice cap up 20 feet. This mass of ice moved the falsework, which consisted of more than 1,000 piles driven deep into the bottom of the Copper River 40 feet below the surface. That falsework, carrying a mass of unfinished steel for the bridge, had to be put back.

As in Rex Beach's fictional scene of falsework moved by spring breakup, all hands were on deck to drive steam from engines into feed pipes to melt or chop the ice clear of the piles. Inch by inch the men dragged 450 feet of towering bridge back into place. The crew sped up the pace and sent home the last bolt of the span at midnight after an 18-hour day. Blocks were knocked out and the third span settled on its concrete bed. At 1 a.m. all the falsework wrecked as the river won its fight an hour after the span had been saved, which saved a year's work.

Unfortunately, Heney would never see his railroad completed. Five months after saving the bridge work at Miles Glacier, he passed away from a lung infection contracted after a trip south the year before.

Courtesy Alaska State Library

Bridge Over Copper Rive
At Childs Glacier

The Irish Prince of Alaska had traveled to Seattle and New York on business in July 1909. A month later he was returning north onboard the *SS Ohio* when the steamship struck a reef in Finlayson Channel, British Columbia. There were 188 passengers and 88 crewmen aboard – three crewmen and a wounded soldier lost their lives, according to insurers Lloyds of London.

Heney, who some sources say first went below deck to try and rescue his horses, jumped off the ship and swam to one of the lifeboats. Since there was no room in the boat for him, he held onto the stern as its occupants rowed to shore. He caught a cold during the ordeal, which developed into pulmonary tuberculosis.

His robust health never returned. Following completion of the first phase of his contract with the Alaska Syndicate after the railroad reached Tiekel on November 30, 1909, Heney again traveled to New York the next year to update the Katalla Company on the progress of the railroad. He returned to Seattle to spend the winter and died there on October 11, 1910.

His men carried on and completed the tracks the next year. A copper spike, to signify the last spike of the railroad construction, was driven into the rail at Kennecott on March 29, 1911, by Chief Engineer E.C. Hawkins and Superintendent Samuel Murchison. The final cost

Courtesy University of Alaska Fairbanks

P.S. HUNT. 1928. END OF COPPER RIVER AND NORTHWESTERN RY. KENNICOTT, ALASKA.

A train carrying members of the National Geographic Society Katmai Expedition of 1918 leaves Cordova and crosses a trestle built by Michael J. Heney in 1906.

came to $20-$25 million, which in today's dollars would be around $600-$700 million.

The Kennecott mines that it served were among the nation's largest and richest with ore of unequalled quality anywhere. The first train full of copper left Kennecott on April 8, 1911, in 32 rail cars and was valued at $250,000. The Alaska Syndicate formed the Kennecott Copper Corporation four years later, which included the Kennecott Mines Company, the Copper River and Northwestern Railway, and the Alaska Steamship Company. The new company named Stephen Birch its first president.

The last train ran from Kennecott to Cordova on September 11, 1938, after producing an estimated $200 million (almost $4 billion today) worth of copper ore. At least 50 percent of which was profit that was used to purchase mines in Arizona, Nevada, New Mexico, and South America. The Kennecott Copper Corporation became the nation's largest copper company.

When the timber trestle over the Copper River at Chitina went out with the 1939 spring thaw, the railroad route was forever severed.

The Kennecott Corporation donated the railroad right-of-way to the United States "for use as a public highway" in 1941.

By the early 1960s, the Alaska Department of Transportation had extended the Copper River Highway to Mile 59. But the Good Friday earthquake on March 27, 1964, damaged 28 bridges and delayed further construction until the highway was extended to Mile 72 and south 20 miles from Chitina by 1972. Bridge 339 washed out in 2012, which cut access and now the roadbed from Chitina to McCarthy forms the McCarthy Road.

ALASKA'S IRISH PRINCE
BY LAUREL DOWNING BILL

Michael James Heney, known to many financiers as the Irish Prince of Alaska, took to the tracks as a young lad. The Canadian was born on October 24, 1865, to farmers near Stonecliffe, Ontario. The son of Irish immigrants ran away from home at 14 to work on construction of the Canadian Pacific Railway. His railroad dreams were cut short, however, when an elder brother found him and took him back to the family farm.

In June 1882 the man who built the first two railroads in the Great Land headed west to work as a mule handler for the CPR crew at Elkhorn, Manitoba. He soon moved on to laying track. Wanting to learn all he could about railroad building, Heney joined a survey crew and worked in the mountains of British Columbia during 1884-85 where he gained a thorough understanding in all aspects of railway construction. When the final spike was driven into the CPR line, the then-21-year-old felt ready to head out on his own as an independent contractor.

Courtesy Free Encyclopedia

Michael J. Heney

Heney received many construction contracts from the Canadian Pacific Railway, and in 1887 he moved to America and built the Seattle Lake Shore and Eastern Railroad in two years. He became known as "the boy contractor."

It was during construction of a mine hydraulic plant at Anchor Point, Alaska, in 1896, that he became fascinated with the north country. And at the peak of the Klondike Gold Rush, he made a preliminary survey of the White Pass to assess the

His Eminence.

Michael J. Heney, seen here walking on the White Pass trail during construction of the White Pass and Yukon Railway, was respected by those who worked for him.

feasibility of a railroad route to haul prospectors and gold between the Yukon interior and tidewater in Southeast Alaska. A chance encounter in the lobby of Skagway's St. James Hotel with surveyors of Close Brothers and Company of London, a British financial business that was thinking of building a railroad from Skagway to Whitehorse, led to him being hired as a labor foreman. He supervised a crew of 1,000 men and traveled by horse between camps to check on progress. It didn't take long for him to take on a more important role, and he completed the last two-thirds of the 100.7-mile White Pass and Yukon Railway as contractor of record.

The last spike of this famous railway over the Chilkoot and White Pass trails was driven into the track at Caribou Crossing (Carcross), Yukon Territory, on July 29, 1900. This project propelled Heney's reputation internationally as he became known as an exceptional railway contractor.

Big Mike, as many of his men called him, next turned his attention toward building a railroad to Alaska coal and copper claims in the Copper River Valley. Heney, with support of Close Brothers and engineer Erastus Corning Hawkins – with whom he had worked on the White Pass route – founded the Copper River and Northwestern Railway.

P.S HUNT C3897   LOOKING DOWN THE MAIN BUSINESS STREET OF CORDOVA, ALASKA

After railroad contractor Michael J. Heney chose where he wanted to start building his Copper River and Northwestern Railway from Prince William Sound to the Kennecott copper fields, the town of Cordova sprang up. By 1908 businesses lined its main street.

Heney surveyed and filed a right-of-way for a route that would start at what became Cordova, follow the Copper River north to Chitina and then continue 60 miles to Kennecott. He then began constructing tracks to the Kennecott mines in 1906.

However, the Kennecott Copper Corporation – a partnership of J.P. Morgan and Company and the Guggenheims' American Smelting and Refining Company that became known as the Alaska Syndicate – did not think Heney's route was feasible to reach its copper claims since there were two glaciers in its path. Instead, they began building their own railroad from Valdez. When that route didn't work out, the Americans attempted a railroad from Katalla. A few months later, a huge series of storms wiped out those plans and the Syndicate was forced to pay Heney $250,000 ($7.5 million today) for his right-of-way and gave him the contract to complete his railroad late in 1907. Heney then began working for Daniel Guggenheim.

Courtesy University of Washington

On November 30, 1909, the Copper River and Northwestern Railway had reached the Tiekel River, completing the first phase of Michael J. Heney's contract with the Alaska Syndicate. Workers lived in a tent camp along the river, seen here, while they worked that section.

Construction of the Copper River and Northwestern Railway was completed when a copper spike was driven into the track at Kennecott on March 29, 1911, although Heney was not among those witnessing the historic event. Alaska's Irish Prince died just shy of his 45th birthday on October 11, 1910, from a lung infection he'd contracted the year before after the *SS Ohio* sank on its voyage from Seattle to Alaska.

Heney, buried in Calvary Cemetery in Seattle, Washington, left an estate worth more than $1 million (more than $30 million today) to relatives, associates, Catholic charities, and Alaska Natives in care of Episcopal Bishop Peter Trimble Rowe. Today a mountain range, a mountain peak and a glacier near Cordova all bear his name.

The following pages reveal what the *Chitina Leader* newspaper reported following the ceremony that drove the final copper spike into the Copper River and Northwestern Railway tracks at Kennecott. As you read the account, keep in mind that $1 in 1911 would be $32 in 2022 after adjustment for inflation.

Note: *Aunt Phil's Trunk added the photos in this article to enhance the reader's understanding of this massive project.*

Chitina Leader 1911
Railroad Completed to the Copper Belt
Copper Spike is Driven at Mine

Cordova Now in Close Touch With Famous Bonanza Mine at Kennicott, a Big Producer of Fabulously Rich Ore

By Will A Steel

The goal has been reached. 3:30 p.m., Wednesday, March 29, 1911. At a cost of over $20 million.

The Copper River & Northwestern Railway, from Cordova to Kennecott, 196 miles.

Wednesday afternoon will ever remain a memorable occasion in Alaska. It records an event that will have important significance throughout the United States. At the time recorded the last rail was driven into place by a copper spike that marked the completion of track laying on the new railway that runs from seaport terminus of Cordova to Kennicott, the end of the line as at present projected.

At the interior terminus is located the renowned Bonanza copper mine; 800 feet beyond the big concentrator and ore bins, on the mountain side opposite one of the largest glaciers in the northland, with a beautiful perspective of snow-covered mountain peaks, frozen rivers and timbered valleys, the modest ceremonies were witnessed that records the accomplishment of one of the most gigantic and daring enterprises known to the commercial world.

Interior Terminal, Kennecott, Alaska of Copper River & Northwestern RR.

The Copper River and Northwestern Railway terminated at the Bonanza Mine at Kennecott, seen here as final copper spike was driven into tracks on March 29, 1911.

The day was most propitious. The sun shone brightly and the crisp, invigorating air, with the thermometer registering 38 degrees above zero, had an inspiring effect on the interested spectators. A tense and anxious feeling was evidenced until the last act was performed that declared the practical completion of the building of the railroad to the end of the line. And it was the obliterating of frontierism from a hitherto remote section, bringing rapid communication and making available all the comports of civilization, in the development of that vast domain tributary to the Copper, Chitina, Nizina and other unnavigable rivers.

All present realized the full import of the advent of steel rails in the awakening of a new empire of hidden wealth that is destined to soon woo thousands of adventurous prospectors and operators, who will produce mineral values in such quantity as will startle the world.

Driving of the Copper Spike

On Monday Chief Engineer and General Manager E.C. Hawkins left Cordova for the front, in Superintendent Van Cleve's private dining, sleeping and observation car. Accompanying him were J.F. Van Cleve, Superintendent, and R.J. Barry, general freight and passenger agent of the new railroad; E.A. Hegg, photographer; and Will A. Steel, editor of the *Cordova Daily Alaskan* and the *Chitina Leader*. At Chitina the party was joined by J.C. Martin, manager of the Orr Stage Line.

This was the first through train that had gone over the entire trackage of the new railroad. After spending the night at camp 146 the train went on to Kennicott arriving Tuesday afternoon within a quarter of a mile of the end of the line. Shortly beyond a trestle of 256 feet was being put in, which delayed track laying until the following morning. However, the trestle was completed and trackage laid to the ore bins and concentrator of the Bonanza mine before noon Wednesday. After lunch the additional 800 feet of steel was laid and the final ceremonies occurred at 3:30 Wednesday afternoon.

When all was in readiness the golden, or in this instance, the more appropriate copper spike, was placed in position by Mr. Barry. It was then driven in turn by chief Engineer Hawkins and General Superintendent Samuel Murchison. Faithful old engine No. 50, puffing and whistling, stood on the track a few feet in the rear, with a large portrait of the late M.J. Heney over the headlight. The spectacle was witnessed by a couple of hundred workmen, officials and a few other interested spectators. Prior to the act of driving the spike, in response to a suggestion by Mr. Hawkins, the assemblage stood and bowed and uncovered heads in memory of the late and much beloved contractor, Mr. Heney. Afterwards Mr. Hawkins made a short address, in which he expressed the appreciation of himself and the Katalla Company for the splendid organization built up by Mr. Heney and so able perpetuated by Mr. Murchison, and for the effective and harmonious work performed by the contracting department.

Afterwards there was general congratulations and Mr. Murchison took occasion to extend his grateful appreciation to Mr. Hawkins and the Katalla Company for the many courtesies extended and the able assistance rendered his people. The several engines then blew whistles and the workmen and all others present gave way to much rejoicing.

The telephone wires had kept pace with the railroad construction and General Manager Hawkins telephoned a message to Cordova, to be cabled to Seattle and there telegraphed to New York, informing the owners of the railroad that the copper spike had been driven. The following morning several replies were received at Chitina, expressing the sincerest congratulations for the splendid work so expeditiously performed by Mr. Hawkins and the contracting company.

Shortly after the important finish the special train left and passed over the new and unballasted track for 50 miles at the rate of 20 miles an hour. The night was spent at Mr. Murchison's headquarters, camp 146. Thursday morning the run was made to Chitina, where Mr. Hawkins left the train, expecting to remain several days between that point and Kennicott. With the rest of the party Superintendent Van Cleve took his car down to mile 54, where he and Mr. Barry rendered valuable assistance in cleaning the snowslides.

A Glorious Accomplishment

The completion of the Copper River & Northwestern Railway marks an important epoch in Alaska's history. While equally as daring railroad accomplishments may have been undertaken in other parts of the world, it is doubtful if there has ever been another project that has been so successfully carried on under more adverse and trying conditions.

For nearly three and a half years past, men numbering into the thousands, from the highest officials to the laborer who shoveled mud or snow gave of the best that was in them. At times over 6,000 men were employed, while at the end the number had decreased to about 500. During the period of construction such adverse conditions were encountered and surmounted as are very seldom met with in other parts of the world.

Much of the work on the several steel bridges was done when the thermometer was from 35 to 50 degrees below zero, or when raging torrents or huge icebergs carried by swift currents, made foundation work almost impossible. In constructing, understanding, scientific knowledge, broad intellect, physical force, and even unto their heart's blood, to a work that shall forever be down to the credit, to the glory of the capitalists who made it possible, and to the benefit of the thousands who will make of the new section a land of rich development.

Route of the New Railroad

The tide water terminus is at the land-locked town of Cordova, on an inlet of Prince William Sound. Then, as Mr. Swergal describes it, the road effects a sea level passage of one of the coast spurs of the Chugach Range at the junction of Eyak Lake and Eyak River, some six miles from Cordova, the only point of easy penetration to the interior from the southern Alaska coast. After leaving this mountain pass the road is laid on a tangent of 13 miles, passes the old Russian trading post at Alaganik, crossing the rioting delta of the Copper River by means of modern steel bridges at what are known as Flag Point, Round Island and Hot Cake channels. Fifty miles from Cordova occurred one of the greatest engineering feats of modern times; the second crossing of the main channel of the Copper by the erection of the Miles Glacier cantilever bridge, embattled on either side by the mighty Childs and Miles Glaciers, both presenting a defiant wall of ice 300 feet

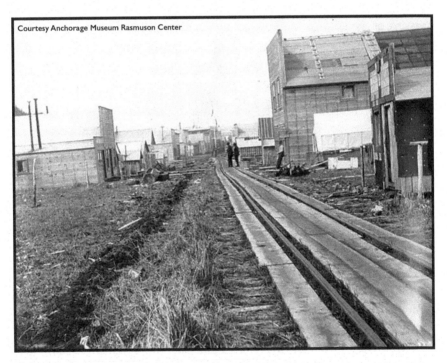

Courtesy Anchorage Museum Rasmuson Center

The Copper River and Northwestern Railway tracks went through the Alaska Native village of Eyak, seen here, about six miles from Cordova.

above and 100 feet below the river and three to five miles in length. Here, in summer, thousands of tons of ice fall into the river in single masses almost hourly, accompanied by thundering roars. These masses of ice throw monster waves across the river, leaving the salmon high on the banks to be gathered by prowling bears and passing prospectors and Indians.

From the glaciers the line extends in a general northeasterly direction along the Copper, over the Baird Glacier Moraine (a field of earth hidden ice), and on through the panoramic Wood Canyon, surpassing the grandeur of the Alps, and on to Chitina, the coming copper city of the North. This is also the point of connection between the railroad and the Orr stage line for carrying passengers and the U.S. mail to and from Fairbanks and other interior sections. Leaving Chitina through a solid rock tunnel, the railway makes the third crossing of the main channel of the Copper immediately above the mouth of the Chitina River, and there climbs to the bench lands skirting the Kotsina. One hundred and forty-nine miles from Cordova, the crossing of the Kuskulana River is made by means of a modern steel bridge 238 feet above the ice bound floor of the gorge, thence on through the valley of the Chitina to the famous Bonanza copper mine at Kennecott, 196 miles from Cordova. This is in the heart of one of the world's greatest copper regions, and it also promises great wealth in gold.

Magnificent Steel Bridges

Everyone connected with the railroad is proud of the fine steel bridges that were rerected under most trying climatic conditions, at a cost of over $2,500,000. From the very start it was generally known that the problem of bridging the Copper River from the foot of Glacier Lake and the edge of Child's Glacier, was one of the most perplexing problems and hazardous feats that the management had to contend with. Two abutments and three piers were decided on to support the necessary 1,550 feet of steel. With the current rushing past at a reckless rate of speed and carrying the immense icebergs, which find their way out of the lake, the problem of bridging the river proved a most difficult one.

Work was started on the first caisson in April 1909. In building it a railroad track was laid over the ice, and a monster pile driver, resting on the ice, drove the piles necessary to support the wave of the caisson. In early

May when the caisson was ready to slip into place the ice began to break and it was necessary to carry on the work by means of an aerial tramway. In placing the other caissons in the middle of the stream by the aid of compressed air, huge icebergs were continually careening and bumping the sides of the caissons.

But this work was finished and the piers completed that summer, followed by the placing of the falsework, which permitted the setting on and riveting of the steel pieces so soon as they were received in the spring of 1910. The work of putting the spans in place went on satisfactorily until toward the finish of the third span in May. The ice had been running for a week past, moving two or three inches each day, and had at various times seriously interfered with the falsework or trestling from which the men were working. Had the ice carried away this piling and framework it would have been impossible to have completed the bridge that season. But fortune favored the brave efforts of a heroic class of steelworkers and when the break came two days later the time of danger had passed. The last span was built over a portion of the river that is distant from the main channel and was not affected by the floating ice. It was completed in June 1910.

The total cost of the bridge was about $1.5 million. In the construction of the two abutments and three caissons about 18,000 cubic yards of concrete were used, while in the bridge there are 5 million pounds of steel. The first span of the bridge is 400 feet long; the second 300 feet; the third and cantilever span 450 feet, while the fourth is 400 feet. Chief Engineer Hawkins received valuable assistance in this great work from A.C. O'Neel, bridge engineer, who was directly in charge of the work. He labored with untiring zeal in supervising and directing this great undertaking, with the loyal assistance of foreman of bridge construction, Chas. McDonald, the steel foreman, Chas. Dwyer, and a corps of faithful steel men.

The work of crossing the Kuskulana gorge, 238 feet high, was staged October 23, 1910 and completed the following Christmas day. This bridge consists of three half-camel back spans and is 500 feet long being three spans of 150, 200 and 150 feet. The construction of this bridge presented difficulties not heretofore encountered in the other steel bridges of the road. The extraordinary height of the structure, together with the swiftness of the water in the chasm that it spans, rendered the erection of falsework

Construction of the bridge over the Kuskulana River gorge, seen here. posed challenges.

infeasible. These conditions necessitated constructing the bridge by the cantilever trick. That is, the central span, which actually crosses the gorge, is suspended from the first span by cantilever rigging attached thereto. When the gorge or central span was completed, the wedges in the cantilever rigging were slacked off, permitting the span to settle in place at its union with the third span on the other side of the gorge. Engineer O'Neel was compelled to work his men much of the time with the thermometer 20 to 45 degrees below zero.

The Flag Point bridge at mile 27 is 1,300 feet in length with spans as follows, in feet: 300, 150, 150, 175, 175, 175, 175. It was completed in August 1909. Almost a continuation of this bridge is the Round Island structure at mile 28. It is 560 feet in length, with two spans of 300 and 260 feet each, and was completed in May 1909. These two bridges were built at a cost of $560,000. The Hot Cake bridge at mile 34 is 525 feet long with three spans of 175 feet each. It was finished in November 1909, and cost $230,000. The steel in the five bridges weights over 20 million pounds.

The construction of the steel bridges was done directly by the Katalla Company, while the wooden bridges and trestles were built by contractor Heney.

Wooden Bridges, Trestles and Snowsheds

Between Cordova and Chitina there are 129 bridges, with a length of 42,988 feet, or 8.15 miles, which were built at a cost of $590,000. This side of Miles Glacier, mile 47, there are 40 bridges, length 17,963 feet costing $256,000. From Miles Glacier to Tiekel, a distance of 52 miles, there are 42 bridges length 15,459 feet, costing $18,000. From Tiekel to Chitina, a distance of 32 miles, there are 47 bridges, length 9,566 feet, costing $163,000. The longest bridge is across the Copper River just beyond Chitina, at mile 132. It is 2,790 feet long, or a little more than a half mile. The west approach to the Miles Glacier bridge is nearly as long. The Gilahina bridge is 890 feet long, from 80 to 90 feet high, and was built in eight days.

The superintendent of bridges is P.J. O'Brien and he made many notable records in the construction of wooden bridges and trestles. With the thermometer always down to zero and as far below as 50 degrees, Mr. O'Brien completed 6,700 feet in 35 days, after January 7, 1911, working with an average of 48 men. The total cost of the bridge and trestle work on the Chitina branch has not yet been determined.

In order to protect the tracks from snowslides and drifting snow, 3,030 feet of substantial sheds were built. At Round Island, mile 28, 703 feet were built and at Ambercrombie Canyon, between miles 53 and 54, there are 2,727 feet. These sheds were built at a cost of $101,000. As a result of the past season's experience and observation it has been found necessary to erect additional sheds, which will be done before next winter.

Equipment of Railroad

Everything is of the most modern and substantial character and includes 15 locomotives, eight coaches, 256 cars, four steam shovels, two rotary ploughs, one wrecking crane, track driver, two spreaders, one dozer, all of

SNOW SHED MILE 52, C.R+NW.RY.

Above: Snowsheds, like the one seen here at Mile 52 of the Copper River and Northwestern Railway, were built to protect the tracks from snowslides and drifting snow.

Below: As the photo below shows, heavy snows can cause problems for rail construction and operation. While the average snowfall in the United States is about 28 inches per year, the route along the Copper River and Northwestern Railway is 135 inches per year.

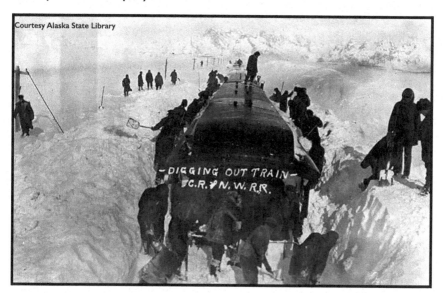

—DIGGING OUT TRAIN—
C.R.+N.W.R.R.

which were purchased at a cost of $750,000. This motive power runs over a standard gauge railroad with 70-pound rails to Chitina, and 60-pound rails on the Chitina branch to Kennecott. Native ties have been used throughout, while all of the track fittings, sidings, frogs, switches and other ap-standards.

The motive power was built by the American Locomotive Works and includes several consolidation engines of the most modern type equipped with electric headlights and used exclusively in the hauling of passenger and mail trains. Two snow rotaries are in constant readiness to give battle to the snow and prevent blockades. The rolling stock is of the latest approved pattern, the freight cars ranging from 60 to 100,000 pounds capacity, with a large complement of auxiliary cars for construction and maintenance purposes. A table d'hote dining car service is maintained on all passenger trains between Cordova and Chitina, the service of which is unexcelled on the standard railways in the states, insuring appetizing meals in comfort at all hours.

Preliminary Work on CR&N Railway

After the Alaska Syndicate acquired the Bonanza mines, under ownership of the Kennecott Mines Company, the necessity was at once apparent for the construction of a railroad to reach their valuable copper properties and also to open up what was considered a rich mineral belt running to the north and south of the Chitina, Nizina and other rivers. Engineer M.K. Rogers decided that the cheapest route was north from Valdez, and in spring 1905 he secured rights and stated to build from Valdez. The difficulties of getting through the canyon and the high grades necessary in climbing the mountains brought discouragement.

In the fall of 1905 the valuable coal deposits of the Katalla fields began to be generally discussed and the Alaska Syndicate was impressed with the necessity of taking the coal question into consideration in the construction of a railroad. Work was suspended at Valdez and Mr. Rogers directed his attention to Katella and the Copper River country. It was then decided to build from Katella, in preference to Valdez or Cordova, active work starting in the early spring of 1907. Efforts to construct a breakwater and secure a suitable harbor at Katalla soon met with unsatisfactory results, after trestles had been built, 10 miles of grading done and eight miles of track laid.

In June 1907, the Syndicate secured the services of E.C. Hawkins, formerly chief engineer of the White Pass & Yukon Railway. He came north on July 1 to study the whole situation. For over three months he tramped over the various suggested routes for reaching the Bonanza mines. He held in mind the necessity for starting at tidewater at a common point to tap both the copper belt and the coalfields, with the lightest possible grade. He also desired an open harbor the year round, with deep water and secure anchorage, where a large fleet of vessels might be safely sheltered.

Mr. Hawkins satisfied himself that Cordova offered more advantages than any other point, even though the cost of constructing from there would be greater than from some other port. He went to New York and at a meeting of the Syndicate in October, reported in favor of discontinuing work at other points and starting from Cordova. The meeting decided on the line from Cordova.

On November 15, 1907, Mr. Hawkins was made chief engineer and general manager of the Katalla Company, organized for the purpose of constructing the railroad, and which positions he continues to hold. He was placed in absolute charge of the engineering and construction work.

The first contract was for rebuilding the old part of the Copper River Railroad five miles out from Cordova and new construction to Ambercrombie, or Mile 54. Track was laid to this point by October 30, 1908, with the exception of the bridge crossing the river at Mile 49. The next contract was to Tiekel, or Mile 101, whch was completed on December 1, 1909. The road was competed to Chitina, or Mile 131, on September 12, 1910. Track was laid to Kuskulana, Mile 149, October 23, and the steel bridge across the river was completed December 25. The trestle 880 feet long and from 80-90 feet high was built across the Gilahina River, Mile 160, in eight days, and trains were running over it January 28. For the rest of the distance the actual tracking laying in the dead of winter and over ice and snow progressed at the rate of nearly a mile per day not including the building of trestle, until the end of the line was reached on the afternoon of March 28, 1911.

Some Items of Expense

Some of the most expensive rock work in railway building has been

The sounds of explosive dynamite and powder filled the air as parts of mountains and canyons were blown away to build the Copper River and Northwestern Railway.

encountered, ranging from nominal amounts to $220,000 per mile. Faces of mountains and canyons were literally torn away by tremendous charges of dynamite and powder. Practically along the entire line north of Miles and Childs glaciers the very mountain summits echoed and re-echoed again and again the martial-like sound and explosions proclaiming the indomitable will and physical hardihood of the industrial soldiers of peaceful progress blazing a way for the enrichment and convenience of generations to come. There were 5,680,000 cubic yards of excavation, of which 3,140,000 were of solid rock. Great quantities of explosives were used, at a cost of $375,000. Over 1,200,000 yards of gravel were moved by steam shovels, at a cost of $290,000.

Already $8.3 million has been paid labor for wages, exclusive of the wages paid for contract station work. Fuel was an important item and cost $610,000. Over $375,000 was paid for lumber and ties, while the government will receive nearly $100,000 for stumpage. The cost for piling aggregated $118,000. An expensive item was the rails, for which $1,110,00 was paid. Building wagon roads and trails so as to transport materials cost $78,000. This big and substantial wharf at Cordova cost $136,000. An expensive item will be the 190,000 tons of freight received by sea and much of which came by rail from the Eastern states. The charges for this item will likely run up to over $2 million.

Effective Hospital Service

In the employment of thousands of men there are necessarily man accidents. It has always been the policy of both the Katalla Company and M.J. Heney to afford the maimed the best possible accommodations and the best medical assistance obtainable. During the period of construction work for the contractor, Dr. F.B. Whiting has acted as chief surgeon, which position he also filled during work on the White Pass and Yukon Railway.

To know Dr. Whiting is to know a man who stands high in his profession, and a man who is possessed of boundless energy and a sympathetic heart. Any distance or hour of the day or night would find him responsive to a call of distress. He is a man of strong organizing ability, and the selection of his assistants he secured the best men obtainable. His hospitals have been provided with the latest and most up-to-date instruments and facilities for the treatment of patients. Some of the operations performed required the highest skill of his profession, which merited the exceptional success that his efforts earned. As a result, there were surprisingly few fatalities.

At present the main hospital is at Mile 146, where Dr. Broderick is the assistant. As work progressed others have been maintained at Miles 55, 96, 101, 123, 133, 182 and 191.

The Katalla Company has always maintained a splendid hospital at Cordova. Until last summer it was in charge of Dr. W.W. Council, when he gave way to Dr. Smith, who has since been in charge. Other hospitals have been maintained by the Katalla Company at Mile Glacier, for the benefit of bridge workers, and at Ambercrombie Canyon, when the snow sheds were being built, and at Kuskulana, when the bridge was erected.

Alaska Syndicate

The men who have financed the Copper River & Northwestern Railway are M. Guggenheim Sons and J. Pierpont Morgan, with their friends. They formed a combination for working purposes known as the Alaska Syndicate. The first purchase for $3 million of mining claims, including the Bonanza mine at Kennecott 196 miles into the interior, made necessary the building of a railroad to reach this property. After having experts examine the many mining claims that were then located by various individuals and companies in what is known as the Copper River District, a conclusion was reached that sufficient tonnage would be available soon after completion of a railroad to warrant the construction of a standard gauge, high-class railroad.

Several million dollars were spent in the effort to establish the proper seacoast terminal, including Valdez and Katalla, before deciding Cordova was the most desirable and feasible point to reach the coal and copper fields. From that time forward the work has been prosecuted with diligence and without interruption. As estimates for the costs were submitted the Syndicate endorsed the expenditures and promptly supplied the necessary money. The financiers are represented in New York by S.W. Eccles, who has very largely reflected the policies of the Syndicate and conducted their business from that end.

The Katalla Company and Railway

This company was formed for the purpose of constructing the railroad. Certain contracts were awarded to M.J. Heney on a percentage basis, while the construction of the steel bridges and certain other work after the contractor and turned over a completed division, was performed by the Katalla Company. Of this company S.W. Eccles of New York is president, while E.C. Hawkins is vice-president and general manager.

Mr. Hawkins was given practically absolute authority on matters of construction, which involved the expenditure of many millions of dollars. He had the absolute confidence of the financiers who built the road. They early realized his wonderful genius as an engineer and railroad builder, and he was always regarded by them as a man of sound judgment, unswerving integrity and of exceptional energy.

To Mr. Hawkins, more than any one man, is due the credit for the accomplishment of one of the greatest engineering feats and best pieces of pioneer construction ever attempted in the United States. After his preliminary plans were complete, there was necessity of the almost continuous exercise of his fertile brain to meet and dispose of the many complex and unusual questions that were arising in all quarters. His mental and physical strength were at times tried to their utmost. But his courage never failed, and today he can look upon the accomplishment of a gigantic work with the consciousness that his duties were not only well performed, but that the results merit him the highest possible credit and honor.

Through his kindly consideration for all employees Mr. Hawkins won their confidence and regard to such an extent as is seldom enjoyed by a head official. And in return the loyalty and energy they displayed redounded to the advancement of the work and to the credit of all concerned. During the past three years Mr. Hawkins has had valued assistance and co-operation from all of the employees, and particularly the following head officials: Alfred Williams, assistant engineer; C. E. Harrison and L. J. Caswell, division engineers; G. H. Spangler, special engineer; A. C. O'Neel, bridge engineer; J. W. Covert and H. A. Brown, assistant bridge engineers; S. Corner, chief draftsman; Fred W. Hawkins, Philip Caleb Corser, L. M. Price, Henry Dyo, T. W. Secrest, E. C. Eby, Daniel Boyle, Homer McHadley, C. E. Wingate, J. C. Scurry, S. A. Walker, S. E. Sellows, C. J. McCain, T. C. Brill, B. Dreitenstein, W. J. Ford, W. A. Richelsen, resident engineers; W. S. McCune, chief timekeeper.

In the operation of the Copper River & Northwestern Railway the resident officials are E. C. Hawkins, chief engineer; J. R. Van Cleve, division superintendent and master mechanic; R. J. Barry, general freight and passenger agent; W. J. Ford, auditor; I. W. Young, storekeeper; L. Wernicke, division engineer.

The general officers at the New York and Seattle offices are as follows:

S.W. Eccles, president, New York; F. W. Hills, comptroller, New York; J. H. Young, vice-president, Seattle; C. J. Jones, traffic manager, New York; D. H. Jarvis, assistant treasurer, Seattle; W. E. Bennett, secretary, New York; W. H. Bogle, attorney, Seattle; J. K. MacGowan, purchasing agent, New York; W. B. Sprague, assistant purchasing agent, Seattle; Kenneth Kerr, industrial agent, Seattle.

M.J. Heney, Contractor

The contract for the grading, track laying and trestle work of the railroad was awarded to M. J. Heney, who had been the contractor for the White Pass & Yukon Railway. Mr. Heney at once proceeded to affect an organization that was characteristic for its loyalty, strength and efficiency. He surrounded himself, as heads of the different departments, with men of experience and exceptional ability, who soon justified his wisdom by proving themselves able and faithful, remaining loyal unto the end.

Heney was in the wreck of the steamer *Ohio* in August 1909, but later proceeded to Cordova and directed and labored with his old-time energy, until he left for the states on December 6, 1909. He proceeded to New York, but soon returned to California, where his weakened condition developed into pneumonia and heart trouble, from which he died October 11, 1910. The thousands of men who were in his employ grieved and mourned over his death with such deep feeling and sincerity as is seldom witnessed in this generation. But to all M. J. Heney was a friend, and not a taskmaster. He was loved and respected by all his men and the public generally.

As during his previous contract Mr. Heney had as his first lieutenant Samuel Murchison. He has much of the same force and many of the characteristics of his chief. When the absence and illness of Mr. Heney required that he assume full responsibility, Mr. Murchison never faltered, but took hold and labored with a fidelity and energy that endeared him to his chief and won him the favor of all the employees. Since the death of Mr. Heney the work has been under the absolute direction of Mr. Murchison, and he has made for himself such a record as will forever establish him as one of the foremost and successful railroad builders of the country. He has a splendid knowledge of men, and his kindly and courteous treatment of his employees resulted in securing their confidence and loyalty to a marked degree and with such results as is only achieved by men of giant force and great consideration.

The personnel of M. J. Heney, contractor, is composed as follows: General superintendent, Samuel Murchison; superintendent of bridges and buildings, P. J. O'Brien; superintendent of transportation, W. C. Robinson; superintendent of motive power, H. R. Simpson; superintendent of track, A. L. McCoy; general foreman, Daniel Hedican; chief surgeon, Dr. F. B. Whiting; chief storekeeper, Archie Shiels; assistant storekeeper, Thos. Fitch.

The Heney company has considerable work still to perform before turning over to the Katalla Company the remaining section from Chitina to Kennicott. Filling in ties, completing trestles, ballasting, and some general work will keep the present employees busy until the 15th of April. On that day Mr. Murchison will turn over the last section of the railroad to General

Manager Hawkins, and from that time on all necessary ballasting and additional improvements on the railroad will be performed by the Katalla Company.

The work of the Heney company has been energetically and skillfully performed. Some delay was occasioned by reason of discovered ice seams and slides in heavy rock work. This delayed the building of the Kuskulana bridge until an extreme bitter season, and naturally resulted in necessary delay in the completion of the work. Otherwise it was up to schedule and such delay as there was is attributed to the elements.

The direct reason for the construction of the Copper River & Northwestern Railway was to reach the mining property of the Kennecott Mines Company, which had been acquired by the Alaska Syndicate for a consideration of $3,000,000. This property now consists of 32 lode claims and 18 placer claims, embracing a total acreage of 3,240 acres. Practically the only development was on the Bonanza group, which had $6,000,000 of rich copper ore in sight. But it was apparent from the start that the Syndicate would not be justified in building a standardized modern railway to carry the tonnage of their own property. They realized the prospective development of many greater producers on claims close to the railroad and so decided to build a substantial and permanent road, in the belief that development would give ample tonnage.

The Bonanza mine is located upon a high ridge between Kennecott glacier and McCarthy creek. It is six miles above the foot of the glacier and three miles from the town of Kennecott, where the concentrator and ore bins are located. The mine is 1,500 feet above the timber line, at an elevation of about 4,500 feet, with a good trail leading to it. The ore is practically pure chalcocite, or copper glance, and is stained upon the surface by copper carbonates. Comparatively little work has as yet been done in the development of the mine. There are about 1,000 feet of tunneling and 150 feet of raise. Possibly 2,000 tons of ore has been taken out, most of which will run 65 per cent, and some higher, in copper.

The ore is conveyed by a three-mile tram to the concentrator and ore bins. Ore is now being sacked, preparatory to shipment over the railroad to Cordova, from whence it will be taken to the Tacoma smelter. It is expected that the ore will run over $200 per ton and that 1,500 tons will net $300,000.

When the smelter return is announced within two or three weeks, it is believed that the high value of the ore, and in much great quantities, will startle the mining world. And it certainly will prove a stimulus to prospectors and those who are at present interested in the Kotsina-Chitina copper belt to exert greater effort in the discovery of valuable properties and the development of those already acquired.

Last year the Kennecott Mines Company took in over the trail the machinery for a sawmill. After that was established, sufficient lumber was cut to supply the 200,000 feet necessary for the erection of a large concentrator building 44 feet wide of six stories of benches ranging from 16 to 22 feet. Other construction consists of tram terminals, transfer bunkers, ore chutes and 375 feet of snow sheds between the mine and ore bins.

The sawmill also furnished the lumber for a two-story addition to the main office or headquarters, a new cottage, another bunkhouse, with

Courtesy Alaska State Library

This is a bird's-eye view of the Kennecott mining operations around 1911. Note the supports for tram used to transport copper ore.

sleeping, reading, sitting and bathrooms for 20 men, and a warehouse. In addition to the erection of buildings around the Bonanza property, a dam is being constructed across National Creek near the end of the tramway for the purpose of furnishing a sufficient head of water to operate the machinery for the crushers and concentrators, as well as furnishing power for the electric and steam plants to be installed.

The general manager of the Kennecott Mining Company is Stephen Birch. The superintendent is E. B. Emory, who formerly worked for the Guggenheims in Mexico.

Kotsina-Chitina Copper Belt

When the charge is so flagrantly made that the Alaska Syndicate has practically all the copper in the interior of Alaska, it may be interesting to know that their four groups of 40 claims are a very small part of the 200 groups of 4,000 copper and gold claims that have been located by other individuals and companies. These locations have been made in the Kotsina-Chitina copper belt. This is a tract of mountainous country, east of the Copper River and embracing the watersheds of the Kotsina, Kuskulana, Gilihena, Strelna, Lakina, Nizina, Kennecott, Chitistone and Chitina Rivers with their tributary streams, notably, Nugget, Elliott, Dan, Chititu, Young, and Glacier creeks.

One of the biggest companies operating in this part of Alaska is the Great Northern Development Company. E. F. Gray is one of the owners and also general manager. Associated with him are Phillips, Dodge & Co., of New York, part of the Amalgamated copper combination. This company has already expended $800,000 in development work and improvements, employing 140 men last season on two properties located at Copper Mountain and on the Kotsina. Several thousand feet of tunnel has been driven and large bodies of ore uncovered. This year work on a larger scale will go on and a branch line of the railroad will likely by built 12 miles up the Strelna to the property. Three or four miles distant, near the Kuskulana Glacier, are the Dillman properties, worked by the Alaska United Copper Exploration Company. Considerable work has been done on the Finch group and the tunnels show rich bodies of glance and bornite. A crew of men this season expect to open up the property so as to make it an early shipper. Assays show from 30 to 45 percent copper. This company is also working the Westover group on the mountain side above Dan creek. As the work progresses values hold good, and the lead of bornite ore retains its width of 16 feet. Assessment work is being done on other properties.

The California-Alaska Development Company, composed of Capt. A. E. Lathrop and San Francisco parties, will work their Kotsina properties this season on a larger scale than ever. Others operating on the Kotsina are the Hubbard and Elliott, the McCarthy company, and the Guilianeau Mining Co. The Cushman properties on the upper Strelna, the Deyo and Price group and others, will be worked. The Mother Lode Mining Co., beyond Kennecott, and the Millard company, which owns the Nikolai mine, propose to work on a larger scale than ever, as does also the Blackburn Mines Co.

The Dan Creek Mining Company is operating extensively on Dan creek. The Birch brothers and Jim Galen have taken in considerable hydraulic machinery to work their placer ground. Geo. Max Esterley has taken in machinery and expects to take out several hundred thousand dollars in placer gold from Dan and Chititu creeks. The Kernan company will also operate on Dan creek.

Scores of other operators will assist this year in disproving the theory that the Guggenheims have gobbled up all the valuable copper and gold properties in this district.

Rates on Ore

While the rates on the transportation of ore have not been officially announced by the railroad company yet, it comes from a reliable source that the maximum rate per ton will be $20, with the minimum running down to about $5 per ton. The price will be graduated in accordance with the value of the ore, as is the custom of all railroads in mining countries. Usually ten percent of the value is charged. Most of the ore in the Copper River country will run from $50 to $250 per ton in copper, and the freight rate as quoted will be more than satisfactory to them. As one operator declared, he expected to and would be perfectly willing to pay 20 percent of the smelter returns.

Some Interesting Facts

About fifteen per cent of the railroad is composed of bridges and trestles.

Stephen Birch, one of three managing partners of the Alaska Syndicate, established a homestead for what became the town of Chitina, seen here in 1909.

The railroad is on a water grade from Cordova to Chitina. On the Chitina branch to the end of the line except two pusher grades, the maximum is 1.15 per 100 feet.

Joe Redmond, chief blacksmith for the contractor, fashioned the copper spike that was driven at the end of the road by General Manager Hawkins, of the Katalla Company, and General Superintendent Samuel Murchison, of the contracting company. It was cut from a solid piece of native copper, taken from the bed of Chittitu creek, a stream near the Bonanza mine. The spike was afterward drawn and will be properly inscribed and sent by Mr. Hawkins to the head office in New York, as the first return received from an investment of over $40 million. Mr. Redmond also presented Mr. Hawkins as a personal memento, a copper horseshoe with nails projecting to be used for penholders, and a pick and shovel acting as a back holder.

One of the hardest worked and most conscientious officials in the service of the Copper River & Northwestern Railway is J. R. Van Cleve, superintendent and master mechanic. His ability and energy are towers of strength in the operating of the new railroad.

A half million tons of steel rails have been laid since January 7.

When the Katella branch line is constructed from Mile 39, the distance from the coal mines to Cordova will be 93 miles.

Any timber cut by the railroad up to Mile 89 had to be paid for, as it was within the government reserve. Practically the only available timber in the entire reserve is near Mile 13, where there is fine native spruce, which was largely used for ties and piling. With this exception a selected quality of Puget Sound Douglas fir was used for all timber work. Three and one-third cents for each tie cut was paid to the government.

When the railroad reached Mile 54 a steamboat landing was established and until the end of last season three steamers, the *Tonsina*, *Chitina* and *Nizina*, were used to transport freight and supplies for the railroad up the river. The cost was $1.07 per ton per mile. The cost of building these steamers was $215,000.

During the summer of 1909 the ferryboat *Gulkana* was used to transfer supplies from the railroad at Camp 49 across the Copper River to connect with the rails. Until the Miles Glacier bridge was completed last summer, the supplies were taken across on scows drawn by cables and donkey engines.

Courtesy Alaska State Library

The steamer Gulkana, seen here in front of Miles Glacier, transferred supplies from Camp 49 across the Copper River to connect with railroad tracks. It often had to dodge chunks of glacier ice.

THE MAN BEHIND THE WORDS

BY LAUREL DOWNING BILL

As in his best-selling novel, *The Spoilers*, published in 1906, Rex Ellingwood Beach based his story *The Iron Trail* on true events of the time. He wove his tale around the real life of railroad contractor Michael James Heney and added a bit of romance to spice up the story of building the Copper River and Northwestern Railway between Cordova and Kennecott during 1906-1911.

Beach followed the siren's cry of "gold!" after the precious metal was discovered in the Yukon a few years earlier. The 19-year-old convinced his lawyer brothers, Elmer and Raymond, to grubstake him on his first gold-seeking adventure during the summer of 1897 after the *Portland* and the *Excelsior*, loaded with ore from the rich Canadian gold fields, docked in Seattle and San Francisco. The newspaper headlines announcing the big strike that followed the "gold ships'" arrival drove more than 100,000 people to head to the Klondike. However, along with Beach, only around 30,000 actually made it.

The lure of quick riches was enticing during this time in American history due to a series of financial recessions, bank failures and high unemployment. The Klondike was "just far enough away to be romantic and just close enough to be accessible," historian Pierre Berton once said.

Most of those heading north took steamers to Southeast Alaska, landing at either Skagway or Dyea, and then climbed the infamous Chilkoot Trail. But others, like Beach, chose the "rich man's route," an all-water trail. Hopeful prospectors hopped aboard steamships leaving Seattle and other West Coast ports and traveled around the Aleutian Chain to St. Michael. There they connected with flat-bottom sternwheelers for the 1,500-mile trip up the Yukon River to Dawson. At first, a ticket cost $150 (almost $5,500 in 2022 dollars). Within months, that same ticket cost $1,000 (close to $36,000 in today's money).

However, many travelers discovered the Yukon riverboats on which they'd booked passage did not exist and found themselves stranded at St. Michael. Others jumped on boats that started up river too late in the season and got caught in the river's ice. They were forced to spend the winter in Circle City or Rampart.

Beach, who'd been studying law in Chicago and working for his brothers when gold fever hit him, was one of those who settled in Rampart. He spent the winter of 1897 and spring 1898 in a cabin located about 600 miles from his original destination of Dawson City.

He found work with ex-ranger Bill Joyce, one of the first prospectors on the Yukon. Beach earned $5 a day and beans working a hand-hewn windlass at Joyce's claim on Little Minook Creek.

Beach credits Joyce with many of his story ideas. The then-70-year-old prospector often dropped into Beach's tent in the evenings to spin yarns and share tales of adventure.

Courtesy Alaska State Library

Miners that traveled the all-water route transferred from large steamships to smaller riverboats, like the *Nora* pictured here, to carry them up the Yukon River from St. Michael to Dawson City.

Rampart Blossoms

Two hundred and thirty miles downstream from Fort Yukon is the almost deserted village of Rampart. Its existence can be traced to half-Russian/half-Native prospector John Minook, who discovered gold in 1893 at the mouth of Minook Creek – about 700 miles downriver from Dawson.

"Were it not for the Klondike, Minook would itself have caused a stampede from the United States," wrote Pierre Berton in his book, *The Klondike Fever.*

Established in 1897, Rampart served as a river supply point for gold placer mines in hills and creek valleys south of the Yukon. Its name refers to the range of low mountains through which the river runs and forms the "ramparts" of the Upper Yukon.

When Rex Beach arrived there in 1897 with his fur-lined sleeping bag, a rifle, a dog-skin suit and mandolin, the town's population had reached 1,000. Dilapidated cabins brought $800 and lots fetched up to $1,200.

New strikes in Minook Creek, Idaho Bar, Quail Creek and Eureka Creek, all within 30 miles of Rampart, triggered a rush to the area in 1898. Some estimates suggest the population swelled to more than 10,000 people during its heyday. Residents enjoyed hotels, saloons, a library, fire department, hospital, stores and a newspaper.

Its boom was short lived, however, as new strikes in the Upper Koyukuk River and the discovery of gold on Anvil Creek – which led to the birth of Nome – drove the town's population out to try their luck elsewhere. By 1903, when gold was discovered in what became Fairbanks, records indicate that only a community of Natives remained among the abandoned businesses and homes.

THE MAN BEHIND THE WORDS

Beach's early life may have prepared him for his northern adventure. Born in Atwater, Michigan, on September 1, 1877, to Henry Walter Beach and Eva Eunice Canfield, a schoolteacher, he spent his childhood watching his father and older brothers thresh buckwheat on his father's farm. The family left the Grand Traverse Bay region when warmer climes lured his family south in 1887. With little money to spare, the Beaches joined a few other families that chartered a commercial fisherman's schooner to sail them to Florida.

The 103-day voyage of the *Fair Play* took the then 9-year-old Beach through a lake to Chicago, then a narrow canal that linked Lake Michigan with the Illinois River, then on down to the Mississippi and onward to the land of sunshine.

His father squatted on deserted land that had once been a Civil War military reservation just outside of Tampa and again began farming – he later added chickens, hogs, horses and cows. Young Beach became the family's sales representative for the laying hens, until at age 14 he entered the prep department of Rollins College at Winter Park. (Although he did not graduate from Rollins, Beach received an honorary Bachelor of Science degree and Doctor of Literature in 1927, served as the first president of the Rollins Alumni Association from 1927-1940 and presented an honorary degree to Admiral Richard E. Byrd in 1938.)

Beach cut short his last year of education at Rollins and headed to Chicago to attend law school and follow in the footsteps of his brothers. He later said his plans included joining their law practice, making himself a partner in the firm and then becoming a Justice of the U.S. Supreme Court.

He hungered to get rich quick and eat well. However, he found the meager wages he earned as his brothers' go-fer in 1896 did not come close to helping him with either issue. He remedied the latter after learning the Chicago Athletic Association kept a well-stocked training table filled with food for its athletes. The ever-adaptable young Beach convinced the captain of the football team that he had played every position in the game and wanted to sign up.

Once the captain agreed to try him out, Beach bought a Spalding book of rules and studied it thoroughly because he knew nothing

Young Rex Beach competed on the track team while attending Rollins College.

of the game. He ended up playing left tackle for the remainder of that season and then went on to join the club's aquatic team the next spring. He found water polo produced fewer injuries while it allowed him to continue to eat the club's culinary delights.

When news of Klondike gold spread later that summer, Beach figured his get-rich-quick dream may come to fruition. He used part of the grubstake he coerced out of his indulgent brothers to purchase a fur-lined sleeping bag, a rifle, a dog-skin suit and a mandolin. Loaded with his "outfit," Beach set off toward Dawson in search of his fortune.

By late autumn, he and many other Klondike-bound adventurers had to turn back at Fort Yukon due to low water in the flats and tales of famine at Circle City and Dawson. The group settled in Rampart for the winter.

The next spring he learned he and the others had missed their chance at Klondike gold. Those who had made it to that promised land had staked all the good claims.

During the two years that followed, Beach found odd jobs and did a bit of prospecting. But he did not find any motherlode to pad his pockets. In fact, by winter 1899 he was flat broke when he returned to Chicago to continue his legal studies.

Rex Beach lived in this cabin during his stay in Rampart.

But he couldn't shake the lure of the northland – especially now that some inexperienced miners had found gold on the beaches of the Bering Sea at a place called Nome. Mining laws did not apply to this new discovery since the surf carried the golden ore from the sea onto shores that were public property.

Beach contracted with an engineer to build simple machinery to wash gold from the sand and caught the first ship north with his invention in the spring of 1900. He became one of thousands dumped on Nome's shore together with tons of freight, mining and building supplies, fuel and more. The now-22-year-old found the once-isolated stretch of tundra fronting the beach transformed into a rip-roaring tent and log cabin city filled with prospectors, gamblers, claim jumpers, saloon keepers, women of ill repute and a multitude of con men. He also found that gold along the beach above low tide had been picked clean. He had to go farther out into the surf to look for his pay streak.

It didn't take long for him to realize he didn't have the strength to combat the resistless forces of Nature. A fierce storm battered the "golden sands" for three days and broke the dredging machines.

In fact, that massive storm spelled the end for most novice miners in Nome. The Poor Man's Gold Rush played itself out by the end of 1900, and after the storm destroyed the business district and the beach mining operations, thousands left on boats heading south. Some – like Beach – stayed behind and continued on with placer mining, but by 1910 Nome's population had dropped from 20,000 back to around 2,000.

For all his labors, Beach ended up with about $25 (about $900 in 2022 dollars) worth of gold from his beach operation.

He melted the ore and turned it into a button, which later was stolen.

The intrepid young man spent another couple of years playing the mining game. He worked for himself and others, stampeded to new discoveries where he did have a bit of luck finding gold and tried his hand at a few other ventures along the way.

But he finally decided he wasn't cut out to be a prospector – or a

Courtesy Alaska State Library

Rex Beach and other miners used sluice boxes to mine for gold on the beach.

THE MAN BEHIND THE WORDS

lawyer. He returned to Illinois with his Far North experiences locked safely away in his head.

Beach hired on as a salesman for a Chicago company selling construction materials. He again became a member of the Chicago Athletic Association's water polo team and helped the team win second place at the St. Louis Olympic games in 1904, the same year his father died. However, the International Olympic Committee considered the match an exhibition game, so the team did not receive an Olympic silver medal, according to Rollins College archives.

It was around this time that a chance meeting with another man who had been in Alaska sparked an idea that would lead Beach into writing for a living.

"Back in Chicago, I was selling firebrick, lime and cement when I met a Yukon acquaintance who told me he had sold a story of one of his mining experiences for $10," Beach later recounted. "There was an empty desk where we were standing. I snagged a chair and wrote."

Back at the turn of the last century, $10 was worth nearly $365 in today's money. So Beach hunkered down and began writing fictional tales based on his gold-rush experiences.

This was not his first foray into writing. Beach had worked on *The Sandspur*, the Rollins College student newspaper, while attending prep school. He published two short stories for that college literary endeavor in 1896: A "Strange Experience" and "The Convict's Story." He also had worked on a few plays for opera houses while in the Last Frontier.

Beach sold his first story, "The Mule Boy and the Garrulous Mute," to

Rex Beach began writing for a living after he learned he could earn at least $10 for a story about the North Country.

McClure's Magazine in 1903. *Pardners*, a series of short stories about life in Alaska and the West, debuted in magazine form in 1904. It was published as a book in 1905.

That same year he also crafted the events surrounding crooked Nome politician McKenzie and his willing partner Judge Noyes into a nonfiction series of articles titled "The Looting of Alaska" for *Appleton's Booklovers Magazine.*

That series became one of his most famous novels, *The Spoilers*, after he added some fictional characters and events. Beach wove his tale with two Yukon adventurers who duke it out over a gold claim, a beautiful saloon girl and a crooked gold commissioner and judge. First serialized in *Everybody's Magazine* in 1905, the book – published by Harper & Brothers – became a bestseller in 1906.

Later that year, Beach reworked the novel into a play, which ran for two-week runs in Chicago and New York before it went on the road for a few years. Later the up-and-coming author contracted with the Selig Corp. to release a film version of his novel for 25 percent of gross profits.

Beach truly was a pioneer novelist who got in on the ground floor of the movie business. He became the first American author to insert a clause about movie rights into his contracts. In 1914, *The Spoilers* graced the silver screen as one of the first feature-length silent films – only 11 years after the first-ever silent movie, *The Great Train Robbery,* debuted.

That 12-minute flick produced by Thomas Edison was directed and filmed by Edison Company employee Edwin S. Porter and was the first narrative movie that told a story. The 1903 movie led to opening permanent movie theaters and birthing the future film industry. It played across the country in 1904 and then in 1905 at the first "nickelodeons," theaters in which movies cost a nickel to watch.

The Spoilers was put to film a total of five times: in 1923, as another silent film; in 1930, just three years after the first "talkie," *The Jazz Singer,* came out; in 1942, with John Wayne playing Roy Glenister, Marlene Dietrich portraying Cherry Malotte and Randolph Scott acting as Alexander McNamara; and again in 1955 with Jeff Chandler as Glenister, Anne Baxter as Malotte and Rory Calhoun as McNamara.

Like Jack London, whom he admired, Beach's exposure to adventure, frontier towns and unexplored lands helped him create settings that captured peoples' imaginations. His mingling with steadfast and hearty men and women chasing golden dreams in harsh circumstances while greed, corruption, villains, and heroes surrounded them became fodder for short stories and essays that sparked a fire in most who read them.

After the overnight success of *The Spoilers*, which paved the way for Beach to become one of America's favorite authors, he married his sweetheart in 1907. He'd met Edith Greta Crater during his stint in Nome.

Stirred by romantic stories of the golden North, she had given up her successful career as an actress in Colorado and came to Alaska with some friends. Although her friends did not stay long, the Denver girl ended up running a successful hotel and living in a small cabin nearby – which is where this woman from a "very good family" had a brush with lawlessness that earned her the moniker "the Wag Lady."

Courtesy Library of Congress

Edith Greta Crater, sitting in the back seat of a car in 1911 driven by her husband, Rex Beach, became known around Nome as the Wag Lady.

Beach recounted the particulars surrounding her association with a gang of thieves in *Personal Exposures*.

Because of her kindness to a bullet-wounded member of the Wag Boys gang who showed up on her doorstep one day, the group of thieves adopted her. They often dropped off gifts, which they'd stolen, to thank her for her medical services to their compatriot. Thus she became known as the Wag Lady.

Greta, as she was otherwise known, did not approve of the group's actions and did not want any part of their ill-gotten goods. But the gang was steadfastly loyal to her and continued to watch out for her needs. When she fell ill during a typhoid outbreak, the gang even stole Nome's only cow so Greta could get much-needed milk for her recovery.

Beach was smitten with the Wag Lady, who he described as "the loveliest creature I had ever seen. Slim, blonde, with a head of yellow hair that had never been touched up; she had a pair of deep dimples that looked as if they had been poked into her cheeks by a mischievous finger."

While Beach was crazy about Greta, some sources claim he managed to find time to work on his novel *The Barrier* while on his honeymoon. The action-packed love story that takes place during the Klondike gold rush made the bestseller list in 1908.

His next book, *The Sliver Horde* released in 1909, is set in a fictional Bristol Bay town, Kalvik. It tells the story of a down-on-his-luck gold miner who discovers a greater wealth than gold in Alaska's salmon run and opens a cannery. He must overcome the relentless opposition of the "salmon trust," a fictionalized Alaska Packers Association, that undercuts his financing, sabotages his equipment, incites longshoremen to riot and bribes his fishermen to quit.

Beach knew the land about which he wrote. He had traversed through the Katmai region in search of gold after hearing a tip about a big strike on the upper reaches of the Kuskokwim River. He and a friend he'd met in Rampart, Roy Norton, hiked through Katmai Pass with an outfit that included a sled, tent, stove, two light fur robes and a meager supply of food. They picked up an Aleut guide and five dogs at Katmai Village and more dogs when they reached Savonoski. But when the group finally made it to cannery settlements in Bristol Bay, the men learned that there had been no gold strike on the Kuskokwim. The rumor was false.

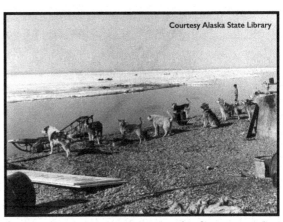

Courtesy Alaska State Library

Sleds and dogs were a common mode of transportation during the gold-rush years.

But the knowledge Beach gained of the area, and the workings of the canneries at the time, struck gold when he wrote *The Silver Horde*. The book made the bestseller list in 1909 and also was turned into a successful movie twice – a silent film in 1920 and a talkie in 1930.

Beach's work helped set the public's mind about both Alaska and the Yukon. He published more than 30 novels, dozens of short stories and novelettes and authorized 32 film adaptations of his work.

Critics say he wrote in the "school of realism," as his stories were of romance and frontier adventure aimed at young men. Plots featured ordinary, hard-working people who were forced to confront forces of nature and corruption. His heroes overcame adversity through violence, loyalty to the cause and to each other. In keeping with Beach's own philosophy of rugged individuality, his characters persevered through their own actions, not by relying on government entities to assist them.

His books were popular among the general public but others were not as enthralled with his stories.

"Regular people loved his books, but intellectuals and critics did not like his stuff, referring to them as the 'he-man school of literature,' or 'pot boilers.' Beach cried all the way to the bank," wrote Florida historian Mike Miller, according to an article titled "Adventure novelist called Lake Hopatcong home" written by Mart Kane that appeared in the *Lake Hopatcong News* on Sept. 5, 2014.

"Big hairy stories about big hairy men," wrote James R. Belpedio of Becker College in Worcester, Massachusetts, when discussing film adaptations of Beach's works.

Even Alaska historian Stephen Haycox stated that many of Beach's works are "mercifully forgotten today," according to Wikipedia.

Westbrook Pegler, Pulitzer Prize winner and syndicated newspaper columnist, stated that he discounted by 60 percent the stories of Alaska hardships as described by Beach, Robert Service and Jack London.

However Beach stood by his description of life in the North.

"I take no offense at being called a fiction writer," Beach wrote in *Personal Exposures*. "I've been called worse things right to my teeth but actually neither London nor any of the rest of us overwrote the hardships of life on the brown bean frontier and I'm sure any sourdough will subscribe to that statement."

But Beach did not want to be known solely as the author of Alaska stories. So he and his bride headed to Panama around 1909 to check out jungle life and research the massive canal project that was under construction to see if other story ideas might percolate.

Begun by France in 1881 and taken over by the United States in 1904, the 51-mile waterway connecting the Atlantic and Pacific oceans across the Isthmus of Panama was approaching completion when the Beach's arrived. It officially opened on August 15, 1914.

Beach found the country and its people fascinating. His trip resulted in his next literary success, *The Ne'er-Do-Well*. The story, published in 1911, is about a rich playboy who is kidnapped by his friends, drugged and put on a ship heading to Panama. He finds work on building the Panama Canal to earn passage home and becomes a man through the process.

Even though Beach wanted to branch out and write stories that were not based in the wilds of Alaska, there was a tie between Panama and the Last Frontier. Once the canal opened in 1914, there was no need for all the equipment that had been used to create it, so much of it made its way north via steamships to work on the Alaska Railroad project that began in 1915.

Beach's next fictional tale, *The Net* published in 1912, features an American man who travels to Sicily, gets tangled up with the Mafia and spends a couple of years trying to uncover the identify of a mysterious don. Following *The Net* came *The Iron Trail*, published in 1913, that tells the story of building a railroad across the rugged Alaska frontier of Prince William Sound.

The prolific author then began popping out almost a book a year and developed a devoted following that remained loyal to his works into the mid-1930s.

Beach and his wife lived in New York during the first few years of their marriage. But when they visited friends in a lakeside community in New Jersey during the summer of 1910, they fell in love with the area. The couple bought a house in Lake Hopatcong in 1911 and spent their summers at their vacation home, which they called Mañana, for the next five years.

"Mr. Rex Beach, the novelist, has been at his summer home since May 15 and intends to remain for the season unless business calls him away. He has already started a new book," reported the *Lake Hopatcong*

Rex and Greta Beach spent five summers at their second home, which they called Mañana, seen here in 1911.

Breeze on July 1, 1911. The book may have been his novel, *The Ne'er-Do-Well*, which came out later that year.

Courtesy Sebring Historical Society

Beach traveled between Mañana and his New York home often, according to an article in the *New York Times*, dated September 9, 1911.

"I can't work here," Beach was quoted as saying about Lake Hopatcong in the article. "I'd rather swim or fish. There's an old fellow lives across the lake that I go fishing with, and he and I

Rex Beach, seen here on Lake Hopatcong in 1912, loved to spend time on the water.

are great tillicums – that's Indian for pals or chums. Of course, I'd rather swim or fish than write. But writing is a good game. Such a good game it's a wonder to me the police don't get after us for taking money for it."

The successful novelist said he spent his mornings writing, and then enjoyed tennis, boating, swimming, or fishing during his afternoons at the lake.

Two years later, the *Lake Hopatcong Breeze* reported that Beach was working on a novel about New York City's social life. The article said he'd wanted to write it the year before, but the public had wanted a northwestern story, so he wrote *The Iron Trail* instead.

It was while he was in Cordova researching that railroad story that Beach had a painful attack of what he thought was snow blindness. However, it turned out to be iritis, an inflammation that affects the colored ring around the pupil. The cause is often unknown, but it can cause severe vision loss, even blindness.

Beach traveled blindfolded on board a ship to Seattle, where specialists examined him, gave him drugs, and put him in a pitch-black hospital room for many days. He suffered bouts of iritis for the next 10 years.

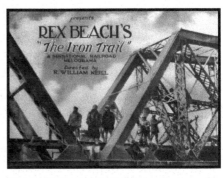

The Iron Trail **was made into a silent movie, as advertised on this movie card, in 1921.**

"In spite of the best medical attention and the utmost precaution I seldom went more than a few months – sometimes only a few weeks – without one," he wrote in his autobiography.

He lamented that one of the biggest disappointments in his life was that he could not serve in the military during World War I due to this ailment. He desperately wanted to do his bit for the war effort.

Beach and Greta looked after soldiers in their home, volunteered to write and produce Red Cross propaganda and did anything else that came their way to help the war effort. But Beach never felt those efforts were enough.

"… on the whole I felt pretty useless and envied every man in uniform. When I met one, I wanted to throw him down, take it off and wear it home."

But Beach did manage to write a few more novels in between bouts of iritis: *The Auction Block* (1914); *Heart of the Sunset* (1915); *Rainbow's End* (1916); and a series of short stories in *The Crimson Gardenia* (1916).

The Beaches sold Mañana in 1916. The structure burned in April 1920, but a similar home was rebuilt immediately on the site.

Beach served as president of the Author's League from 1911-1918, and as such he urged authors to follow his example and put film clauses into their publishing contracts and rework their publications into screenplays. Often his advice fell upon deaf ears, however, as many believed that cinema was beneath them. But for those that did listen to Beach, he led the way for them and later authors to reap greater profits by exploiting other media outlets for their works. He helped define "what the 20th-century author of popular literature became by mid-century: an independent entrepreneur," according to James R. Belpedio in his article about Beach written for encyclopedia.com.

He had a passion for financial success and "viewed his mind as a create factory producing a marketable product. Writing involved raw material, production, and sales. The end result was profit," Belpedio added.

Beach also wrote a brochure, titled "The Miracle of Coral Gables," to promote the new 1926 planned city real estate development in Florida. He received $25,000 for that piece of work, which equates to almost $430,000 in 2022.

He used some of his profits to purchase 7,000 acres near Sebring, Florida, and became a successful cattle rancher in the 1930s. He also wrote another novel in 1935, *Wild Pastures*, set in cattle lands around Sebring. He then bought another 2,000 acres.

The novelist had an avid interest in experimental farming and devoted himself to celery and flower bulb husbandry. In 1937, he encouraged his alma mater, Rollins College, to participate in nutritional studies on produce grown by Dr. Charles Northen of Orlando's Colloidal Institute. He also invested in Easter lily bulb growing in Mexico, and later transferred operations to Florida. Rumor has it he made a second fortune by growing gladioli and Easter lilies.

That he moved to Florida makes sense since his family moved there from Michigan in the

Rex Beach, 1925

Rex Beach turned his attention to ranching and farming in Florida in the mid-1920s and 1930s.

1880s. His fruit farmer father had good luck with fruit trees in the warmer clime.

Once Beach and wife Greta returned to the sunshine state, they spent their lives dividing time between their New York penthouse and their Sebring farm. The lure of Alaska had faded – until Beach received a letter from his guide during the time spent in Cordova and the Copper River area researching for *The Iron Trail.*

Joe Ibach, who had been a prospector, miner, and trapper before becoming Beach's guide, wrote to invite him to his cabin on an island near Icy Straits in Southeast Alaska. Ibach, who now was fox farming, also mentioned that he'd made a promising discovery of gold quartz and "mountain leather," a strange mineral so rare that no one knew much about it.

Mountain leathers are flexible, sheet-like formations of asbestiform minerals. The sheets resemble leather and are made of minerals like palygorskite, actinolite, saponite, sepiolite and tremolite.

Beach began thinking about the offer and realized that "Alaska had been so long forgotten that it was new; it was being reborn, and the story of that rebirth might be worth telling," he wrote in his autobiography.

So in August 1935 he again headed to Alaska via steamer. Only this time Beach had a cabin instead of having to stretch out under a grand piano or share space with sheep as he had on previous voyages north.

When the ship docked in Juneau, Beach met up with humorist Will Rogers and famous aviator Wiley Post, who were on an adventure to fly around the world. Joe Crosson, one of Alaska's most skillful and daring pilots, also was in town. The group ate dinner together, shared tales well into the evening and then met for breakfast before Rogers and Post took off for Fairbanks. Within a few days Beach learned that the pair had crashed and died near Point Barrow on August 15. Their deaths plunged Americans into deep mourning.

From left: Walter Hall, Wiley Post, Rex Beach, Joe Crosson and Will Rogers. The men visited at an airplane hangar in Juneau in August 1935.

The Associated Press asked Beach to write a story about the tragedy, so he flew to Fairbanks shortly after Crosson had taken off to collect the bodies of their friends. There he saw none of the "days of old." He felt none of the country's old-time glamor, no dog teams, no lively variety theaters, and no abundance of whiskered prospectors.

Beach next went to investigate the new Matanuska Valley Colonization project in Palmer, as he also had accepted an assignment to write about it. He found the flimsy town of tents and rough lumber more in keeping with the Alaska of old.

"The hullabaloo and confusion against that background of stumps and raw soil was like a scene from one of my early stories," he later wrote.

Although he appreciated the adventure of the 200-plus families who relocated from several northern states to create farms in the wilderness, he never thought that U.S. President Franklin D. Roosevelt's New Deal agricultural experiment would recoup the cost of its establishment. Beach estimated it cost the federal government around $50,000 or more to bring each farmer north and set him up with land, a home, and a grubstake.

He wrote that if other resettlement projects across the United States proved as costly in proportion to their size, "it was bad news for taxpayers."

Rumors soon started spreading that it cost around $125,000 to bring each colonist to the valley. With taxpayers still reeling from the devastation of the Great Depression, it is little wonder that many of them questioned the wisdom of establishing an agricultural community in remote Alaska.

But Anthony J. Dimond, Alaska's Delegate to Congress at the time, stood firmly behind the colonization of the Valley.

"The Matanuska Valley farm settlement plan is both humane and economically sound," he said. "The fact is, if it be a fact, that mistakes made in the setting up of the colony give no reason to condemn it. The settlers are being helped to get into a position to help themselves and this is the best sort of aid."

The mayor of Seward during that time agreed.

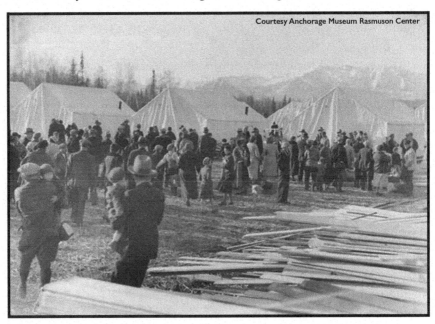
Courtesy Anchorage Museum Rasmuson Center

Rex Beach thought the Matanuska Valley Colonization Project was a waste of taxpayer money.

"I was in Washington, D.C., during the time of organization of the Matanuska Colonization Project and did all I could to help it," Don Carlos Brownell said. "I consider the colony now working so perfectly at Matanuska to be the greatest single enterprise ever put into operation by the government for the future development and growth of Alaska."

A traveler named Dan Noonan wrote an account of his observations in the developing settlement during the fall of 1935, which appeared in the February 1936 issue of *The Alaska Sportsman*. He said he thought the experiment was a good use of taxpayers' money, too.

"Every new venture has its pitfalls, every undertaking where things are done which really amount to something has its mistakes, but after the din and controversies have died down and this colony is functioning as it is intended it shall function, all Alaskans will be glad that the Territory at last has a 'breadbasket.'"

However, since local produce wasn't competitive with food shipped from Seattle, the Matanuska cooperative ran into problems marketing. Many colonists eventually abandoned the project to pursue other ventures like mining; some left the territory, and a few remained and eked out a living through the land.

After touring the colonization project, Beach made his way to his friend's cozy cabin near Icy Straits and heard more about Ibach's life on the island, fox farming and his mineral discovery in Glacier Bay.

Ibach then told Beach that he had a big problem with his Glacier Bay claims. He explained that President Calvin Coolidge had issued a proclamation in 1925 that created the Glacier Bay National Monument, which withdrew about 1,800 square miles from mineral entry.

Since the monument's

Courtesy Alaska State Library

Miners had legal problems mining their claims in Glacier Bay, seen here, after President Calvin Coolidge created Glacier Bay National Monument in 1925.

THE MAN BEHIND THE WORDS

creation, Ibach said he had not been able to work his recorded claims, which were legal under the terms of the proclamation, because the land office told him he would be defacing the park and could be fined or jailed. In essence, he would be trespassing if he worked his legal claims.

However, Ibach also needed to do at least $100 of assessment work every year to hold his property. The poor man was truly placed between a rock and a hard place and had been trying to clear his titles for the past 10 years.

Ibach's dilemma eventually led Beach to the halls of the U.S. Congress. Working closely with Dimond, who served as the territory's delegate from 1933 to 1945, the pair managed to get legislation passed that permitted mining within the monument.

The World in His Arms, released in 1946, was Beach's last novel written about Alaska. It's a love story set in the 1850s and features a San Francisco in its infancy and the Russian-American capital of Sitka. The 1952 movie version, starring Gregory Peck, Ann Blyth and Anthony Quinn, became the eighth most popular movie at the British box office in 1952, according to the December 18, 1952, issue of Sydney, Australia's *The Sunday Herald*.

Beach's passion for writing began declining once he moved to Florida. Although he did develop and write more than 40 episodes for an unproduced radio series based on his autobiography during the 1940s.

He began losing his good health in 1944 and became depressed after Greta's death on April 15, 1947, following a long illness. Beach developed throat cancer that same year and eventually had to use a breathing tube, as well as a feeding tube.

Devastated by his wife's death, and tired of suffering the pain of cancer and increasing loss of sight, Beach shot himself in the head on the morning of December 7, 1949. He was 72.

His and Greta's ashes were combined and placed in a grave, marked by a marble slab, at the Rollins College campus near the Alumni House. Beach's books, notes, letters, photographs, and manuscripts are also at the college.

He sold everything he wrote, except for the radio series and an unfinished novel he was writing when he died. *Woman in Ambush* was published posthumously in 1951.

Beach and his most famous novel, *The Spoilers*, were honored in 2009 by naming a public pedestrian-bicycle trail after them. Dubbed "Spoilers Run," the trail is near his New York residence in Dobbs Ferry.

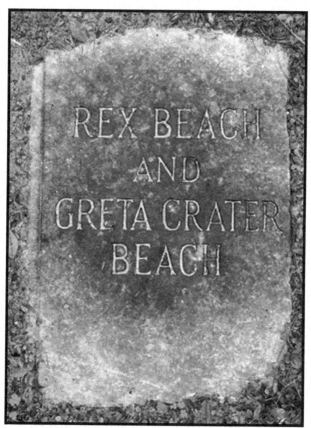

This marble slab on the campus of Rollins College at Winter Park, Florida, marks the grave of Rex and Greta Beach.

L I S T   O F   W O R K S

B Y   R E X   B E A C H

Novels

Pardners (New York: A.L. Burt Co., 1905 – 10 short stories)
The Spoilers (New York: Harper & Brothers, 1906)
The Barrier (New York: Harper & Brothers, 1908)
The Silver Horde (New York: Harper & Brothers, 1909)
Alaskan Adventures ((New York: A.L. Burt Co., 1909)
Going Some: A Romance of Strenuous Affection (New York: A.L. Burt Co., 1910)
The Ne'er-Do-Well (New York: Harper & Brothers, 1911)
The Net (New York: Harper & Brothers, 1912)
The Iron Trail (London: Hodder and Stoughton, 1913)
The Auction Block (New York: Harper & Brothers, 1914)
Heart of the Sunset (New York: Harper & Brothers, 1915)
Rainbow's End (New York: Harper & Brothers, 1916)
The Crimson Gardenia And Other Tales of Adventure (New York: Harper & Brothers, 1916) (short stories)
Laughing Bill Hyde And Other Stories (London: Hodder and Stoughton, 1917 – short stories)
The Winds of Chance (New York: A.L. Burt Co., 1918)
Too Fat to Fight (New York: Harper & Brothers, 1919)
Oh, Shoot! Confessions of an Agitated Sportsman (London: Hodder and Stoughton, 1921)
Flowing Gold (New York: Harper & Brothers, 1922)
Big Brother and Other Stories (New York: Harper & Brothers, 1923)
The Goose Woman and Other Stories (New York: Harper & Brothers, 1925)
Padlocked (New York: Harper & Brothers, 1926)
The Mating Call (New York: Harper & Brothers, 1927)
Don Careless and Birds of Prey (New York: Harper & Brothers, 1928)
Son of the Gods (New York: A.L. Burt Co., 1929)
Money Mad (New York: Cosmopolitan Book Corporation, 1931)

Novels (Continued)

Men of the Outer Islands (New York: Farrar & Rinehart, 1932)
Beyond Control (New York: Farrar & Rinehart, 1932)
Hands of Dr. Locke (New York: Farrar & Rinehart, 1934)
Masked Women (New York: Farrar & Rinehart, 1934)
Wild Pastures (New York: Farrar & Rinehart, 1935)
Jungle Gold (New York: Farrar & Rinehart, 1935)
Valley of Thunder (New York: Farrar & Rinehart, 1939)
The World in His Arms (New York: G.P. Putnam's Sons, 1946)
Woman in Ambush (New York: G.P. Putnam's Sons, 1952)

Films Based on Novels

The Spoilers (1914)
The Auction Block (1917)
Heart of the Sunset (1918)
The Iron Trail (1921)
Fair Lady (1922)
The Spoilers (1923)
Big Brother (1923)
Winds of Chance (1925)
The Goose Woman (1925)
The Auction Block (1926)
The Barrier (1926)
The Spoilers (1930)
The Silver Horde (1930)
Flowing Gold (1940)
The Spoilers (1942)
The Avengers (1950)
The World in His Arms (1952)
The Spoilers (1955)

Courtesy Library of Congress

Portrait of Rex Beach in 1900

BIBLIOGRAPHY

Find A Grave, https://www.findagrave.com/memorial/58170893/rex-ellingwood-beach

Florida Backroads Travel, "Rex Beach: Rollins College and the Spoilers," https://www.florida-backroads-travel.com/rex-beach.html

Highlands News-Sun, "More than just a famous author" by Robert Miller, Sept. 1, 2018

Lake Hopatcong Breeze, "Adventure novelist called Lake Hopatcong home," July 1, 1911

New York Times, "Rex Beach house in Jersey burns," April 27, 1920

Personal Exposures, Rex Beach. (New York: Harper & Brothers, 1941)

Online Literature, Rex Ellingwood Beach, www.online-literature.com/rex-beach/

Rex Beach, Wikipedia, http://en.wikipedia.org/wiki/Rex_Beach

Rollins College Archives, Rex Beach, https://lib.rollins.edu/olin/oldsite/archives/150EBeach.htm

Sebring Historical Society Archives

The Spoilers, Rex Beach. (New York: Harper & Brothers, 1906)

The Iron Trail, Rex Beach. (New York: Harper & Brothers, 1913)

MORE BOOKS FROM
AUNT PHIL'S TRUNK

Winner of the Literary Classics International award for Best Nonfiction Series in 2016, the *Aunt Phil's Trunk* Alaska history series is filled with entertaining short stories and hundreds of historical photographs that share Alaska's colorful past!

"I sampled one before going back to critical activities, but it's like sampling a new flavor of a gallon of ice cream. 'Even a gallon is a sufficient sample,' you grumble as you try to get your face into the carton to lick the bottom." – Larry Winebrenner, reviewer

These history books are available for $19.95 each at www.AuntPhilsTrunk.com.

Volume One
Early Alaska up to 1900

Volume Two
1900 to 1912

Each book in this highly acclaimed Alaska history series shares easy-to-read short stories and dozens of historical photos that captivate readers from ages 9 to 99.

Be sure to check out specials on our website, AuntPhilsTrunk.com.

Volume Three
1912 to 1935

Volume Four
1935 to 1960

Volume Five
1960 to 1984

Spell of the Yukon
and Other Verses
$14.95

The Call of the Wild and
Other Northland Stories
$19.95

Sun Swings North

$19.95

The Spoilers

$19.95

Winner of 2018 Silver Medal in Best of Education category from Literary Classics International

Aunt Phil's Trunk Alaska History Curriculum now available! www.AuntPhilsTrunk.com

Online Alaska History Course https://aunt-phil-s-trunk.teachable.com/p/ alaska-history-course

Aunt Phil's Trunk of Alaska Trivia $9.95

How much did the largest gold nugget found in Alaska weigh? What is unusual about fireweed? Which Alaska glacier is larger than the state of Rhode Island?

You will learn the answers to these and many more questions when you get *Aunt Phil's Trunk of Alaska Trivia*. Its 104 pages are filled with fascinating facts and crosswords, word searches and sudokus that will tease your mind and broaden your knowledge of America's Last Frontier.

Sourdough Cookery $14.95

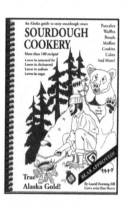

More than 100 heart-healthy recipes are featured in the *Sourdough Cookery* cookbook, which comes with authentic, 120-year-old Alaska sourdough starter!

Along with recipes for low-fat, low-sugar, low-sodium breads, biscuits and buns, you will find treats like Cranberry-Chocolate Cake, White Chocolate Cherry Muffins and Apple Pumpkin Bread – all made with egg, sugar and sodium substitutes. However, each recipe includes how many real eggs, how much sugar and other items are needed for those who want to bake with the "loaded" ingredients.

Muckluck, Alaska $14.95
Where Nothing Ever Happens

Muckluck, Alaska – Where Nothing Ever Happens, released August 2012, is written by Alaska author Lisa Augustine, edited by Laurel Downing Bill and published by Aunt Phil's Trunk LLC.

Readers will be enchanted as they travel through this 200-page fictional tale about life during 1930s-1940s in the Last Frontier. As told through the voice of 95-year-old Kate, a lifelong Alaskan, the stories ring true of small town Alaska in days gone by.

Alaska Children's Books

www.AuntPhilsTrunk.com

Raven's Friends $9.95
Alaska Animals Far and Wide

Raven's Friends, Alaska Animals Far and Wide, released June 2012, is written and illustrated by Kim Sherry. Children ages 3-8 will love this book as they follow its narrator, Raven, through 32 pages filled with colorful illustrations and poems that share facts about animals that call Alaska home.

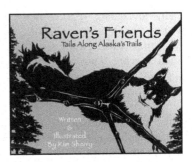

Raven's Friends $9.95
Tails Along Alaska Trails

Raven's Friends, Tails Along Alaska Trails, released June 2013, is written and illustrated by Kim Sherry. Children ages 3-8 will love this book as they learn new things about animals that travel along Alaska trails. These 32 pages are filled with colorful illustrations and poems.

The Dragline Kid And Her
Golden Wish $9.95

The Dragline Kid and Her Golden Wish, released July 2014, is written by Alaska author Lisa Augustine and beautifully illustrated by artist Melody Trone. Children ages 3-8 will delight in this story of a little girl who dreams of finding a gold nugget in Alaska's wilderness.

Alaska Animal Alphabet Practice Book
$14.95

Children ages 3+ will have fun learning how to write the alphabet – with both capital and lowercase letters – through a tracing technique. There is a handdrawn Alaska animal that begins with each letter on each page. Children also can learn their numbers from 0 to 11 in the back of the book.

Author Solutions – Adults

Journals for Self-Discovery, Fiction and Poetry Writers

Daily journaling is a wonderful habit. These workbooks provide prompts to jump-start your creative juices. Each journal features 31 idea-creating suggstions for the writer to ponder and expand upon.

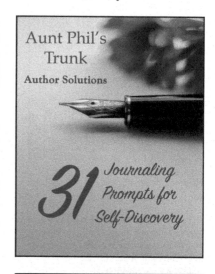

They also provide space to make daily observations and jot down ideas for new stories or poems.

Self-Discovery Writers 31 Journaling Prompts $14.95

Sample prompt: Name three to five people you'd like to meet this year? Why did you choose these people?

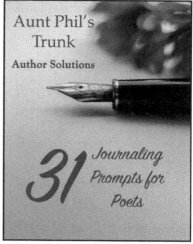

Fiction Writers 31 Journaling Prompts $14.95

Sample prompt: Philip rechecked his to-do list: groceries, bank, post office. What was he forgetting? Oh, yes - the private detective.

Poetry Writers 31 Journaling Prompts $14.95

Sample prompt: Describe a single memory of your grandmother's (or the typical grandmother's) kitchen. Write a poem about that memory.

Author Solutions – Children 8-12 Years

Journals for Self-Discovery, Fiction and Poetry Writers

Daily journaling is a wonderful habit. These workbooks provide prompts to jump-start your child's creative juices. Each journal features 31 idea-creating suggstions for the child to ponder and expand upon.

They also provide space to make daily observations and jot down ideas for new stories or poems.

Poetry Writers Kids 31 Journaling Prompts $14.95

Sample prompt: Make a list of five-ten words that begin with the same letter (like alley, apple, allergy, etc.). Then use the words throughout the lines of verse.

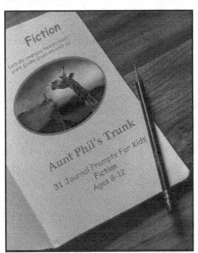

Fiction Writers Kids 31 Journaling Prompts $14.95

Sample prompt: Write a story about going on a jungle safari. What will you pack and what animals will you see?

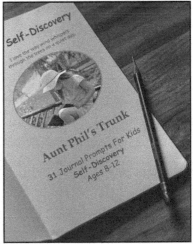

Self-Discovery Writers Kids 31 Journaling Prompts $14.95

Sample prompt: Who is your favorite person on the planet? What do you like most about that person?

30-Day Writing Challenges

Journals for Encouraging Kindness and Gratitude and Discovering Your Purpose
$9.95 each

Sample prompt: How can you be kinder to someone who annoys you?

Sample prompt: Write about someone who makes your life better.

Sample prompt: What are your greatest assets that can help propel you along the path toward your life's purpose.

MORE BOOKS FROM AUNT PHIL'S TRUNK

Made in USA - Kendallville, IN
13742_9781940479378
09.17.2022 1259